WHAT O

Beautiful Bandit is an
appoint...with just t
drama, and suspense.
for tired souls and an inspiration for hungry hearts.

—*Sharlene MacLaren*
Award-winning author, the Little Hickman Creek and
The Daughters of Jacob Kane series

Loree Lough's writing once again shines. Lough crafts characters in a way that makes it feel as though you are right there
with them. She has woven words together in a way that hooks
you immediately and encourages your excitement to discover
the outcome. This is a book you will want to read several
times over!

—*Penny Zeller*
Author, *McKenzie*, book one in the Montana Skies series

Fresh, vivid, and lively, *Beautiful Bandit* inspires giggles, cap-
tures the heart, and makes the world beyond the pages disappear. (It does, too!)

Best-selling author, Th

Beautiful Bandit promises to give readers a rollicking love story with entertaining characters, along with a wonderful storyline. After reading the opening chapter, I was hooked. You'll be pulled in by Loree's outstanding gift for storytelling.

—*Rita Gerlach*
Award-winning author, *Surrender the Wind*

Loree Lough has once again melded her mastery of words with her innate understanding of people to create two characters you can't help but love. With history, adventure, and a little romance tossed into the mix, this first book in the Lone Star Legends series promises a story that will delight and encourage you.

—*Laurean Brooks*
Award-winning author, *Journey to Forgiveness*

Loree Lough throws the reader into the wilds of West Texas in 1888, complete with the unrelenting heat and suspicions. She peoples the book with strong characters who have nothing in common and a lot to lose. A real page-turner.

—*Lena Nelson Dooley*
Award-winning author, *Minnesota Brothers* and
Love Finds You in Golden, New Mexico

I can count on Loree Lough for a deeply engaging story and characters who come to life on the first page. With the richness of Loree's vivid descriptions, readers can feel the powerful emotions as they sizzle between Kate and Josh.

—*Debby Mayne*
Author, *Love Finds You in Treasure Island, Florida*

Loree Lough makes you feel as though you are there as she paints a beautiful picture. The tension mounts quickly in this romance as conflicts abound. *Beautiful Bandit* is a page-turner, one to keep readers up at night!

—*Lori Twichell*
Reviewer, fictionaddict.com

Kate Wellington is vulnerable and very real, and Stetson-wearing Josh Neville grabs your heart in the first two pages. Loree Lough's sharp, finely honed writer's voice is the melody behind this song, and her depth-infused characters and compelling story will have you turning page after page to keep up with their adventure. Plant your feet firmly in the stirrups and wind the reins tight around your hands—this is one great ride!

—*Sandra D. Bricker*
Award-winning author,
Love Finds You in Snowball, Arkansas and *The Big 5-Oh!*

The catchy title *Beautiful Bandit* sets the scene for another gutsy, entertaining book by veteran storyteller Loree Lough. This first book in the Lone Star Legends series is a beautiful tale of love, suspense, and courage. Loree is a master at grasping the emotions of a woman's heart and the determination of a man's will. With her remarkable characters, authentic historical details, and hint of intrigue, Loree has crafted another rich romance… a delightful story that leaves them eagerly anticipating the next two books in the series.

—*Irene Brand*
Author of more than seventeen novels, including *Broken Bow, Where the River Flows*, and *A Husband for All Seasons*

I love historical fiction with a lot of intrigue and romance. Make the outlaw a woman, and you grab me all the more. Filled with suspenseful twists and turns, *Beautiful Bandit* made me breathless with anticipation. It's riveting.

—*Michelle Sutton*
Award-winning author, *It's Not about Me!*

Whether she's writing upbeat contemporary or dramatic historical romance, Loree Lough writes with a flair for character, emotion, and suspense. *Beautiful Bandit* is so intriguing, it kept me turning the pages and wishing I was in 1888 Texas!

—*Robin Bayne*
Award-winning author and compiler, *Words to Write By*

Beautiful Bandit

Beautiful Bandit

Loree Lough

ω

WHITAKER
HOUSE

BEAUTIFUL BANDIT
Book One in the Lone Star Legends Series

Loree Lough
www.loreelough.com

ISBN: 978-1-60374-225-2
Printed in the United States of America
© 2010 by Loree Lough

Whitaker House
1030 Hunt Valley Circle
New Kensington, PA 15068
www.whitakerhouse.com

Library of Congress Cataloging-in-Publication Data

Lough, Loree.
 Beautiful bandit / by Loree Lough.
  p. cm. — (Lone Star legends ; bk. 1)
 Summary: "Texas rancher Joshua Neville rescues a hapless runaway who calls herself Dinah Theodore and finds himself falling in love with her, but when he learns that she is wanted for robbery and murder under the name Kate Wellington, he must discover the truth about her past, help her to accept God's forgiveness, and decide whether their love is meant to be"—Provided by publisher.
 ISBN 978-1-60374-225-2 (trade pbk.)
 1. Ranchers—Texas—Fiction. I. Title.
PS3562.O8147B43 2010
813'.54—dc22
                      2010013100

2 3 4 5 6 7 8 9 10 11 12 **Ⱳ** 18 17 16 15 14 13 12 11 10

Dedication

To my dear readers (many of whom have become cherished friends over the years), whose lovely letters inspire me to keep writing.

To my steady-as-a-rock husband, who feeds my confidence.

To my daughters and grandchildren, whose belief in my talents never falters.

To every one of the wonderful people at Whitaker House, whose hard work and faith in my abilities made the Lone Star Legends series possible.

A special, heartfelt thank-you to Courtney and Lois, my wonderful editors, whose insights and guidance helped make *Beautiful Bandit* an even better story.

Above all, to my Lord and Father, who blessed me with a talent for storytelling and provides the ideas and the energy to share His Word at every opportunity.

A Letter from Loree

Precious Friends,

Oh, how I love hearing from you, whether by way of the mailbox out front or the one in my e-mail program! When your letters arrive, I stop whatever I'm doing and sit down with a cup of tea to enjoy my mini visit with you. I praise the Lord as I read your good news, and when you share tribulations, I pray He will see you through every trial. Is it any wonder that so many of you have become treasured friends over the years?

In 1994, the Almighty called me to write faith-based fiction, and, seventy-four novels later, it's *you*, my precious friends, who inspire me to continue. My goal with every story is to provide you with entertaining, exciting, Spirit-filled tales that feature characters who, just like we do, face tragedy and trauma…and work their ways toward grace by following the pure, bright light of God's mercy and love.

The Lone Star Legends series will transport you to Eagle Pass, Texas, just miles from the Rio Grande. I hope you've tied your bonnets on good and tight, because, oh, how different things were in 1888! Once there, you'll meet the rowdy, blond-haired, blue-eyed cowboy cousins with hearts as big as the Texas sky, and the tough yet tender women who tame them with love and patience—and the power of prayer.

I hope you'll write soon to tell me how much you enjoyed this trip to the Wild, Wild West in this first book of the series, *Beautiful Bandit*. Until then, I pray the Father will shower you and those you love with joys too numerous to count!

Warm hugs and God's blessings to you!

*T*he hot, sticky air in the banker's cluttered office made it hard to breathe. Josh ran a fingertip under his stiff collar as the image of cows, dropping by the thousand, reminded him of why he'd come to San Antonio. Selling a couple thousand uncontaminated acres from his family's ranch, the Lazy N, was the only way to protect the land that remained until they were able to get the anthrax infection under control.

He did his best not to glare at the decorous Bostonian, Griffen, sitting beside him. It wasn't the Swede's fault, after all, that the disease had killed so many of the Nevilles' cattle. In his shoes, Josh would have snapped up the land just as quickly. Trouble was, now this la-di-da Easterner would move to Eagle Pass, bringing his never-been-out-of-the-city wife and children with him. Worse yet, Josh had a sneaking suspicion that the former printing press operator would make a regular pest of himself by asking about the Texas climate, irrigation methods, when to plant, and only the good Lord knew what else. If that didn't earn Josh a seat closer to the Throne, he didn't know what would.

Few things agitated him more than sitting in one spot. Especially indoors. Confusion at how these fancy gents managed to look so calm and cool only added to his restlessness. He hung his Stetson on his left knee, mostly to occupy his hands in some way. Now, as the banker explained the terms of the agreement, Josh stared hard at the bloodred Persian rug under his boots and searched his mind for something else to focus on, anything other than the wretched document that would transfer ownership of Neville land to this foreigner. Moving his Stetson to his right knee, he remembered the day he'd bought the hat, and how he'd purchased another just like it one year later, when business at the Lazy N had put him back in Garland. One for riding the range, one for his wedding.

Strange, he thought, how Sadie could appear in his mind's eye from out of nowhere, even after three long years without her. He forced her from his mind. This get-together was more than painful enough without his dwelling on the most agonizing period of his life. Josh exhaled a harsh sigh, hoping the banker and the Swede hadn't heard the tremor in it. For his agitation, he blamed the oppressive heat. His empty stomach. The ten-day ride from Eagle Pass that had left him so bone-tired, he couldn't sleep, even on the hotel's pillow-soft mattress. *A body would think that an establishment with Persian rugs and velvet curtains could afford to provide some cold water for its clients*, he thought, loosening his string tie as Griffen asked yet another inane question. *Father, give me the strength to keep from grabbing those papers and hotfooting it out of here without making the deal!* he prayed silently.

Sadly, his thoughts were doing little to distract him from the grim truth.

He had cast the single dissenting vote at the family meeting, and the decision to sell the land had become even more odious to him when it had been decided that, as the only Neville with a law degree, Josh would be responsible for transacting the sale. He groaned inwardly at the sorry state of affairs, leaning forward to hide the tears that burned in his eyes. He loved every blessed acre—especially *those* acres— that made up the Lazy N. He'd built a small but solid home for Sadie and himself on that section of the ranch, and having to hand it over to someone else hurt almost as much as burying Sadie had.

Griffen, God bless him, had been the one to suggest that Josh hold on to the precious acre where she had been buried, along with their twins, who had died at birth. When Josh had asked permission to visit their graves from time to time, Griffen's pale eyes had darkened a shade, and he had said, "I'd be a wreck in your position. We will build a fence around the land to make sure your little family is never disturbed." But Josh had known, even as he'd nodded in agreement, that having to cross Griffen property to reach his family would only heap one misery atop another.

Josh grabbed his Stetson and, with his elbows propped on his knees, spun it round and round as he watched, through the window, two men dismount sweaty horses and tether them beside two others with empty saddles. They looked as tense and restless as he felt, and he wondered what unfortunate family business had brought them to the bank today.

"If you'll just sign here, Mr. Neville," Thomas Schaeffer said, redirecting Josh's attention to his own, unfortunate family business.

He accepted the banker's fountain pen. As its freshly inked nib hovered over the document, a bead of sweat trickled down his spine, and he felt a disturbing kinship with the fat hen his ma had roasted for dinner last Sunday.

Outside, the wind blew steadily, swirling street grit into tiny twisters that skittered up the parched road before bouncing under buggies and scurrying into alleyways. Even the burning breeze would feel better than this choking heat. "Mind if I open the window? I'm sweatin' like a—"

"I'd much rather you didn't," he said, peering over the rims of his gold-trimmed spectacles. "The wind is likely to scatter our paperwork hither and yon."

Hither and yon, indeed. Josh had read sayings like that in literature, but what kind of person actually used that sort of language in everyday speech? His musings over the annoying situation were interrupted by the sounds of shuffling foot-steps and coarse whispers from the other side of the banker's office door.

The commotion put a stern frown on Schaeffer's heat-red-dened face. "I declare," he said through clenched teeth, "I can't take my eyes off that fool assistant of mine for fifteen minutes without some sort of mayhem erupting." Blotting his fore-head with a starched white hanky, he continued grumbling, "Looks like I'll have no choice but to replace him." Shoving the eyeglasses higher, he lifted his chin and one bushy gray eyebrow—a not-so-subtle cue for Josh to sign the paper.

So, gritting his teeth, Josh inhaled a sharp breath, scratched his name on the thin, black line, and traded the pen for the banknote Schaeffer handed him.

On his feet now, Griffen grabbed Josh's hand. "T'ank you," he said, shaking it, "been a pleasure doing business wit' you, Neville."

Unable to make himself say, "Likewise," Josh forced a stiff smile and pocketed the check. "You bet." God willing, the worst was behind his family now.

The burnished, brass pendulum of the big clock behind the banker's desk swayed left with an audible *tick* as the men prepared to go their separate ways.

It swung right as gunshots rang out in the lobby.

Schaeffer and Griffen ran for the door, but a flurry of activity outside drew Josh's attention back to the window.

Tick....

It was the twosome he'd seen earlier, now joined by another man and a woman, scrambling up into their saddles. A lumpy burlap sack rested on the meaty rump of the biggest man's mount, and sunlight glinted from his pistol.

Tick....

Now Josh knew why the bunch had looked so nervous before. They'd been just about to rob the bank! He yanked out his sidearm, pulled back the hammer with one hand, and threw open the window with the other, hoping to get off a shot or two before the robbers were swallowed up by the cyclone of grit kicked up by their horses' hooves.

Tick....

Perched on the sill, Josh took aim at the shoulder of the fattest bandit, just as the woman's pony veered right, putting her square in the center of his gun sight.

Tick....

She looked back as Josh released the pressure on the sweat-slicked trigger.

Tick....

Quick as you please, she faced front again, her cornflower blue skirt flapping like a tattered sail as she was swallowed up in a thick cloud of dust.

Mark my words, girlie, that one's trouble. Big trouble. The purty ones always are."

Nobody was better at taking a man's measure than Etta Mae Samuels, proprietress of Silky's, the saloon where Kate Wellington sang for her supper. If she'd heeded her boss's advice, Kate would be crooning "Jeanie with the Light Brown Hair" and plinking the keys of Etta's battered Chickering & Sons piano right now, instead of walking the soles off her boots by night and resting, hidden behind boulders and trees, during the daylight hours. If only she could make it to Mexico before the Texas Rangers or the Frank Michaels Gang caught up with her.

Kate Wellington, she thought ruefully, *your life is way out of tune.* She might have felt even sorrier for herself, if not for the fact that she had no one to blame but herself for her predicament.

All last month, Frank Michaels had sat front and center at Silky's, asking to hear "Sweet Betsey from Pike," "Yellow Rose of Texas," and "Get Along, Little Dogies" and tossing coins onto the stage each time she filled a request. He'd treated her to dinner, bought her posies, and plied her with compliments that set her heart to fluttering and her cheeks to flushing. Then, a week ago, he'd invited her to join him for an ice cream, and when he'd asked if she minded waiting while he made a quick withdrawal at the bank on the way there, well, how would she have been able to refuse such a gentlemanly request?

At the door, he'd jerked her close and whispered, "Do as you're told, and no one will get hurt." When she'd opened her mouth to protest, he'd rammed a gun barrel into her ribs. "One word," he'd hissed, "and it'll be your last."

Nodding like a marionette, she let him lead her inside. "Tell that pasty-faced old hen to fill this up," he rasped, handing her a burlap sack. "Remember—do as I say, and nobody gets hurt." Using his chin as a pointer, he made sure she was aware of the teller, assistant manager, and two customers he'd shoot if she didn't comply.

Trembling, Kate plopped the bag onto the counter. "Put all the money into this sack, Claribel, and be quick about it. He isn't afraid to—"

Frank jabbed the gun deeper into her side.

"We aren't afraid to shoot," she said instead.

The woman's face went sickly white as her fingers fumbled with the bills. Then, the lead started flying, and in less time than it would have taken to say, "You promised no one would get hurt!" two more men stormed through the doors, guns blazing. The bank patrons and employees started toppling like dominoes, and Kate knew, as Frank dragged her outside, that she'd see that grisly image every time she closed her eyes.

For a moment, as they were mounting up, Kate locked gazes with a man staring out through a window of the bank. She almost shouted, "I'm not one of them! I'm a hostage!" But her spinelessness had already cost four lives, and the fear that he might become the fifth made her clamp her teeth together. She watched the stranger draw his gun and take aim in her direction, and she held her breath, hoping that he was a good shot. She deserved to die the same, awful death as those poor, innocent people in the bank.

"Get moving!" Frank bellowed as the man in the window slowly lowered his gun.

The same question was still echoing in her head as she limped along the hardscrabble path: Surely, he'd believed she'd been involved in the robbery. So, why hadn't he killed her when he'd had the chance?

If he had, her aching feet wouldn't be competing with the twinge in her back, and she wouldn't be cold and tired and hungry. Had she pulled a muscle, falling from the window in the Loma Vista Beer Saloon's storage room? Or was the pain a result of walking miles and miles in dressy boots not made to withstand rugged terrain?

Kate knew she was living on borrowed time. As she was the only witness to the robbery and murders, what choice did Frank and his gang have but to hunt her down and silence her?

And to think she'd believed he intended to propose marriage! Why, he'd bamboozled her, just as surely as Axel Ayers bilked city slickers with his "pea under the walnut shell" game. Axel's victims had lived to refill their purses and pockets, but her foolish infatuation had cost four good people their lives, and not even the fact that the nose of a revolver had been digging into her back seemed a good enough excuse for her cowardice.

If she'd refused to participate, if she'd warned Claribel, if she'd tried to grab the gun barrel, or something, Frank probably would have killed her where she stood. But Kate had no family to mourn her, whereas Claribel had a husband and grandchildren, and those poor men had wives and children.

Immediately following the holdup, she'd thought of little else as the Frank Michaels Gang had zigzagged across the countryside to confound the Texas Rangers. The only times she'd been distracted had been at night, when Frank would boast about how quickly he'd taught his little "Katie toy" the price of resisting. Oh, she'd learned to silently endure his torture, but nothing—not threats to slit her throat or promises of fancy clothes—could keep her eyes from exposing her unadulterated revulsion. And so, Frank had taken to blindfolding her each time he violated her, using the same, grubby rag with which he had tied her hands to the saddle horn.

With no family and little hope of ever having one, thanks to what Frank Michaels had done to her, Kate felt like she didn't have much to live for. But if she really believed that, why had she fought so hard to survive his brutality? And why had she escaped the first chance she got "You'll have plenty of time to puzzle that one out," she said to herself, her breath puffing white into the inky air as she slumped, exhausted, to the cold ground, "once you get to Mexico." She could almost hear the rowdy voices and clinking glasses of the Mexican cantinas Etta Mae's customers so often talked about. Surely, she could find work in one of them, tickling the keys of an out-of-tune piano and crooning popular melodies for the patrons.

And then, an idea flitted into her head, one so good and so bright that it inspired a tiny smile. "You can learn to live on just a few pesos," Kate whispered to herself, "and send money to Claribel's husband, and the wives and children of—"

She couldn't bring herself to say, "The men who died because of your cowardice." Instead, she made a solemn oath to do everything she could to make up for what she'd done—or, more accurately, what she hadn't done—at the bank.

Kate pushed herself back to her feet and pressed on, trying to ignore the cold night air, her parched throat, and her growling stomach, hoping with every agonizing step that Frank wouldn't be waiting on the other side of the next rise, that the Rangers were too busy looking for Frank to worry about following her.

Because, for the first time since Frank had taken her captive, Kate Wellington had a good reason to live.

*J*osh yawned and stretched the kinks from his neck, wondering when he'd last felt as dog-tired as he did now. "Sure will be good to pull up for the night, won't it, girl?" he asked his horse.

Callie responded by quickening her pace, as if she understood that several pans of oats and water would be hers when they stopped for the day. She wouldn't have had to make the trip at all if Josh had taken Pa's advice. But few things annoyed him more than wasting money, and that's just what he would have done by purchasing a two-way train ticket to San Antonio.

Josh could have shaved two days off the ride if he'd been willing to push Callie harder. But as much as he wanted to ride under the familiar, wrought-iron gate that spelled out "Lazy N Ranch," he saw no point in making his loyal mare pay the price for his family's decision to make a land-for-money deal with Griffen.

Callie's stomach growled, and, as if on cue, so did Josh's. Another hour, maybe two, and he'd treat himself to some of the jerky he'd bought on his way out of town. His purchases—coffee, oats, biscuits, jerky, carrots, and matches—would have cost half as much at home. One more reason to thank the good Lord that he lived on the outskirts of Eagle

Pass, where the annual church bazaar stood in satisfactorily for big-city noise and activity.

The sun went down, and so did the temperature, making a fire seem mighty appealing. Josh directed Callie toward a flat spot near a small grove of scrub pines he'd spotted.

"Atta girl," he said, patting her neck as she slowed to a stop. Both his boots hit the dust as he added, "Let's hope our campfire won't lure scorpions—or bandits."

He'd worried about both almost from the moment he'd ridden out of San Antonio. It hadn't taken long to tell the sheriff what he knew about the holdup at the bank. He'd done his best to describe each man, but that hadn't been easy, since all but one had had his face hidden behind a bandanna. That was, all but one and the girl.

If the sheriff had asked his opinion, Josh would have told him the gang's best bet would be to head south, not west. That's where he'd have gone, anyway. But the sheriff hadn't asked, and as Josh had watched the posse ride out, he hadn't been able to help feeling uneasy. Like a dark cloud, the dubious sensation had shadowed him, meaning he'd had to sleep with one eye open every one of the five nights of his trip. Still, it would feel mighty good sliding into his soogan after washing down a biscuit and some bacon with a cup of hot coffee.

It was completely dark when he finally stretched out under the night sky. Callie, her belly full of oats and carrots, nickered from where he'd tethered her to the branches of a scrawny blackbrush shrub, reminding him of the last trip on which he'd bedded down beneath a canopy of stars. It had been two years ago—just over a month after Sadie had joined Jesus—that Josh and his cousins had driven a herd toward a Nebraska packing house. During those sweltering, dusty days, the boys tried to cheer him up by cracking jokes as they yee-hawed and whistled to keep the cows together. At night, the dogies lowed in happy harmony to Daniel's guitar, while Paul plucked the Jew's harp and Micah hummed into his harmonica. Ordinarily, Josh would have crooned along, but with Sadie's passing so fresh in his mind, he'd counted stars in silence, instead.

Now, he tucked his hands under his head and smiled a little, thinking about Sadie's first Thanksgiving as a Neville. "The good Lord did your mamas a favor," she'd teased, "putting just one boy under each roof!" Josh's mother had pointed out that God had more than made up for it by delivering giggling girls to each Neville house—four sisters for Paul, three for Micah, six for Daniel, and two for Josh—all of whom had bonded instantly with Sadie, despite the fact that she'd grown up as the only child of elderly parents.

Pushing himself up on one elbow, Josh used a gnarled whitebrush branch to stir the coals. Sparks floated toward the heavens, and he recalled how much Sadie had loved the stars. "God's diamonds," she'd called them.

Callie snorted, then pawed the dirt and whinnied. Josh strained his ears, sitting up all the way to distinguish between normal noises of the night and whatever had spooked his usually unflappable mare. He quickly dismissed the hoots of owls, the symphony of crickets, and the shrill *peent* of a nighthawk and focused on a sound that fell somewhere between a moan and a sigh, coming from behind a boulder near Callie's tree.

Instinct made him palm his pistol. Witnessing the robbery and murders in San Antonio had made him edgy and restless. The gang of outlaws could be anywhere, and, after all his family had suffered in order to obtain the banknote hidden in his boot, he had no intention of giving it up without a fight.

Inching along toward the source of the sound, he eased back on the hammer of his gun, wincing at the barely audible click that seemed to crack like thunder in the near silence.

"Please," came a tiny, frail voice, "please don't shoot."

What's a young'un doing way out here in the middle of nowhere? Josh wondered. But he'd volunteered to help the Rangers round up enough rustlers and bandits to know they had more than just cards up their sleeves. It wouldn't have surprised him in the least if it was an outlaw imitating a child. "Hands up," he growled, "and on your feet."

"I—I can't."

He'd already assumed the "ready, aim" position. Now, as Josh took those last few steps, he adopted the "fire" stance, fully prepared to drill the phony-voiced crook full of lead if he had to.

However, it was not a child, but a woman. When he rounded the rock, she was on her knees, facing him, both arms high in the air. She was not much bigger than a child, and Josh couldn't tell if her head-to-toe trembling was caused by fright—for her bright-green eyes looked twice the size of Callie's—or if the chill in the air was to blame. Seeing that she wielded no weapon, he lowered his own. "Are you out of your mind, sneaking up on a man in the dark?" he snarled, holstering the gun. "That's about the best way I know to get shot!"

Hugging herself, she said, "I—I just hoped to come closer to the fire...once you'd gone to sleep, that is. I would've been gone before you awoke in the morning."

How long had she been skulking around these parts, to have worked out a plan to snare a few moments of warmth? She looked oddly familiar, though, for the life of him, he couldn't say why. "Looks like you've been yanked through a keyhole at the end of a rope," Josh said, helping her up. "What in tarnation happened to you, missy?"

It must have been feminine self-consciousness that prompted her to pat her snarled, coppery hair and smooth her wrinkled, brown skirt. Sweat and grit had stained what had likely once been a fine, white shirt, and those boots—clearly not made for hiking any distance—were covered in trail dust.

He'd never been able to stand seeing a female in distress, even one who looked as though she'd just climbed out of the coal bin. So, he invited her toward the warmth of the flames, and, when she appeared to be limping, he scooped her up in his arms. She weighed hardly more than his saddle, and her pained grimace told him that under the grubby blouse, she hid bruises, maybe even a cracked rib or two.

Dropping to one knee, Josh eased her to the ground near the fire. The instant he draped his blanket over her shoulders, she clutched it tightly to her and leaned so close to the fire that he worried she might topple face-first into it.

"Easy, now," he said, "unless you want a mouthful of hot ashes." Uncorking one of his canteens, he held it out to her. "Are you thirst—"

She grabbed it, pressed it to her lips, and gulped.

"Whoa, too much at once, and you'll end up with a powerful bellyache."

She quickly wiped the back of one hand across her mouth. "Sorry," she gasped. "Didn't mean to behave like an ungrateful pig."

He shook his head to let her know that she needn't apologize, noting how odd it was that, so far, she hadn't looked him square on for longer than an eyeblink.

"I haven't had anything to drink in days," she added.

Or a bath, he thought, *and probably not a bite to eat, either.* He fetched a chunk of jerky and two biscuits from his saddlebag, then held them out to her. "Slow and easy, now, hear?" he said as she accepted them with an eager look in her eyes.

"Thanks," she said around the first mouthful.

He plopped down beside her, careful not to sit too close, and rested his forearms on his knees. "So, what's your story?"

Brows high on her forehead, she stopped chewing. "Story?"

"I've made the trip between Eagle Pass and San Antonio several dozen times. Saw my fair share of lizards and bobwhites and even a cuckoo or two on the trail, but you're the first woman. There's sure to be quite a tale about why you're out here, all by your lonesome, lookin' like you do."

She finished chewing and swallowed, then ran her dirty fingers through her tangled hair. "I...." Frowning, she looked everywhere except at him, as if somewhere deep in the blackness, she'd find an explanation to satisfy his curiosity. "I don't know how I got out here."

"Is that so? Well, I don't mind admitting that sounds more than a mite suspic—"

The tears glittering in her eyes silenced him, and though nothing she'd done or said so far justified it, a long-forgotten sentiment echoed in his heart. He wanted to ease her fear, make her feel safe. "Let's start with something easy, then. Like, your name?"

Staring into the fire, she chewed her lower lip. "I—I don't remember."

"Don't remember?" he echoed her. Josh had met some addle-brained women in his day, but every last one had at least known her own name! "Did you fall from a horse? Wander away from a stagecoach accident? Get thumped on the head by a robber?"

A minuscule gasp escaped her lips, and, for a moment, she actually looked him square in the eye. In that instant, he knew without a doubt that something sinister *had* happened to her. Then, just when he thought he might have made some headway, she hid her face in her hands. "What day is it?" she mumbled through her fingers.

"Wednesday."

"Is it—is it still May?"

This country was ripe with swindlers, each with a unique scheme to steal a man blind. Could it be that she had donned this clever disguise to relieve him of his family's money? "Yep, still May."

She dropped her hands but kept her eyes fixed on the fire. "Did I hear you say you're returning from San Antonio?"

He answered yes, thinking he'd have to be deaf not to hear the strain in her voice.

"We aren't, by any chance, headed to Mexico, are we?"

Maybe she *had* suffered a blow to the head. She'd said "we." Did that mean she expected to travel with him from here on out? Josh sure hoped not. Because the last thing he needed was a woman adding to his worries. Especially one without a horse. And one who reeked of trouble.

He picked up the whitebrush branch again and shoved the pointy end into the fire. For all he knew, she had a derringer tucked into one of those little boots; the glowing end of the stick might just come in handy if she decided to aim it at him. "We're a good three days' ride outside of Eagle Pass." Josh didn't know why, but when she blinked in response to his curt tone, he gentled his voice. "Mexico—is that where you're headed?"

"Yes. At least, I think so."

That was an afterthought, if ever he'd heard one. But something told him that he could hammer at her all night and still end up with more questions than answers. Better to let her finish the meat, have another swallow of water, and get a couple of hours of sleep. Maybe her memory—if that was her problem—would wake with her at first light.

Once she'd finished devouring every crumb of biscuit that had fallen into her lap, Josh tidied his makeshift bed and helped her slide into it. For a minute there, as she blinked up at him gratefully, he was tempted to press a comforting kiss to her forehead, the way he did when tucking in his sister's little boy for the night. "G'night," he murmured instead, fighting the urge.

In place of a reply, she treated him to a shy, little smile that started his heart to pounding like a parade drum. Josh blamed his reaction on the life-altering events of the past few weeks—events that, one by one, had threatened to make him stagger. Since Sadie, no woman had turned his head, and he couldn't allow himself to acknowledge that the waiflike woman near the fire could change that fact, even if she was the cutest little slip of a thing he'd ever laid eyes on.

Wrapping himself in Callie's saddle blanket, Josh leaned back against the tree where she was tied, smiling to himself as the woman slipped into a fitful slumber. His grin faded, though, when she began to mutter and groan. In the fading firelight, he saw her expression change from worry to horror. "What do you make of it, Callie?" he whispered.

The horse snorted, as if to say, "You've got me by the feet."

The woman hadn't seemed able to bring herself to look at him, whereas Josh couldn't make himself look away from her. Even contorted by apparent anguish, her face reminded him of an innocent angel, and he shook his head, wondering about his earlier wariness. *Without all that grit and grime, she'd likely be downright gorgeous*, he thought.

The mare bobbed her head as if she agreed with his silent assessment.

When the sun rose, maybe its rays would reveal evidence of a head injury to explain his midnight visitor's peculiar behavior. In the meantime, Josh could count two good reasons to content himself with watching her sleep.

For one thing, she had the prettiest face he'd ever seen. She was prettier than any of his sisters. Prettier, even, than Sadie, though he felt like a lout admitting that, even to himself. For another, as long as he kept a guarded eye on her—and kept his boots on—the money his family would use to repopulate their herds would remain safe.

If only he could be as sure about the safety of his heart.

4

*K*ate felt terrible about lying to the good-looking cowboy, but what other choice did she have? He could have been an off-duty Texas Ranger, for all she knew. Or, worse, some ruffian who'd once ridden with the Frank Michaels Gang.

He was kind to share his food and water and to insist that she take his bed near the fire. And it had been mighty nice that he hadn't pressed her for too many details, especially considering it was plain to see he was chomping at the bit to learn more—lots more—about her history.

He looked vaguely familiar, but that didn't surprise her. She'd lost count of how many men had visited Silky's as they'd passed through town. Maybe this soft-spoken, trail-weary fellow had been one of those who'd asked her to sing his favorite ballad.

On the off chance he was just an ordinary man, going about his ordinary business, he was far better off—and far safer—not knowing the truth about her. In the morning, after she'd gotten directions to Mexico, she'd ask his name and pray for his well-being as she headed south.

In the meantime, she figured she'd better come up with a new identity for herself. Even if the cowboy didn't resume his interrogation, she was bound to run into someone else between here—wherever "here" was—and Mexico, and the next inquisitive fellow might not be a gentleman.

And then, there was the matter of the wanted poster that featured her portrait. Hunger and thirst had driven her into the last town she'd passed. As she'd stood, gawking, at the black-and-white likeness of herself, Kate's heart had beat so hard, she'd worried it might just burst clean through her shirt. "WANTED," the top line said, and below it, "KATE WELLINGTON, DEAD OR ALIVE." Beneath that, "FOR MURDER AND ARMED BANK ROBBERY." And, finally, in bigger, bolder letters, "REWARD."

What a silly little fool she'd been, believing no one had been witness to what had happened that day in the bank. It was yet another reason to change her name. And she'd stop wearing her hair loose and free, the way the artist had drawn it in the picture, and style it in a sensible bun. She'd also trade her attractive dress for humdrum attire. The changes would save her skin, and if they spared the cowboy from having to choose between letting her go and delivering her to the Texas Rangers, who'd make her one of the only women in history to be sent to the gallows, they'd be worth every uncomfortable moment.

She agonized over it all night, pulling at his scratchy, brown blanket, punching at the ratty quilt he'd rolled up to be used as a pillow, then berating herself for how spoiled she'd become. The third-floor bedroom Etta Mae provided as part of Kate's weekly pay came furnished, complete with thick towels and crisp, white sheets, a colorful coverlet, and a fat, feather pillow. On her small balcony, she could sit, sipping tea, as she smiled and waved to the townsfolk down on Main Street. And when the delectable scents of chicken-fried steak and beef stew woke her taste for solid foods, she had a standing invitation to help herself to anything in the kitchen, any old time her hungry heart desired. She could almost taste the melt-in-your-mouth mashed potatoes and vine-ripened tomatoes served by Dinah and Theodore, Etta Mae's cooks.

Kate had grown accustomed to her pampered lifestyle, but those days were long gone, thanks to her fanciful, doltish decisions of late. If she hoped to fulfill her dream of sending money to the families of Frank's victims—and she most certainly did—she realized she'd need to learn to make do with rough covers, unyielding head cushions, and scarce food. She'd better get used to clothes that looked like she'd borrowed them from a scarecrow, too.

The thought brought her attention to her soiled shirt and tattered skirt. How could she expect a future employer to hire her when she looked like a ragamuffin? And yet, with no money, and no prospect of procuring any, how would she replace her ragged outfit? Discouraged, Kate exhaled a weary sigh.

Dwelling on the situation won't change it, she scolded herself, *so don't!* Her thoughts and energy would be better spent on solving her dilemma, starting with putting herself on the Mexican side of the Rio Grande. The Texas Rangers' jurisdiction stopped at the border, though, in all truthfulness, dying at the end of a rope seemed a far, far easier way to go than enduring whatever torture Frank would inflict—before ending her life.

The fear welling up inside her reminded Kate of a day from her childhood, when the mighty Mississippi had surged above its banks, feeding on houses and businesses like a raging, gluttonous fiend. Miraculously, she and her mama had escaped the water's greedy appetite, but many others hadn't been so lucky. If she closed her eyes, Kate could still hear their terrified cries for help. She could pray for another miracle like that, but why would God answer the prayers of a sinner like her?

Swallowing hard, Kate licked her lips. A sip from her rescuer's canteen sure would taste good right about now. She lifted her head and saw him staring toward the horizon. What had captured his attention so completely? The Rangers, maybe. Or Frank's gang. She needed to leave this place. Leave this man. Because, whether the approaching riders were lawmen or lawbreakers, he could pay a hefty price for helping her.

If she could depend on her traitorous, pampered feet, she'd grab one of his canteens and run for the border. But logic quickly fizzled that thought. Even if she knew which way to go, he'd saddle his horse and catch up to her in no time. He'd been kind and gentle so far, but then, she hadn't riled him, either.

You could try honesty for a change, you little ninny....

Maybe. Yes, that might just work. If she played her cards right, perhaps he'd offer her one of his canteens, or even loan her a dollar or two, provided her story was pitiful enough. Of course, she wouldn't be able to pay him back.

Just listen to you! You're turning into a little swindler, hardly better than Frank Michaels, himself! She'd come from hard and humble beginnings yet had never been tempted to steal or beg. Did having both sides of the law on her trail excuse her sinful thoughts? Kate didn't think so. But she couldn't risk putting this kindly cowboy in danger just to save her own skin.

The world began to glow with deep, purple light, indicating that the sun would soon rise. Kate rolled over in her crude bed. *Not much time left to dream up a believable story,* she told herself. Her stomach churned, telling her with each growl and grumble that the food the cowboy had shared last night hadn't done much to ease her days-old hunger. Oh, for another bite of stale bread and salty beef!

The thought of eating made her think again about Etta Mae's cook, Dinah, and her strapping husband—also Etta Mae's manservant—Theodore. Dinah, who was Irish, and Theodore, who had been born in London, had moved to San Antonio by way of New York City and Chicago. With no children of their own, they were only too happy to treat Kate like a surrogate daughter. "Etta Mae told me about yer brutal da," Dinah had said to Kate just a few months ago. "It does me old heart good, Katie-girl, that ye took the high road." The older woman would always roll her eyes at the painted gals known as "Etta's Girls." "I know ye'd make more money doin' what they do for a livin', but, ah, the price ye'd pay to drop those extra coins into yer purse on payday!"

Kate had been proud of herself when that conversation had ended, but she didn't feel that way now. But she had no one to blame but herself for the self-loathing swirling in her heart, for her own poor choices had put her on this tough and lonely road. She could only hope that smarter decisions in the future would put her back on the right road again.

Just then, the idea popped into her head so quickly, it was all she could do to keep from bolting upright and shouting, "Yes! That's *it*!"

"Well, you gonna sleep all day?"

The sudden sound of the cowboy's voice startled Kate, and she muffled her squeal in the bristly bedroll. Land sakes! She'd become a jumpy little wretch. Just because Frank Michaels was a brute and a beast didn't mean this man would duplicate the torture he'd inflicted on her! Tossing the blanket aside, she got to her feet. "Do I smell coffee?"

"You do, but don't get your hopes up—all I've got to go with it is jerky. And some more biscuits, if you're tempted."

"Sounds like manna from heaven." She shook the dust from the blanket, then began folding it into a tidy square. "Anything I can do to help?"

In place of an answer, he looked at her feet. "Not limping much this morning, I see."

She returned his friendly smile. "Amazing what food, water, and a good night's sleep will do for a girl." He didn't need to know that she'd hardly slept a wink.

"Don't know where my mind was last night," he said, handing her a blue mug speckled with white. "Clean forgot to introduce myself."

"I forgot a few things, myself," Kate admitted as the sharp scent of fire-brewed coffee floated into her nostrils. She held out her right hand. "Dinah Theodore," she said when he took it. "Pleased to make your acquaintance."

"Josh. Josh Neville." One corner of his mouth lifted in a wry grin. "So, where are you from, Dinah Theodore?"

It sounded odd hearing her new name spoken aloud that way. "Chicago, originally. Moved to San Antonio with my father, who worked for the railroad." At least that last part was true.

His left brow rose slightly, the way Etta Mae's always did when she caught one of her ladies in a fib. Maybe Kate didn't have to worry about becoming a savvy liar, after all. But before the good-looking cowboy started asking about Chicago—questions she wouldn't be able to answer, as the only thing she knew about the place was that Dinah and

Theodore had been married there—she helped herself to the smallest biscuit. Tearing it in half, she returned the rest of it to the pie tin. "So, which way is Mexico?"

Josh pointed south. "It's a four-day ride from these parts. I reckon it'll take three to four times that long to walk the distance, and I don't rightly know how you hope to get that far without a horse and food and water, or a coat and hat, especially wearin' those things you call boots."

Don't let him see that you're flustered, Kate, she commanded herself. And then, *Stop calling yourself Kate!* Later, while she trudged south, she could count the steps by chanting her new name and figuring out the facts about her new life, reciting them so they'd roll right off her tongue in response to inquiries. Why, she could even make up a song to help her remember that she'd left Kate Wellington in San Antonio to become Dinah Theodore! "Do you know where to find the nearest town?"

"Why?"

She shrugged. "Well, as you so astutely pointed out, I'm in need of sturdier shoes."

"You passed half a dozen towns between here and San Antonio. Why didn't you stop at any of them for, uh, 'sturdier shoes'?"

"I—I didn't notice any towns." Had she told him where she'd started her journey? Kate honestly couldn't remember. If she hadn't been terrified of running into Frank or one of his men, or someone with a silver star on his shirt, Kate might have risked stopping to ask a shopkeep if she could perform some menial chore in exchange for a used housedress, a pair of socks, and a hat to protect her head from the unrelenting sun. Right now, that was neither here nor there. "Can you recommend a particular road I should follow?"

"To get to Mexico, you mean?"

Kate nodded.

Josh waited a long time before answering, and she shifted uneasily under his intense scrutiny. Finally, he calmly refilled his coffee mug and said, "I didn't get much sleep last night, so I had plenty of time to wonder: What in tarnation are you running from?"

5

*T*he blood ran cold in Kate's veins. They'd exchanged, what, a few dozen words since he'd found her cowering behind that boulder? How could he have taken her measure so quickly?

"Woman doesn't just appear out of nowhere in the middle of the night, looking like she's been wrestlin' with a wildcat." He paused and, shaking his head, exhaled a deep breath. "All I'm saying is, you'll be defenseless out there all by yourself. If the critters and scorpions don't get you, the two-legged animal who put you in that shape might." He took a swig of his coffee. "I'm heading that direction, anyway, so it isn't like I'd be going out of my way."

Was he offering to let her ride with him? Surely, he wasn't serious. But, if he was, what price would he extract for going to so much trouble?

"You've got my word: long as you're with me, you'll be safe."

Except for Theodore—and, briefly, Frank—Kate had never really trusted a man in her life. Her father's ongoing barroom brawls had ultimately been the end of him, and, after his death, her mama, desperate to put a roof over their heads, had married the first fellow to ask, then drowned the pain of his abuse in rye whiskey. Though the sheriff had called it a suicide, even the then twelve-year-old Kate had known that her stepfather was responsible for her mama's death. He probably would have killed Kate, too, if he hadn't figured out she was more useful as payment for a poker debt.

She hadn't hung around long enough to find out if the bearded winner would bully her the way he bullied everyone else in town. Instead, Kate had sold her mama's cameo and stuffed her meager possessions into a pillowslip. In spite of the lies of a dozen deceitful young men who'd vowed to save her, she'd miraculously remained a virgin—until the night of the bank robbery. Did this stranger really expect her to believe she'd trust him just like that, simply because he gave her his word?

As if he'd read her mind, he said, "I can see you're not too sure if I'm reliable or not. So, here are a couple of questions you should ask yourself." Josh held up his forefinger. "First, what choice do you have?" He paused, and then his middle finger joined the first. "Second, how much worse could it be with me than it was with…"—he reached across the space between them to gently trace the still-tender bruise on her jaw—"with the pig who did *that* to you?"

It took every ounce of strength and willpower she could muster to keep from bursting into tears. Because like it or not—and she most certainly did *not*—the handsome cowboy was right. Tears prickled behind her eyelids. If she answered him now, they'd flow like rain from a downspout, and there was no telling when they'd stop.

"Seems to me, a gal who walked all this way knows how to take care of herself. Leastways, in most circumstances. But just in case you're still not convinced," Josh said, rummaging in his saddlebag and pulling out a gleaming, pearl-handled revolver, "you can shoot me if I step out of line."

Well, that settled it. Either the man was out of his mind, or he was telling the truth.

Kate couldn't think of a time in her life when she'd wanted—no, *needed*—to trust someone more. Slowly, she wrapped her hand around the grip of the revolver, and as she turned it this way and that to inspect it, he cautioned her, "It's loaded, so you might want to take care where you aim it."

The muzzle, she noted, had been pointed at his heart. Kate eased the gun into her lap as the irony of the situation provoked a giggle that started deep in her gut, then bubbled up and spilled out until it became breathy, full-blown laughter. The wanted poster in that little town said she'd committed armed robbery *and* cold-blooded murder, and yet, until this moment, she'd never even held a gun, let alone fired one! If he took the time to consider her sanity, chances were slim to none that he'd let her keep it after this display.

"Next town we come to is about half a day's ride south," he said, as calm as you please. "I'll go into a store while you wait at the border with Callie. I'll buy you a couple of skirts and shirts, a pair of boots that'll hold up in the weather, a hat to protect your pretty hair from the sun...."

Wait at the town's border? It could be only one of two things. Either he'd figured out that she was on the run from the law, or he was embarrassed to be seen with her. Kate could hardly blame him. Why, she'd seen drunks and scalawags who'd looked more presentable!

At this point, Kate couldn't tell tears of mirth from tears of fear, frustration and confusion. Had he given a thought to how she'd repay him for his generosity? Maybe he had a lazy wife and ten boisterous boys waiting for him in Eagle Pass, and he planned to take her home to cook and clean until the debt was repaid. Kate doubled over with laughter at the thought, because Frank would never think to look for her in a place like that!

Surprisingly, the cowboy continued, as composed as any man had a right to be, considering the company he'd chosen to keep. "You'll need your own blanket. And, can you ride?"

"A horse, you mean?" she managed to squeak out. Clearly, he'd decided to ignore her peculiar behavior. Maybe his wife was lazy *and* crazy, and he was accustomed to women behaving as if they'd gone completely mad. "Yes, yes, I can ride—"

"Then we'll get you a horse and saddle, too."

It seemed to Kate that he'd done more than just a little thinking last night. "You should know that I have nothing but the clothes on my back, such as they are." Hands up in supplication, she suddenly felt quite serious. "I have no way to repay you," she added.

Josh shrugged and topped off his coffee. "Haven't been to church in a couple of years, so let's just consider this the tithing I haven't done."

"Tithing—like I'm a charity case?"

"I hate to be blunt, but that's exactly what you are." He held up a hand to forestall any argument she might make. "A temporary situation, I'm sure."

Then he did the strangest thing. He smiled. Smiled! And, because Kate had never been on the receiving end of a genuine smile—at least, delivered by a man other than Theodore—it touched her. Profoundly.

Maybe it was a sign that she really could start over with a brand-new name and begin a brand-new life. Hope glowed inside her for the first time in a very long while. Kate took a deep breath. "Thank you, Mr. Neville. This is by far the nicest thing anyone has ever done for me."

"You can call me Josh," he muttered.

She ignored the flush of embarrassment that colored his tanned cheeks. For now, she had to find ways to convince herself that Kate Wellington was dead and gone, and that, as Dinah Theodore, she had a chance to live a normal life.

Kate had never been particularly pious, but she knew how much she owed God, for He'd saved her. She owed a debt of gratitude to Josh Neville, too, though he hadn't yet spent a penny on her.

6

*T*he following afternoon, as they rode side by side, Dinah pointed west. "What are those mountains?"

"The Anacachos. Not the highest peaks I've seen, but a pretty view, just the same."

"The view would be a lot prettier without those storm clouds."

Josh nodded. He'd had his eye on the dark sky since just after sunup.

"How bad do you think it'll be?"

Bad enough that we'll be lucky to avoid lightning strikes, he thought. "If memory serves me correctly, there's a little shack three or four miles ahead." He hoped they'd make it that far before the skies opened up. "Can you cook?"

Dinah let out a soft, dainty laugh that eased into his ears like music.

"A little."

He didn't know how to read the grin that slanted her beautiful lips. It could have meant either that she mostly turned vittles into charcoal or that she'd picked up more than her share of kitchen skills along the way.

"How 'bout you?" she asked, quirking one well-arched brow.

Josh told her about the many times he'd manned the chuck wagon when his family hadn't been able to find a cook to accompany them on cattle drives, and he admitted that his talents with trail food were limited to fried potatoes with canned beans and meat. "Never heard a complaint as the men walked away from the fire," he said, grinning.

"Well, I have firsthand knowledge of your abilities with biscuits and beef jerky."

She punctuated her comment with a merry wink that buzzed through Josh's veins like a tiny lightning bolt. And when she winced and wriggled in the saddle, he asked, "Been a while since you sat on a horse?"

"I'll answer that by asking if you have any liniment in that bag of tricks of yours."

"I reckon I can spare a drop or two."

Thunder rumbled in the distance, drawing Josh's attention back to the heavens. And because even the smallest bonnet in the store had been too big for her head, Dinah's hat caught a draft of wind and drifted up and then down to the ground. Josh brought his horse up, intending to fetch it, but she slid down from her saddle and grabbed it before he could even make the offer. In no time, she was back on the horse, tying a perfect knot under her chin.

"I was hoping not to need these bothersome ribbons," she said, frowning slightly, "but unless I want this pretty cap to become a nest for a family of jackrabbits out there in the brush, guess I'd better use them."

Chuckling, Josh shook his head. The girl had a knack for making the best of things, no doubt about that. Had a knack for looking pretty in even the plainest of clothes, too. Put that same dull, brown skirt and simple, white shirt on another woman, and the ensemble would look downright dreary.

Hopefully, she'd keep looking straight ahead. Or up. Anywhere but into his face. For she'd surely wonder what thoughts had turned his cheeks as pink as a silly schoolgirl's! It had been a long time since a woman had inspired such feelings in him. Two months shy of three years, to be precise. He blamed his mind-set on the tricky ride to San Antonio, when he'd been baked by sun and drenched by rain. On the heart-breaking reason he'd gone there in the first place. On the fact that his promise to deliver Dinah to the Mexican border meant adding a day, maybe more, to his already too-long trip, and the fact that he'd been dog-tired when he'd found her. Or, more accurately, when she'd found him.

Josh didn't really regret his decision to accompany Dinah to Mexico. His brain never would have let him rest, wondering about all the awful things that might happen to her, alone in the middle of nowhere. Seeing her safely across the border would ease his conscience, and, maybe, as they traveled together, she'd learn that not every man she met up with wanted to use her as a punching bag. *What kind of man would strike a woman?* he wondered. *Especially one so tiny and delicate and—*

"So, Josh, who's waiting for you at home?"

She'd caught him ruminating. Again. Tugging at his hat brim in hopes that it would hide yet another blush, Josh chuckled. "If I named them all, I'd talk myself hoarse."

Dinah inhaled a breath so deep, it lifted both of her shoulders. "Oh, Josh, how I envy you!"

A boyhood memory surfaced from out of nowhere. Once, during a ride into town with Ma, the wind had caught hold of her favorite scarf. Billowing like a white sail, it had soared high into the sky, then fluttered like a wounded dove before settling to the ground. Halting the team, he'd jumped down from the wagon to fetch it, and, to this day, he felt bad about the way his callused hands had snagged the fine fabric.

He felt himself frowning because he couldn't figure out why Dinah's voice just now had reminded him of the soft, silky feel of his ma's scarf.

Clearing his throat with the intent of clearing his head, too, he sat up straighter in the saddle. *What on earth has gotten into you?*

"I'm an only child, myself," she said. "My father died when I was only nine, and Mama didn't waste any time getting herself a new man."

Josh didn't know what to make of the sarcastic tone that punctuated her admission, but she didn't give him much time to speculate.

"Ma died, too, before...before she and my stepfather could have more children."

He noted her extra emphasis on the word "step," meaning she hadn't approved of her substitute father. Josh waited, but Dinah didn't elaborate on her story.

The period of quiet tempted him to pull out his pocket watch. Instead, he counted the silent seconds by the steady clip-clop of the horses' hooves. He couldn't imagine his sisters allowing this much time to pass without filling the void with chatter, and he had to admire a gal who didn't need to hear the sound of her own voice every waking moment.

Then, it hit him like a pebble to the forehead. That bit about her father dying and her mother remarrying had been the only personal information Dinah had shared about her past. What if her ability to stay quiet for more than a minute at a time wasn't an agreeable character trait, at all? What if, instead, she was harboring a secret, one she couldn't risk revealing by a slip of her tongue in a moment of mindless chatter?

When Dinah had told him she couldn't remember how she'd ended up alone, out there in the middle of nowhere, looking as if she'd just fought off a pack of coyotes, he'd believed her "I don't remember" story. And why wouldn't he have, when he'd witnessed dozens of falls or blows to the noggins of ranch hands that had resulted in their missing minutes, hours, and even days once they had come to? Also, what about the time when, at the age of ten, he'd tumbled from the hayloft and lost consciousness? It had been only because of his cousins' unrelenting taunts that he'd stopped claiming to be nine. To this day, he couldn't explain what had happened to that entire year of his life.

Pity had made him believe her story at first, but Josh found himself believing it less and less. Few things riled him more than idle chitchat, but he realized he'd better figure out a way to get her to open up, or he might miss an opportunity to learn crucial information about her.

"The fella who did that to your face," he ventured, "was he your husband?"

She stared straight ahead, toward the unending ripple of flatlands, then cast a worried glance over her shoulder, squeezing the saddle horn so tight Josh heard a quiet squeak.

"I made a lot of poor decisions in my life, but that one?" She met his eyes. "That one was downright stupid."

She paused, and Josh's suspicion grew, because, doggone it, she seemed intent on making him pull the story out of her, word by word. "Well," he drawled, "not every man is cut out to be a husband."

Her gaze skimmed the horizon again. He was about to ask what she was looking for when she said, "He wasn't my husband."

Well, at least he didn't have to worry about some deranged madman popping up on the other side of the next rise, looking to drag his woman home, where she belonged. "That's a relief." If he'd taken time to think a minute before speaking, he sure as shootin' wouldn't have said *that*. Because, now, she'd figure he had designs on her, and—

"Why?" Dinah tilted her head and met his gaze, her brow furrowed in befuddlement.

For as long as Josh could remember, his pa had been fond of saying, "Facts are facts." The man—whomever and whatever he was to Dinah—had given her a terrible pounding. The swelling would go down, and the bruises would fade, but the jagged cut on her jaw would probably leave a scar. And that wasn't counting the scars that had been left in her head and on her heart.

The mere thought of someone bigger and stronger laying hands on her made the hair stand up on his neck, made him want to inflict twice the damage on the hide of that two-legged swine. "Well," he said through clenched teeth, "if he manhandled you this way while he was only your beau, think what he'd have done if he were your husband. Some men believe saying 'I do' makes a woman their property, like furniture or livestock."

She emitted a tiny groan. "He wasn't my beau, either. At least, not then."

Well, that got his mind to whirling! "So, then...." Josh thumbed his Stetson to the back of his head. "What sort of work did you do back in San Antone?"

She sat so stiff and straight, it looked like somebody had strapped her to a board. "I know what you're thinking," she snapped, "but you're wrong!"

"What am I thinking?" His question prompted her to lift her chin another notch. He watched as she pressed a palm to her chest and then blinked and huffed and wiggled her shoulders, the way his sisters did when they were feeling flustered.

"I'll have you know that my grandmother taught me to play the piano. She taught me to sing, too. And it came in right handy after my mama died, because—"

"You were—you were a dance hall girl?" Josh didn't know what surprised him more, his reaction to that last bit of information or the quiet laughter his question provoked. He took a lot of pride in the notion that he'd conducted a long and careful study of his mother and sisters and probably knew more about women than most other men. But something told him if he lived to be a hundred, he wouldn't figure this woman out!

"No, I wasn't a dance hall girl. My clothing and my pay weren't nearly that glamorous." She punctuated the admission with a wistful sigh. "I plunked the keys of a beat-up piano and sang for my supper. That's all."

Josh sighed, too, but his was a sigh of relief. While he'd never been one to frequent saloons, he knew as well as any cowboy that dancing ladies usually did a whole lot more than just dance. And he didn't want to think of Dinah doing that, no matter what circumstance might have driven her to such work.

"My cousins and I do our fair share of crooning out on the trail. Keeps the cows calm. The horses, too." Dare he put her to this test? "Ever heard of a hymn called 'I Need Thee Every Hour'?"

"Heard of it! Why, as a little girl, I used to sing it in church all the time—solo, I'll have you know!" Dinah took a swig from her canteen, then cleared her throat and launched into the first verse of the hymn.

Josh had heard the tired, old saying, "She sings like an angel," but until that moment, he hadn't believed it could be true. Now, as the pure, clear notes lilted from her lips, he smiled.

Then, with no warning whatever, Dinah stopped, and the peace that had settled over him whipped away, just as quickly as that gust of wind that had stolen her hat. "Why'd you stop?" Josh was flabbergasted at the tremor in his voice.

"Because," she answered, "I thought you were going to sing *with* me!"

She laughed—an entirely different kind of music to his ears—and Josh wanted to bring their horses to a halt and dismount so he could haul her out of that saddle and wrap her in his arms.

Instead, Josh removed his Stetson and ran a hand through his hair. While he debated whether to say, "Maybe another time," or "Throat's too parched," a deafening thunderclap sounded overhead.

"Gracious! That likely sliced two years off the end of my life!" Dinah exclaimed.

Chuckling, Josh said, "Well, I hear tell those last two are the roughest years on a body anyway."

A second, louder explosion roared down from the clouds, interrupting his attempt at humor. He pointed. "That shack I was telling you about is just over the next rise." Oh, how he wanted to erase that look of fright from her face! "How fast can you ride?"

Until then, her eyes had been as wide and round as pie plates, but they narrowed when she replied, "Depends." Before he had a chance to ask what she meant, Dinah giggled. "How fast do you suppose this horse can run?"

Josh was about to find out if Dinah Theodore really was too good to be true, or more work than she was worth. He dug his heels into Callie's sides and lurched forward as the skies opened up. Between Callie's hoofbeats hammering the earth and the big-as-nickels raindrops pounding the brim of his Stetson, he couldn't hear Dinah's horse. Josh shot a glance over his shoulder, and there she was, about a furlong behind him, pressed flat against her mare's neck, soaking wet and smiling into the wind.

Oh, she was some woman, to be sure. He faced forward again and, despite the rain pelting his cheeks and the lightning flashing around them, smiled, too. An unexpected notion entered his head—a crazy, foolish idea that puzzled him no end.

He didn't want to take Dinah to Mexico. He wanted to take her home.

7

*A*fter releasing the bit from Callie's mouth and securing her to the hitching post, Josh threw back the oilcloth that was protecting a chest-high stack of firewood. "Thank God," he said, "for the man who took the time to chop this wood and was kind enough to leave it for us."

Kate nodded in agreement, and, by the time she had removed the bit from her own horse's mouth and tethered the animal beside Josh's dapple gray, he'd piled half a dozen small logs in the crook of his arm. "I feel horribly guilty," she admitted.

"Guilty?" he said, frowning as he reached for another spindly log. "Why?"

His stern expression unsettled her. If only she'd learned how to read more in a man's countenance than whether he was the type to tip her for a song well sung. For a reason she couldn't define, the prospect of holing up with Josh in this tiny cabin frightened her more than riding on the open prairie, where Frank could easily put a bullet right between her eyes without being witnessed. She hid her fear behind the practiced smile reserved for Etta Mae's customers. "Because we'll be inside, warm and dry, and these poor horses will be out here in this storm."

His left eyebrow quirked as a corner of his mouth lifted in a wry grin. "Aw, now, you oughtn't fret over it. They're just horses, and they're used to being outside in foul weather. Besides, we've got 'em tethered on the side of the shack where they'll be blocked from the worst of the wind."

"If they're so accustomed to being outside in foul weather, why do they flinch with every thunderbolt?"

His smile vanished like smoke, and he grumbled something unintelligible under his breath. His mouth formed a small O, as if he'd planned to say something, then stretched into a thin line. "You'd best get on inside."

One foot on the porch, the other in the muddy puddle below the bottom step, she harrumphed. "And you'd best do the same." Pointing, she indicated the stream of water pouring from the brim of his hat onto the logs in his arms. "The poor nomad who was the last to stay here wouldn't be very happy to know you wasted all his efforts to leave us with dry wood. I'm sure he could've taken the tarp to keep himself warm and dry, instead."

It was Josh's turn to harrumph. "Unwritten rule," he said, walking past her, "to look out for the man who comes behind you." The door opened with a loud squeal, and he disappeared inside.

Callie huffed, and Kate's horse echoed the sound. *If only there was a way to get you both inside, out of the storm,* Kate silently lamented.

Josh's voice cut through the dark interior of the shack. "You gonna stand there all afternoon, letting the wind and rain in here?"

Kate took a small step forward. "I just can't do it," she said, darting back to the horses.

"Do what?" she heard him yell. Then, "Where in the world are you going?"

"The least we can do is get their saddles off," she shouted into the wind. "How would you like it, standing in this awful storm with all this weight on your back?"

"Wouldn't like it one bit, which is why I aimed to do just that once I got a fire started."

How he moved from the woodstove to her side in an eye-blink and never made a sound, Kate didn't know. But there he was, his big hands gently plucking hers from Callie's cinch. "You know how to build a fire?"

Was it her cold, wet clothes or his nearness that sent a chill up her spine? Nodding like a simpleton, Kate blinked. My, but he was a good-looking fellow, with those piercing blue eyes and long, black lashes.

"Takin' care of horses is men's work," he said.

"But the job will go twice as fast if we work togeth—"

He wrapped his gloved fingers around her wrists. "Go on inside, out of this mess," he insisted, "and get a fire going. We're going to need it to dry our clothes and cook up something for supper."

Half a step closer would bring her near enough to embrace him—and, oh, how she wanted to! She was shivering from her hat to her stockings as raindrops ran down her face and beaded on her lashes, and it would have made perfect sense to do as he'd suggested. But not even nature's wrath seemed too high a price to pay for the warm comfort of an embrace.

"Go on, now," he said, using his chin as a pointer. "The sooner you start a fire, the sooner we can warm up."

Get moving! said her brain. But her feet refused to obey. Her earlier fears gone now, Kate wondered how much safer she'd feel, wrapped in those powerful yet gentle arms.

"Are your ears filled with water?"

"Are my—what?"

"Either you didn't hear me just now, or you're doing the most convincing impression of a stubborn mule I've ever seen." Smiling, Josh set both hands on her shoulders, and her heart fluttered at his proximity. Ever so gently, he turned her until she faced the shack and gave her a gentle shove. "Inside, before I throw you over my shoulder and carry you in there."

Finally, her traitorous feet obeyed, and she plodded forward. She'd just put one soggy boot on the bottom porch step when she heard him say, "You'll find matches in my saddlebags." How could she have mistrusted a man who had no problem with her rifling through his gear? Nodding, Kate hurried into the dank, little hovel and walked face-first into a sticky cobweb.

"And close the confounded door," he said as she spat and sputtered and plucked at the web. What sort of silly twit did he think she was? She grumbled inwardly at how calmly he'd announced that he'd take care of the "man's work" while she busied herself inside, doing "woman's work." And yet she couldn't help smiling, despite the stink of wet mud coming up through the cracks in the floor and the steady *plop, plop, plop* of rain seeping through the thatched roof. The sudden urge to tidy up the place and make it cozy seemed more important than the fact that her soggy skirt and petticoats were leaving a trail of dime-sized drips all over the floor.

"You do know how to make a fire, right?" came Josh's voice from outside.

"Hmpf," she said as she rummaged through his saddle-bags to find the matches.

Minutes later, thanks to some old twine and twigs she'd found in the cupboard drawer, she had a good base fire going. By the time Josh dug through that teetering heap for more dry logs, the bottom of the stove would be aglow with hot coals.

Leaving the stove door ajar to increase the flow of air over the kindling, Kate slung a blanket over the rope that stretched from one side of the room to the other, then grabbed the broom and began whacking down cobwebs. "Pity it isn't part of the 'unwritten rule,'" she muttered to herself, "to clean up for the next man—"

At the sound of Josh's boots thudding across the porch, Kate fell silent. She put the broom back where she'd found it and flung open the door. "Good thing you wrapped our spare clothes in that oilcloth of yours," she said as he dropped another load of firewood near the stove. "I've got a good base going and made us a privacy screen, so you can change into some dry things." She sounded bossy, even to herself. "If you've a mind to, that is," she added in a softer tone.

"Don't mind if I do," he said, "but ladies first."

She could tell by his no-nonsense expression that he meant it, so she grabbed one of the two outfits he'd bought her in Uvalde and ducked behind the blanket. She was down to her petticoats when he said, "Let's pray that the good Lord will see fit to dry our wet clothes by morning."

"Morning?" But even as the word slid past her lips, Kate knew what a foolish question it had been. It would be dark soon, and they certainly couldn't travel in this weather. Of course, they'd have to spend the night here. Alone. Way out in the middle of nowhere.

"I've seen storms like this before," he went on. "If it lets up by daybreak, I'll be surprised."

During the weeks Kate had been forced to travel with Frank and his gang, she'd had plenty of time to think about the character traits and tendencies of men. Just because her stepfather and Frank Michaels had been brutally abusive was no reason to judge all men as beasts and bullies. Josh Neville didn't seem any more likely to force himself on her than 99 percent of the men she'd entertained in the saloon. Still, it wouldn't hurt to keep her distance from him, just in case. And if anyone found out that she'd spent a night alone with a man, it wasn't likely to damage her already tarnished reputation. She'd been making the best of bad situations for as long as she could remember. She'd gotten herself into this mess, and she'd get herself out, somehow.

"I noticed some tin cans in the cupboard," she said, mustering a courage she didn't feel. "They're not labeled, but if I can find something to open them with, I might just be able to rustle us up a decent supper."

Squatting in front of the stove, he said over his shoulder, "I'll show you how to use a hunting knife to do the job."

He eased three slender logs onto the glowing coals and closed the stove's door with a clang. Then, getting to his feet, he said, "It'll take a while before this beast gets hot enough to cook anything on it. Might be better if we just finish off those muffins I bought in Uvalde."

"Coward."

"Coward?"

"Afraid I'll start a bigger fire on the stove than you made in it?"

Her playful smirk woke those feelings inside him again, the ones he'd thought he'd never experience again. But before he could tell her that he had complete confidence in her cooking abilities, a gigantic dollop of water leaked through a hole in the roof and landed with a noisy *plop* on her head.

"Goodness," she said as a second drop splashed onto her head, "that might feel refreshing, if my hair wasn't already soaked to the scalp." She punctuated the admission with a shiver and a giggle. "So, you're sure, are you, that this storm will last all night?"

"Could end sooner, but I don't think so."

Dinah rolled her eyes. "Well, for the love of honey biscuits, even I could have come up with an answer like that!"

The logs popped and sizzled, making her jump. My, but she looked tiny, standing there near the rough-hewn table. "How tall are you?" he asked, out of curiosity.

"Don't rightly know. Last time my mama got her yardstick after me, it wasn't to take my measure."

"Now, why don't I have trouble believing that?" Using his rain-soaked bandanna, he wiped down two of the four rough-hewn chairs.

She relieved him of it, looking shy and frightened when their fingers touched. "Let me do that—woman's work, you know?" she said, winking. Then, pointing at the blanket, she added, "You should get out of those wet things."

Josh quickly did as she suggested. For one thing, it made perfect sense to comply. For another, he didn't like the cold, clammy feel of his clothes sticking to his skin. Mostly, though, he'd gone along with her suggestion because she'd looked downright concerned while delivering it—the way a loving wife might.

By the time he came out from behind the curtain, she'd lit every lantern in the place. "Feels good to be warm and dry, doesn't it?" she said, adding his sodden clothes to her own on the table. Then, one by one, she wrung the water from each article of clothing into a dishpan while humming a happy little tune.

Josh picked up a sock and started squeezing the water from the toe, thinking that if they both worked at it, they could make the job go more quickly.

"Oh, no you don't," Dinah said, grabbing the sock from him. When he started to protest, she held up a finger. "This is woman's work, too," she said with calm authority, then pointed to the nearest chair. "Take a load off, cowboy."

Like an obedient child, he sat. "Are you hungry?"

"I'll tell you a little secret about me," she whispered, leaning closer. "I have a serious medical condition."

Josh felt a surge of worry.

"My mama called it a hollow leg."

A wave of relief and amusement mingled in his mind, prompting a quiet chuckle. Being this near to her roused a recollection of when they'd stood outside earlier, Dinah staring up at him and looking for all the world like a drowned angel. She'd been close enough to kiss, if he'd wanted to— and he'd wanted to, all right!

So, why hadn't he?

His stomach growled, rescuing him from having to come up with an answer.

Dinah took the blanket from the rope and folded it into a tidy square, just as she'd done with the one he'd loaned her the night he'd found her, cold and cringing, behind that big rock. She draped his socks over the rope, then patted her flat stomach. "My mama always used to say you could feed me to overflowing, and then, in ten minutes, do it all over again."

"That's what Lucinda and my ma say about me."

But Dinah didn't seem to have heard him. She stood at the door with her nose pressed to the wood, peering through the cracks. "In case you're wondering," he joked, "I think it's raining out there."

"I thought I heard something. Sort of like thunder, only—"

He heard it then, too—hoofbeats closing in on the shack, hard and fast.

"I count three men," she said, her voice raspy, as if she believed whispering would keep them from stopping. "They must have seen our lights. And the smoke from the stovepipe."

Josh was on his feet in a heartbeat. "Get your pistol," he barked. "Put it in your boot. And I know it's warm in here, but put all your clothes back on. Everything, wet or dry."

That got her attention. When she turned, her eyes sparkled like emeralds. "Even my hat?"

"Even your hat."

Concern flickered in the green orbs. "But—but why?"

"Whoever they are, they've a mind to get in out of this mess, same as us." As he spoke, he shoved his own revolver into his belt and shrugged into his jacket. "And if they're bandits, they'll take anything that isn't nailed down or tacked on, that's why."

It took most of his willpower to tear his gaze from hers. He hated scaring her, but if it meant keeping her safe, so be it. Fully dressed, he peered through the opening between the window frame and the wooden door. "You know how to use that thing?" he asked without looking around.

"I—I think so."

Fear rang loud in her voice, and he turned around. "Just pull back on the hammer, aim, and fire." He forced a grin. "Just be sure you're aiming at the man you hope to stop, not me."

Dinah nodded, which told him she knew it would take only minutes for the riders to hitch their mounts out front, and that, seconds later, they'd burst through the door. He then realized that he had only minutes to teach her a thing or two—lessons that could very well save her life. And, quite possibly, his, too. He gripped Dinah's shoulders and gave her a gentle shake. "Did your mama ever say, 'Do as I say, not as I do'?"

Another nod.

"Well, keep that in mind once they're inside, in case I have to do or say something that doesn't seem to make sense. I think we'll be all right."

"Y-you *think* we'll be all ri—"

"What did I promise you out there on the trail?" he interrupted her.

The way she stood there, trembling and blinking up at him, told Josh he'd been right. Brutal bandits—or outlaws of some sort—had been responsible for her predicament and her paranoia.

"You said…." She licked her lips and straightened her shoulders. "You said I'd always be safe with you."

The thundering hoofbeats stopped.

The riders had arrived.

In no time, they'd step inside and shake the rain from their coats. Could he convince her in the next few seconds to trust him completely? "Did you believe me?"

She bit down hard on her lower lip. "I did. And I believe you now, too."

"Good. Then follow my lead. Got it? And quit lookin' so all-fired scared. We'll just pretend to be a nice married couple who came in here to wait out the storm. Bandits are like cougars; if they smell fear, they'll be all over you."

Dinah took a gulp of air and let it out slowly as the door burst open and slammed against the wall.

In all his years, Josh had never seen a larger man. Rain poured down his coat in torrents and formed puddles between his muddy boots. He was chewing a thin twig that extended out of the right corner of his dark-mustached mouth, and, in one swift move, he shrugged out of his slicker, exposing a rifle—and a badge. "Gus Applegate," he said, extending a beefy hand toward Josh.

Josh breathed a silent sigh of relief as he gripped it. The encircled silver star was all the proof he needed that these men were Texas Rangers.

"Sorry 'bout the mess, ma'am," Gus said to Dinah, stepping into the center of the room as his comrades stomped inside behind him. "I'd sure as shootin' like to know who riled ol' Mother Nature, 'cause that's one powerful-bad storm out there!" As the door closed behind the last of the Rangers, he said, "So, what brings you nice folks out here in this weather?"

"Just heading home from doing business in San Antonio," Josh said in as casual a voice as he could.

Gus gave Dinah a quick survey. "Long way for a purty young thing like this to ride." He scowled at Josh in disapproval. "And dangerous, to boot."

"Tried to talk her out of coming with me," Josh said, shrugging, "but—"

"No need to say more," said the second Ranger. "Women. Can't live with 'em, can't live without 'em." Chuckling at his own joke, he stuck out his hand. "Shorty McAllister. And you are?"

"Neville," Josh said, shaking it. "Josh Neville."

The third man stepped up and offered his hand, too. "Name's Ephram Bradley, but, mostly, folks just call me Stretch."

"Not 'cause he's tall, mind you," Gus put in, "but 'cause he can take two hours to tell you what he ate for breakfast."

After a moment of jovial laughter, all three hung up their coats and hats. They leaned their rifles against the wall, Josh noted, but kept their sidearms. Not that he blamed them. It was reassuring to have his own Colt belted to his hip.

"What sorta business put you in San Antone, if you don't mind my askin'?" Shorty said.

Josh had witnessed a Gatling gun demonstration a while back, and if he hadn't seen it with his own eyes, he never would have believed any weapon could fire a thousand rounds in a minute. Well, Shorty McAllister talked even faster than that. He stood barely taller than Dinah, but his stance—chest puffed out and chin raised high—made it clear he wanted an answer, whether Josh minded giving it or not. Since he'd never liked playing cat and mouse, he said, "Anthrax epidemic killed off a thousand head of cattle, and now the land where they'd been grazing is tainted. Had to sell some acres to make up the loss, and the only interested buyer wouldn't pay up unless I met him on his own turf. So...." Josh let a nonchalant shrug finish his sentence, hoping he hadn't offered too much information, because, in his experience, that's what made a man look guilty.

Gus muttered a curse. "You don't mean to say you've got cash on your perso—"

"No, no," Josh assured. "Banknote."

Stretch, red-faced from struggling to get out of his wet boots, grunted. "Good thing, too, 'cause we've been tailin' Frank Michaels and his gang of murderin' thieves. Last we heard, they were hidin' out somewhere close by."

Josh heard Dinah's tiny gasp, but before he could figure out what had provoked it, Shorty said, "We been doggin' 'em for nigh onto a week, now. Almost had 'em, too, when this confounded storm muddied up their tracks." A quick look at Dinah stopped him as effectively as a hand clamped over his mouth. Narrowing one eye, he said, "Hey, don't I know you from someplace?"

A nervous giggle exploded from her mouth. "It's the funniest thing," she said, "but people tell me that all the time." Looking at Josh, she added, "Don't they, darlin'?"

Josh hoped his forced smile didn't look too fake. "Guess you just have one of those faces, *darlin*'."

The Ranger stared hard at her for another second or two and then shook his head. "Nah, ain't that. I'd bet my next paycheck that I know you from someplace." He gave a shrug. "Don't worry none. It'll come to me before long."

He stepped closer to his comrades, who were lighting cigarettes and talking. On the heels of their raucous laughter, the threesome picked up where they'd left off, griping about how the Frank Michaels Gang had left half a dozen bank heists, train robberies, and dead bodies in their wake between here and San Antonio.

"We'll get 'em," Stretch snarled, blowing smoke toward the ceiling. "They got a female with 'em now. Don't matter none that she's an outlaw; she'll slow 'em down, sure as I'm standin' here, simply 'cause she's a woman."

Josh glanced at Dinah, whose rosy cheeks had paled to a chalky gray. He reached her just in time to catch her as she fainted.

*W*hen Kate opened her eyes and looked into Josh's worried face, her first impulse was to comfort him. He'd been so kind, so sweet, so gentle. And so generous....

Then, reality set in, and she remembered where they were, and why. But she couldn't figure out what was causing the loud hammering in her ears—the ferocity of the storm or her hard-beating heart.

Blinding flashes of lightning sparked through cracks in the cabin walls, each one waking a white-hot memory: Frank's threat to slit her throat if she ran off; the ghastly image of Claribel and the men he'd shot; her own name emblazoned on the wanted poster. She also formed a clear, mental picture of herself swinging at the end of a rope.

The men's voices sounded hollow and distant, reminding her of hot, summer days from childhood, when she and her playmates would take turns diving into the millpond behind her grandmother's house, their smiling faces easily identifiable through the water's translucence, their shouts nearly as muted and murky as the pond's spongy floor.

Kate sipped from the canteen Josh pressed to her lips, wondering how long she'd been out. Not long enough, she prayed, for the Rangers to study her face, because surely the one who'd thought he recognized her would have put two and two together.

"Well, sir," Stretch said, "if I had me a cigar, I'd light it up in your honor." He slapped Josh's shoulder. "My wife swooned, too, purty near ever' time she was expectin'. Don't rightly know *why* carryin' a young'un makes women keel over thataway, but...." He chuckled and gave Josh's back a friendly slap. "So tell us, boy, when's the baby due?"

Josh looked every bit as confused as Kate felt. His gaze fused to hers, as if he hoped she'd send him a suitable response by way of the invisible thread that locked their eyes together. If the lawmen believed she and Josh were married—and why else would a self-respecting man and woman be out here in the middle of nowhere together?—maybe they hadn't figured out who she was.

At least, not yet.

"Thank you," Kate said, trying to change the subject. "But I'm fine. Really." She sat up, then tried to get onto her feet. "I don't know what came over me. I've never fainted, not once in my entire life!"

And it was true. That's why, when the unfamiliar, woozy sensation had tickled the edges of her consciousness, she hadn't recognized it for what it was. And why, when the room had started spinning and everything had turned a muddy yellow, she hadn't tried doing anything to avert the episode.

"Well, y'ain't never been pregnant before, that's why," Shorty pointed out.

She couldn't afford to dally. The quicker she set about the business of stoking the fire, making coffee, and rustling up something for the men to eat, the better. Performing mundane chores would give her a good excuse to keep her back to the Rangers and give them less of an opportunity to match her face to the crude drawing on the wanted poster.

The instant she stood up, a second wave of dizziness overwhelmed her and nearly put her right back on the floor.

She ended up in Josh's arms again, instead.

"You scared me half out of my wits," he said, tucking several stray wisps of hair behind her ears before setting her down gently but keeping his arms around her.

The heat of a blush warmed her cheeks. Did she feel hot and clammy because so many men had crowded into the small, damp space? Because the woodstove was radiating heat? It certainly couldn't be because Josh held her so tenderly—could it?

She pressed both palms to his chest and stood at arm's length from him. Frank had held her this way, and look where that had gotten her!

Then, she remembered what Josh had said just moments before the first Ranger had burst through the door: "Follow my lead." Later, when they were alone, she'd confess how much she admired his acting skills. If his performance had nearly convinced her of his genuine concern for her, surely the Rangers had fallen for his act, too.

Well, two could play that game. "The next time you tell me not to skip a meal," she said, touching a fingertip to the end of Josh's nose, "I promise to listen," and, just for good measure, she tacked on, "dear."

A corner of his mouth lifted as brawny fingers closed around her wrist. Pulling her closer, Josh said, "See that you do, love."

The word reverberated in her head and echoed in her heart. The way he'd said it—accented by the caring glow that emanated from his blue eyes—made her wonder if love would ever be part of her future. What man in his right mind would want her after what Frank had done to her? "I'm fine," she said, wriggling free of his grasp. "I think the fire's hot enough to get a pot of coffee brewing. I'm sure the Rangers could use a cup."

His eyebrows shot up so fast that Kate half expected to hear the impact as they slammed into his hairline. But any amusement roused by his expression was quickly forgotten as she stepped away from his protective presence. A sense of longing and loneliness instantly settled over her. How could she miss him when he was standing no more than three feet away?

She shook off the silly, romantic notions. Even under normal circumstances—which, granted, these certainly were not—she and Josh could never be more than passing acquaintances. Maybe he did have a wife and a handful of children waiting for him at the ranch. And he had no idea that he'd elected to help a wanted criminal cross the border into Mexico. A damaged and tainted criminal, no less. Besides, for all she knew, he could be putting on a good act, just as Frank had done when she'd first met him. What if, in time, Josh turned out to be just as vicious and violent? Kate shuddered inwardly. *I can't survive another ordeal like that!* Frowning, she stepped outside long enough to set the coffeepot on the porch. A few minutes out there in the driving rain would be adequate to fill it with enough water to rinse out the dust; a few more minutes, and she'd have what she needed to brew a pot of coffee.

The picture of Josh surrounded by a loving spouse and adoring children stirred envy in her like none she'd ever experienced, and Kate didn't like the feeling. Not one little bit.

You've been in tight situations before, she admonished herself, searching the small, crowded sideboard for coffee mugs. *So, why is this one upending your ability to reason?*

Her rummaging turned up a dented washbasin, three bent spoons, and a crusty, cast-iron skillet. Finally, behind a white-enameled stew pot, she spotted half a dozen blue mugs speckled with white, just like the two in Josh's saddlebags. She loaded them into the washbasin and headed for the door.

"Where in tarnation are you goin', girl?" Shorty asked, standing in her way.

"To fill this with rainwater so I can rinse the coffee cups." Closing her eyes, Kate blew a puff of air into one of the mugs, and Shorty stepped back to avoid inhaling the cloud of dust she'd stirred up. "You wouldn't want to drink coffee out of that, now, would you?" she asked him.

"I've swallowed that and then some on the trail." Narrowing both eyes, he leaned closer. "I feel it only fair to warn you, I aim to take you with me when I leave here."

Take me…? Maybe she had been unconscious long enough for him to remember why she looked familiar. Kate's heart ached, wondering what Josh would think when the Rangers put her in handcuffs and read off the charges against her.

But why did she care so much about the opinion of a man who easily could be another Frank Michaels?

Josh tensed at Shorty's comment, but he relaxed when Gus said, "There he goes, dreamin' again."

"Aw, you're just jealous," Shorty countered, "on account o' I have a chance of gettin' me a purty wife who can cook and clean, but your bachelor days are gone like yesterday's biscuits."

"Now, let's give credit where credit's due," Stretch put in. "Gus's missus ain't much for bakin' pies and such, but let's not forget that she won the tobacco spittin' contest at last year's county fair."

Gus rubbed his forehead and groaned. "I don't know what I ever did in my miserable life to get stuck ridin' with the pair of you." Then, he elbowed Josh good-humoredly. "Besides, Shorty there would have to win a fight with you if he hoped to take little Miss Puff-in-the-Cup home with him. Ain't that right, young feller?"

Dinah looked as helpless now as he'd felt earlier, when Stretch had asked when her baby would be born. If a fib could erase the fear in her big, green eyes, he'd pay his penance to the Almighty later. "Much as I'd hate to get into an altercation with a Texas Ranger, Gus is right," Josh said, winking at Dinah. "Little Miss Puff-in-the-Cup is spoken for."

Taking a seat at the table, he watched her exhale a relieved breath, then scurry for the door. Now, why did he have the feeling that if a storm weren't raging out there, she'd run south just as far and as fast as those tiny feet would carry her?

During the next hour, she made coffee and threw together a crude meal made up of beef jerky, canned beans, and biscuits made from the lard and flour she found in the cabin. She served the meal on mismatched plates and bowls from the cupboard, and, amazingly, managed to keep her back to them while she cleaned up afterward, too. If the Rangers had noticed, they didn't show it or say so, but her secretive behavior sure had Josh's mind spinning.

While the Rangers swapped good-natured barbs, Josh made a decision. When the weather quieted and the Rangers headed out, he'd have a heart-to-heart with Dinah. Until then, he thought, tilting his chair back on two legs and propping both boot heels on the table, he was more than happy to sit and surreptitiously watch as she did everything humanly possible not to attract attention to herself.

The ruse seemed to be working, if the Rangers' bored yawns and frequent head bobs were any indication. Interlacing his fingers behind his head, Josh leaned back in his chair and closed his eyes, content to imagine Dinah in his kitchen at home, humming as she performed wifely chores—and not just as his pretend wife, either.

*K*ate's hope had been that the riders wouldn't recognize her. If she needed proof that God had heard her, there it was, in the form of three soundly sleeping Texas Rangers and one rancher who had decided to play possum. For a while, anyway. The fact that he felt it necessary to keep an eye on her at all times hurt her feelings, and Kate didn't mind admitting it. If the Rangers weren't suspicious of her, why was he?

But that was being unfair, and she knew it. Josh had put his life on the line by agreeing to deliver her to the Mexican border. She'd heard it said that the Texas Rangers always get their man—or woman. If these men figured out who she was, they'd haul her in, and they'd have no choice but to arrest him, too, for aiding and abetting. Only God knew how long it might take to conduct the investigation that would prove Josh hadn't participated in the robbery, or in the murders of three innocent men and a faultless woman.

Kate shivered at the memory but quickly shook it off. She had to stay alert and aware, and how could she do that if her thoughts kept turning to that awful day? Especially considering what her mama used to say: "You're a terrible, *awful* liar! Why, every thought in your head is written on your face, plain as day!" Etta Mae had also noticed her transparent nature and had commented on it almost as often as her mama had, making her more determined than ever to avoid looking the Rangers in the eyes. For that very well could be all it would take to seal her fate.

As they'd gobbled up the pathetic meal she'd scraped together, the men swapped stories about how each of them had survived conditions far worse than this—tornadoes, blizzards, even a hurricane or two.

As Josh had stoked the fire, he shared his own account of being stranded for nearly a week in a shelter just like this one. It had poured steadily for days, he said, filling the Rio Grande to overflowing. Fascinated by the tale—and the man who told it—Kate slumped onto the seat of a rickety, wooden chair, propped both elbows on the table, and rested her chin in her upturned palms. Josh told them how the waters had come closer and closer, hour by hour, to the door, and how, by the time they had reached the porch, he'd run out of food and had taken to eating bugs and sodden weeds. Kate sat there and listened, spellbound.

And that's when he put the poker down and caught her staring.

All three Rangers turned in their seats to see why he'd stopped talking so suddenly, and why his expression had changed from intense concentration to fond warmth. They chuckled when he winked at her, and when he sent her a flirty grin, their bawdy laughter bounced off every wall.

What a pickle he'd put her in! The Rangers were behaving like schoolboys, but they weren't fools. If they entertained a wary thought or two about her, her reaction here could make the difference between looking like a woman in love— or a woman wanted by the law.

"Even after all this time," she said, "he still has the power to make me blush like a schoolgirl."

The men were quiet for all of a second before another round of boisterous laughter filled the room. Josh hadn't taken his eyes off her, not once since he'd looked up and caught her staring. If his smile alone could double her heartbeats, even under such intimidating and crowded circumstances, how might she have reacted if she had gone ahead and embraced him when the whim had struck her?

Feigning a yawn, Kate got to her feet. "I hope our bedding is dry by now," she said, testing the blankets that hung near the stove, "because I'm about to fall asleep standing."

"Just like a horse!" Shorty said.

His comment reminded her that all of their horses were out there in that awful weather. She couldn't imagine being tied to a post while the wind blew the rain sideways, not to mention the blinding lightning and deafening thunder.

She didn't understand the emotions tumbling in her head and in her heart. Before Frank had kidnapped her, she'd always been a realist, a both-feet-on-the-ground woman who took pride in how far she'd come in life by dint of hard work, stubborn determination, and keen instinct. She understood the impracticality of bringing the horses inside, but that didn't stop her heart from aching for them. They worked so hard, endured so much, and didn't ask for more than some hay or oats and enough water to wash them down. How unfair and unkind it seemed, making them stand out there in that mess.

Without warning, her eyes filled with tears, and her lower lip began to quiver.

Though she tried to hide it, Josh saw.

"Now look what you've gone and done."

All eyes were on her. So much for trying not to call attention to herself.

Then, Shorty jabbed a thumb into his chest. "Who, me?"

Stretch and Gus echoed the question in turn.

"Sounds like a flock of owls in here," said Josh.

The Rangers gave that a moment of thought. Then Gus said, "Aw, there ain't no such thing." When the others frowned in confusion, he explained, "Owls travel alone. Don't you boys know nothin'?"

"Hmpf." Stretch shook his head. "For your information, professor, owls don't travel. They *fly*."

"If flyin' ain't travelin', I sure as shootin' don't know what to call it."

The conversation went from abstract to silly in a matter of seconds, and in the silence that followed Gus's last remark, Kate's stifled sobs became a fit of giggles.

"Land sakes," Stretch said to Josh, "you better hope that young'un of hers gets born sooner, not later." He held one hand beside his face, hiding his pointer finger behind it. "She'll drive you plumb loco if she keeps this up!"

Gus harrumphed, then stood up and stomped over to the corner where he'd tossed his bedroll. "I've had enough jabberjawin' for one night." With two flicks of his wrists, he made himself a pallet on the floor. "I sure as shootin' hope you fellers don't aim to keep those lanterns glowin' all the blessed night," he growled. "We've got a long, hard ride ahead of us tomorrow."

Shorty took a peek at his pocket watch. "Gus is right. Maybe, if we all just turn in, the storm will blow over, and we can head on out of here come daylight."

"What time is it?" Kate asked him.

He snapped his watch shut. "Eight-o-five." Without another word, he fixed himself a bed across from Gus. He'd barely made himself comfortable when he sat up. "I've got it!"

"What's got you bellowing like a bull moose?" Stretch asked.

"I know why our little mama-to-be looks familiar."

While her heart hammered, Shorty grinned. If he realized she'd been featured on a wanted poster, would that have been his reaction?

Hopefully not.

"Don't she put you in mind of your sister, Stretch? The youngest one, who lives in Abilene?"

Stretch sat up, too, and stared so hard at Kate that she thought surely her blushing cheeks would catch fire.

"Y'know," the man said, "I have to admit that she does favor Rosa some. Mostly, around the eyes." He nodded, then settled back onto his bedroll. "Now that you've solved your little mystery, you think we can maybe get some sleep around here?"

"Yeah," Gus barked. "Like I keep sayin', we have a lot of territory to cover tomorrow." He flapped his blanket. "And you newlyweds keep the billin' and cooin' to a minimum, now, y'hear?"

Stretch chuckled. "Seems the least you can do since we left you both of the cots, so's the li'l mother-to-be can get a good night's sleep."

Josh sent her a silent message by way of those oh-so-blue eyes, but Kate couldn't manage to decipher it. She rubbed her temples and tried to remain calm. How had things gotten so far out of control?

She'd gone along with the charade to keep the Rangers from guessing her true identity. Thankfully, the plan had worked—so far. But, now, she faced a whole new dilemma, for in going along with the plot, she'd inadvertently dragged Josh into her quagmire of a life. Earlier, Stretch had said that after a good night's sleep, things would look fine. She wanted to believe that, but something told her things wouldn't be fine for Kate Wellington, aka Dinah Theodore, for a very long time. If ever.

10

*L*ast night, amid the men's droning snores, Kate had spent hours tossing and turning, despite the fact that Josh, bless his kindhearted soul, had stacked his mattress on top of hers for extra padding. He'd made himself a bed of blankets on the floor and, to quiet her protests, insisted it was cooler down there.

But she'd known better.

The shack had been constructed from the crudest of materials. A mere twelve inches off the ground, the warped and sagging floorboards acted like a wick, drawing moisture from the rain-soaked earth beneath them. Kate told him the Rangers were feeling the damp and the chill of this stormy night, and, as proof, she'd pointed out the way each had burrowed deep beneath his blanket.

"Every one of us has slept outside on nights this bad, or worse," he'd quietly countered. "This beats trying to catch a few winks in the blinding rain. I know it, and so do they."

And, with that, he'd turned the lamp down so low that it barely glowed at all and had fallen promptly to sleep, leaving Kate wide awake to ponder her situation. All through the night, though the rain drummed loudly on the shack's roof and the wind rattled its walls, Josh and the Rangers slept soundly. Maybe he hadn't exaggerated, and the little hovel's shelter seemed like a mansion compared to the conditions outdoors. Between snores, Kate heard Shorty's pocket watch counting the endless, slow-moving minutes and reminding her that her chances of living a normal life were ticking away, steady beat by steady beat.

Shortly before dawn, Kate was relieved to hear the wind die down and the rain stop falling. She sneaked outside to check on the horses, feeding them oats and then treating them to one bite apiece of the carrots Josh had bought for Callie. He treated that horse better than her stepfather had treated her mama, and far better than Frank had treated her! If he could show that much caring and thoughtfulness to his horse....

She couldn't afford to entertain such thoughts. Kate sat down on the front porch step, her chin perched on her fist, as she recalled the few young men who'd inspired notions of a home and family—and had made hasty retreats the minute she'd declared that she intended to stand at the altar with a soul as pure-white as her wedding gown. She didn't think she'd ever live long enough to figure out why they'd believed a girl with no parents deserved less respect than the girls with whom they'd gone to school and attended church. With every passing year, her dream of marriage and children had seemed less likely to come true, and her belief that she'd die a lonely, solitary death had sharpened.

And then, along came Frank, with his swashbuckling charm and lavish lifestyle, treating her as though she were a gift from heaven and saying everything she so desperately needed to hear.

Disgusted, she got to her feet and paced the only grassy spot near the shack. "Fool," she scolded herself. "Stupid little ninny."

She heard footsteps, but not in time to silence herself.

"What're you doing out here all alone, talking to yourself?" Josh asked, placing his hands on his hips.

The sight of his handsome face sent a shiver down her spine. She caught sight of the coffeepot brimming with clear rainwater and said, "Just trying to figure out how I'm going to make coffee without waking our guests."

He took a small step closer to her. "I wouldn't worry about it. They're the ones who said they have a lot of ground to cover today."

This was how it had begun with Frank, and she'd rather die than go through that again! Kate hurried for the porch and retrieved the coffeepot. "Guess I'll get this on the stove. The water's ice-cold. It'll probably take forever to heat up."

One blond brow rose in response to her abrupt departure and change of topic. "Well," he started, "just don't keep to yourself *too* much."

She might have asked why if he hadn't quickly added in a low voice, "Wouldn't want to rouse their suspicion. Again."

His remark reminded Kate that her resemblance to a Ranger's sister had already stirred some misgivings about her. Thanks to Stretch, the matter had been cleared up, at least in the Rangers' minds.

While the coffee brewed, she busied herself trying to pull together some semblance of a breakfast. As the men devoured the oatmeal mush and sad flapjacks made from stale flour and sugar Kate had found stored in rusting, dented tins in the cupboard, she thought of the stories she'd read as a little girl about knights in shining armor who rescued damsels in distress. Though Josh rode a dapple gray instead of a great white steed, he'd saved her all the same.

With trembling hands, Kate poured the coffee. She barely heard the chorus of thank-yous as she distributed the steaming mugs, because her head was too full of memories of all the thoughtful things Josh had done since finding her on that cold, frightening night.

Josh's fingers touched hers when he accepted his cup, and the brief caress lit a boyish light in his long-lashed eyes. But she didn't trust herself to make smart decisions about men. Especially not after Frank. Besides, what if Frank was out there somewhere, skulking in the hills, waiting for the Rangers to leave so he could make good on his promise? "I'll slit your throat if you leave," he'd threatened her more than once, "to keep you from testifying against me." As long as Josh stayed with her, he was in just as much danger as she saw.

Josh had said he lived in Eagle Pass, but Kate didn't know where, precisely. He'd mentioned a big family, but she didn't know if it included a wife and children. He'd talked about his ranch, but it could be the size of the shack or as vast as the horizon, for all she knew. Had he really been on his way home from San Antonio when he'd found her? Or had that been just another chapter of his "follow my lead" story to keep her from knowing the truth?

If it had been a lie, it meant he had his own secrets, and the thought sent a shiver down her spine. During her hours with him, Josh hadn't provided many details about himself, partly because she'd been so wrapped up in self-centered thoughts about her own problems that she hadn't asked. Yet, unless he'd robbed a bank and murdered innocent civilians, he was still too good for the likes of her.

Kate sighed, tired of whipping that same, dead horse. Self-pity was an ugly thing, and she needed to shed it, and shed it fast. What this situation called for was a healthy dose of acceptance. *Maybe then you can stop dwelling on thoughts about "poor, poor, pitiful me."*

An hour later, as the scents of male sweat, wet leather, and strong coffee mixed with the sticky air, Kate didn't so much as crinkle her nose. What business did she have complaining about anything? Days ago, she'd escaped the vicious hands of the vile Frank Michaels and staggered into a stranger's camp, and she hadn't wanted for a single thing since then, thanks to Josh.

He was sitting in the chair he'd ended up sleeping in, tilting back on two legs and leaning against the wall nearest the door, with both arms folded over his broad chest and one booted foot crossed over the other. As Kate gazed at his weather-worn, lightly whiskered face, she fought the affection smoldering inside her. If he did have a wife, how much like a princess she must feel to wake beside him, care for him, and *be* cared for *by* him. That, Kate decided, was the stuff fairy tales were made of!

A thought popped into her head so suddenly that it evoked a tiny gasp. It was a good idea, too, a selfless act that would at once show him how sincerely she appreciated all he'd done for her.

As she gathered up the empty breakfast plates and coffee mugs, she heard the Rangers say that they planned to head for Fort Stockton, where they'd join up with some other Texas lawmen and uniformed soldiers. They were none too happy about Governor Hogg's command to round up the *banditos* who'd been terrorizing the citizenry, because, as Gus pointed out, "We've got our own rotten fish to catch right here."

By "fish," he meant Frank Michaels and his gang. Kate knew that as surely as she knew her name wasn't really Dinah Theodore. Frank deserved to be caught, deserved to pay for the death and destruction that clung to him like a depraved shadow.

"Soon as we've mollycoddled the governor," Gus had snarled, shaking a fist, "them low-down varmints are *ours*."

Hopefully, with the Rangers hot on his trail, Frank would be too busy keeping his own throat out of the hangman's noose to hunt Kate down and slit *hers*. Still, it was only slightly comforting to know that while the Rangers were doing their duty at Fort Stockton, she was safe from them.

There was just one thing left to worry about, as she saw it: separating from Josh before her precarious situation put him in real jeopardy. There'd be plenty of time, once she crossed the Rio Grande, to worry about how she'd repay the man who could never return the affection she was beginning to feel for him.

But, oh, if only he could....

Suddenly, he was standing right in front of her.

"You all right?" Josh whispered, interrupting her musings.

Kate met his eyes and knew in an instant that she'd better run far and fast if she hoped to stay one step ahead of her feelings for this man. Unable to trust her voice to sound steady, she only nodded.

He gave her shoulder an affectionate squeeze. "I'm a man of my word, remember?"

Of course, she remembered—that was part of her problem!

You'll be all right, she told herself, *once you don't have to look into his beautiful eyes, once he is no longer near enough to touch, once—*

"No reason to fret, Dinah. You're safe as a baby in its mama's arms."

If only, she thought again.

There was no harm in dreaming it was possible for an upright man to love a woman with a sullied past and an uncertain future. Those dreams would get her through many a long, lonely night. They would simply have to be enough.

No sooner had the Rangers ridden off than the pounding downpour resumed. Josh had endured similar scenarios enough times to understand the misery of each muddy step as the rain pelted their cheeks and the wind nipped at their ears. He felt a tweak of sympathy for them, because he knew only too well that no matter how well a man thought he'd covered himself, the water and cold always found a way to work themselves right down to his skin.

He'd promised that Dinah would be safe with him, and he saw no point in making her ride through this miserable weather, especially after everything she'd already endured. It was after six at night when the clouds finally parted, and they went outside in the fresh air. "Twilight," he said, "my favorite time of day." And when she didn't respond, he added, "We might as well take advantage of having a roof over our heads one more night."

As she stood beside him, staring silently at the sooty sky, he couldn't help but notice how tiny she seemed, how vulnerable and childlike. Couldn't help but wonder what had caused this sudden mood shift, either, because, up till recently, she'd been cheerful and chatty, no matter what. He remembered the terror in her eyes when the Rangers had ridden up. He had seen a lot of frightening things in his twenty-seven years, but nothing had scared him that much. Even now, just thinking about it made him want to wrap his arms around her, defend her from threats of any kind.

He'd expected her to relax some once she realized the riders were lawmen. When she hadn't, Josh had been left with two conclusions: She'd participated in a crime and feared punishment, or she'd witnessed one and had reason to believe the perpetrators' retribution would be far worse. Either way, at least he had a partial explanation for the sorry shape she'd been in when he'd found her.

She turned slightly to look up at him. "Hungry?"

Josh patted his thigh. "Feed me now," he said, grinning, "and in ten minutes, you can do it again."

The reminder of their earlier exchange inspired a smile—my, was she a beauty when she smiled!

"Guess I'd better get busy, then," Dinah said, heading for the cabin. "I'll see what I can whip up."

"Did those fool Rangers devour all our grub?"

"They left a few crumbs," she said over her shoulder. "Maybe I'll make soup and biscuits."

He wanted to ask what she hoped to put into the soup pot, but his stomach growled, as if on cue. "Sounds good."

He wanted to follow her, too, but he stayed put, intent on taking full advantage of this rare opportunity to get a good look at her, head to toe. Until now, she'd been sitting, riding, bustling around the kitchen area, or standing too near for him to see much more than her lovely face—not that he had a mind to complain about that.

The top of her curly-haired head didn't quite reach his shoulder. She'd taken to pulling the soft curls into a tight bun, worn at the back of her head. A time or two, he'd been tempted to pluck out the hairpins, just to watch her tresses spill down over her slender shoulders like a cinnamon-colored cascade. He'd resisted, of course, just as he'd struggled against the urge to find out if her full, pink lips felt as soft as they looked.

She had feet so small and dainty that when he'd bought her a pair of boots, he'd had to shop in the children's sizes. How they held up a full-grown woman was anybody's guess.

And full-grown she was, with attractive curves, a smile that could charm leaves from the trees, and eyes that twinkled like big, green stars.

Stars—Sadie's favorite of the heavenly bodies. An image of his wife materialized in his brain, and, with it, the memory of his last moments with her. "Don't grieve too long," she'd rasped. "Love will come along again, and, when it does, I want you to welcome it." Ah, but she'd been something else, that bride of his. She'd clung to life like a drowning man might cling to a branch extended to tow him ashore. She'd made up her mind to hold on until she'd wheedled that promise out of him. "All right," he'd finally agreed. "If love comes along again, I'll welcome it."

If he'd had children to raise, he might have understood why almost every female in his life—aunts and cousins and sisters alike—seemed driven to match him up with the second Mrs. Josh Neville. Riding home from a church social last fall, his youngest sister, Susan, had scolded him, saying, "Priscilla is a lovely girl. I declare, Josh Neville, it's as if you're not even trying!"

He hadn't needed to try with Sadie, but Josh hadn't wanted to rile his sister further by pointing it out.

Months later, Josh had had a similar set-to with his eldest sister, who'd confessed that she'd gone to a lot of trouble rigging the boxed lunch auction to ensure he'd end up with her best friend's cousin. "Did you ever stop to think that if you looked harder, you might just find something close to what you shared with Sadie?" she'd asked him.

Why should he settle for close when he'd had *it?* "I'm content living alone," he'd said. And he had been, too, right up until the moment he'd gotten an eyeful of the battered bundle of nerves cowering behind a boulder in the dead of night.

Almost from the start, something in Dinah had called to something in him, and, more and more, his heart wanted to answer. He didn't understand it, he couldn't give it a name, but the sensation had grabbed hold and refused to let go.

Maybe it boiled down to a man's need to protect a woman.

Maybe he was just overtired from being on the road for so long.

He could hear her in the cabin, humming and clattering as she "threw something together" for their supper. "Better get ahold of yourself, Neville," he grumbled. What if the abusive beast she'd escaped was searching for her? An important question. So, why hadn't he asked it earlier, along with dozens of others? Were his sisters right? Was he the least inquisitive man in Texas?

Frowning, Josh pocketed both hands and stared up at the charcoal sky, where a million stars winked around the snow-white moon. A gentle wind riffled his hair, and he took a deep drink of it. The stifling heat had departed with the storm, but nature was fickle and undependable. Tomorrow might be a good day to travel south, but it just as easily might be a repeat of eye-smarting sun and skin-puckering temperatures. Riding in the rain definitely had its benefits when compared to certain, other conditions.

Experience told him they wouldn't see a repeat of today's weather, but he had the uneasy feeling he hadn't seen the last of life's storms.

12

*T*hey rode in silence during the early morning, and Kate couldn't help but wonder what was going on in that handsome head of his. Even in profile, she could see the taut set of his jaw, his brows dipping low in the middle of his forehead.

He'd been quiet at supper last night and at breakfast this morning, too. That hadn't surprised her, considering the recent oppressive heat, which had stifled even her energies for conversation. When the warmth had faded with the storm, she'd blamed his silence on the clammy stench of damp leather and wet blankets left behind by the Rangers. But after the cool breeze had cleared the cabin of foul odors, she'd run out of excuses and explanations for his distant behavior.

Until the lawmen's arrival, Josh had been unrelenting in his need to hold her gaze when they spoke, to the point of dipping his head to maintain eye contact. It had been unnerving, at first, but in time, she'd grown more comfortable with it. But he'd barely met her eyes since the Rangers had disappeared over the horizon the previous morning.

When they'd bedded down for the second night—Josh on a pallet on the floor, she on the rickety cot against the wall—he'd said, "Peaceful dreams, Dinah, and may God's angels watch over you." His simple, soft-spoken words had rocked her to the very core, stirring tears and a thick sob that prevented her from saying anything more than, "You, too."

She'd stared into the darkness for hours, listening to his steady breathing, wondering how to slip away without waking him. Climbing out of the cot and tiptoeing directly out the door wouldn't pose a problem, for she'd worn her boots and jacket to bed. She'd also placed her hat atop a well-packed saddlebag to make it easy to grab on her way out. The challenge would be in hoisting the heavy, leather saddle without setting off a series of creaks and squeaks.

Kate tried to be single-minded about her decision to leave Josh for his own good. And, every few minutes, her brain would shout, "Now!" and she'd grip the blanket, determined to throw it off and swing her legs to the floor.

But memories of the moments leading up to his sweet, good-night wish had shouted louder....

Before they'd gone to bed, Josh had thrown his saddle over one shoulder and stepped onto the porch, filling Kate with a surge of panic. Had he determined that enough was enough and decided to leave her before she could leave him? Unable to quiet her curiosity, she'd blurted out, "Josh? Where are you going?"

He'd turned and tucked in one corner of his mouth, studying her face. "Just thought I'd bed down out here under the stars," he'd said, his voice a gentle murmur, his frown softening with care and concern. "But I'll stay inside, if you want me to."

Her own expression must have told him that she wanted very much for him to stay inside, for he'd given a quick nod, winked, and dropped the saddle onto the floor.

And so, throughout the night, Kate's conviction that she needed to leave battled the blooming love in her heart. Ultimately, she had fallen into a deep sleep and dreamed about the many kind things Josh had done for her in the short time they'd been together.

When she'd awakened at daybreak, she'd seen him in the doorway, silhouetted by the morning sun. "Horses are saddled," he'd said, "and there's coffee on the stove."

Kate had gulped down half a mug of the murky liquid and taken one last look at the cabin—the closest thing to a home she'd had in nearly a month—before closing the door quietly behind her.

"We'd best get moving," Josh had announced when she'd stepped up beside him. Then, he'd planted both leather-gloved hands on her waist and hoisted her into her saddle.

"Thanks."

He'd snapped a two-fingered salute off the brim of his Stetson and said, "Welcome."

And he hadn't uttered a syllable since then.

She hadn't thought it was possible to miss the sound of a man's voice. But she did.

She hadn't thought she'd yearn to look into those captivating, blue eyes of his, but, right now, Kate would have welcomed even his most intense scrutiny.

Golden pinpricks of sunlight glinted from the whiskers covering all but a thin, white scar that was angled across his chin like a boomerang. She wondered how he'd earned it, then decided that, perhaps, some lighthearted banter might brighten his dark mood.

"So, how did you get that scar?" she began.

Josh ran a glove-tipped finger over the spot. "Fell off the barn roof when I was nine."

She gasped. "The barn roof! Whatever were you doing up there?"

He shrugged. "Aw, just boyish antics."

"Were you hurt badly? Other than the gash to your chin, I mean?"

"Nah."

Kate pressed him further. "No broken bones? Not even a cracked rib?"

"Nah," he repeated. Just like that.

Question.

Answer.

Polite and matter-of-fact.

What in heaven's name had she done to rile him? She had half a mind to ask him that, too. But since they'd soon be parting ways, perhaps she was better off not knowing. It might make leaving him easier to do. "Are you hungry?" she asked him next.

He sent her a quizzical look. "You fed me two biscuits not more than an hour ago."

And your point is? She decided not to voice her frustration. "Well," she began, "it's hot. And windy. And the past few days have been...well, they haven't been the easiest. I mean, I seriously doubt that when you left San Antonio, you expected to meet up with the likes of *me*. Or that you'd find yourself buying clothes and boots and—and wind up stuck with me for days and days. I'm just saying that it wouldn't seem peculiar at all, your being a big, strapping man and all, if you were hungry, even though you'd only just eaten a short while ago, because—"

"Dinah?"

"Yes, Josh?"

"Relax."

Relax? What made him think she was tense? Surely not the fact that she'd been rambling nonsensically! "I might be able to—if a certain person around here could speak in more than single-word sentences."

He glanced left, right, then leaned forward slightly and patted Callie's neck. "Where's this taciturn person she's referring to, I wonder?"

When Callie snorted, Josh chuckled.

"Go ahead. Make fun of me. But *you* try riding for hours and hours with someone who doesn't talk, and see how you like it."

"I have."

Kate bit back the groan in her throat. Gripping the pommel tightly, she turned in her saddle. "You have what?"

"I have ridden for hours with someone who doesn't talk."

He shot her a quick glance, and, in that instant, she recognized the by-now familiar grin. "I can't think of a time when I've let more than a few minutes of silence pass between us," she protested.

For some absurd reason, he laughed, and lovely as it was to hear, Kate bristled, because she didn't have a clue what he found so funny.

Once his moment of amusement passed, Josh cleared his throat. "So, let me get this straight—you've been chattering nonstop as a favor to me?"

Based on everything he'd said and done since scaring the wits out of her that night at his camp, Kate had no reason to believe he would intentionally insult her. Was it possible she'd misjudged him? That his question had an underlying purpose? Perhaps, his gentlemanly behavior had limits, and because she'd overstayed her welcome, the pressure to maintain the act had grown burdensome. That would certainly explain the silent treatment he'd been giving her!

Lifting her chin, she straightened her spine and stared straight ahead. "Ninny," she muttered to herself. "If you'd left when you wanted to—"

Josh whipped off his hat so fast, it created enough breeze to muss her bangs. "I knew it!" he exclaimed, startling both horses.

She decided not to give him the satisfaction of asking what he'd meant. She'd let him get a good taste of what it had been like, coping with sustained silence and gruff, monosyllabic responses!

But inquisitiveness got the better of her. "Knew what?"

"That something was up."

All right, so the man is sleep-deprived. Hungry. Worried. Annoyed at having been thrust into the hero role on the heels of a family crisis. And made poorer by more than a few dollars because he generously insisted on buying me food and clothes and…oh, bother. Kate's irritation died a sudden death. What sort of ungrateful, heartless, selfish person would allow herself to feel anything even remotely akin to frustration with a man like Josh Neville?

"I saw you packing last night," he said, interrupting her self-recriminating tirade, "and I had a feeling you might ride off on my horse."

That had her sitting up straight in the saddle. "Your horse? But—but I—I thought—"

Josh's grating harrumph stopped her stuttering.

"If you thought I can afford to give horses away, you thought wrong. What *I* thought was, I'd get you safely to Mexico, just as I promised, dressed in clean clothes and decent boots; I'd make sure you had a job and a place to live; and then I'd lead this horse back to Eagle Pass."

So, if she had left last night, as planned, Josh could have had her arrested as a horse thief. Kate didn't know which shamed her more—that he actually thought her capable of stealing from him, or that she'd been foolish—no, *stupid*—enough to think he'd give her such an expensive gift. The humiliation of it ached all the way to the soles of her oh-so-decent new boots. "Oh, Josh," she finally managed to say. "I'm sorry, truly sorry."

His expression said, "For what?" But his lips remained a taut line.

Don't you cry, you pathetic, little weakling, don't you dare cry! A sob ached in her throat, but she pressed on. "I'm sorry for everything. For taking your bed that first night. For costing you so much money. For keeping you from your family. For believing you'd—for making the mistake of—for thinking that—for—"

"Whoa," Josh said, bringing both horses to a halt. He slid from his saddle and, holding his horse's reins, grabbed hers and pointed at the ground. "Get down from there, missy. I need to have a few words with you."

It galled her that he was treating her like a spoiled child—mostly, because that's exactly how she felt. She'd hear him out, and, once he'd gotten a few things off his chest, she'd politely ask him to point the way to Mexico. He had a pencil stub and an envelope in his saddlebag—she'd seen them when she'd been looking for the matches. Kate still had the pistol he'd given her to prove she had nothing to fear from him, and she made a mental note to give that back, too, just as soon as he tore the flap off that envelope and wrote down where she could send the money to repay him.

That is, if she made it to Mexico and found a job.

Would she ever dig herself out of this hole? By the time she sent money to the families of the people Frank had killed, and sent still more to Josh, she'd be lucky if she could afford bread and water for herself. *You'll have plenty of time to feel sorry for yourself later, when you're alone on the trail,* she told herself. She started to dismount, thinking she might as well get this over with.

"Dinah, watch out for that—"

His warning came a tick in time too late, for she'd already rolled her ankle on the rock beneath her heel. Tears stung her eyes as she collapsed onto the sandy soil. The last thing she wanted to do was add to Josh's burdens. But she'd broken that same ankle as a girl, playing leapfrog on the slippery rocks in her grandmother's pond. If she hadn't broken it again, it would be a miracle.

Oh, sweet Jesus, she prayed silently, *I know I don't deserve it, but I sure could use a miracle right about now.*

N o woman in his life had ever exasperated him—or touched him—the way Dinah Theodore did. She'd crumpled to the ground like an empty flour sack, and if she'd hurt herself, well, it would be his fault. If only he hadn't commanded her to climb down from her horse, as if he were General Houston himself, and she, a lowly private.

Kneeling beside her, Josh said, "Don't try to move it. If it's broken, you'll only make it worse."

Grimacing, she nodded.

He'd given Dinah his word that she'd be safe with him. Had given her a loaded pistol to underscore that fact. But now, he felt like a bully, a cad, and a heel, because his surly mood had put this scene in motion. The irony wasn't lost on him, even as he condemned his impatience, that the reason he'd stopped the horses in the first place had been to put an end to her ongoing apologies. Now, he was the sorry one. Sorrier than he'd been in—well, at the moment, Josh couldn't recall anything he regretted as much.

"Goodness gracious, sakes alive," she whimpered, her shoulders sagging. "Now look what I've gone and done. I've upset you. Again." Lifting her chin, she got onto her knees. "I've broken bones before—this very one, as a matter of fact—so please don't worry. I'm not made of porcelain, you know. I know you're anxious to get home, so I promise not to slow you down." She shot him a crooked little grin. "I can still ride. Really, I can! You might have to help me into the saddle, and out of it when we stop, and I'm sorry about that, but—"

"Dinah," he interrupted her, grabbing her wrists, "for the love of all that's holy, will you please stop talking?" His mood vacillated between guilt and frustration. "Stop saying you're sorry. You have nothing to apologize for!"

In this position, they were eye to eye for the first time, and the intense glow of the sun left little to the imagination. He noticed the sprinkling of freckles across the bridge of her nose. Saw for the first time blue flecks that glittered in her green eyes. Despite her womanly features, she seemed so young, so inexperienced, and so innocent.

Dinah looked as transfixed as he felt. She swallowed, hard. Widened those remarkable, riveting eyes. Raised her perfectly arched brows. He could tell she was holding her breath, and he could feel her pulse pounding through the fingers of his gloves. Josh frowned with self-loathing at the doubt that was etched in her delicate features. But there was no time for lingering here, gawking at her pretty face. "We'd better head out."

One corner of her pretty mouth lifted in a tiny grin. "'Cause we're burnin' daylight?"

He wanted to say, "No, 'cause if we don't head out, I'm liable to kiss you right where you sit." Instead, he said, "Yeah, 'cause we're burnin' daylight."

Josh wanted to gather her close and admit how much he'd come to care for her. Wanted to pledge that he'd never speak a cross word to her again. That as long as they were together, he'd protect her from rain and wind, from whatever might—

"Then, I guess we'd best get going."

"First, let's have a look at that ankle. If it's broken, it might need a splint."

"And if it isn't, it'll puff up like a bullfrog's throat, and I'll never get my boot back on."

"Good point," he said. "I'll have a look at it when we stop for the night."

She nodded, and as Josh held out a hand to help her up, she didn't hesitate to take it. So, he was furious with himself for not thinking to use both hands, because Dinah lost her balance when she stood up and had to lean on him for support. Not that he minded having her so close, of course.

He held on tight, determined not to let her fall again. But he knew without a doubt that if they stood this way a minute longer, he'd find out firsthand if those extraordinary lips felt as soft and tasted as sweet as they looked. "Let's get you back on the horse," he said. "Start out sidesaddle, so you won't bang your ankle on the horn."

Dinah took a deep breath.

With one hand on either side of her waist, he said, "Ready?"

Another nod. Then, with her eyes closed tight and her lips taut, she said, "Ready when you are."

"Up you go."

Once her backside hit the saddle, a high-pitched yet barely audible "Ouch" squeaked from her mouth. And then, she laughed. "Whew," she said, fanning herself. "I'm glad that's over!"

Well, I'm not, he thought, heaving himself up onto Callie's back.

"You want to hear something funny?" she asked as they cantered south.

Leave it to Dinah to find something comical about an injured ankle. "Sure."

"I'm famished."

He grinned. "Want to hear something funnier?"

She matched his smile, tooth for tooth. "Sure."

"Me, too."

A moment of silence ticked by as they stared into each other's eyes. Their laughter started slow and low, escalating in pitch and volume, until both Dinah and Josh were breathless and wiping tears from their eyes. How long had it been since he'd laughed like that? Had he ever laughed as long or as hard? If so, he couldn't remember when.

"Think I can dig some food out of my saddlebags without falling off my horse?"

"A man can hope."

Half an hour later, after polishing off a stale biscuit and a strip of jerky, Josh found that his good humor had soured like milk left too long in the sun. Every clip-clop of the horses' hooves moved them closer to Mexico, and he couldn't imagine saying good-bye to Dinah; he didn't want to think about the fact that, once he did, he'd probably never see her again.

He would cross the river with her, accompany her into some little border town, help her find a job and a room to rent. He'd check the place out to make sure it was safe for a woman on her own, and, if it wasn't, he would insist that they move on to another town. That way, at least he'd know where to find her, if he had a mind to.

"So, who do you know in Mexico?"

"No one."

"I don't get it," Josh admitted. "Why Mexico?"

Something akin to a shadow darkened Dinah's expression before she looked away. Shrugging, she said, "It's just—it's just something I have to do. Call it a girlish dream."

A foolish dream is more like it. "You're not afraid of *banditos*?"

He wasn't sure what name he'd give to the expression that skittered across her face. Apprehension? Fear? "Lots of outlaws down there, you know," he went on. "Very shady characters, according to the newspapers. No surprise, if you think about it, because the U.S. Marshals and the Texas Rangers can't touch 'em once they cross the border."

Dinah blew a whiff of air through her lips. "So I've heard. But that's a—"

A chance she'd have to take? If only she'd trust him with the secret that had put her on the run! How bad could the truth be?

"It's getting dark," he observed.

"So it is."

Small talk, Josh thought with a mental harrumph. He'd never been any good at it. And he wouldn't have had to deal with it now if he hadn't stuck his nose where it didn't belong. "Let's pull up over there," he said, indicating a tall pine. "I'll rustle us up some firewood while you—" He remembered her ankle. "Actually, you sit tight. As soon as I get a fire going, I'll take a look at that foot of yours."

An hour later, as the night matured around them, she appeared to be resting comfortably in a splint made of branches held in place by strips of cloth torn from his blanket. He had determined that her ankle wasn't broken, but it had been twisted badly. They'd dined on jerky and stale biscuits, washed down by tepid water, and she seemed calm and content.

Josh tossed another log onto the fire. "I've been thinkin'."

She stretched languorously. "Do tell," she said around a huge yawn.

He grinned. "I'm thinkin' you shouldn't go to Mexico."

That certainly woke her up!

"My gut tells me you haven't thought this through," he went on.

Dinah tilted her head and regarded him for a moment. "You're wrong. I've given it a lot of thought."

She was downright beautiful in the firelight, and he cleared his throat. "Then you must've hit your head sometime before you lit out for Mexico."

"Hit my...."

He scooted closer and took hold of her hand, giving it a gentle squeeze. "You're not thinking straight, Dinah. Now, I know you think you're strong and smart and capable, but you're just a little slip of a thing." He nodded into the endless darkness. "And it's dangerous down there."

She looked at their hands, then met his eyes. "Josh, I—"

"How do you expect to hunt for work with that ankle of yours?"

Her eyelashes fluttering, she started, "I—"

"And, even if you find a job, how will you do it in the shape you're in?"

Her frown deepened.

"How will you pay your rent without a job?"

Dinah stared into the flames and sighed.

"I'm right. You know I am."

A second, perhaps two, passed before she said, "Right about what?"

"That you haven't thought this through."

"I had everything all worked out, until…." She lifted her injured foot. "Until this."

"Come home with me."

She turned her head so quickly that a lock of long, luxurious hair gently whiffed his cheek. "You're joking, right? What would your wife and children think? What would—"

"My wife died three years ago, giving birth to twin boys, who died, too."

"Oh, Josh," Dinah whispered, pressing the fingertips of her free hand to her lips. "I'm so sorry. How sad and—that's just—it's just awful, that's what!" And then she threw her arms around his neck and hugged him tight. After a moment, she leaned back, but only slightly. "You need me to help care for your other children, is that it? Like a governess, or a—a housekeeper?"

"I live alone," he admitted, his voice sounding quiet and gravelly, even in his own ears. "No wife. No other children. Just me."

Her brow furrowed. "But you said—" Dinah pursed her lips. "Didn't you say you had a big family in Eagle Pass?"

Josh started counting on his fingers. "Parents, sisters, cousins who have wives and young'uns, and we all live in houses on the same ranch. My ma could use some help running the big house." Later, he'd tell her about Lucinda, his mother's housekeeper, and his unmarried sister, who helped take care of the home.

"But, my ankle— What help can I possibly be, limping around like a—"

"You can sew, can't you?"

She waved the question away as if swatting at an annoying mosquito. "Well, of course. Can you name a woman who can't?"

"Then you can darn socks and sew buttons back onto the field hands' shirts. There are bound to be dozens of chores you could do, sitting down." He could tell that he had her attention by the way she was chewing her lower lip, the way her eyes were flashing. "And, once your ankle heals, you can do more." He hoped she wouldn't say that when her ankle healed, she'd leave.

"What would your poor mother say?"

"About what?"

She groaned. "Why, about your bringing a stranger into her house—one you found wandering around, alone, dirty, and bruised, in the middle of the night, one who can't earn her keep because of her own clumsiness!"

Knowing Ma, he expected her to say, "It's about time you brought a woman home to meet me!" But that wasn't the answer Dinah needed to hear. Josh cleared his throat. "She'd say, 'Thank heaven, I finally have some help taking care of this big, drafty, old house.'"

"How far from here to your—hey, wait a minute," Dinah said, narrowing her eyes. She sat up straighter. "I thought you said you lived alone!"

"I built *my* house with my own two hands, but I spend a fair amount of time at the home place." He couldn't bring himself to tell her he'd built the house as a wedding gift to Sadie, and that he hated it more than anthrax now that she wasn't around to share it with him.

It was clear by the way Dinah sat there, wide-eyed, that she was considering his offer. "Why not sleep on it?" he said, giving her hand another little squeeze. Then, he moved to the opposite side of the campfire and spread out his bedroll. "G'night, Dinah," he said over the flames.

"G'night, Josh. And thank you."

"For what?"

"I don't know what I'll decide to do after sleeping on it, but, whatever it is, it can't change the fact that you're very sweet to offer to take me home."

Sweet? The last thing he wanted her to think was that he was sweet.

"Who would've guessed...?"

Did he really want to ask what she meant by that? "Guessed what?"

"That, in such a short time, you'd become such a dear friend."

Her words touched him. But they disappointed him, too, because Josh didn't want to be her friend. He wanted to be more. So much more.

But that was plumb loco, since what he knew about Dinah Theodore, he could put in one eye.

14

"Well," Josh said, "there it is. The Lazy N Ranch… home."

He sat with one hand atop the other on the saddle horn, staring straight ahead. The view was impressive, to be sure, and Kate squinted, looking for a house, a barn, or a fence that might indicate a property line. Instead, the rise and fall of the gently sloping hills seemed to go on forever, some wearing a blanket of lush, green grass, others draped in brilliant gold, which seamlessly blended the earth and the vivid blue sky. "Where is the ranch?"

Josh swept one arm from left to right. Surely, he didn't mean that all of this land made up the Lazy N! "How many acres?" she asked.

"Two hundred thousand—now."

Kate had always lived in a city, or on the fringes of one, in houses surrounded by small yards. As a child, she would spent the summers with her grandparents, who'd owned two acres on the outskirts of Dodge City, and even that space had seemed as vast as an ocean to her. She couldn't visualize two hundred thousand acres. "How many were you forced to sell?"

"Hmpf," he snorted. "See that bluff over there?"

Kate followed the imaginary line he'd drawn with his forefinger.

"Used to be ours from there," he pointed, "to there." He gave another snort. "Ten thousand acres gone, just like that."

She wondered how many cows had died of anthrax to force a sale that enormous. "And the contaminated area—where is that?"

Josh nodded. "Just over that rise, there. Nearly five hundred acres, all useless now."

"But, that's not forever, right?"

He tore his gaze from the distant horizon and fixed it on her face. "No. Not forever. But the land will be useless for generations."

Despite the shadow cast over his face by the brim of his hat, there was no mistaking the pain that shimmered in his eyes. He loved this place, just as surely as he loved his family. Kate didn't have the heart to ask him how long it would be before it was again safe to graze cattle there. Of course, she'd heard of anthrax, but she had no idea what it was. Perhaps, in the next few days, she'd learn more about it. She wanted to know about everything and anything that was of the slightest importance to this wonderful, gentle man. "Is your family expecting you?"

Josh's mouth slanted in a wry grin. "I'd bet my saddle that George has eyes on us right now."

"One of your brothers?"

"No, I don't have any. At least, not by blood. Just four cousins, raised like brothers." He paused, then added, "George might as well be blood kin, though. I've known him almost all my life."

His reply made her wonder if, in addition to selling off acres, he'd been forced to let go some of his trusted employees, too. But it wasn't a question she wanted to ask for fear of waking more sad memories. "I'm sure they'll be thrilled to see you."

Josh turned his attention back to the trail. "I reckon."

"How long have you been away?"

"Twenty-one days."

The way he enunciated each syllable told her that, to Josh, it might as well have been twenty-one months. It dawned on her suddenly that, very shortly, he'd introduce her to his family. She wanted to make a good first impression, especially on his mother—if that was even possible under the circumstances. "What will you tell her?"

Josh faced her and thumbed the Stetson to the back of his head. "Ma, you mean?"

"Yes." Why the response had come out sounding like sandpaper grazing a rough board, Kate didn't know. She knew only that the mere mention of the family matriarch caused her breaths to come in short, shallow bursts. She prayed he wouldn't say, "Why, I'll tell her the truth, of course." Because what woman willingly invited a stranger into her home—especially one who looked, as Josh had said on the night they met, like she'd been dragged through a keyhole at the end of a rope?

"What will I tell her about what?"

"Well, about what you're doing with the likes of me, for starters. And about why you brought a complete stranger into her house, and—"

"Dinah," he interrupted her gently, "settle down."

"That's easy for you to say. You aren't the one dropping in unexpectedly at the poor woman's home."

He sat quietly for a moment, then exhaled a sigh. "I guess I see your point. So, I'll just tell her how I ran into you during the ride home, and that, when I realized you were hurt, I offered to put you up until your ankle healed." He shrugged. "She's always welcomed my friends. No reason to expect it'll be any different this time."

What he'd said sounded reasonable, except for one word: *friend*. But she'd gone over and over that argument a hundred times in the privacy of her mind, each time coming to the same conclusion: enforcing an arm's-length distance in her relationship with Josh was the right thing to do. For his sake, anyway.

Until now, her life had rarely brought her face-to-face with the thorny side of doing the right thing. Sticking to her plan would test far more than her resolve; it would also determine the strength of her character.

"Is your ankle bothering you?"

"Not really."

"Then, why the long face?"

"I was just thinking that maybe I should clean myself up a mite. It'll be hard enough meeting your family for the first time without looking as scruffy as a barn cat."

"You look beaut—you look fine. Just fine."

Kate felt herself blush as she tucked several stray wisps back into place. "How long will it take us to get from here to the house?"

"Half a day, maybe longer."

Her heartbeat quickened at the realization she'd meet his mother that soon. "Is there a creek or a stream nearby where I might wash up a little?"

"Yeah, but unless they got some rain from that storm we just rode out, it's hard to know if there'll be any water moving in it."

"Is it very far out of the way?"

"Nope."

And with that, he clicked his tongue, and Callie dutifully moved forward, inspiring Kate's horse to do the same. "Have you named her yet?" she asked, patting her coffee-colored neck.

"Nope."

Please, Lord, don't tell me we're back to one-word replies for the rest of the ride!

"She's a lovely animal," Kate said. "Seems a shame for her to go through life without a name."

"What do you suggest?"

"Brownie?"

Josh smirked. "Very original."

"How about Chocolate, then?"

"I thought women were supposed to be natural-born poets."

Giggling, Kate said, "You thought wrong." Then, "How did you choose Callie's name?"

That inspired a chuckle. "Long story."

"By your own words, we have half a day, maybe more, before we arrive at your mother's house. I think there's time for you to tell it."

He sent her a sidelong glance, then launched into the story. "My grandmother, Mee-Maw, hates wastefulness, so she saved every leftover scrap from every dress and skirt and curtain she ever sewed. Kept them in flour sacks and pillow-slips—dozens of them—and when she got too feeble to get around much, she started turning them into quilts.

"Callie, here, never met a fence she couldn't jump, and the day I brought her home, she leaped over the corral gate like it was knee-high to a grasshopper. She moseyed right on up to the front porch, where Mee-Maw sat stitching, and learned right quick that if she kept the old woman's chair going, she could earn some sweets.

"She earned herself a place in my grandmother's heart that day, pressing the chair's rockers like a bellows pedal. And that very day, Mee-Maw made this purty saddle blanket out of strips of calico."

"What parts of the story did you leave out?"

Even in the shade of his Stetson, she could see his confused grin. "Beg pardon?"

"You must have edited out a lot of details, because you said it was a long story, and telling it took you hardly any time at all."

He gave another shrug. "Just the same, that's how Callie got her name."

Kate added that bit of information to her quickly growing list of reasons to like Josh Neville. How thickheaded of her to think moodiness explained his short, staccato replies. He was a man of few words; it was as simple as that.

And she intended to pay a lot closer attention to each one from here on out.

S usan, Josh's youngest sister, grabbed his hand and led him into the library. "Oh, Josh," she gushed, "Dinah is simply adorable!"

"You can say that again," his older sister, Sarah, agreed. "Now, tell us the truth—Ma is out of earshot. Where did you *really* find her?"

Flanked by smaller, feminine versions of himself, Josh knew that his chances of escape were slim to none, but he estimated the number of steps from the stove to the door, just in case an opening presented itself. "I've already told the story half a dozen times."

Susan jabbed a bony finger into his chest. "Then, that's how many times you fibbed, brother dear."

He'd promised Dinah that he wouldn't tell his family the details of how they'd met, and he aimed to keep that promise. Besides, what if they asked a question he couldn't answer? The information she'd volunteered was slim, at best. "I think I hear Ma calling you—"

"I do believe I might be forced to ride into town and fetch Reverend Peterson."

He frowned at Sarah. "What for?"

"I'm worried about the state of your soul, Joshua Amos Neville, that's what for. Maybe the reverend can talk the good

Lord into forgiving you for all the lies you've piled one on top of the other. Why, you haven't been home a full day, and I'd wager you've already told dozens!"

All right, so he'd said a few things to sidetrack them. Was it his fault that the reality of the situation and their perceptions of it were miles apart? Josh loved his sisters dearly, but he didn't trust them a whit. Experience had taught him that even if they placed their right hands upon the Good Book and vowed to keep the story to themselves, everyone within fifty miles of Eagle Pass would have heard a distorted version of it by week's end. And what if the monster who'd abused Dinah happened to be passing through town and got wind of her whereabouts? If Josh had to spew a fountain of fibs to protect her, he'd do it in a heartbeat. Did that make him a sinner? He supposed it did. But he'd much rather ask the Lord's forgiveness for telling a few lies than beg His mercy when the truth put Dinah in danger. "Like it or not," he said, "that's the story."

His sisters exchanged wary glances and then rolled their eyes. Susan threw up her arms in frustration. "He's impossible!" she exclaimed, letting both hands fall at her sides.

Sarah faced him head-on with one hand on her hip, the other wagging a finger in his face. "I bet Ma could get the real story out of you!"

That was true, Josh conceded to himself. But if he put his list of reasons not to admit it next to the list of the tales he'd told, the former decision would win, hands down.

"All right, Mr. Stubborn-as-a-Mule, tell me this, then: When do you think you'll marry her?"

Leave it to Sarah to ask the one question he couldn't answer without spilling the whole pot of beans. If he said that he couldn't wager when he'd marry a woman he'd met just a few days ago, well, there went his story that he and Dinah were old friends. If he denied having feelings for her, Sarah would see through him as through window glass. So, he did the next best thing—he told a different truth. "Don't know as she'd have me, even if I asked."

Susan rolled her eyes. "Please. I've seen the way she looks at you."

"And hangs on your every word," Sarah added.

"And follows your every move."

Sarah giggled. "The girl is positively smitten with you, brother dear!"

Josh faked a hearty laugh. "'Smitten.' I declare, Sarah, where do you come up with such words?"

"From books," she retorted, "you illiterate cowboy, you."

He didn't point out that, of all the Neville cousins, only he and Micah had gone to college, and that, to accomplish the feat, they both had read stacks and stacks of books, including a few tomes that weighed nearly as much as he did. It was far better to let her think she'd won their verbal sparring match. So, Josh tried changing the subject. "What's for supper?" he asked, patting his stomach.

"How would I know?" Sarah clucked. "Surely, you weren't gone so long that you forgot that Lucinda doesn't allow other people in her kitchen."

"Ah, the lovely Lucinda." He nodded thoughtfully, then added, "She has always welcomed *me* in her kitchen. With open arms, I might add."

"Sarah said 'people,'" Susan teased, kissing his cheek. "You know as well as I do that the bighearted woman has a soft spot for creatures and critters." She turned on her heel and headed for the foyer. "Now, I'm off to find that pretty young lady you brought home, and to see if she'd like to soak in a nice, hot bath."

Sarah pressed her lips to Josh's other cheek, then stepped back, feigning a chill. "You might want to give some serious thought to heading over to your place for a little while," she said, wrinkling her nose, "because you could use a bath, yourself."

Susan popped back into the doorway long enough to add, "And a shave."

Once they were gone, Josh had to admit that they were right. Twelve days on the trail after leaving San Antonio—no, thirteen, counting the stopover in the storm-racked shack— had taken their toll on him. Smiling, Josh rubbed his whiskered chin. Yes, he cherished his sisters dearly—and loved the silence they'd left behind almost as much.

"Got a minute to talk, son?" came his father's voice from the other side of the screen door.

"Sarah and Susan just laid down the law," he said, stepping onto the porch. They've ordered me to bathe and shave before dinner."

Matthew Neville chuckled and dropped onto the seat of the double-wide swing. "Couldn't hurt to wash the trail dust from your face, I suppose."

Josh leaned back against the porch railing and crossed both arms over his chest. "Reckon you want a detailed account of what happened in San Antone."

Nodding, Matthew said, "You reckon right. But that can wait. No point covering the same ground more than once. When everybody is at the dinner table, we'll talk about rounding up the brothers and their boys. I'm sure they'll be interested to hear all about it, too."

Josh hadn't yet decided whether to tell his family about the bank robbery, since a report like that would only rile the menfolk and terrify the women. He'd prayed on it, night after night, and had come to the conclusion that if the good Lord believed the story should be told, He'd send a signal. And, since none had been delivered yet, Josh took it to mean it was best to keep the news to himself, at least for the time being.

"Now, about this young woman you've brought home," Matthew said, breaking into his thoughts.

"Dinah?"

"Dinah, yes. Is there anything you'd like to tell me?"

Josh ran the question through his brain a time or two, trying to determine what, exactly, his father wanted to hear.

"I couldn't help but notice that scar on her jaw."

Sometimes, Josh reasoned, the truth beat a story all the way to town and back. "Don't rightly know how she came by that," he admitted. "But I can tell you this—she looked a whole lot worse than she does now when I came across her on the trail."

"You—you found her?"

"Halfway between here and San Antone, hunkered down behind a boulder, shivering and half-starved, and looking like she'd just gone three rounds with a prizefighter."

"And lost."

Josh nodded.

"Then, your ma was right."

"About what?"

"She had a feeling the poor girl's story about falling from her horse was more fable than fact."

"Well, that is how she twisted her ankle. I was there when it happened."

His father settled back in the swing. "And the rest of it? Were you there for that, too?"

"No. She hasn't offered an explanation for the rest of her bruises, and I haven't pressed her for one."

"I understand." His father got to his feet and rested a strong yet gentle hand on Josh's shoulder. "You might want to warn her to have something ready to tell your sisters when they ask about the cuts and bruises, because you know as well as I do that they're bound to ask."

Josh needed only to remember the conversation he'd just had with the pair of them to realize the accuracy of his father's remark.

"I'm proud of you, son. Not every man would step out in faith that way, rescue a woman in distress."

Rescue? The word implied he'd performed a heroic deed. If there was a man out there who'd have done anything differently, Josh would like to meet him, because it might be interesting to come face-to-face with a truly heartless human being.

"I know you did us proud in San Antonio, too." With that, Matthew headed for the barn, leaving Josh to ponder their exchange.

He gazed out at the Lazy N land—land that reached far beyond the horizon and represented nearly half a century's struggle to grow roots in the dry, Texas soil. Over the years, his grandfather and father had told tales of a hundred calamities, and how they'd muscled their way through each. This latest tragedy had taken a heavy toll, but they'd survive the anthrax, too.

Josh should have felt safe and secure, here on home turf. Should have felt encouraged and strengthened by the land

and the knowledge that the blood of hardy men and women flowed in his veins. So, how was he to explain the sense of foreboding that was closing in around him?

It wasn't an entirely new sensation. He'd felt a similar sense many times on the trail, when cougars and coyotes or bandits and rustlers would stalk the Nevilles' herds. With his nerves on edge, he'd stare hard into the darkness, ever alert, always ready. And although being prepared hadn't thwarted every raid, the feeling that something was coming had protected Josh and his men against many a surprise attack.

Yes, danger was lurking nearby, that much was certain. But how would he defend his family against a foe he couldn't identify?

The better question was, how closely connected were this gnawing sense of doom and Dinah's presence at the Lazy N?

16

If the simple skirts and plain shirts Josh had bought her on the trail hadn't soaked up all that rain and dust, Kate would have been wearing them now instead of the frilly, pink gingham dress Sarah had loaned her.

With her hands on her hips, Kate did a slow twirl in front of the tall oval mirror, unable to decide which pained her more—her injured ankle, or the fact that a New York designer had created the dress. She had no use for the puffy sleeves, expansive bustles, feathered hats, and button-up boots that stretched the term "high fashion" to the snapping point, in her opinion. She didn't think that a getup like this would flatter a dressmaker's dummy, and yet, here she stood, cloaked from head to toe in the ridiculous thing.

An hour earlier, as she'd been dozing contentedly in the warm, sudsy waters of a deep, tin tub, Josh's sister, Sarah, had rapped at the door and peeked her head in. "We appear to be about the same size, Dinah," she'd said, her friendly smile brightening the room, "so you're more than welcome to borrow one of my dresses until you've had time to launder and press your own things."

After her bath, when she'd first gotten a look at the dress Sarah had in mind, Kate had oohed and aahed with as much gratitude as she could muster—a big mistake, as it had turned out, for her exaggerated enthusiasm had only encouraged Sarah to race back to her room to gather accessories to complete the outfit: bizarre, feathered combs to hold back her hair and an enormous cameo ring to wear on her finger.

Now, staring hard at her reflection in the mirror, Kate fought back tears, reminding herself that, in a day or two, when her own clothes no longer reeked of mildew, she'd be able to wear them instead of the dress. But shedding the phony identity she'd invented for herself was something else, altogether; she couldn't afford to cast it off if she hoped to save her own skin.

In a matter of weeks, she'd gone from being a self-sufficient young woman to someone who'd come to depend on one man for her every need. How had her life become so completely overturned? From the shiny, high-heeled shoes on her feet to the white feathers in her hair, there was no hint of Kate Wellington to be seen. Would any remnant of her true self linger once this mess was behind her?

Kate clenched her jaw, determined not to cry. A girl who'd gotten into a fix like this through no fault of her own would have had a right to feel sorry for herself. At least, for a little while. But someone like she, whose circumstances were of her own making, had no business wallowing in self-pity, not even for a—

"Dinah?"

Josh's voice interrupted her thoughts.

"Ma says to tell you dinner's on the table."

Kate pinched her cheeks and bit her lips for a touch of color, just as her mama had taught her to do all those years ago.

When she opened the door, Kate stifled a tiny gasp. She'd never seen Josh all bathed and powdered and shaved before. The crisp, white shirt served the dual purposes of accenting his bronzed complexion and intensifying the blue of his eyes beneath his brow of still-damp hair, which glowed like spun gold. She hadn't noticed before because of his vest and suede jacket, but in those smart, black trousers, it was impossible not to notice his trim waist and flat stomach. "My, but you clean up nicely," she said, trying to cover her astonishment with levity.

"I was about to say the same thing to you."

"Really?"

"Really."

"Hmpf." In response to the confused arch of his eyebrows, she said, "If anybody had asked if I thought men liked frilly, fussy clothes, I would have said they dislike them even more than I do."

Immediately, she regretted her words. *Goodness, what if Sarah heard that?* Kate glanced up and down the hall. "Please don't say anything to your sister," she whispered. "She's been so generous and helpful, and I wouldn't want to hurt her feelings or seem ungrateful."

Josh grinned. "What do you have against pink?"

"It isn't the color I object to, but the style—if you can call it that." She flapped both arms. "I'll bet if I jumped off the roof, these sleeves would hold enough air to bring me gently to the ground."

He held out his arm. "Just like one of those hot air balloons."

"Exactly!" she said, laughing as she linked her arm with his.

"I don't mind admitting," he said with a chuckle, "that you amuse me, Dinah Theodore."

His words should have been comforting. They ought to have broadened her smile and heightened her joy at being this close to him after so many hours apart. Instead, a curtain of gloom closed around her, and as surely as a bucket of water can snuff a fire, his compliment cooled her warm mood.

"How's that ankle?"

Oh, but he was perceptive! Though she still wore a cheerful smile, he'd sensed the subtle shift of her temperament and attributed it to her injury. She decided it was better to let him think that than to admit the real reason. "It's a little achy," she admitted, "but nothing I can't tolerate."

With no warning whatever, he slid one arm under her knees, wrapped the other around the small of her back, and scooped her up, just as he had on the night they'd met. It should have frightened her then, but it hadn't. How could she fear a man who held her as gently as if he thought she might break?

He carried her down the long flight of steps as easily as a basket of line-dried linens and lowered her carefully to the floor at the bottom of the staircase. "Easy, now," he instructed her. "Lean on me."

"I most certainly will not."

Her refusal must have baffled him, as indicated by the faint furrow etched between his eyebrows.

Kate didn't want to be responsible for dampening his mood, too, so she smiled and added, "I've been leaning on you for days, it seems. It's high time I stood on my own two feet, don't you think?"

His face relaxed—a little, anyway. Clearly, that hadn't been the answer he'd been looking for, but she supposed it was close enough.

"When your ankle is healed, I'm all for it. Until then, you'll lean on me—or I'll pick you up again. Just think of the impression you'll make on my kinfolk you haven't met yet if their first eyeful of you is—"

"Fine. All right. If you insist. Whatever you—"

"Is that you out there, Josh?"

"Yes, Ma—and I've got Dinah with me."

"Well, stop your lollygagging, the both of you, and get in here. We've been holding dinner for you."

The massive grandfather clock near the front door counted out the hour, and Kate's heart pounded twice for every resonating note. This meeting would be different, she knew—very different—from the casual hellos and polite pleased-to-meet-yous they'd exchanged earlier. This time, his sisters wouldn't be able to rescue her with an offer to show her to her room. This time, she'd join them at the family table, where making conversation and eye contact alike would be required.

"How many are usually at dinner?" she whispered to Josh.

"Depends on how many ranch hands are riding the range, and how many were close enough to get cleaned up in time for the meal." He shrugged. "Some days, twelve or fifteen. Others, twenty-five or thirty."

All seated at the same table, at the same time? Kate would have asked the question out loud if they hadn't rounded the corner at that exact moment.

Josh's father rose from the chair at the head of the wide table, which seemed to stretch out forever. Kate tried to count the heads that turned when she and Josh stepped through the arched doorway, but by the time she reached seven, Matthew Neville had reached them. "Here, son," he said with a grin and a wink. "Let me help you with that."

"Matthew, honestly," Josh's mother, Eva, chided him. "She isn't a sack of potatoes."

The rest of the family laughed as the father and son guided Kate into the chair between theirs. She sat down, took a deep breath, and smiled sheepishly, keenly aware that except for the steady tick of the big clock, the room had fallen completely silent. Even the youngest child had stopped squirming and giggling to fix his gaze on the woman seated to his grandfather's right.

"Matthew, Josh," Eva Neville said, "please sit down so we can say the blessing. Everything's getting cold, and you know how Lucinda feels about that."

A short, husky woman burst through the swinging door that connected the dining room and kitchen. "Yes," she said, wagging an index finger, "Lucinda does not like cold food." She shot a playful wink at Josh. "You are forgiven, señor, but only because we have a guest today."

Lucinda took her place beside Eva as Matthew stood and cleared his throat. "Dear Father in heaven," he began, setting off a chain reaction of clasping hands and bowing heads that rustled from one end of the table to the other. "We ask Your blessing on the humble servants gathered around this table. Watch over us, Lord, especially those whose work keeps them in the fields. Bless the hardworking hands that grew and gathered this food, those that prepared and served it, and those who will share Your bounty here today. We praise Your most holy name, amen."

Beautiful Bandit ᦞ 137

A chorus of amens followed the prayer. Then, the young man directly across from Kate smirked. "Way to go, Matthew—just the way I like my blessings. Short and sweet, nice and neat."

"Sam!" Susan exclaimed. "Will you never learn?"

Her husband feigned surprise. "Learn what?"

"To show a little respect, especially regarding prayers. What sort of example is that for—"

"Oh, leave him be, honey," Josh's mother said. She looked at Kate to say, "We often refer to Susan's husband as one of our 'outlaws.'" Then, smiling sweetly at her son-in-law, she said, "And, oh, we do love and cherish our family clown, don't we, children?"

"Yes, we love him," Sarah echoed.

And the rest of the clan agreed as spoons clattered against serving bowls.

"Who's that pretty lady, Mama?" asked the boy seated between Sam and Susan. "Is she Unka Josh's new—"

"Her name is Miss Theodore," Susan quickly responded, "your Uncle Josh's...." She glanced at her brother. "His friend."

The child looked from Kate to Josh and then back again. "I'm Willie, and I'm thwee," he announced, holding up three pudgy fingers, "and I know how to count to twenty-five. Want to hear?"

Kate started to say she'd love to—anything to shift the focus of their attention from herself to the boy—but Susan intervened. "Maybe you can show her after you've finished your dinner," she said. "Right now, the only thing I want you to count, Willie, my love, are those peas as they move from your plate to your belly."

The child did as he was told but kept his eyes on Kate. *Such a charming child*, she thought. And, much to her surprise, sadness shrouded her. The boy was yet another reminder that she'd probably never have children of her own.

Thankfully, the amiable conversation among the Neville family members and their beloved employees drowned out her sorrow and continued until the last slice of pie disappeared. To Kate's great relief, she hadn't been asked a single question about her life or her background, and although she'd seen many stares at the bright-red scar on her chin, no one mentioned that, either. Hopefully, their curiosity would remain at this level until she bade them a grateful good-bye.

Fifteen minutes later, the field hands returned to work, and the Nevilles scattered to perform their various duties.

Josh was the last to head out. "Will you be all right if I leave for a few minutes?"

"Of course, I will," Kate said, getting to her feet. "I'm not a helpless invalid, you know." As if to prove it, she balanced on her good foot and began gathering plates—until Lucinda put a stop to it.

"You should not use the foot, *señorita*," the woman said, relieving Kate of the stack of dishes. "I will be back in *un momento* with something from my kitchen that you will like, I think."

"If you're smart," Josh said, grinning as he donned his Stetson, "you'll do as she says."

"I wouldn't dream of disobeying her."

"She and George have been with us since I was in diapers. They never had young'uns of their own, and since they can't go back to Mexico, we're all the kin they've got."

"But didn't you say Mexico was just a few miles away, on the other side of the Rio Grande?"

"It isn't the distance that's keeping them here."

Kate had read newspaper articles about conflicts between Texans and Mexicans. While it was wonderful that two families who should have been enemies had adopted one another, she would have asked what, exactly, prevented Lucinda and her husband from going back to their native land if Lucinda hadn't chosen that moment to return for the rest of the dishes.

Grinning, Josh saluted and left her alone with Lucinda, who chattered nonstop as she went about her work. "I have something that will make it easier for you to walk, *señorita*. You sit while I get it for you."

As Willie had all through dinner, Kate did as she was told.

She glanced around, admiring the moss green, velvet drapes flanking the French doors, the glossy, mahogany furnishings spaced tastefully around the room, and the tapestries of wild horses that hung above the sideboard and serving cart. Miniature rainbows glittered from the elaborate chandelier, and sunlight gleamed off of the polished brass candlesticks on the mantel. How had the Nevilles managed to bring so many fine things to a place so remote?

Then, Lucinda returned carrying a cane of knotted wood. "This once belong to *mi padre*. He use it much in the last years." Smiling, she ran her fingertips over the curved handle, then met Kate's eyes. "She will help you get around, but you will use only when you must be on your feet, *sí*?"

Kate accepted the cane and stood up, giving it a brief test. "Thank you, Lucinda," she said, hugging the woman. "This is so thoughtful of—"

"Ho-kay," she said, forefinger ticking back and forth. "Enough gratefulness. Come. I have prepared a place for you in the parlor."

The cane did make walking easier and more comfortable, and as they walked the length of the hall, Kate thanked Lucinda yet again. In the parlor, she saw the "place" Lucinda had fixed up for her—a chair with bright, floral cushions, which sat near a bank of windows overlooking the front lawn. Beside the chair was a big, straw basket filled with vibrant fabrics, and on the matching footstool sat a black, metal box.

"My sewing kit," Lucinda said, opening the box.

Peeking inside, Kate saw several dozen spools of thread of every color imaginable. Needles, pins, and a small pair of silver scissors were nestled neatly in the velvet-lined lid.

"Josh say to me that you can sew?" Lucinda said, relieving Kate of the cane.

"It's not my greatest talent, but I can mend a sock or take up a hem."

"*Bueno!*" Lucinda exclaimed as she hung the cane over the arm of the chair. "Then, you will sit. You will sew and enjoy the breeze and the pretty picture out the window. When I have finished the dishes, I come back to see if you need anything."

And, just like that, she was gone, leaving Kate alone again, this time to admire the ornate chairs and plush rug in the parlor. Amazing, she thought, that the Nevilles had managed to carve civilization from the untamed territory around them.

Outside, the sound of a dog barking drew her gaze to the window. It was hard to believe that, somewhere beyond the serene hills, where rows of corn waved and cattle grazed contentedly, Frank Michaels was doing his best to confound the Texas Rangers.

When he hadn't been torturing her, he'd occupied himself by sipping brandy and playing cards, and she'd used those hours to study him. During her weeks of captivity, she'd come to understand the way his demented mind worked. Frank considered himself better-looking, better-dressed, and better-educated than anyone he knew. The only opinion that mattered was his own, and, somehow, he found a way to blame every one of his missteps and mistakes on someone else. The definition of *stealing* was "taking what does not belong to you"—unless your name happened to be Frank Michaels. He'd stop at nothing to protect the only living being he truly loved: himself.

Was he aware that the Rangers had been temporarily sidetracked by their assignment from the governor? Of course, he did. Nothing escaped Frank's notice.

Just then, a haunting thought caused the breath to stick in her throat. If Frank knew the Rangers were busy elsewhere, what would prevent him from hunting her down and making good on his threat to keep her from testifying against him?

Kate hands trembled so violently that it took her five tries to thread the needle. She plucked a brown wool sock from the basket and slipped it over her left hand. It could have belonged to any man on the Lazy N Ranch, but on the chance it might be Josh's, she pressed it to her cheek and closed her teary eyes.

After a moment, she poked the needle through the thick wool, picking up a thread on one side of the hole and connecting it to a strand on the other side. And then she pricked her finger. There was just a small droplet of blood, but she didn't want to risk staining Sarah's dress, so she popped her fingertip into her mouth.

Risk. The word echoed deafeningly in her head.

As long as she stayed here, the Nevilles were at risk. She'd seen firsthand how little value Frank put on any life but his own. He'd kill them all if that's what it took to get to her.

It was more important than ever that she take Lucinda's advice and rest that ankle, for the sooner it healed, the better. She needed to leave as soon as possible, to lure Frank as far as possible from these wonderful people.

Kate Wellington and Dinah Theodore had a lot in common, including experience that proved doing the right thing could be excruciating.

*B*eneath a cloudy haze of cigar smoke swirling in a Kansas City saloon, Frank Michaels sat in a chair tilted back on its rear legs, the sole of his boot pressed against the edge of the table to keep his balance. "So…?"

The scruffy man standing across from him shrugged. "So, what?"

Frank Michaels had never been a patient man. Learning how to pace himself, to wait, and to bide his time had been the toughest lessons of his life. The only lesson tougher? Learning not to let his impatience show.

The other men seated at Frank's table stiffened as their boss's eyes narrowed to mere slits. He inspected the glowing tip of his cigar, then met the bearded man's eyes. "So, Ben," he repeated. "Where is she?" He drew out every word.

The man's Adam's apple bobbed once before he croaked, "In Eagle Pass."

"Alive?"

"Alive."

"Ben, Ben, Ben," Frank said, dragging on the cigar. "You disappoint me."

Ben cleared his throat and shifted his weight from one foot to the other. "Couldn't get a clear shot," he said, his voice wavering slightly.

Frank blew a stream of smoke directly at his face. "And what, pray tell, prevented you from doing what I paid you to do?"

"Hmpf. Ain't seen no money yet."

Frank's lips drew back in a thin, sinister smirk. "You haven't been with me long, Ben, so it's no surprise, really, that you don't know me very well." He took great pride in his precise diction, his practiced tone, both self-taught skills. He flicked an ash at Ben's feet, and then, using the cigar tip as a pointer, counted his men. "You might want to consider buying a drink for Tom and Amos, here. I'm sure they'd be glad to enlighten you on the subject of how I don't tolerate shirkers." His smirk became a sneer when he added, "I don't pay them, either."

"But I rode hard, Frank," Ben protested feebly. "Rode more'n two weeks, sometimes in mighty foul weather." He slapped his sweaty hat against his thigh. "Nearly got snake-bitten once, and come within spittin' distance of a cougar a time or two, but I kep' on a-goin'. An' when I finally did catch up with your girl, there were half a dozen Rangers with her."

"Texas Rangers?"

Ben lifted his bristly chin. "That's what I said."

"And they didn't haul her off to jail?"

"No, sir. The lot of 'em lit out in a terrible rainstorm, leavin' her with that fella she was with."

That the Rangers were on the trail didn't worry him. To Frank's knowledge, no wanted posters with his name or face existed, and there was a very good reason for that. He'd made a practice of settling into a town before relieving its good folks of their money. Courting a local girl, experience had taught him, provided the perfect cover; if any witnesses survived the robbery—and, mostly, they didn't—they'd identify her, not him or his men, since hers was the face and name they recognized and remembered most.

Hearing that the Rangers had closed in on Kate didn't surprise him, but the news that she wasn't traveling alone—now, that *was* troublesome. She was a chatty, fickle little thing; no doubt, she'd bared her soul to her companion. And the type of man she'd attract? Well, she was a beauty, not even he would deny that. The image of her flashed in his memory—big, green eyes with thick lashes and long, luscious curls that a man could drown in….

Frank took another puff of his cigar and nodded pensively. She had the look of a savvy, sophisticated woman, but he'd never met anyone more naïve. He'd bet every dollar of his next heist that this "fella" she'd hooked up with had played the hero role, thinking it might just get him a cut of the loot. Frank nearly laughed out loud at the thought, because, by now, the poor, dumb fool had figured out that the only way to get any affection from Kate was to take it by force. By the time he figured out she didn't have access to the loot, well, that would only add insult to injury. Did Frank dare hope the idiot would do his dirty work for him?

"Mind if I order up a beer, Frank?"

"As a matter of fact, I do. Tell me more about this 'fella.'"

Ben's stupefied expression made it clear that he had no idea what information Frank wanted. "What's he look like, for starters—tall? Fat? Old?"

"I don't hardly see what that's got to do with anyth—"

"Did he look familiar?" Frank didn't move, save for narrowing his eyes.

"Like somebody on a wanted poster, y'mean? No, can't say I ever saw the man before. He weren't nothin' special. If he hadn't been with your girl, I probably wouldn't have paid him no mind."

"Let's get something straight right here and now, Ben—she most assuredly is not my girl."

Out of the corner of his eye, Frank saw Tom and Amos exchange a disbelieving glance with Ben, but he chose to ignore it. *Let them think anything they please.* "If I had a mind to link up with a woman, it wouldn't be someone like Kate." But the words sounded false and hollow, even to his own ears. Unlike the women he'd used in other towns, he'd genuinely enjoyed spending time with her. Yes, she was delightful to look at, but she was so much more. Once, he'd sneaked in to a practice session and heard her playing Beethoven. She crooned popular tunes, but she could sing classic ballads as beautifully as any prima donna, as far as he was concerned. She could discuss politics or history, music or art, and make it sound equally fascinating. In truth, if he had a mind to link up with a woman, it wouldn't be with someone like Kate. It would *be* Kate.

On the night of the robbery, the boys had warned him to get rid of her, but he'd convinced them she could prove useful—she could cook their meals and scrub the trail dust out of their clothes. She'd performed those duties handily, but not without making it patently clear that she found him contemptible and disgusting. He didn't tolerate disrespect, and he didn't put up with betrayal. By running off like she did, Kate had violated both rules, and he hadn't slept the night through since, worrying that, to keep her own pretty neck out of the noose, she'd draw the Rangers a map to his favorite hiding places.

His only hope of saving his own neck was to find her before they did.

He took a long draw on the cigar. "So, tell me, Ben, why didn't you take care of 'the fella she was with'?" He blew a ring of smoke and poked the glowing cigar tip through it. "Especially after the Rangers rode off into the raging storm, and your odds improved?"

Ben narrowed his eyes and thrust out his chest. "You callin' me a liar, Michaels?"

Chuckling softly, Frank gave a nonchalant shrug. "Calm down, Ben, because I'm really not in the mood to kill anyone tonight." And then he waited while the meaning of his carefully chosen words sunk in. Did Ben realize, Frank wondered, that he'd taken half a step back? That everyone within earshot could hear him swallow? "You can take this to the bank: If I was at all confident that your story is more tale than truth, our kindly barkeep over there would have already sent for the undertaker."

Ben ran a shaky hand through his hair. "Well, but, still—if I was lyin', I wouldn't've come here to let you know where you could find—"

In an eyeblink, Frank went from annoyed to angry. "Don't insult my intelligence by pretending you're here for any reason other than to collect the money you *think* you earned," he said through clenched teeth.

The man might as well have been a five-year-old boy being told by his daddy that there'd be no dessert after supper since he hadn't done his chores. "B-but—but, Frank—I *did* earn it! You hired me 'cause I'm a good shot, and 'cause I got no qualms about killin', but even I can't take out five Rangers."

"Which was it, Ben? Five Rangers, or six?"

The gunman stood blinking, shaking his head. This time, he ran trembling fingers through his beard. "Five, six, what difference does it make? They each had two good hands, and a revolver, a rifle, a shotgun…." He whipped out his Colt, quick as a flash. "And all I had was this."

Tom and Amos scooted their chairs back. The plinking piano fell silent, replaced by the rumble of boot heels as the bar patrons raced for the door.

Frank leaned forward, letting the front legs of his chair hit the floor. Propping one elbow on the table, he stared at his cigar as he rolled it between his thumb and forefinger. True, he'd hired the man for his skills with a gun. But he'd seen Ben shoot and knew that *he* was faster. Slowly, calmly, he took a long pull on the cigar and let the smoke escape slowly, slowly…. "Take care where you point that thing, Ben."

Ben gave the warning a moment's thought, then cocked his wrist so that the barrel was aimed at the ceiling instead of at Frank.

"Better," Frank said. "Much better." He inhaled another mouthful of smoke and then let it out deliberately. "Now, then. I want to be sure I heard you correctly," he said, watching the smoke curl toward the ceiling. When the last blue wisp slithered into the rest of the fog, he began counting, touching his thumb to a different finger in succession. "You trailed her. You found her. You saw the Rangers, then you didn't even try to get her, because she was with some 'fella.'" Staring hard through the smoke, he added, "Would you say that's a fair summary of what you've said so far?"

Ben swallowed again, harder this time. "Yeah, I guess you'd say that 'bout sums it up."

"I guess so." Then, "When's your birthday?"

The man tucked in his chin. "My birthday?"

Frank let out a sigh of exasperation. "Yes, Ben. Your birthday."

"October—"

"Interesting," Frank said, cutting him off. "Mine is August 12." He grinned over at Tom and Amos. "Maybe one of my women will bake me a cake."

He noticed that as his men laughed at his joke, the bartender cowered behind his cash register and every windowpane glowed with the wide eyes of the men who'd scurried outside with their jiggers of whiskey and steins of beer. Evidently, the time he'd spent with that dime novelist a year or so ago had paid off, albeit in a cockeyed sort of way. Despite the lack of wanted posters, they'd all recognized him from the description the writer had woven into his story. Chest puffed and chin high, he leered back at every face because not one had the courage to fetch the sheriff or his deputy, for fear of becoming the latest statistic in Frank Michaels's murders.

If they'd asked him, Frank would have admitted they had nothing to fear. He hadn't just been joking when he'd told Ben he wasn't in the mood to kill anyone tonight. Bullets weren't cheap these days, and he saw no point in wasting them on the likes of these cowards. Oh, he'd shoot if he had to, but he hoped he wouldn't have to. He didn't believe in making the same mistake twice; far better to let his fury build so that, when he got his hands on Kate Wellington and looked into those beautiful, green eyes, he wouldn't be tempted to spare her life a second time.

The novels and newspapers said he'd gunned down nearly two dozen men. Who was he to tear down their castles in the sky, especially when those fantasies delivered the respect he craved? Truth was, he'd killed only six. Five, if he didn't count the gap-toothed boy in Durango who, when Frank had caught him eavesdropping as he and the boys had been planning their next heist, had jumped from the second-floor window of a hotel. One less loose end. Frank hated loose ends.

He didn't like the unsettled feeling roiling in his gut, either. According to Ben, the Rangers had left without Kate, meaning she probably hadn't told them anything. The only logical reason he could come up with was that the shame of having been touched by the notorious Frank Michaels outweighed her fear of what he might do if he caught up with her.

He did his best to overlook the disappointment and hurt that notion aroused and focused instead on the thought that if that's how she felt, he might just have caught a lucky break.

Then, he remembered what she'd said before he'd passed out on the night she'd run off: *"Someday, you'll pay for every evil thing you've done, Frank Michaels. It could be tomorrow, or next year, or even ten years from now, but you will pay."* He'd laughed it off at the time. But with the memory of her words, Frank also remembered the conviction gleaming in her enormous eyes.

He might have caught a lucky break, but she might just wake up one morning and decide that today was the day he'd pay.

Frank didn't want to kill her now any more than he had on the night of the San Antonio bank robbery, but what other choice had she left him?

He pulled a silver dollar from the pocket of his trousers. Oh, how he loved the way it caught the light as he turned it heads up, tails up. Holding it like an auction paddle, he gave it a little wave, then tossed it to Ben, watching as it flipped end over end before being swallowed up by the man's free hand.

"Consider that payment for your nonproductive Eagle Pass tip." Before Ben could accept or reject the offer, Frank said, "Now, I've got a tip for you."

The man's scowl lessened when he heard the unmistakable sound of Frank's pistol, cocking under the table. "If you want to live to see your next birthday in October, you might want to return that Colt to its holster, friend."

Moments later, once Ben was gone, the piano player resumed his tune, and the bartender started splashing rye and beer into the glasses of the men who'd come back inside. Laughter mingled with the sounds of cards being shuffled and the saloon hall girls' skirts swishing. The near-fatal incident seemed all but forgotten in every mind, except for that of the man who sat quietly with his back to the wall, playing solitaire and calculating how many banks, stagecoaches, and trains he could rob between Kansas City, Missouri, and Eagle Pass, Texas.

"Meester Neville, he try to get fireworks," Lucinda said, handing Kate a fresh basket of mending, "but just like last year, he realize it is *imposible*."

Kate continued her darning as George frowned. "You will wear out the poor *chica*'s fingers," he told his wife. "Where you find all these shirts with no buttons and skirts with torn hems?"

"In the laundry basket," she said matter-of-factly.

He responded with a resigned sigh, then smiled at Kate. "One of these years, Meester Neville will order those fireworks, and the train, she *will* bring them. Is good that he never gives up, no?"

She started to nod when Lucinda got up and left the parlor, waving both hands beside her dark-haired head, muttering, "Men, *siempre los soñadores*. Why not be happy with what they have instead of wishing for *el imposible*?"

"There is a difference, *mi amor*, between dreaming and hoping. What can it hurt to dream a little more, anyway?" George plopped his floppy-brimmed hat onto his head. "But all in good time, *sí*? All in good time." From the doorway, he added, "Maybe you should not try so hard to keep up with the sewing, or my Lucinda really will wear your fingers to nubs!"

On the heels of a good-natured laugh, he left her to thread her needle, and from out of nowhere, a tall, good-looking cowboy stepped up beside her and held out his hand, startling her so badly she nearly pricked her finger again.

"I was in San Arroyo when you arrived the other day. Been busy on the river acres ever since. Name's Daniel," he added when she took it, "but mostly, they call me Dan around here." He winked conspiratorially and whispered, "And you can wipe that confuzzled look off your face. *Soñadores* means 'dreamers.'"

His mustache grazed her knuckles as he kissed her hand, and then he gently let go.

She watched him ease onto the sofa across from her. "You're a man of many talents, I see."

It was his turn to look confused.

"You move like a cat," she said, to answer his unspoken question, "and you're a mind reader, to boot."

Dan shot her a crooked grin.

"Well, it's a pleasure to meet you, Dan. I'm K-Dinah—Dinah Theodore." Would she ever get used to calling herself that?

"So, how'd you hurt your foot?"

"I'm ashamed to admit it to a rancher, of all people, but I fell off a horse."

"Ah," he said, "I guess you didn't see me wobble into the room."

"I didn't see *or* hear you! Perhaps you ought to put bells on your boots."

Dan stood up and walked back and forth between her hassock and the sofa to show her his limp. She couldn't bear to ask if the hitch in his step was caused by pain or permanent damage to his leg. "How'd you hurt *your* foot?" But even as she asked the question, Kate knew he'd injured more than just his foot.

He perched on the arm of the sofa. "Well," he drawled, "I hate to admit this, being a rancher and all, but I fell off a horse."

He smiled when he said it, and yet Kate sensed an underlying despair to go with his story.

Nodding, Dan added, "Fell off my horse—and landed square in the middle of a stampede."

Kate had heard stories about cattle stampedes, and the mental picture of thousands of thundering hooves—plus the imagined sound of the terrified bellows of cows and men—made her wonder how Dan had survived. If he wanted to tell her about it, she'd listen. Otherwise, she would not meddle. He had as much right to protect his secrets as she had to protect hers! Pretending to hunt for a button that matched those on the shirt in her lap, she asked, "When did it happen?"

"About three years ago."

Her heart ached for him. She'd been off her feet and coping with the pain in her foot for only a few days. It must have been quite a fall to have left him with so pronounced a limp, three years later. "Were you laid up for very long?"

"Couple of months." He shrugged slightly. "Broke some ribs, cracked my skull—which, they tell me, put me out like a light for almost a week—but the leg...." Dan shook his head. "The leg took the brunt of it."

"I'm so sorry, Dan."

"Don't be. God has perfect timing. I was right where I needed to be when Sadie died. It gave Josh something to do, acting as my round-the-clock nursemaid." He chuckled at the memory. "Some days, I didn't make it easy on him, asking for this and whining about that, but it gave him a purpose, and I think that took his mind off all he'd lost, at least for a time."

Kate didn't know which cousin she felt sorrier for, Dan or Josh, but she wouldn't let her pity show, for she had already figured out that pride ran deep in the Neville men.

"Now that I think of it, it happened in June, right about this time. We were moving a herd to Kansas City and were hunkered down one night when rustlers spooked the cows. It was the first time Josh wasn't with us on a drive, and I think that's part of the reason he threw himself into caring for me afterward."

He'd stayed home to mourn, Kate realized, and, in that moment, it was Josh she felt sorrier for.

"Wasn't like he could have done anything to prevent it. Except he convinced himself he'd have been where I was, and since he fancies himself a better rider...." Dan grinned slightly. "June never was my favorite month, but at least now I have a specific reason to dislike it—other than the unpredictable weather, that is."

Kate had never given much thought to things like that. In her mind, one month was pretty much like another. It had been like that, at least, until Frank Michaels had come along.

She'd met him at the beginning of May, and he'd managed to sweep her off her feet in no time, so that, by the fifteenth of the month, it had taken nothing more than a simple invitation for ice cream to embroil her unwittingly in a plot of murder and robbery. By Sunday, May 27, she'd escaped the horrors of being held his captive, and she'd wandered into Josh's camp on May 30. The days following that had been a blur of harsh weather and Ranger encounters, hard-riding days and cold, dark nights. And, through it all, Josh had done his best to make her feel safe and protected, right up until June 7, when they'd ridden side by side onto Lazy N land.

And here it was, June 15—one month after the haunting holdup. Kate swallowed an impatient sigh. If not for Frank, she'd be in Laredo with Etta Mae right now, shopping for a new piano and pricing glassware for the saloon. Not only would she have been spared Frank's brutality, but she wouldn't have needed to hide behind a phony name. Instead, she'd be traipsing around town, free as a dove, introducing herself as Kate Wellington, Etta's singing piano player, and partaking in lively festivals and picnics, parades and Fourth-of-July fireworks displays.

Then again, she wouldn't have met Josh.

Kate couldn't help but think that something was fundamentally wrong with her. It couldn't possibly be normal to conclude that going through all she had had been more than worth it because it had led up to meeting a nice cowboy.

"Penny for your thoughts," Dan said, interrupting her reverie.

"Sorry." She rubbed tiny circles into her temples. "I tend to be a bit of a daydreamer sometimes."

Dan smiled. "Don't you worry. He'll come around."

Had her emotions been that obvious? This time, Kate didn't stifle her sigh. There didn't seem to be much point in asking whom Dan was referring to, and so she didn't.

He got to his feet. "See you at supper, then?"

"Yes, of course."

"Good. It'll be nice having a pretty face across the table to look at for a change." He started for the hall but stopped

158 ⌒ Loree Lough

just short of the doorway. "You ought to give George's advice some serious consideration," Dan said, pointing at her sewing. "You're good at that. And fast, too. But the man is right—you keep it up at this pace, and Lucinda just might wear your fingers to nubs!"

Kate gasped with pretend shock. "Surely, you're not suggesting that I give the work less than my best, I hope, or that I devote more time to each repair than necessary!"

"Way I heard it, you're leaving the Lazy N as soon as that ankle of yours heals, anyway. So, you might as well just slow down. Let nature take its course, and maybe that hardheaded cousin of mine will come around before you head south."

Kate smiled as he shuffled from the room. It seemed she could add "perceptive" after "proud" to the list of attributes of the Neville men.

*D*o you think you're up for a ride into town?"

When Josh's mother asked the question, common sense told Kate that her ankle hadn't healed quite enough for her to take a long, bumpy wagon ride, but she was so flattered at the invitation that an enthusiastic "Yes!" popped impulsively from her mouth. Besides, her eyes were red and burning, her fingers stiff and sore, and her shoulders aching from days of sitting hunched over her sewing. Sometimes, she almost suspected Lucinda of deliberately removing buttons and letting out hems for the sole purpose of keeping Kate off her ankle. She couldn't help but smile to picture the kindhearted woman scouring every bureau and wardrobe for articles of clothing to add to the pile.

"I think some time spent away from this stuffy, old house will be good for you," Eva said. "Besides, it'll give us a chance to get to know each other better. Just in case that boy of mine comes to his senses sometime soon."

In case what? Kate thought. What had Josh's mother seen or heard to make her say such a thing? But Eva Neville never gave her the chance to ask. In fact, the woman talked incessantly from the moment the buggy started rolling. Halfway to Eagle Pass, Kate's throbbing ankle made it nearly impossible to pay close attention as Eva talked about the weather—which, according to her, was unseasonably hot, even for West Texas—and listed the stores they'd visit in sequential order.

"I'm so glad you let me talk you into wearing a proper lady's bonnet instead of that lopsided thing you had on your pretty head when you rode in with Josh."

Lopsided thing? Kate loved that hat! It had provided protection from the unrelenting sun and had kept the pounding rains from blinding her, and, most important, Josh had chosen it for her. She smiled a little, remembering the way he'd patiently showed her how to cinch the stampede string that encircled its brim just tightly enough so that the hat would stay on, even if the most powerful wind gusts threatened to blow it "hither and yon." Her smile grew as she remembered those three little words that had started him laughing so hard, he'd hardly been able to breathe, and how it had taken minutes before he'd collected himself enough to tell her about how that "starched shirt of a banker" had used the phrase.

"I thought you looked lovely in Sarah's pink dress the other day," his mother was saying, "but with your peaches-and-cream complexion and all those freckles, and your lovely, auburn hair, oh, how well yellow becomes you!" She gave Kate's hand a gentle pat. "And did you know that yellow just so happens to be Josh's favorite color?"

Earlier, when Kate had checked on the clothes she'd washed—the ones Josh had bought for her in Uvalde—she'd been disappointed to find that, despite the thorough scrubbing she'd given them, they still smelled like a damp mop. Josh had warned her not to leave them rolled up in her saddlebags, and it upset her to think she might never be able to wear them again. Not as upset as Lucinda, who, once she'd gotten a whiff of them, had insisted on scrubbing them herself.

Hopefully, when Kate returned to the ranch, the shirts and skirts would have dried smelling like sunshine and the fresh, Texas air, because she didn't want to keep borrowing clothes from Sarah. Josh might like yellow, but she had a feeling he wasn't any fonder of fussy ruffles and superfluous lace than she was.

She felt the heat of a blush color her cheeks, inspired in part by regret that she knew almost nothing about her handsome hero. If it hadn't been for Eva's casual comment, she wouldn't have known about his favorite color. What about the rest of his favorites? Did he prefer his potatoes fried or mashed, with gravy or without? Did he favor apple pie or spice cake? After all he'd done for her, she should have known a lot more about him.

"Tell me, Dinah dear, what's *your* favorite color?"

The question had seemed to come out of nowhere, and so did Kate's answer. "Green," she said, without even thinking.

Eva turned slightly on the wagon seat to meet her gaze. "You don't say! I never would have guessed, what with those beautiful, green eyes of yours!"

For the first time since she'd put on the ridiculous, frilly bonnet, Kate found something to like about it: the awning of white toile that poured from its crown provided exactly the right cover to hide her blush, although she didn't know why the compliment should have embarrassed her. Flower petals and tree leaves were green, and so were—

"Look, *señora*," George said, pointing. "The hotel roof."

"Ah, marvelous!" Eva exclaimed, clapping her gloved hands. "That means we're only about a mile outside of town." She adjusted the black, satin bow of her bonnet. "Any minute now, the courthouse will come into view, then J. W. Riddle's grocery store, though it's silly to call it that when he has every sort of item imaginable for sale in there! Oh, how I wish you could come inside and prowl around with me. It'd be such fun to see the look on your face when you realize how much merchandise that man has managed to stock on his shelves!"

Before long, George parked the wagon in the shade of some trees beside the store, then helped Eva climb down.

"I won't be long," she said, patting Kate's knee. "Are you sure you'll be all right out here all alone, dear?"

Kate smiled, amazed at the depth of fondness she'd developed for this woman in such a short time. "I'll be just fine. Take your time, and don't worry about me. I'll have plenty to keep me entertained, watching the goings-on in the street."

"Well, I'll have George come back to check on you in a few minutes, just in case." And with that, Eva and George went off in separate directions to run their errands. They weren't gone five minutes when Kate saw a small group—two men and a woman—gathered at the courthouse directly across the street. They were huddled around a flyer tacked to the big board beside the door. She couldn't make out every word of their animated conversation, but when she heard one of the women say "never heard of" and "woman bank robber" all rolled into the same sentence, her heart nearly leaped out of her chest.

As the small group dispersed, Kate acknowledged that it very well could be her own image on the poster, and, if it was....

If it was, she had to get it. Had to tear it down from the bulletin board and destroy it so that no one in Eagle Pass, no one at the Lazy N, would know her true identity. Because she couldn't allow them to find out how deep her selfishness ran—so deep that a threat on her own life had caused her to stand by in self-preservation as others were senselessly slaughtered. They'd hate her and question what had prompted them to welcome her into their home, into their world. Especially Josh.

She tried to imagine how he'd feel once he learned that she'd lied to him, duped him, and used him for no reason other than to save her own skin. The thought roused an ache inside her that rivaled the pain of burying her mama. If crossing the street would keep Josh and his family safe from the truth about her, then she had to do it, even if it caused a setback in her recuperation. Eva had mentioned that the bank would be her next stop, and to get there, she'd need to pass right by the courthouse. She could not see that poster!

Kate swallowed. Hard. She estimated the distance from the buggy to the bulletin board to be twenty feet, definitely no more than twenty-five. Even with her lame ankle, she didn't think it would take her more than a minute to reach the bulletin board. Add a few seconds to grab the poster, unnoticed, and another minute back to the wagon—yes, she could do it. Failure wasn't an option.

Hooking her cane on the edge of the wagon to make it easier to reach once she hit the ground, Kate carefully lowered herself to the ground and started up the alleyway. The street was empty when she reached it, and she began slowly hobbling across. Hopefully, it would stay that way until she made it back to the wagon with that poster safely tucked into the pocket of her purse. But hurrying, she quickly realized, caused her ankle to ache almost as much as when she'd first twisted it. If she wasn't careful, she'd do far more than just slow its healing; she might very well cause permanent injury. Still, she pressed on, reminding herself with every painful step how much more it would hurt if Josh and the rest of his family discovered the truth about her.

Her heart was pounding, droplets of perspiration were trailing down her face from her temples to her chin, and she didn't need a mirror to know that her curlicue bangs were plastered to her forehead. A bead of sweat trickled down her spine and puddled just beneath the bustle of Sarah's dress. She could blame the heat of the day for the condition the dress would be in when she got back to the Lazy N, but nothing would explain away the wanted poster.

As she limped up the courthouse steps, she entertained the unlikely hope that, once she reached the bulletin board, she'd see a sketch of some other female bank robber. She even thought about praying that would be the case, but her prayers would have been in vain. For when she reached the top of the steps, she stood, slack-jawed and wide-eyed, staring at her own face staring back at her, just as she had in that small town immediately after she'd escaped from Frank. Any one of a hundred people in San Antonio could have described her to the artist. Asked to name which one, Kate would have guessed it had been the bank manager, for Mr. Schaeffer had seen her running ahead of Frank and had called out her name.

Looking at the poster wasn't exactly like gazing into a mirror, but the artist had come jarringly close to duplicating her features. Her stomach lurched and her heart beat doubly fast when she read again the bold, black letters:

WANTED
KATE WELLINGTON
DEAD OR ALIVE
FOR MURDER AND ARMED BANK ROBBERY

At the bottom of the poster was the word "Reward." Many men had turned to bounty hunting to make ends meet. She'd recognize Frank and his men and could easily hide from them—if they didn't see her first—and Texas Rangers were easy to spot because of their silver stars. But just about any man could be a bounty hunter. How was she to hide from them?

Kate glanced left, then right, and then, satisfied no one was watching, she ripped down the poster and stuffed it into her purse. It was too soon to breathe a sigh of relief, but she couldn't help feeling a flash of reassurance. Now, if only she could make it back to the wagon, unnoticed!

"What you got in that li'l yeller bag o' yours, miss?"

A tiny scream burst from her mouth as Kate whirled around to face a boy who looked barely more than ten years old. He stood on the top step, clutching a gray pistol in his grimy hands.

She'd seen his type in San Antonio plenty of times. The threadbare clothing and tattered boots told her times were hard at his house, and the fear flashing in his brown eyes led her to believe he hadn't quite become an expert mugger. Yet.

During those dark days as Frank's captive, she'd overheard boastful tales about how growing up dirt-poor had motivated him and his men toward petty crimes that later turned them into career criminals.

It wasn't likely that anything she said or did would have a lasting impact on this youngster, whose desperation drove him to steal, but how would she live with herself if she didn't at least try? "I certainly hope that's a very realistic wood carving you're holding, young man," she said, forcing a tone of bravado she didn't feel into her voice.

"This ain't no carving, lady," he snarled, holding the weapon higher. "This here's my pa's Colt, and it's got his bullets in it, too." His eyes narrowed menacingly, and he added, "Now, you'd best hand over that li'l purse of yours, or you'll find out right quick just how real it is."

"You want my purse as a present for your mother?"

Both eyebrows disappeared into his mop of tangled bangs as he whipped the frayed, wool cap from his head. "A present?" he barked. "What kinda fool talk is this? I only want what's inside it. Now, hand it over, or else!"

If he kept shouting that way, someone was bound to notice. Kate couldn't afford to let that happen, for his sake or for her own. Narrowing her eyes, she took a half step closer. "What's your name, little boy?"

"Say," he sneered, "I *ain't* no little boy. Turned nine on my last birthday." He used the gun as a pointer. "Now, you give me that purse, you hear, or—"

She'd heard it said that desperate people did desperate things, and in that instant, she understood the full impact of its meaning. In one second, Kate hooked the end of her cane around his wrist and pinned it to the wall. In the next, his pistol clattered to the wooden walkway, and, despite the pain it caused her, she used her injured foot to hold it in place. Before he had a chance to react, she grabbed a fistful of his shirt and gave him a good shaking. "Have you ever heard of Frank Michaels?"

"Y-yes'm," he said, blinking enormous, brown eyes. "Read about 'im in a book my pa has."

She couldn't afford to waste another minute trying to reason with this aspiring criminal. Fear and tension coursed through her veins, and she aimed every bit of the resulting adrenaline at him. "Then I expect you already know that he's as mean and evil as the devil himself."

He gave a shrug and smirked, and it horrified Kate to realize that he saw Frank as a hero of some sort. She gave the fabric of his shirt a slight twist and leaned in closer. "How many men do you suppose he's killed?"

"Dunno, lady," the boy croaked out. "Lots, I reckon."

"Well, here's something I'll bet you don't know: Frank Michaels and every one of the murdering robbers who travel with him got their starts in the thieving business by robbing ladies of their purses."

That struck a chord, as evidenced by the giant gulp he took.

"Is that what you're working toward—to become a thieving killer who's feared and hated by all, who will most surely die a slow and grisly death at the end of a rope—that is, if some bounty hunter doesn't put a bullet in you first?"

Tears shimmed in his eyes as he stuttered, "N-no, ma'am. I just wanted—I—needed—I thought—"

"Here's something to think about, young man. Next time you want or need something, go to church and ask the pastor to help you instead of terrorizing decent, law-abiding citizens!" She felt like a hypocrite, talking and behaving this way, but she would deal with her guilt later. Right now, she had to do her best to set this boy straight, and, hopefully, silence him, as well.

Kate kicked the gun off the step, and it landed with a quiet thud in the dusty road. Using her free hand, she pointed at it. "You'd better think long and hard next time you try to take what isn't yours, because someone might take that from you, just like I did, and use it on *you!*"

Shaken by fear, and also appalled at the level of her fury, Kate turned him loose. "Now, you'd best go and find your mother before *I* find the sheriff!"

"Y-yes, ma'am," he blubbered, scurrying down the courthouse steps. He threw a last, astonished look over his shoulder as he bent to retrieve his pistol, and she read it to mean he wouldn't soon forget meeting her! *Well, good,* she thought as she watched his small, raggedy boots pound down the street, raising small puffs of dust with every footfall.

As she made her way back to the wagon, Kate felt exhausted, and not only from the painful physical exertion. Later, alone in her room at the Lazy N, she would thank the good Lord for helping her grab the placard and shoo the would-be purse snatcher without being seen. Even if He didn't hear her prayer, she knew nothing short of heavenly intervention could have saved her from what had almost happened just now.

Hopefully, the boy would think about what she'd said.

Hopefully, the crumpled poster hidden in her purse had been the only copy.

Hopefully, Josh's mother would be too tired to chatter all the way back to the ranch, because Kate had a lot to think about, starting with how lucky she'd been that no one had seen her take the poster and that no one had heard or seen her run-in with the boy.

Hopefully, she'd catch her breath before Eva or George returned and wondered what had gotten her panting like she'd just run a race. What would they think if they found her sweaty, red-faced, and trembling? *Calm down,* she ordered herself. *Just take a deep breath and get yourself under control. Focus on something else, like the buildings lining Main Street and*

the people bustling about on the sidewalks. Because this is likely
the only time you'll ever see Eagle Pass.

If she hadn't been so preoccupied watching a couple of
pups frolicking in the street, she might have noticed the tiny
separation between the lacy curtains in the front window of
the hotel.

And if she'd seen the dark gaze fixed upon her, Kate
Wellington, aka Dinah Theodore, would have run for her
life.

I s'pose life in Maverick County has seemed a mite boring to you since the big uprising back in March," Josh kidded Shad White, the deputy sheriff, as they stood inside the entryway of J. W. Riddle's grocery store.

"Hmpf. Unlike you rowdy Neville boys, I can live without constant excitement."

"Aw, give us a break," said Dr. Lane, the local physician, elbowing him. "You'll probably have it etched onto your tombstone: 'Here Lies Shad White, Captor of Mexican Deserter Antonacio Luis.'"

"Stow it, Lane. It ain't every day there's a gunfight right here on Ryan Street."

Josh chuckled. "I'll grant you that, White."

Jack Dillon, the customs inspector, added his two cents' worth. "What lawman comes to a melee without his gun?"

Shad squinted one eye. "Jack Dillon, I'll thank you to keep your nonsensical opinions to yourself. If not for those three Mexican soldiers—who showed up just in the nick of time, I don't mind admitting—you'd have been in a pickle, too!"

The good-natured repartee continued until Dr. Lane winked, effectively silencing his comrades. "So, did you read in the *Eagle Pass Times,*" he said, his booming voice echoing throughout the store, "that ol' Riddle, here, has been spending more time with the bank president these days than at his own store, stocking his shelves?"

Eleanor Holbrook, the mayor's wife, hustled up to the group to add her voice to the mix. "Well," she huffed, "no wonder the bread and confections supplies have suffered of late. He'll have to change his advertisement from 'Corn, oats, and meal always on hand' to 'Whenever we get around to it.'"

The men joined in her laughter as Riddle sidled up to the group, puffing on a fat cigar. "We'll always have fresh bread," he said, "no matter how many hours I spend down at the bank." He winked at Mrs. Holbrook. "And our fine, family flour is just as fine as always, and I'll thank you not to forget it."

"You just let me be the judge of that, my dear Mr. Riddle," she said. "And, speaking of flour, I'll take three pounds, if you can tear yourself from your cronies long enough to measure it up for me."

As Riddle went to fill her order, Dr. Lane changed the subject. "Don't know about you boys, but I'm not sure that irrigation ditch they're proposing is worth the time and our tax dollars."

Josh listened for a moment as several men shared their opinions on the subject. When there was a lull, he said, "Tell me, White, what happened to that new wanted poster I saw on the courthouse wall earlier today?"

The deputy frowned, then stepped outside and, bending at the waist, squinted in the direction of the courthouse. "Well, I'll be a coyote's cousin," he said, shaking his head. "Looks like them confounded hoodlums got another one." Facing the men again, he shook a fist. "If I get my hands on 'em, they're gonna sit on one cheek for a good, long while, that much is certain!"

The mayor's wife sashayed up again, her shopping basket stuffed to overflowing with goods. "Whatever do you suppose they *do* with those wanted posters?" she asked no one in particular. Then, she shook her head, which set the feathers of the stuffed bluebird nesting in her bonnet to fluttering. "Makes a body wonder where their mothers are while those young'uns go running through the streets, making mischief, doesn't it?"

Every man in the group had heard enough of the woman's "When my boys were young" tales to know they were about to hear another one.

"Lovely hat," Dr. Lane said in a not-so-subtle attempt to change the subject and avert her story.

"Indeed," the deputy agreed, stroking the curved ends of his long mustache. "And you look mighty fetching in that dress, too."

Mrs. Holbrook whipped out a lace-edged hanky and fanned her flushed cheeks. "Listen to the lot of you. Why, I don't spread butter on my toast anywhere near as thick as you boys are spreading the flattery!" She tucked the hanky into the cuff of her sleeve, then fiddled with the black netting on her hat. "But you can be sure that I'll tell the mayor that the next time any one of you comes to his office begging a favor, he's to do whatever you ask!" With a girlish giggle, she headed for the door, her bustle swaying, her bluebird bobbing.

The minute her button-up boots hit the walk, the grocer leaned on the worn, wooden counter and shook his head. "The four of you need to repent and confess your sins to Reverend Peterson come Sunday morning."

"Sins?" Dillon said, befuddled. "What sins?"

"Your lie about liking that hat, for starters," Riddle thundered. "Why, I'll wager that I'd catch more field mice with that thing than I do with those newfangled traps I'm sellin' over there. And you boys go on, actin' as if you think it's purty, just to escape another story about her 'amazing sons.'" He chuckled. "Well, if you want my honest opinion, that's a lie of omission!"

The doctor tucked both thumbs under his suspenders. "Well, sir, you know what they say about *those*." With his chest puffed out, he lowered his voice an octave and said, "Opinions are like armpits—everybody has a couple, and, mostly, they stink.'"

Though Josh pretended to join in on the tomfoolery, his primary focus was on that wanted poster—and why it had been there one minute, gone the next.

Earlier, when he'd stepped into the hotel to ask how the owner, Mrs. Connors, was feeling after her bout of influenza, she'd invited him to share a snack of tea and crumpets. An import straight from London, the poor, old gal had lost the last of her kin when cancer had claimed her husband's life a year earlier. Aside from the businessmen and honeymooners who rented rooms at her hotel, she had few folks to visit with, so Josh hadn't been able to bring himself to refuse the offer. While Mrs. Connors had gone to fetch a tray, Josh had strolled up to the open window, hoping to catch a passing breeze, and had seen Dinah glance right and left before snapping what appeared to be a wanted poster from the board next to the courthouse doors. It hadn't surprised him to see her there in town, because he'd heard his ma issue the invitation at breakfast. What had surprised him, though, had been her apparent determination to get across the street and read the placards posted beside the courthouse doors.

The mayor sometimes tacked up information about town meetings, and, once in a while, the pastor would post something about a church picnic or a traveling preacher. But, mostly, it was the place where Shad White hung his wanted posters—on the rare occasion he got his hands on them—to alert the good folks of Eagle Pass that they should be on the lookout for Mexican bandits, cow rustlers, murderers, train robbers, and the like.

He'd watched the Martin boy slink up the courthouse steps, and it had taken only a moment to figure out that he was up to no good. Though Josh hadn't been able to hear the exchange between the boy and Dinah, her tense posture and stern facial expressions had made it clear that she was giving the boy a tongue-lashing he wouldn't soon forget.

Then, Josh had noticed the toy pistol, which had made him want to rush across the street and give the boy a piece of *his* mind, too. But, as he'd reached the door, Josh had seen that Dinah had the matter well in hand. Chuckling under his breath, he hadn't been able to help but admire her. Hadn't been able to help but think she'd make a wonderful mother someday. And, as the boy had skulked away, looking guilty and afraid and a whole tumble of other things he couldn't give a name to, he'd wondered why Dinah looked so guilt-stricken and afraid.

"Will you know which poster was taken once you see the bare spot on your board?" he asked the deputy.

"Darned tootin' I will. Never hung one of a female robber before."

Josh swallowed. It was then that he remembered the female robber from the bank in San Antonio—and her striking resemblance to Dinah. "Got another to take its place?"

"No, and ain't that just a sorry shame!"

"Can you describe this female robber?"

The men exchanged curious glances, and Josh hoped he hadn't asked one too many questions. Everyone in town knew the Nevilles had taken in an injured, young woman. If they put two and two together, they might start asking questions of their own. "I'm just wondering, so we'll know who to be on the lookout for."

White frowned and crossed both arms over his chest. "And just why are you so bent on finding out about it?"

"Yeah," the doctor agreed. "Don't think I've heard you ask so many questions since—" He fell suddenly silent and, blushing, clamped his mouth shut.

White shuffled his feet, and Dillon cleared his throat.

Josh bit back his desire to finish the sentence with a terse, "Since Sadie got sick, you mean?" A splinter of guilt pierced his heart because the glow of Sadie's memory had faded considerably since Dinah had stumbled into his camp, disheveled and distressed. Before that, he'd thought of his young wife several times a day, but, since then, whole days had passed without his giving Sadie a single thought. It seemed to Josh that he should have been the one standing there, red-faced and stammering, not these good men.

"Well, enough of this hee-hawin'," White said. "I got work to do over at the jail."

The others seemed only too happy to disperse. Donning their hats, they quickly left J. W. Riddle's grocery, leaving Josh alone to hope he was wrong. What kind of man replaced the memory of his deceased wife with thoughts of a woman who very well might be a murdering bank robber?

At this thought, Josh admonished himself again. Dinah Theodore was the picture of charity and selflessness. And even if she were the same woman pictured on that wanted poster, there had to be some sort of explanation—a setup, for example. He simply couldn't reconcile what he knew about Dinah with the profile of a cold-blooded killer and bank robber. Admittedly, he had a lot more to learn about her. And he was all the more eager to get started.

*E*arly in the morning of the Fourth of July, Kate ambled into the kitchen, hobbling only slightly now. Lucinda had been cooking since dawn. There was nothing unusual about that, for the woman always awoke long before daybreak to prepare an enormous breakfast for the ranch hands. But the Neville family didn't believe in doing anything halfway. Today, the usual plates of flapjacks and bowls of fried potatoes joined casseroles of scrambled eggs, platters of crisp bacon, and baskets of biscuits spread on the cookstove and tables. As Lucinda added a plate of sweet rolls and jars of apple butter and jam to the lineup, Kate saw George on the other side of the window, cranking the spit to ensure the enormous pig roasting above the fire would cook clean through.

"Goodness," she said, wrapping a big, white apron around her waist, "he's been at that for days, it seems. When does the poor man sleep?"

Lucinda scooped a chunk of butter from the churn and plopped it into a bowl. "He likes to think we believe what he says—that he and Cal work in shifts," Lucinda said, laughing. "But Cal will tell you what I already know: George seldom takes a rest." She winked. "That man, he love cooking the pigs!"

Kate smiled. "Before I climbed into bed last night, I opened my window to catch a breeze and got a whiff of that pork, and I dreamed of food all night long. It's a miracle I didn't devour my pillow while I slept!"

Lucinda gave a hearty chuckle.

"What's left to do to get things ready for the big celebration?" Kate asked her when her laughter subsided.

There were tablecloths to iron, Lucinda said, and plates and flatware to be distributed, and pies and cakes and biscuits to bake.

Kate slid onto the seat of a kitchen stool. "I can handle all of the baking from right here. And the ironing, too."

Her announcement earned a warm hug of appreciation from Lucinda, who then pressed a floury palm to each of Kate's cheeks. "All I will say is, Josh better make up his mind *lo antes possible*."

Kate was well aware that everyone at the Lazy N had a theory about her relationship with Josh, and that they'd all been subtly pressuring him into admitting it. But the poor man didn't even know her real name—and, if she had anything to say about it, he never would.

Lucinda continued, "Something tell me this pretty patient will hop far away soon as she can again squeeze her foot into her boot." She planted a motherly kiss on Kate's brow. "Now, you sit," she ordered, "while I bring the iron from the pantry. Then you will keep Lucinda company, and while you press the tablecloths and napkins, we will pray *Señor* Josh wake up before your ankle is completely healed, *sí?*"

Lucinda had made no secret of the fact that she prayed, morning and night, for Josh to ask "Dinah" to marry him. Somehow, the woman had gotten it into her head that marriage would be good for them both. Every morning, as Kate stepped from her comfortable feather bed and found that her ankle hurt less than the day before, she was reminded of Lucinda's prayers for a complete recovery.

She had no cause to resent the woman's relationship with her Maker; Lucinda had lived a good life and deserved to have His ear. But Kate didn't have the heart to tell her that, while the Lord may have answered many of Lucinda's other prayers, those involving her would not take shape.

When she was a child, Kate and her mama had been regular churchgoers. Her faith had been strong, her trust in the Lord deep and steady. But her pa's death and her ma's suicide, followed by her stepfather's abuse and later attempt to use her to pay off a poker debt, had changed all that. How could she trust in a Being who had allowed her to become an orphan? If He was all-knowing, wouldn't He have seen those events brewing? And, if He truly was all-powerful, why hadn't He prevented them?

When she'd set out on her own at the tender age of twelve, Kate had stopped going to church. She had prayed from time to time, but since the Almighty had never seen fit to answer, she'd eventually stopped doing that, too. Building a wall between herself and God had been so much less painful than admitting He didn't think her worthy of His time. Maybe, someday, He'd show her the reasons why He'd abandoned her, but, until then, why risk heaping disappointment atop the hurt by asking for things that would never be delivered?

Kate admired Lucinda's confidence in the Lord. But why wouldn't she believe, when, in answer to her prayers, the Lord had delivered a cure when George had nearly died from cholera and had brought them safely across the Rio Grande, despite a ferocious clash between two bandit gangs? Lucinda had prayed for work, and the Nevilles had hired her and George; she'd prayed for a home, and a small cottage had been provided as a part of their salary. So, when Lucinda asked God for the quick and complete healing of her ankle on her behalf, the woman had no reason to believe He wouldn't answer her.

It confused Kate no end to admit that she only half wanted that healing, because, once she could stand and walk and run again, she'd have to leave this wonderful place and the wonderful people who called it home.

Self-pity grew into sorrow as she faced more cold, hard facts: If the Texas Rangers realized their error in riding away from the shack without her in tow, they could track her to the Lazy N and cart her off to jail to await a trial. And with no one to testify on her behalf, the judge would probably assume that she'd willingly participated in the bank heist, and only Lucinda's beloved God knew what sentence the man might hand down. Even worse than that, Josh and his family would see her as guilty, too.

If, on the other hand, Frank and his cohorts found her before the Rangers did, the Nevilles and every one of their loyal employees would pay a price for her cowardice and stupidity. Like it or not—and she most certainly did not—Kate had no choice but to put this place behind her.

Far, far behind her.

She could only hope that the God who answered Lucinda's prayers would allow her to hold fast to the fond memories she'd made during her time with the Neville family, because she'd have little else to warm her cold, lonely heart when she left them.

"Here you go, *carina*," Lucinda said, interrupting her gloomy trance. "The iron—be careful! *Está caliente!*"

Kate had been so lost in her thoughts that she hadn't heard the woman come back into the room, let alone set the tool onto the hot stove to warm it up. If she knew what was good for her, she'd get a handle on her musing, because Frank was more mountain lion than man, stealthy and silent and capable of pouncing before his unwitting prey realized that a predator had been stalking nearby.

Kate exhaled a long sigh as Lucinda plopped a small pile of red-and-white-checkered tablecloths and napkins onto the tabletop. "Call me when the iron cools, ho-kay, so I can heat it up again for you?"

A huge sob of self-pity ached in her throat, and Kate didn't trust her ability to speak without letting it out. So, instead, she fixed a stiff smile onto her face and spread the first napkin onto the ironing pad.

Oh, how she'd miss this dear, sweet woman!

How she'd miss everyone at the Lazy N, from Josh's warmhearted, welcoming parents to sweet, funny Sarah, who seemed determined to turn Kate into her living, breathing look-alike, to Susan, who took her jobs as Sam's wife and Willie's mother so seriously that she sometimes forgot to smile.

Then, there were Josh's cousins, affectionately known as the "Bible Boys," because, like their fathers before them, each bore a name taken straight from the pages of the Good Book.

Joshua, the eldest of the foursome, played the big brother role very well, always making himself available to lend an ear or offer advice—or to dole out some good-natured teasing.

Daniel, just two months younger than Josh, had long ago become the family's self-appointed comedian, cracking jokes and poking fun at himself every chance he got. He'd shared with Kate his dream of someday becoming a pastor, but, for now, family duty called louder than seminary.

It hadn't taken her much time at all to figure out that Micah, lovingly dubbed by the family as the "Quiet One," was anything but! She almost didn't mind those nights when sleep eluded her, because, more often than not, he'd join her on the big, covered porch for long conversations. It was easy to tell that this cousin had developed strong views on an extensive collection of topics—and he wasn't afraid to share them!

Like his biblical namesake, the youngest male cousin, Paul, loved to write, and he scribbled in his notebook every chance he got. When Kate had asked to read his work, he'd agreed, on the grounds that she promised never to tell anyone what he'd written. She'd thought it a shame that he wanted to keep those skillfully crafted poems all to himself, and so she'd been trying to think of a way to talk him into sharing them. The idea had come to her after dinner one night, when little Willie had sung a Bible verse set to a tune for easier memorization. That same evening, Kate had suggested that Paul set his sonnets to music, and, within the week, almost everyone at the Lazy N had been singing his beautiful words.

Kate found it hard to believe that she'd been able to develop a deep, powerful bond with each of them in such a short period of time. Even more amazing was that they seemed to feel the same way about her. As she spread a napkin onto the ironing table, she remembered a poem she'd read years ago, in which the author had written about the pain of sacrifices made in love. If she thought for one minute that God would hear her prayers, she'd ask Him to help her learn to live without these good people. Because leaving here was the right thing to do—and also the most heartbreaking thing she could imagine.

*K*ate leaned against a porch post and surveyed acre upon acre of gently undulating hills, some peppered with contented cattle, others shimmering with emerald-green stalks of corn. A sense of pride bubbled inside her as she watched the cows lumber lazily in search of sweeter grass. How much more delightful would it feel, she wondered, if she'd earned the right to drink in this beautiful panorama by dint of her own sacrifice and hard work, as the Nevilles had?

Closing her eyes, she slowly inhaled, drinking in the heady scents that rode the dry, Texas wind, savoring the sensation as each current caressed her cheeks, as every wisp of wind tousled her hair. *Learn it by heart,* she told herself, *because, too soon, all of this will be nothing but a beautiful memory.*

The breeze picked up and set the hems of the tablecloths flapping like red-and-white-checkered flags. Lucinda had told her how Cal, the blacksmith, had fashioned the metal clamps that held them in place, adding that he was a man of many talents. He'd made the two-story arch that welcomed one and all to the Lazy N Ranch from wrought iron. If she needed a new wooden spoon, Joseph, the carpenter, would carve one. And, if the handle of her stew pot ever came loose, George would fix it. Kate realized that everyone associated with the

186 ⌒ Loree Lough

Nevilles had been absorbed into the family, and their pride and love for one another was as obvious as the ache in her heart.

This was no time to dwell on her disappointments and regrets. Lucinda still had many chores to do, and she needed Kate's help to complete them all before the guests started arriving.

She focused on the long makeshift tables separating the back gardens from the nearly parched creek bed and knew they'd soon bow under the weight of platters of fried chicken and bowls mounded high with potatoes and biscuits. For now, only stacks of stoneware plates and baskets of flatware had been neatly positioned at the head and foot of each table. Kate had seen similar displays at town festivals and city fairs, but never so much in one place, all for one family!

She quickly corrected herself, for the feast wasn't just for the Nevilles. The ranch hands, their families, and most of the neighbors would attend, as well. She'd met a few of them, but most were total strangers. She didn't need to shake their hands and exchange friendly greetings to know they'd do everything in their power to make her feel part of the community.

She was counting along as the big clock in the hall gonged eleven times when a heart-stirring, baritone voice interrupted her thoughts. "You look mighty pretty today."

She turned slightly to face him and willed herself not to react to Josh's handsome smile or the warm light emanating from those oh-so-blue eyes. Under other circumstances, Kate might have returned the compliment, for he looked regal in his bright-white shirt and the dark-blue string tie, which matched his trousers. He'd slicked back his shoulder-length, golden curls, and she resisted the urge to tuck a wayward lock of hair behind his ear. "Thanks," she said, one hand fluttering at the collar of her blouse—one he'd bought her while they had been on the trail. Why, oh why, she wondered, facing the fields again, did she feel as though she might cry?

He leaned closer. "Will you come inside with me?" His breath tickled her ear when he added, "I'd like you to meet my grandmother."

She had just returned from her sister's house in Amarillo. Forcing a smile, Kate met his gaze. "So, I take it she's recuperated from her long trip?"

"I reckon. But even if she hasn't, I've never known her to miss a party." He took her elbow and led her into the house. "She's in the parlor, sipping lemonade. Ma made it special for her, since it's her favorite drink."

"Goodness, she must feel like a queen, with lemons being so hard to come by—"

"Trust me," he said, quirking one brow, "my grandmother is one woman who doesn't need lemonade to feel like a queen!"

"Well, I suppose that's her right, considering all she did to help turn this ranch into a successful operation."

Josh stopped dead in his tracks and blocked her path. "I don't think anyone has ever acknowledged that before. At least, not out loud." One corner of his mouth lifted in a grin. "You're something else, Dinah Theodore. Mee-Maw is going to love you."

He started for the foyer, but she grabbed his wrist and stopped him. She had to stall him so that she could gather her wits, plan a few good answers to the woman's inquiries. "Before we go in," Kate whispered, "do you mind answering a few questions?"

Josh glanced at the fingers she'd wrapped around his wrist, then fixed his azure gaze upon her face. "Such as?"

She couldn't very well admit that the prospect of meeting the family matriarch terrified her, now, could she? But it had been her experience that older people had a knack for spotting phonies—and a tendency to say exactly what was on their minds. What if Josh's grandmother gave her a thorough interrogation, took her measure, and…. The thought was too unnerving to complete!

"Why do you call her Mee-Maw, instead of something more dignified?"

Josh chuckled. "It's no big mystery," he began, taking her hands in his own. "When the lot of us were knee-high to boll weevils, 'Mee-Maw' was easier to say than 'Grandma.'" He shrugged a shoulder and arched one eyebrow. "It won't take a minute for you to figure out that she wouldn't feel the least bit comfortable with something more…'dignified.'"

Kate exhaled a shuddering breath.

"Oh, don't tell me you're afraid to meet a kindly old woman—"

"Of course not." But even before uttering the final word of her sentence, she felt the heat of a blush creep into her cheeks. "It isn't that I'm *afraid*, exactly. It's just—well, I want to make a good impression, that's all." She swallowed. "How much…. What have you told her about me?"

His eyes narrowed slightly, his smile became a wily smirk. He studied her face in silence for a moment before saying, "That you're on the run from the Texas Rangers, who hope to hang you for murder and bank robbery."

Kate snatched back her hands, wondering as she shoved them into her apron pockets if it was possible for a human heart to thump so hard it could leap clean out of a person's chest. Her skin grew clammy as a chill snaked up her spine, just as it had that night in the shack. Waves of wooziness fogged her brain, and her mouth went as dry as fresh-picked cotton. She pressed her back against the cool, plaster wall, shut her eyes tight, and slid slowly to the floor.

"Good gravy!" Josh said, crouching beside her. "What in tarnation…?" She opened her eyes, and he lifted her chin on a bent forefinger and studied her face. "I was only—"

"Joshing?"

Her feeble attempt to lighten the mood fell on deaf ears—that much was evident by the stern set to his manly jaw. "I know you believe you've been helpful, spending all that time on your feet to help Lucinda, but I think you're in more pain than you'll admit. And I think you've been skipping meals, too."

Kate blotted her forehead with the hem of her apron.

"Well?"

"Well, what?"

"Am I right?

"I suppose I have missed a few breakfasts and suppers."

He pursed his lips.

"Really, it doesn't hurt all that much."

"But you wouldn't tell me if it did, would you?"

No, Kate thought, *I would not.*

"I didn't think so." He stood up, then helped her to her feet. "Think you can stand on your own without toppling over like a tower of Willie's building blocks?"

"I'm fine."

"So you say."

"If I say I'm fine, then I'm fine!"

"And if I say I don't believe a word of it...." Josh guided her farther into the foyer, and stopped short of the parlor door. "Why, you're hardly limping at all. That's pretty amazing, considering...."

Considering? Did it mean he was surprised at how quickly she'd healed? Or that he thought she'd faked the twisted ankle so he'd take pity on her and bring her home? Probably the latter, if his stern expression was any indication. Kate mustered all the boldness she could and lifted her skirt a tad, exposing the injured foot. "It *is* amazing, isn't it, that something so trifling could be the answer to Lucinda's prayers." Dropping the skirt, she added, "You needn't worry, Josh. Any day now, I'll be out of your hair."

He faced her head-on, both brows low in the center of his forehead. "That isn't what I meant. Surely, you don't think I'd say anything so heartless and—"

"Who's that babbling in the hall?"

Josh gave a sideways nod of his head. "Mee-Maw," he whispered. "Sweet old gal doesn't miss a trick."

Thinking he'd finished talking, Kate made a move to enter the parlor. He stopped her with a powerful hand wrapped around her arm. His lips grazed her ear as he said, "Mark my words, we will finish this conversation later." Then, with one hand on her elbow, he led her into the room and snapped off a smart salute to the elderly woman in the big chair in which Kate usually sat with her mending. "Hey there, beautiful," he said, bending to press a kiss to her forehead. "How's my favorite girl feeling today?"

"If I said, 'Never better,' I'd be lying," she said with a hearty chuckle. "But I reckon I'm not doing too badly—for a 'sweet old gal.'"

Josh rolled his eyes and looked at Kate. "What did I tell you? She doesn't miss a trick."

Kate stood in the middle of the room, clasping and unclasping her hands and grinning like a fool.

Josh pressed a palm to her lower back, gently urging her nearer the chair where his grandmother sat. "This is Dinah Theodore," he said, "the young woman who—"

"I know good'n'well who she is." To Kate, she said, "Step up here, dearie, so I can get a better look at you. My old eyes don't see quite as well as they used to."

Kate inched forward, stopping just short of the ottoman. "It's a pleasure to meet you, Mrs. Nev—"

"Name's Esther, and I can't tell you what a pleasure it'll be having someone call me by my Christian name for a change." She grabbed Kate's hand and gave a tight squeeze. "Good to meet you, girl, good to meet you." She aimed an arthritic finger at the sofa. "Take a load off, and talk with me until the partygoers arrive. Josh, be a good grandson and fetch another tumbler so I can share my lemonade with this beautiful young woman."

"Please don't think me ungrateful, Mrs. Neville, but I couldn't possibly—"

"And why ever not?"

"Well, lemons are so hard to come by, especially at this time of year. And expensive. I surely don't need—"

"I don't need it, either. The good Lord hasn't yet created the body who *needs* the stuff, but He sure as shootin' made a few who need to *share* it!" This time, the crooked finger was aimed at Kate. "Don't make me say it again, girlie," she said with a wink. "The name is Esther."

Josh shrugged helplessly and strode from the room as Kate eased onto the thick sofa cushions.

"Dinah Theodore," Esther echoed. "A good, strong name." She sat back, nodding. "Theodore, Theodore—what is that? English? Welch?"

Kate hadn't thought about the origins of her borrowed name. "I hate to admit it," was her candid reply, "but I have no idea."

"Well, don't you worry your pretty head about it. Things like that might matter in Boston or Baltimore, but here in West Texas, nobody pays much mind to bloodlines. Unless, of course, you're a stud bull or a quarter horse." Laughing, she dabbed tears of mirth from her eyes. "Don't mind me," she said. "But if I don't laugh at my own pitiful jokes, who will?"

Suddenly, Kate didn't feel the least bit intimidated by this powerful, formidable woman. And the credit for that, she knew, went to Esther.

"Lucinda tells me you've been a huge help to her in the time you've been here. Haven't waited to be asked how you might lend a hand. Just jumped in and did what you thought needed doing." She winked. "I thank you for that, Dinah. That poor woman works her fingers to the bone without making so much as a sigh of complaint. She's not getting any younger, either. If you weren't in such an all-fired hurry to leave here, I'd ask you to stay on as Lucinda's assistant."

How would Josh's grandmother know she planned to leave in a day or two, when she'd made the decision only that morning?

"My eyes may not be what they once were," Esther said, "but the Almighty hasn't seen fit to dim my hearing." She chuckled. "Yet."

Kate swallowed hard, wondering what, exactly, Josh's grandmother had overheard.

"Why the long face?" Josh asked as he reentered the room and placed a silver tray, laden with biscuits, ham, and two tumblers of lemonade, on the ottoman.

She was about to ask what he meant when he said, "Ah, I guess Mee-Maw has figured it out, too."

Kate gulped. "I—I—"

"That you plan to leave us soon."

She'd been careful to keep her plans and concerns to herself, and she racked her brain, searching for a thought or worry she might have uttered aloud.

Josh pointed at the tray. "By the way," he said to his grandmother, "Lucinda said to tell you to eat this, or else."

Esther helped herself to a slice of meat. "Or else what?" she asked around the first bite.

"Or else your *medicina* will make your stomach *enfermo*," the housekeeper said, breezing into the room.

Esther snorted playfully. "Sick, my foot." Patting her stomach, she added, "Cast iron, I tell you. Why, I could eat shoe leather and carpenter's nails and not pay a price."

"All the same," Lucinda said, "is better to be safe than—"

"*Enfermo*," the women said in unison.

Lighthearted and touching as the familial interplay was, Kate didn't have much interest in the ongoing interchange between Esther and Lucinda. She much preferred to watch Josh, whose dark-lashed gaze brimmed with tenderness for these two very significant women in his life.

If only he could look at *her* that way someday. Immediately, she sniffed and shook her shoulders at the absurd thought. It brought to mind what he'd said in the hall earlier, when she'd asked what he'd told his grandmother about her. Had there been a rationale for his brusque yet accurate remark? She didn't see how. Besides, Josh didn't seem the good-guesser type.

Yet the possibility that he had an inkling about her true identity further justified her plans to leave this place as soon as she could. Another day or two—three, at most—and her ankle would be almost as good as new, leaving her no rational excuse to stay. After the party, once things quieted down, she'd find a way to get Josh alone, ask him to help her map out a route to Mexico, and assure him that she'd repay every penny.

"Penny for your thoughts," Esther said, startling Kate. When had Josh and Lucinda left the room? But before she could ask, the old woman said, "Lucinda has a cake in the oven, and my grandson is checking on Callie."

Callie? Why would he visit his horse, of all things, so soon before a huge gala?

"He says she's been acting fussy these last few days. *He* thinks she got into some loco weed." Esther winked and chuckled impishly. "*I* say different. In fact, if I was a bettin' woman, I'd bet if that horse isn't carrying a foal, he has to eat his hat."

Kate returned the woman's smile. "Good thing you're not a betting woman, then."

"And why's that?"

"I rather like Josh's hat." The woman's gravelly laughter induced a giggle of her own. "Besides," Kate added, "he has a gift when it comes to horses, but it still wouldn't be a fair bet, considering all your experience."

"Three things to like about you already, and we've only just met."

Kate blinked and waited for the explanation that would surely follow.

"That last remark proves you've got a good head on your shoulders. And it's clear you aren't one of the mindless ewes who'll tack a bustle to your behind and frizz your bangs under a ridiculous hat just because some la-di-da designer from Europe says it's fashionable." Esther sat back and snickered. "Sorry about the little tirade, dearie, but you'll find I'm not one to beat around the bush."

"A practice that's a terrible waste of time, and unnecessarily hard on the shrubbery." But Esther had named only two things. Not that Kate was counting.

The older woman slapped her thigh. "I like you, Dinah Theodore. Not as much as my grandson does, but then, you're his type, not mine."

Now, what had she meant by that?

"Don't tell me you haven't noticed that you've turned my grandson's head. The first gal to do it, I might add, since he buried Sadie."

If she'd ever felt more addle-brained, Kate couldn't remember when. She sipped her lemonade and hoped she was bright enough to swallow it without choking on the pulp.

"You did know that Josh's wife died a few years back, right?"

"Yes," she said quietly, "and I was sorry to hear about it."

Esther exhaled a long sigh. "When I lost my Ezra, I was so miserable that I wanted to climb into the grave right alongside him."

Kate remembered quite vividly how unhappy Josh had looked while telling her that his wife had died delivering twins.

"Josh took it hard, but he never grieved that way. Now, I don't mean to say that losing Sadie didn't pain him, because I'm sure he loved the dear girl." Esther motioned Kate closer and whispered, "But loving her and *being in love* with her?" She clucked her tongue. "Two very different things, in this old woman's book."

Suddenly, the room seemed hotter and stuffier than it had a moment ago, and the air felt thick, making it hard to breathe. Surely she'd misunderstood Esther, because Josh's grandmother couldn't have meant to imply that he'd fallen in love with her!

"I know he sometimes has a standoffish way about him, and that he talks tough, and that the combination can make him seem like he has a heart of stone. But I know that boy better than most, and if you want my opinion, he behaves that way because he thinks it's what folks expect of him." Esther gave a little shrug. "That, and he probably figures, if he walks around like he doesn't give a fig about anything, it'll save him from having to explain how he really feels about things." She paused. "And people." The woman held a finger aloft. "But, believe you me, Dinah dear, that boy has a heart as big as Texas." She aimed the finger in Kate's direction. "So, you take care not to break it, you hear?"

Not knowing what to say, Kate said nothing.

Part of her didn't want to believe Esther, because leaving here would be hard enough without the knowledge that Josh might have feelings for her. And part of her—a very large part—hoped it was true.

For, from almost the moment she'd faltered into his camp, Kate had loved the mild-mannered cowboy who had changed her entire life with nothing more than a gentle offer of help.

*L*eaning against the bark of a towering elm, Josh pretended to inspect the long blade of grass he'd just plucked from the lawn. But it wasn't the straw that captured his interest. Instead, he watched Dinah, standing alone in the shade of the hackberry beside the wraparound porch, smiling at the children who'd gathered to hear one of Mee-Maw's stories.

If he'd ever seen a sweeter face, he couldn't say when.

If he'd ever seen a prettier face....

Josh exhaled the breath he'd been holding and wondered why he always became addle-brained in her presence.

Maybe it was *because* of her pretty, sweet face. That, and her thick, gorgeous hair. Most days, she gathered it in a loose bun, held in place with a wide strip of material that matched her shirt or skirt. And, most days, she hid the graceful contours of her feminine form behind a loose-fitting, ankle-length apron. Today, she'd donned another of Sarah's designs, this one a pale-green dress that hugged her narrow waist and hips. The dry, Texas wind lifted her long, shimmering tresses, and he watched as they billowed out behind her like an auburn cape. Oh, what he wouldn't give to run his fingers through those waves, to find out if they felt as soft and satiny as they looked!

Earlier, she'd rolled up her sleeves to help Lucinda serve fried chicken, and Josh silently thanked God that she hadn't rolled them down again. Closing his eyes, he remembered long, slender fingers and white-as-snow wrists that hovered over food-laden platters as she dropped golden drumsticks and chicken wings onto guests' plates. She was as quick with a joke as she was with a compliment and delighted them all with the quiet trill of her laughter—laughter that sounded more like birdsong than obnoxious giggles. If he concentrated, Josh could hear it, even now.

"You aren't fooling anybody, you know."

The voice startled him so badly that Josh whacked his elbow on the tree trunk. "Never pegged you as the type to sneak up on a fella, Pa," he said, putting as much deference into his voice as he could.

"And I never pegged *you* as the gawking type." He nodded toward Dinah. "Why don't you just go over there and talk to her, instead of standing here, staring like a moony-eyed boy?"

He didn't cotton to being caught in the act of staring, but Josh held his tongue. It was hard to argue with the truth.

"It's been long enough," his father said, and Josh understood perfectly. It had been long enough since Sadie's passing.

He'd thought the same thing, half a dozen times or more, since meeting Dinah. But there didn't seem to be much point in telling her how he felt. "She's just passin' through, Pa," he blurted out. Besides, what he knew about Dinah Theodore, he could tamp into the bowl of his grandpa's corncob pipe.

Matthew dropped a hand onto Josh's shoulder. "Life's short, son. You know that better than most, because you learned the lesson the hard way." He gave the shoulder an affectionate squeeze, then looked at Dinah. "You can't know for sure what she might say about staying until you've asked her." Winking, he said, "Now, I'm going to see what sort of gossip your ma is involved with over there...."

Josh watched his father lumber over to where his wife stood chatting with the pastor and several ladies from church. But his interest in the conversation was short-lived, and soon his gaze slid across the lawn, back to the hackberry.

Much to his disappointment, she wasn't there. He straightened, whipped the blade of grass from his mouth, and did his best to ignore the overpowering ache pounding in his heart. Where could she have gone in an eyeblink?

He tried thinking reasonably. Tried focusing on the facts. Facts such as, the only reason she'd come home with him had been because of her injured ankle. And that she aimed to leave this place as soon as it healed.

Just then, a horrible thought occurred to him: What better time to slip away than in the middle of a boisterous get-together, when no one would notice her absence until the last of the guests had left?

He wouldn't mind her leaving as much if he thought for a minute that she was ready. But that was a lie, and he knew it. Would she really leave without saying good-bye, at least to him? The hot ache in his heart twisted into cold, mind-numbing dread as he admitted, *Yes, she would.* Something— or someone—malevolent still haunted her, and that's why he'd so often caught her staring off toward the horizon, as if she expected that the object of her fears was out there, biding his time for the right moment to finish what he'd started.

Josh had rarely experienced the raw fear he'd observed in Dinah. He hadn't felt it as a young pup, when, during his first trip to a cattle auction in Dallas, the crowd had separated him from his pa. Not at nine years of age, when he'd teetered on the barn roof, where he'd gone to repair the hole made by his mail-order rocket. Not even when Sadie had lain dying.

What's wrong with you? he demanded of himself, looking left, then right, as guilt and disgust hammered hard inside of him. How could he feel so afraid and worried and lost simply because Dinah was gone from his sight?

He made his way to the barn, but she wasn't among the toe-tapping, hand-clapping guests, bobbing their heads in time to the lively hoedown. He faced the fire pit, where a red-faced George was serving up juicy bits of pork to anyone passing by. He also spotted Griffen, though a tick too late to pretend he hadn't.

"Neville," said the Swede, "good to see you, my friend!"

I'm not your friend, was Josh's cynical thought. "Glad you could make it. Where are your wife and children?"

"Still in Boston, but they'll be here soon."

Nodding politely, Josh continued to scan the crowd as Griffen explained how he'd rented three rooms at the hotel, where his family would stay until the construction of their house was complete. "Not home, exactly," Griffen said, "but good enough for the short term." Still no sign of Dinah. Would she take the horse he'd bought her, or would she walk south to Mexico? Would she leave a note to explain why she had to leave, or simply go without a word, leaving him to wonder forever?

"...and once the missus arrives," Griffen was saying, "she'll put on the finishing touches. Nothing like a woman's touch—you know, those 'dainties,' like curtains and doilies and knickknacks—to turn a house into a home."

His voice penetrated Josh's Dinah-fog and brought him back to the here and now. He stood straighter and cleared his throat. "How long before you can send for them?"

"Tomorrow, I will wire the money for their tickets. The little woman wants to arrange the packing and oversee the moving of our things, so, in a few weeks, I expect you will be meeting dem."

"Good, good," Josh said, nodding. "I'm sure you miss them." The way he missed Dinah right now. The way he'd miss her every day until he knew for certain that she was someplace safe. And happy. *Liar.* He'd miss her far longer than that!

Maybe, he was worrying for nothing. She'd probably just gone inside to fetch a bonnet to keep her pretty hair in place.

"I see your mother over there by the spit," Griffen said. "I must t'ank her for inviting me." He grabbed Josh's hand and gave it a hearty shake. "It's good to see you, Neville," he repeated. "If you're in town, look me up. I could use the company. I'll buy you a cup of coffee!"

Josh heard himself say, "Will do," but his mind was fixed on finding Dinah. If he had to, he'd saddle Callie and head south. That didn't make a lick of sense, since he had no idea which road she might have taken, but sense had nothing to do with it. He needed to find her, and, when he did, he'd insist that she come back with him to the Lazy N—to stay.

As he moved toward the flagstone path, Josh wondered what made her think she could get along out there, alone, with no job and no money? He also wondered how he would get along without her!

And then, blessedly, he spotted her, rounding the back corner of the house. He tossed away the blade of grass and half ran to catch up with her. "Wait!" he wanted to shout, or "Dinah, stop!"

Somehow, he found the self-control to hold his tongue. And yet—though he hadn't called her name—she stopped, turned around, and smiled prettily when she saw him. The distance between them couldn't have been more than twenty yards, so why did it feel like two thousand? He wanted to break into a sprint, race up that walk just as fast as his legs would carry him, and, when at last he reached her, he wanted to throw his arms around her and confess the panic he'd felt when he'd thought she'd left him.

When he was close enough to see the merry twinkle in her eyes, she said, "Why, Josh Neville, are you following me?"

He stopped three feet from where she stood with her hands on her hips. "It would appear that I am."

She tilted her head and, with that minuscule motion, turned his ears hot and his palms damp. "Your grandmother asked me to fix her a cup of tea." She nodded toward the back door. "I'd love for you to keep me company while I do."

Josh wanted to tell her he'd like nothing better, except maybe to bundle her in his arms and kiss every freckle on her cheeks and nose.

At his silence, her smile faded. "You're one of the hosts, so, of course, I'll understand if you can't."

She'd misread his hesitation. Oh, how like her to provide him with a good excuse, just in case he didn't want to be alone with her. "I've been looking everywhere for you," he said. "Do I need to say more?"

She lifted her skirts and started up the steps. "Good thing Lucinda keeps a low fire under the tea kettle," she said, "although, if you ask me, it's hot enough out here that one could boil water just by setting a cup in the sun!"

Chuckling, Josh reached for the door handle at the same moment as Dinah. For an instant, while she stood blinking at their tangle of fingers, he thought she might bolt and run. Instead, she said, "You really ought to wear your gloves more often."

Gloves? The last thing he needed while his mind was a muddy mess was to try to puzzle out a riddle!

Dinah took hold of his thumb with one hand, his pinky with the other, and drew an invisible line from callus to callus, like a little girl playing a game of connect-the-dots. Folding his fingers inward, she gave his fist a gentle squeeze. "You're not made of stone, you know. Even big, strong cowboys need a little protection now and then." With that, she grabbed the door handle and stepped inside.

He wanted to comment on how warm and stuffy the room felt. Wanted to pull the window shade down to block out the sunlight and give them some privacy. Considered pointing out, as she spooned sugar into a teacup, that she looked like she belonged here.

"Would you like me to fix you a cup while I'm at it?"

He'd been staring, and she'd caught him at it. Again. Josh might have said, "It's the heat of the stove that turned my face beet-red." But on the chance she hadn't noticed that he was behaving like a wet-behind-the-ears young'un, he chose not to call attention to his ineptness. "No, thanks. Tea is for sick folks and old women."

"Is that what you think?" Her laughter harmonized with the quiet clatter of spoon against china. "And yet, I love the stuff."

And yet? Josh didn't get it, and said so.

Pushing the screen door open with her elbow, she walked outside, talking over her shoulder as she went. "Let's just say I feel a whole lot older on the inside than I look on the outside." When he joined her on the porch, she added, "Thanks for keeping me company, by the way. With all these strangers milling about, it was nice to have a familiar face and voice so near. That was really sweet of you."

There she went again, calling him sweet! She somehow had come to the crazy conclusion that he'd gone looking for her and offered to stay with her while she brewed his grandmother's tea for her sake. Did he dare own up to the truth? He shrugged inwardly. *What could it hurt?* "Didn't do it for you."

Dinah stopped, one foot on the flagstone walk, the other still on the bottom step of the porch, and looked up at him. He prayed for the wisdom to interpret the array of sentiments that flickered across her face, from confusion to pleasure, from sadness to trepidation. If he could make sense of his own jumbled-up emotions, maybe Josh would know how to comfort her—if he should. Feeling oafish and idiotic, he heaved a frustrated sigh. "Guess spending all that time with you on the trail got me so accustomed to having you around that…"—he paused, lifting one shoulder in a helpless shrug—"…that it feels strange when you're not."

With both feet planted firmly on the walk now, Dinah smiled—not that nervous flash of teeth usually reserved for moments when she caught him staring, and not the shy, dimpled grin inspired by his compliments, but a soft, sincere smile of contentment. Oh, what he wouldn't give to make it the only look she'd wear, night and day, for the rest of her life!

Her eyelashes fluttering, she glanced down at the teacup. "I'd better get this to your grandmother before it's too cold to drink."

"Right," he agreed as she started hurrying down the path.

"Coming along?" she called over her shoulder.

"I think I'll just wait for you here, if that's all right," he called after her, hoping she'd heard him.

Josh slapped a hand to the back of his neck. A smart man would back off, do whatever it took to douse the bright-hot flames of new love that smoldered inside him. When it came to Dinah, though, he felt anything *but* smart, a fact that woke a hundred separate doubts and suspicions in his mind.

Because only God Almighty knew if what he'd begun to feel for Dinah would keep him warm for the rest of his days, or burn everything—and everyone—that it touched.

*E*sther seemed perfectly content to chatter with the children gathered around her knees, so, after pulling up a small side table to hold her teacup, Kate headed for the spot where she'd last seen Josh. But he wasn't near the walkway, on the porch, or in the kitchen. Had she misunderstood him when he'd said that he'd wait for her?

She had no business falling for the cowboy, a fact that loomed larger with every passing hour. At first, Kate had told herself that any woman would feel the same way if she'd been rescued from certain doom and then protected by a handsome hero. But it hadn't taken long to figure out that saying something over and over couldn't turn it into truth.

Kate sat down on the top porch step and scanned the lawn. It should have been easy to find Josh among the partygoers, since he towered over just about everyone, but she didn't see him near the bandstand or the food tables, and he wasn't with his parents or his cousins or his grandmother, either. With her elbows propped on her knees, Kate rested her chin in an upturned palm and frowned. "Mindless little ninny," she muttered. "You're foolish and crazy, to boot, and you'd better get ahold of yourself, and do it quick, or—"

"Well, there's an effective way to make sure someone's listening."

Every gloomy thought vanished at the sound of his rich, baritone voice. "I don't always talk to myself, you know," she said, looking up at Josh and hoping the words hadn't sounded as defensive to him as they had to her own ears. Kate patted the space beside her.

He accepted her invitation and lowered himself down to the step. "I see. So, you talk to yourself only when there's no one else around to hear you?"

How was it that he could change her mood from melancholy to merry with nothing but his amazing smile? Kate tried to recall exactly what he'd said earlier, about how spending so much time with her on the trail had made being without her seem odd. The simple memory of it made her heart beat a tad faster.

She looked past him to where Esther sat in the shade, surrounded by a dozen children. "She's quite the entertainer, that grandmother of yours." Better to change the subject, Kate thought, than risk exposing herself for the brainless twit she'd become, thanks to her feelings for him.

Josh followed her gaze. "Few things tickle her more than having a bunch of young'uns around her feet."

Oh, how she wanted to trace the contours of that perfect profile!

It's precisely thoughts like that you need to watch out for! she berated herself. And then, just to be safe, Kate sat on her hands. "She's a natural-born storyteller. Just look at them, hanging on every word she says!"

When he turned and looked into her eyes—deeply— Kate fought the urge to close hers. Because if what they said about the eyes being a window to the soul was true, she didn't want him looking at hers too long and reading the truth that lived deep inside her wretched soul.

One corner of his mouth lifted in a slight smile. "So, tell me, Dinah Theodore, did you inherit those gorgeous, green eyes of yours from your mother or your father?"

Had he put a little extra emphasis on her name? Kate hoped she'd only imagined it; otherwise, it could be a clue that Josh knew more about her sordid past than he let on. "My father's eyes were brown," she volunteered, "and my mama's were blue."

"Well, they're both to be commended, in any case," he said, getting to his feet, "for producing such a stunning end result."

He held out one hand, and she let him pull her to her feet, hoping he hadn't heard the tiny gasp that escaped her lips when his big, strong fingers closed gently around hers. *I'd follow you anywhere,* she thought, *if I thought for an instant I deserved a man like you.*

"Have you had dessert yet?"

Kate shook her head. The way her stomach lurched in his presence, food was the last thing on her mind.

"Then I highly recommend the apple pie. It's by far the best I've ever tasted."

Was that his shy cowboy idea of a compliment? Maybe Lucinda had told him that she'd spent most of the morning rolling dough and slicing fruit.

When they reached the assortment of cakes and tarts, cookies and sweet rolls she and Lucinda had baked yesterday and early that morning, Josh let go of her hand. "I'd cut you a slice of apple pie, but it seems we're out of forks."

Kate watched as he used his forefinger to pick up a dollop of filling that had spilled beside the plate. The mischievous glint in his eyes told her precisely what he planned to do with

it, and she took a step backward, catching her boot heel on
a tree root. She would have landed smack on her unbustled
backside if he hadn't grabbed her wrist.

"Aw, now look what I've gone and done," he grumbled,
frowning at the dab of apple and cinnamon he'd painted on
her palm.

She started to say it wasn't his fault, to tell him not to
worry, because it would wash off with soap and warm water,
and wasn't it fortuitous that she'd rolled up her sleeves earlier? But just as she opened her mouth to let it all out, Josh
brought her hand to his lips and gently kissed away the blob.

"There," he said. "Clean as a whistle."

*Since when has such blatant flirtation been part of his normal
routine?* she thought, watching the thin, blue vein of her inner
wrist counting the rapid beats of her heart. If she'd thought
for a minute her ankle could handle it, she would have run
full throttle to the house and hidden in her room.

Kate wriggled free of his grasp and began gathering up
soiled forks and spoons. "I'll just take these inside and wash
them," she said, plucking two from here, four from there, as
she moved toward the other end of the table, "so Lucinda
won't have to do it. The poor woman has been on her feet
since long before dawn—the same, grueling schedule of every
day. Besides, there's no telling how many people haven't eaten
yet, and there are only so many of these to go around!" At
the sound of her own nervous giggle, Kate winced. She was
rambling and knew it, but she seemed powerless to stanch
the ceaseless flow of nonsensical chatter. "Good thing the tea-
kettle is more than half full on the stove," she added. "That'll
spare me having to boil water to—"

"Dinah," Josh said, pulling her closer, "hush, will you,
please, so I can apologize?"

Clutching the silverware like a shiny bouquet, she looked into his eyes. It wasn't as though he'd given her much choice, what with one big hand at the small of her back and the other behind her neck. "Apologize?" she echoed. "Whatever for?"

"For not doing this days ago."

He licked his lips, and, as his face loomed closer, she realized that Josh aimed to kiss her. As much as she'd yearned for this moment, she couldn't help but think what a horrible mistake Josh was making, because he deserved so much better than the likes of her.

"Well, for the luvva Pete, what are you waiting for, man? Just *kiss* the girl, why don't you?"

The sudden interruption made them both lurch, sending the flatware Kate had collected raining to the grass. Josh pulled himself together first. "Daniel, I declare, for a man with a bum leg, you sure are light on your feet."

His cousin smacked the heel of one hand to his forehead. "Maybe so," he said, "but it seems I'm heavy on intrusiveness. Shame on me for spoiling your romantic moment."

Kate found her voice at last. "Don't be silly. You didn't spoil anything." She bent down to retrieve the fallen forks and spoons, which she began dropping into her apron pockets. "I was just about to go inside and give these a good scrubbing when I lost my footing, you see, and Josh, here, happened to be in the right place at the right time."

Josh's cousin wiggled his eyebrows. "I'll say!" He proceeded to let out a boisterous laugh, and Kate hurried away, dropping more eating utensils into her pockets as she sprinted for the house.

Moments later, alone in the kitchen, she immersed both hands in warm, sudsy water and proceeded to scour every spoon, fork, and plate already in the sink. As she worked, Kate rehashed the scene over and over in her head, searching for the thing she might have done or said to bring about another outcome. But there was no escaping the fact that, if it hadn't been for Daniel's interruption, Josh would have kissed her.

Kate rinsed the dishes she'd washed, then picked up a tea towel to wipe them dry. If only it were as easy to wipe away the memory of standing in the protective circle of his embrace. Yes, he would have kissed her, and she would have let him—a shameful admission, because she had no business letting him believe they could ever be more than just friends!

On the other side of the window, cows grazed in the far pasture while horses frolicked in the corral. Outbuildings that housed plows and tillers had been whitewashed to look their best for the party, and the Nevilles, their friends, and the hired hands laughed and talked and enjoyed the revelry.

Funny how a thin pane of glass could so completely wall her off from sharing in their happiness.

As she scanned the horizon, the all-too-familiar sense of foreboding snaked up her spine. Frank Michaels lurked out there somewhere, like a spider in its web.

If she didn't leave here soon, Kate would lead him right to the Lazy N, where he'd devour the Nevilles one by one.

*D*inah had made herself scarce for the remainder of the party, and even when she joined Lucinda and George to clean up the yard afterward, Josh noticed that she stayed as far from him as humanly possible.

Maybe it had been a mistake to try to kiss her.

And maybe he should have finished what he'd started, Daniel or no Daniel. What better way to show her that he'd fallen Stetson over boots for her—and that there was no turning back?

Josh groaned, and Callie nickered. "What?" he asked, frowning. "You have a better idea?"

The horse bobbed her head as he went back to brushing her, even though her gleaming, gray coat didn't need it. "So, is Mee-Maw right?" he asked, patting her swollen belly. "Have you gone all moody and temperamental 'cause you're gonna be a mama?"

Callie nuzzled his neck and, her ears pricked forward, blew a soft chortle into his shoulder, as if to say, "Are you happy for me, Dad?"

Well, he wasn't.

Nearly a dozen years ago, he'd owned a mare named Mercy. Time had not dulled the painful memory of how she'd suffered trying to birth a breach foal. Born and raised on the Lazy N, Josh understood what every cowboy knew—that such things were part and parcel of ranch life. But that hadn't made putting her down any easier, and he'd vowed as he'd dug her grave that he'd never own a female horse again.

And then, he'd found Callie. Or, more accurately, Callie had found him. From the moment he'd brought her home, he'd done everything he could to keep her away from the stud males. Enduring the good-natured jibes inspired by his decision not to mate her was a heap easier than what might have happened if he had.

She had a spirited nature, one of the things he liked most about her. Regrettably, it was that very trait that had prompted her to jump the corral fence this past spring. She'd been gone four long days when he'd finally given up hope of finding her, and he had prayed that if she'd ended up in the jaws of a cougar or coyote, the kill had at least been quick and painless.

Then, on the fifth day, she'd come home, covered from mane to tail with mud and dust and bite marks, but she'd pranced jauntily into her stall. He'd prayed again, this time that she hadn't met up with a wild alpha stallion out there on the prairie. Almost from the start, his gut had told him that, come January, his worst fears would be realized, and no one at the Lazy N had been able to relieve his worries.

Well, that wasn't entirely true.

He remembered the way Dinah had cared, the night of the vicious storm, when they'd been forced to tether their horses outside the shack in the pounding rain. If he shared his fears with her, she'd not only listen—she'd *understand*.

Josh searched for nearly an hour before giving up hope of finding her. Maybe she'd turned in early. He could hardly have blamed her, because she'd worked as hard as anyone to make the annual Neville Fourth of July pig roast a smashing success.

It was dark when he decided to check on Callie one last time. Moonlight, slanting down from the heavens, was reflected in bright, white shafts on the corral fence, and the black loam of frequently trodden earth contrasted with the shimmering coats of horses, which stood, motionless, save for the soft puffing of their breaths. Recognizing him, Callie pawed at the dirt and whinnied, commanding his attention. Smiling, he sauntered closer. "What's wrong, girl? Did you miss me?"

"So, was your grandmother right? Is Callie going to be a mother?"

She'd spoken softly, yet he lurched enough to startle Callie, and the horse responded with a stern whinny before stomping off to join the others. "You're as bad as Daniel," Josh said, moving closer to where Dinah was perched on the gate.

"Sorry. I didn't mean to scare you."

Josh figured Dinah could probably hear his heart thumping against his ribs, so he didn't bother denying his fright. "What are you doing out here all by yourself?"

She looked into his eyes, then licked her lips—was that a clue that she, too, had given that almost-kiss a lot of thought?

"Couldn't sleep."

"Why not?"

She shrugged. "I had a lot to think about."

The mount he'd bought for her ambled up and nudged her shoulder, and Dinah wrapped her arms around the animal's neck. "Hey, there," she cooed. "Yes, yes, you're a very pretty girl, and I missed you, too." Evidently satisfied with that bit of affection, the horse moseyed back to the group.

"So, what were you thinking about?" How soon she'd leave him? Whether or not she'd say good-bye when she did?

Dinah took a deep breath and then let it out slowly. "Oh, just this and that."

His heart ached—what if she *had* considered leaving? And what if she planned to do it soon? "It's after midnight, you know."

"Is it that late?" She seemed genuinely surprised. "I hadn't realized that much time had passed already."

"How long have you been out here?"

On the heels of a girlish giggle, she said, "I honestly have no idea. It was hot in my room, and when I peeked outside, it just looked so pretty out here. Much too pretty to stay all cooped up inside."

Josh understood perfectly. Given his druthers, he'd rather sleep under the stars than in his bed any night.

Dinah inclined her head. "So, tell me, what are you doing out here at this hour?"

"I couldn't sleep, either."

"But I heard you say earlier that you had to be up before dawn."

"You heard right."

"Then, shouldn't you be fast asleep by now?"

Josh chuckled. "If you ever get to Mexico, you might consider putting that inquisitive mind to work as a reporter for a local newspaper."

Whether she'd chosen to overlook his not-so-subtle hint or didn't have a ready reply, Josh couldn't say. He knew this: her lack of response made him all the more interested in her plans.

"Now, really, be honest. Do you think your grandmother is right? About Callie, I mean. Is she going to be a mama?"

"Yes, she's right. And I'm none too happy about it, either."

"But, Josh! It would mean another little Callie running around—another beautiful horse. What's not to be happy about?"

Josh launched into the story of how he'd acquired—and lost—Mercy, and he didn't stop his tale until he'd brought Dinah right up to the moment when she'd startled him and Callie. Dinah had always been a chatterbox, so it surprised him when she had nothing to say in response to his sad narrative. It baffled him enough to take a step closer to study her face. It was then that he saw the tears in her eyes.

She was even more beautiful in the moonlight, if that was possible. The bright, lunar light painted feathery eyelash shadows on her milk-white cheeks and a crescent-shaped outline beneath her full lower lip. Callie's foal would be a looker—she'd been right about that—but what he'd really like to see were the children he and Dinah would create. Would they have copper-colored curls and big, green eyes, like Dinah had, or blue eyes and straw-colored hair, favoring his features? Maybe, they'd grow up tall and muscular, like their pa, or, maybe, they'd turn out like their ma—short and spunky.

Josh hung his head at the realization that nothing would complete his life quite like the promise of spending the rest of it in a cozy house filled with lively young'uns—and Dinah. But how could that ever happen if she was bound and determined to leave him?

"Why so quiet all of a sudden?"

He leaned both his arms on the gate. "I could ask you the same question."

"I was just thinking how unfair God is, sometimes. On top of everything else you've had to endure in your life, you shouldn't have to worry that you might lose—"

She'd probably stopped short of saying, "That you might lose Callie, too," and he sent up a silent prayer of gratitude for that. Thinking it was bad enough, but hearing the words spoken out loud? Josh could only shake his head in amazement that, yet again, Dinah had read his heart.

"God isn't to blame for anything that's gone wrong in my life," he finally said. "Where would you get such a notion?"

A cynical grunt was her answer.

Several silent moments slid by before she said, "I remember a sermon from when I was just a little girl—something along the lines of, 'The Lord giveth, and the Lord taketh away.' Well, it seems to me He does a whole lot more taking than giving, and it just isn't fair."

In the opalescent glow of the moon, her bruises were invisible. Josh wondered yet again about how she'd acquired them, about the sorry excuse for a man who'd put them there, along with the jagged scar on her jaw. What had her life been like, prior to meeting that two-legged beast? "And what do you think God took from you?"

"Where do I start? My parents, my home, my reputation, my good na—"

She clamped her lips together, but not before he'd heard enough to know she'd almost announced that God had taken her good name.

So, he'd been right all along—she *wasn't* Dinah Theodore. But she couldn't be Kate Wellington. How could the gorgeous little gal who'd cried because some horses had to stay outside in the driving rain be a thief and a killer?

And if she were?

"Why so quiet all of a sudden?" she asked him again, a nervous pitch to her voice.

A brave man would confront her, right here, right now. A smart man would demand to know the truth about her past—and where she aimed to let it take her in the future. But Josh knew good and well that if he were either brave *or* smart, he never would have fallen so quickly and so completely for a beautiful bandit. He felt foolish. Stupid. Embarrassed that he'd let his heart lead when he should have put his head in control, when he should have put God in charge. "Just don't feel much like talkin', I reckon."

Out of the corner of his eye, he saw her stiffen in response to his gruff reply, as if to say, "Fine, if it's silence you want, then it's silence you'll get!" He hadn't meant to hurt her feelings.

But then, he hadn't meant to love her, either.

While she stared straight ahead, Josh stared at her—at that stunning profile, with its upturned nose and full, pouty lips. He didn't know if her name was Kate or Dinah or Clementine, but he did know this: if the woman who stood close enough to kiss had ever played poker, she'd lost every hand. She wore her feelings on her sleeve, written all over her pretty face, in her lovely voice, and in the way she faced adversity with her head high and her back straight. And he loved her all the more for it.

She'd nearly cried just now when he'd told her the story about Mercy. Now, really, how could a woman with a heart that big and a temperament that sweet be guilty of the things printed on that wanted poster?

The soft scent of lavender soap rode the sultry night breeze and floated into his nostrils, and Josh closed his eyes, intent on memorizing it. That way, if she left him—and he was pretty sure that was exactly what she aimed to do—he could summon her scent to dull the ache of plodding through every day of the rest of his life without her.

Several times, as he stood there watching, wishing things could be different, Josh opened his mouth, thinking maybe he'd just throw caution to the wind and blurt out the first thing that came into his head. But, just as quickly, he clamped his molars together. What if "I love you" popped out? What if he asked her real name, asked if she was the woman on the wanted poster, and she confirmed his worst fear—that her bighearted sweetness had been part of her wily, pull-the-wool-over-his-eyes act.

And if none of those things happened? Well, if he didn't know what had gotten them so far off track, how in the world would he get them back on again?

"Honey biscuit?" she suddenly asked, pulling a napkin-wrapped parcel out of an apron pocket.

He wasn't the least bit hungry, but he took it, anyway. "Thanks," he said. At least, with his mouth full, she wouldn't expect him to hold up his end of the conversation.

About the time he polished off the biscuit, Dinah jumped down from the gate and put her hands into her apron pockets. "Here," she said, balancing a shiny, red apple on an upturned palm. "This was supposed to go into the pies, but I remembered how much you and Callie enjoyed the apples you bought while we were on the trail, so I set one aside for each of you." She laughed softly and looked at his horse. "She ate hers in one big gulp, so I guess Esther really is right about Callie's condition."

Grinning slightly, Josh wondered how deep those apron pockets were. But "What's one thing got to do with the other?" is what he said.

Dinah sent him a slanted smile. "She's eating for two, I guess?"

She looked so tiny, so fragile and vulnerable, that he was tempted to say, "I don't want any old apple. All I want is *you*." He might regret it in the morning, but Josh chose not to dwell on that. Instead, he drew her close and rested his chin in her mass of soft, sweet-smelling curls.

Dinah, much to his surprise and delight, nestled into him. A second, perhaps two, ticked by before he felt her shoulders begin to lurch. Josh held her at arm's length, shocked to find tears sparkling on her long, dark lashes. Using the pad of his thumb, he gently brushed them away. "Aw, darlin', what's this all about?"

Wrapping her arms around him, she snuggled closer again. "Oh, Josh, please don't worry about Callie. She's strong and healthy, and her baby will be, too. I'm sure of it!"

And there it was—the comfort and consolation he'd known no one could deliver in quite the same way as Dinah. Instantly, his worries and concerns about her past were gone. He'd live in the moment. What other choice did he have?

"I don't suppose there's a slice of your delicious apple pie left?"

A faint smile tugged at the corners of her mouth as she looked up at him. "I'm afraid you're too late for that." She studied his face, then added, "But there's plenty of peach cobbler."

Josh couldn't remember a time when more unanswered questions had tumbled in his head. Couldn't understand why his heart felt twice its normal size, while his brain seemed to have shrunk to the size of a pebble. Couldn't figure out why, when every rational thought in his head shouted "Stop!" he went ahead and pressed a soft kiss to her lips, anyway.

Or why, when she so sweetly returned it, his heart raced with relief and delight.

*E*veryone at the Eagle Pass Church of God obviously knew that the aisle seat in the second row was reserved for Esther—and the rest of the row for her brood. Kate was just learning this, because this was her first time attending Sunday service with the Nevilles.

Wearing yet another of Sarah's dresses and a hat borrowed from Susan, Kate held tight to Ezra's Bible, on loan from Josh's grandmother, and followed the woman to the left side of the church. But even with the well-worn Good Book in her lap, she felt like a pariah. And a fraud. Because, if these good people knew just how far she'd strayed from the Lord and all that was holy these past months, they might just relegate her to the vestibule rather than to Esther's left in the family pew.

The voices of parishioners, buzzing like bees in a hive as they exchanged "Good mornings" and "Howdy-dos," mingled with the swish of taffeta skirts and the almost-out-loud whispers of children as the church filled with worshippers. Kate started to stand up so that Josh's cousins wouldn't have to clamber over her feet, but Esther held her down. "If they'd gotten here on time, like we did," she announced loudly enough for them to hear, "they'd have been spared looking like clumsy oafs."

Daniel, Paul, and Micah gave sheepish smiles as they paused to kiss their grandmother's forehead, then settled into the pew on the other side of Kate. Sam, who'd chosen the seat directly in front of Daniel's, turned slightly and chuckled behind a cupped palm. "Your turn for the firing squad this week, eh?"

Susan dutifully shushed her husband.

"Oh, no," Willie said. "What did Pa do this time?"

His mother hushed him, too, starting a chain reaction of snickers from Sarah, Matthew, and Eva.

The hired hands and neighbors Kate had met at the picnic the day before smiled and waved to her, looking genuinely pleased to see her there in the pew beside Esther. What a delight, seeing them! But the one person she most wanted to see hadn't yet arrived.

"Girl, that head of yours is just like a door," Esther said, grinning as she squeezed Kate's knee. "I—I'd as-s-sk who you're looking for…."

Esther stopped talking and stared, wide-eyed and slack-jawed, inspiring a grin from Kate. Hopefully, she'd be as funny and energetic at that age!

"…Ish ah din aw-eddy…."

Kate might have laughed out loud at her silliness if she hadn't noticed the sudden, gray pallor of Esther's face. "Did you tuck your fan into your purse?" she asked, grasping the older woman's hand. The cool yet clammy feel of her skin only added to Kate's concern, for the oppressive heat in the crowded little church had turned everyone else's cheeks a glossy, ruddy pink. Taking hold of Esther's drawstring bag, she rummaged inside yet found nothing but a lace-edged handkerchief. So, she grabbed the old Bible and flapped it up and down to stir the air around Esther.

"Nah gud," Esther mumbled, shaking her head. "Nah gud a' all…."

"All right, then," Kate said, sliding her arm across the woman's shoulders, "I won't bother, since it isn't doing any good at all."

Knowing Esther, she'd view her current situation as a sign of weakness, and she'd hate drawing others' attention to it just as much. Kate glanced around, hoping to catch the eye of Josh's mother or father, or one of his cousins or sisters, but every Neville was engaged in lively conversation.

She leaned left and nudged Daniel, "Will you help me get your grandmother outside?" she asked him quietly.

He craned his neck to get a better look at the woman. "The heat seems to be getting to her," Kate explained, "and I think she needs some fresh air."

Sam overheard that last bit, and, as he got to his feet, Kate hoped the family clown would exercise a little restraint and decorum. But, despite the quiet, efficient way he stepped into the aisle and scooped Esther into his arms, people noticed— and reacted.

The reverend's wife, Pauline Peterson, had just stacked her sheet music on the organ. "What's wrong with Esther?" she asked, her voice echoing through the church.

"Why, Pauline, I do believe she's fainted," answered Eleanor Holbrook. "Oh dear, oh dear!"

"Now, now," Mayor Holbrook said. "No sense getting yourself all riled up or you'll be the next one we'll have to carry out of here." Frowning, he shook his head. "I told that fool, Peterson, not to paint the windows shut, but would he listen? No-o-o."

"What seems to be the problem here?"

"Reverend Peterson!" someone called out.

"It's Esther Neville," said another.

"If you'll all just step aside," Sam growled, "I'll take her into the yard, where she can—"

"Oh, sweet Jesus!" Mrs. Riddle squealed. "Good Lord in heaven, poor Esther has *fainted!*"

The pastor's authoritative, tenor voice silenced them all. "Do what Sam says, people, and get out of his way."

During it all, Esther kept her gaze locked on Kate's, and as Sam marched toward the back of the church, she lifted one pale hand, as if to plead, "Come with me. Don't leave me alone!" Was it just her imagination, or had the left half of Esther's face stopped working in tandem with the right? The poor old woman looked positively terrified, and Kate's heart ached for her.

Dispensing with polite courtesies, she shoved her way through the crowd and ignored the barrage of questions following her to the big double doors at the back of the church. Her only concern was Esther. As they stepped into the sunny churchyard, she heard the fear in Esther's voice as she wailed, "Dah-nnuh! *Dah-nnuh!*"

Years ago, during an influenza epidemic, Kate had volunteered at the hospital in San Antonio, where the doctors and nurses had called upon her time and again to translate the garbled words of fevered patients. Back then, she hadn't been wise to see it as a God-given gift, but she thanked Him for it now.

Spotting several chairs off to the right, she hobbled over to fetch one for Esther. "I'll be right there, Sam," she called, "soon as I drag this—"

"What's wrong with my grandmother?"

She looked up into Josh's worried face and wished everyone else who'd gathered would just go away, including his sisters and cousins, and even his parents. "She fainted," Kate began, "because of the heat. I think. So I asked Sam to bring her out here—to get some fresh air, and—"

As he leaned down to grasp the arms of the chair and lift it out of her hands, he paused and looked deep into her eyes. "Thanks for being there for her." Straightening, he hefted the chair into the shade of the tree, where his brother-in-law cradled a frail-looking Esther in his arms. Once Sam had positioned her in the chair, Josh crouched beside her. "Looks to me like you didn't take your own good advice this morning."

"Whaa?"

Kate had to give him credit. If Esther's slack-jawed face and watery eyes alarmed him half as much as they frightened her, he was doing an exemplary job of hiding his concern.

He patted his grandmother's limp hand. "You skipped breakfast again, didn't you, Mee-Maw?"

Esther leaned back in the chair and tried to shake her head. "Dah-nuhh," she moaned. "Wrrrr Dah-nuhh?"

Kate was beside her in a heartbeat. "I'm right here, Esther." On her knees beside the chair, she added, "It'll take me only a few minutes to head up the road and fetch the doctor. Josh will stay with you while I'm—"

But Esther frowned and flicked the fingers of her right hand, as if shooing away an annoying fly. "No-o-o," she moaned. "Mke thm go-o-o...."

Kate faced the people who had congregated nearby. "She doesn't want the doctor, at least not at the moment." She turned to Esther to see if she'd interpreted her wishes correctly. In response to the old woman's grateful sigh, she faced the group again. "The last thing she wants is to worry you. I think she'll pull herself together faster if you'll do as she asks and go back inside for the service."

Willie tugged at his mother's skirt. "What's wrong with Mee-Maw?" he whimpered.

Susan picked him up and finger combed blond bangs from his eyes. "She's just tired, sweetheart. Don't worry."

"Is she gonna die, Mama?"

Sam slid an arm around his wife's waist. "'Course not, son." He frowned. "He doesn't need to see this," he mouthed to her.

"Your husband's right," Sarah whispered, tugging her sister's hand. "Let's go inside. Mee-Maw's in good hands."

Amid a din of whispers and murmurs, the people slowly made their ways back inside the church, with the exception of Kate, Josh, and his parents.

Esther began to cry softly. "Go-o-o...plll?"

Kate was about to translate her last remark when Josh said, "Mee-Maw, darlin', we can't just leave you out here alone."

His grandmother fixed her teary-eyed gaze on Kate. "Wnn be ln-n-n."

"That's right, Esther, you won't be alone." She directed her next comment to Josh and his father. "I won't leave her side for a moment, I promise."

Matthew looked almost as vulnerable and upset as Willie had. He bent at the waist, resting both palms on his knees. "Ma, surely you don't mean for Eva and me to leave, too."

She locked eyes with her son and gave a firm nod, then reached for Kate.

"It'll be all right, Mr. Neville," Kate assured Matthew, taking his mother's hand. "As you can hear, she's already talking more clearly, even after just these few minutes in the fresh air."

Matthew straightened and, folding his arms over his chest, focused on Kate. "I wasn't aware that you'd earned a medical degree, young lady."

He had every right to be upset, given his mother's condition. Every right to be hurt that it seemed his mother trusted a stranger more than her loved ones. Kate could see the pain and worry on his handsome face, and her heart filled with sympathy for him. "I'm sure the only reason she prefers my company is because I'm a stranger, and I won't fuss over her like a friend or family member might." She didn't need to add the obvious—that no one but she could understand a word Esther was saying. "If she isn't better after the service, we'll send for the doctor. In the meantime, what can it hurt to humor her?"

Eva whispered into her husband's ear, inspiring an exasperated sigh and a firm nod. He grumbled something under his breath, then followed his wife up the front steps of the church. At the doorway, he paused and pointed a beefy forefinger up the road, an unspoken command to fetch the doctor.

Once everyone was out of sight, Josh stood behind the chair and watched as Kate tidied his grandmother's skirts. "Should we do what he asked?" Kate asked him.

"Only if you're sure you can handle things while I'm gone."

She met his wary gaze. "Maybe you'd prefer that I go. I can explain things better, anyway—"

"Maybe you're right."

"Just take care that she doesn't tumble forward," she instructed, marching purposefully toward the center of town and rejoicing that her ankle hardly hurt despite the pressure.

In a matter of minutes, she found herself on the Lanes' porch, breathing hard and knocking harder than necessary.

It never occurred to her to wonder why Dr. Lane hadn't been in church with the rest of Eagle Pass, so when his wife announced that he'd gone to Uvalde to pick up his special-order cigars, Kate nearly stamped her feet in frustration. "Did he leave someone else in charge of his patients' well-being?" she demanded.

The mousy little woman hid behind the door. "I'm afraid not," she squeaked, "but he'll be back first thing in the morning, if it can wait—"

"Well, isn't this a fine kettle of fish?" Kate blurted out. "Esther Neville could be dead by then, but at least the good doctor will have a good smoke to comfort him!"

She turned on her heel and hurried back to the church, praying with every step that the slight improvement in Esther's condition would have increased in the time she'd been gone.

She hoped it for Esther's sake, and for the sake of her children and grandchildren. Hoped it for herself, too, because she couldn't leave the Lazy N while the poor old woman had no one but her to interpret her needs.

*T*hrough trial and error, Kate came up with a method for feeding Esther at mealtimes. Since soup was the only thing Esther could swallow easily, Kate made a big pot of it every night after tucking the woman in. Blotting Esther's mouth with a cloth after every bite was easier on the woman's self-esteem, and it kept her nightshirts tidier, too. Kate discovered that chattering about anything that popped into her head helped distract her charge from the fact that she'd lost control of half of her body and, despite her independent spirit, now needed constant care.

"I think, after breakfast," Kate said, dabbing the corner of Esther's mouth with a napkin, "we'll sit outside in the shade and I'll read to you. Any book you choose!"

Esther nodded despondently and did her best to choke down another spoonful of soup.

Kate prattled on about the weather, little Willie's latest antics, Sarah's newest designer gown—anything but Dr. Lane's dismal diagnosis.

"Or maybe you'd rather dabble with your paints." Despite the doctor's gloom-and-doom prognosis, Kate believed that, with practice, Esther could reclaim at least some control of her now palsied hand. It was clear that she understood every word spoken to her, which was proof enough to Kate that, despite her struggle with words, Esther's mind was intact and functioning perfectly!

"Dah-nah," Esther said, doing her best to squeeze Kate's hand, "I glad...you here."

"And I'm glad to *be* here." Wearing the same, forced smile she'd adopted in the church on Sunday morning, Kate spooned several more drops of broth into Esther's mouth. As she did so, she recalled Dr. Lane's words: "Apoplexy leaves people forever changed."

She hid an involuntary shudder as the terrible word echoed in her head. *Apoplexy.* It sounded almost as ugly as what it had done to Esther, who, just days ago, could have challenged anyone at the Lazy N to a battle of wits—and won! But neither the diagnosis nor the prognosis was as horrible as the last thing the doctor had said: "Prepare yourselves for the worst, because, in my experience, symptoms like Esther's are generally a precursor to—"

"Ah...I know...you want go," said Esther, breaking into Kate's bleak thoughts. "How I...shange...your...? What will...make you stay?"

Kate put down the spoon and wrapped her arms around Esther, mostly to keep the woman from reading her own anxiety. She had promised to stay as long as Esther needed her and had every intention of keeping her word. But the all-too-familiar feeling that somebody was watching, which had prickled the fringes of her mind since her escape from Frank, was spiraling higher, like the growing plumes of smoke that signaled a distant inferno. She knew that she needed to leave before the fire engulfed the Lazy N and everyone who called it home. And Esther had sensed it.

"Don' be 'fraid," Esther stuttered. "Josh...he will keep you...safe."

Sitting back, Kate studied Esther's haggard face. How much did she know, and how had she come by the information?

Esther responded with a shaky nod and attempted a grin. "I...I saw...."

Not a wanted poster, Kate prayed. *Please, Lord, not that!*

"Saw," Esther repeated, wrapping her weakened fingers around Kate's wrist, "saw K-Kate...."

Somehow, she'd always known this moment was bound to happen. It had been a gift from God that no one had figured things out days—even weeks—ago. Kate hung her head in shame.

A moment later, Esther brought Kate's hand to her face, gave it a weak hug, and then, frowning, shook her head. "N-no one saw. Just...just me. In Am...rill...o...."

Her heart pounding, Kate fought back tears. She couldn't bear to meet Esther's eyes. How had the woman managed to hide the disgust she must have been feeling all this time?

"Because...because it's...a mistake." She moved her head side to side. "Can't be...true."

Shame quickly turned into guilt as Kate realized what Esther was trying to say. But the information printed on the wanted poster *was* true—every despicable word of it. She *had* participated in a robbery, and in cold-blooded murder, too, by not standing up to Frank, not refusing to be his puppet.

If Esther had figured things out, chances were good that the rest of the Nevilles had, too. They'd all had occasion to go into town, after all, and may have seen the poster there. It certainly explained why no one had asked where she'd come from, why she hadn't made any attempt to reach out to family or friends, why no one had come looking for her. But how long had they known? And why hadn't they confronted her with what they'd learned and demanded an explanation?

"N-no one else," Esther managed, her forefinger wagging like a metronome on its slowest setting. She swallowed and closed her eyes for a moment before opening them again and focusing on Kate. "Just...just...."

Kate's humiliation and remorse were forgotten when Esther's blue eyes filled with tears of frustration. *Oh, Lord,* she prayed silently, *help me calm her and ease her struggles.* "You were in Amarillo," she reviewed, "so no one but you saw the poster?"

Nodding, Esther heaved a sigh of relief.

Kate echoed Esther's sigh. "I'm sorry, Esther—so sorry to bring this disgrace into your home."

Silence hung in the room like a thick, hot curtain, a hush so complete that Kate heard nothing but the older woman's ragged breaths.

All of a sudden, Esther banged a fist on the table beside her chair. "No!" she roared. "You...are...in-no-o-cent!" And, once she'd commanded Kate's full attention, she narrowed one eye. "In-no-cent!"

Kate understood perfectly, but the importance of her own safety and security paled in comparison to that of convincing Esther to remain calm. Besides, what did it matter who might have seen the poster when, any day now, she'd have to leave the Lazy N, and—

"No!" Esther cried for a second time. "Stay!"

Kate could have listed all the reasons why the woman's order was unreasonable, unrealistic, and unsafe, but, knowing they'd only add to Esther's already agitated state, she held her tongue. "All right," she said, standing up and gathering Esther's soup bowl, napkin, and spoon. "I'm sure I can find an able-bodied male somewhere around here to carry you outside." Moving toward the hall, Kate paused in the doorway. "Have you decided which book you'd like me to read to you?"

Esther looked at the Bible, still open on the table, then met Kate's eyes again.

"The Bible it is, then."

With her head down as she made her way down the stairs and toward the kitchen, Kate mentally reviewed her lists of tasks for the day ahead: spend some time outdoors with Esther, feed her lunch, get her settled for an afternoon nap—and then stow her own, meager belongings into the satchel Josh had bought for her. That way, she'd be ready to run at a moment's notice.

What a pity she no longer had her mama's cameo. Otherwise, perhaps Josh would have accepted it as payment for the horse and saddle and food she would need for her journey. As it was, she could only hope he'd take her word that she'd reimburse him as soon as she found work in Mexico.

In her head, she plotted out the note she'd write. She would begin with a heartfelt *Dearest Josh*, and then go on to admit how she could never fully repay him for all he'd done for her. *I promise to send money every chance I get, until my debt to you is completely paid—*

"Oomph!" Josh said as Kate collided with him, sending the napkin fluttering to the floor and the spoon clattering against the baseboard.

Kate hugged the now empty soup bowl to her chest and gawked at the puddle of chicken broth at her feet. Though most of the mess had been absorbed by her blouse and skirt, some of it had splashed onto his shirt and now dripped onto his boots.

"Oh my goodness!" Kate cried, stooping to retrieve the spoon and napkin. "I'm so sorry!" she exclaimed as she blotted the damp spots on his shirt.

Chuckling softly, Josh wrapped his fingers around her wrists. "Where are you headed in such a hurry?"

She didn't dare meet his eyes. Several things he'd said over the past few days made her suspect he knew the truth about her, too, and the last thing she needed right now was proof of that, written all over his handsome face. "I—I was just headed to the kitchen," she stammered, "to—to wash up some dishes." She let out a nervous giggle. "Guess I need to watch where I'm going. I'm sorry—"

"Stop apologizing." He lifted her chin on a bent forefinger. "So, you spilled a little soup. It isn't as if you killed someone."

Of all the phrases he could have chosen, why that one? Kate got down on her knees and used the napkin to sop up the spill. "Wouldn't want anyone slipping in the puddle," she said, scrubbing as though it was tar, not broth. "I'd better get a bucket of sudsy water and do a proper job, make sure I get up all the—"

Josh stooped, placed one hand on each of her shoulders, and brought her to her feet. "When Mee-Maw takes her morning nap," he said, his eyes boring hotly into hers, "I suggest you try to catch a few winks, too. You look exhausted."

Blinking, she eased out of his grasp and made a beeline for the kitchen. "You should get into a clean shirt so I can put that one into a bucket to soak. Soup can leave an oily residue on fabrics, you know, especially linen."

Somehow, he got to the kitchen ahead of her. His boots planted shoulder-width apart, he crossed both arms over his chest. "Where's my grandmother right now?"

Kate set the bowl and spoon into the dishpan. "Why, she's in her room, patiently waiting for me to find someone who can help me get her outside. I promised to read to her from her Bible."

"She's alone?"

Now, Kate understood the scowl on his face. Of course—he was concerned for his grandmother's safety! "Oh, don't worry. I tucked her in good and tight. She's propped up against her pillows, because it's easier for her to breathe that way, and there are pillows beside her, too, so she can't topple over or fall out of bed."

His expression softened, and he chuckled. "I should have known you'd have everything well in hand. So, tell me," he said, leaning an elbow on the counter beside her—so close, in fact, that she could feel his warm breath on her cheek, "why were you rushing down the hall, if she's safe in her room?"

Kate focused on washing the bowl, the spoon, and the half-dozen thick, white mugs buried in the sudsy water. "I wanted to clean a few things up, to spare Lucinda from having to do it. Then, I hoped to brew Esther a cup of tea and see who might be able to help get her outside for some fresh air—you know, in the shade of the elm, since that's her favorite place? I've promised to read to her from—"

"—from her Bible. Yes, so you said."

"Oh. Yes. I suppose I did. Sorry."

"Dinah, look at me."

Didn't he realize that she *couldn't* look at him? Kate concentrated on preparing the tea for Esther. "Two spoons of sugar," she muttered. "Funny how even Esther admits it's a silly waste. Once, she told me, 'Far better to use it in cake batter or to sweeten pie filling.' And I told her she'd earned the right to fill her cup half full of sugar, if that's what she wanted to do, and do you know what she said?"

"No. And, frankly, I don't care." Josh turned her around so suddenly that she nearly lost her footing. His arms slid around her, providing steady support.

"What do you think you're doing?"

"I came looking for you this morning to apologize—and to thank you."

For a quiet moment, he searched her face, then stepped away, leaving her feeling cold and alone and not nearly as safe as she had felt in his arms. *Better get used to feeling this way,* she thought, hugging herself, *because, in no time, it's how you'll feel all the time.* "Apologize for what?"

He turned his back to her. "For kissing you the other night."

Kate could only presume, by the way Josh hung his head and slumped his shoulders, he really was sorry for kissing her. Was he worried that her tainted nature might rub off on him? Did he realize that, by calling it a mistake, he'd tainted the memory of it for her?

"It's—it's like this." Josh faced her again. "The men in your past haven't been very gentle with you. And I had no right to force myself on you that way."

The men in her past? How many did he think there'd been? Oh, what did that matter? What would any of it matter once she was long gone from here? "It would be less than honest to let you think I saw it as forceful." She matched his stare, spark for spark. "I participated in that kiss, too, remember?"

A crooked smile slanted his lips. "Oh, trust me," he rasped. "I remember."

Well, that took care of the matter of his apology. So, what about his "Thank you"?

As if he'd read her mind, Josh said, "I also want to tell you how grateful I am for everything you're doing for Mee-Maw. She'd be lost without you, and everyone here knows it."

The mention of Esther reminded Kate that the poor woman was upstairs, alone, waiting for her. Not that she'd ever *really* be alone, what with her large, loving family, and all the little children who delighted in playing at her feet. Any one of them would gladly keep her company, read to her from her Bible, brew her cups of sweet tea, and feed her warm broth, one careful spoonful at a time. The Neville women would happily bathe and dress her and braid her long, white hair into buns. And the menfolk would gladly carry her from her chair to her bed to the dinner table and back again.

So why had Esther chosen her as her caretaker?

"You're the only one who understands her," Josh said. "Surely, you know how important a thing like that is for a woman like my grandmother."

"I'm happy—*proud*—to help out," Kate said, meaning it. Then, "Will you help me get her outside?"

Josh straightened to his full height. "Is her wheelchair ready to go?"

Nodding, Kate managed a smile. "That thing is so stiff-backed, I don't know how she tolerates it. And it jostles her so badly, too. That's why I dragged her rocking chair out under the tree early this morning and padded it with pillows from the parlor sofa. I borrowed the little table from the foyer to hold her books and her tea. So, really, all that's left to do is to scoop her up and take her out there."

He was beside her again in two strides. "Tell you what," he said, cupping her chin in one big hand. "I'll carry her outside while you finish up in here."

Locked in his warm gaze, she would have followed him the length of the Rio Grande and back again if he'd asked her to, and, in that moment, Frank and his menacing threats were the furthest things from her mind. "Yes," she whispered, "tea...."

If merely turning away from his gentle smile was this disquieting, how much more difficult would it be never to see him again?

*D*inah's patience seemed to have no limits. Josh watched as she tidied the blanket draped across his grandmother's lap, then fed her tiny sips of sweet tea from a spoon. If she dribbled—and she drooled with nearly every mouthful—Dinah quickly and gently blotted it up, talking and laughing and making silly faces to keep Mee-Maw's mind off her steadily deteriorating condition.

And deteriorating it was, just as Dr. Lane had predicted.

For a while there, it had looked like Mee-Maw might bounce back to her old self. As her speech had improved, her spirits had lifted. But in the few days that had passed since the attack, every symptom had worsened. And Dinah, God bless her stubborn, steadfast soul, refused to admit defeat. "With time and patience, we'll prove that old doctor wrong!" If she'd said it once, she'd said it a dozen times.

Josh had gate latches to repair and barn door hinges to replace. There were cows to milk and horses to feed, and a corral fence post to straighten. If he wrote down every chore, the list would be longer than his forearm. Yet he couldn't make himself leave these dear women—one he'd loved all his life, and one he'd come to treasure in a completely different way.

He sat, leaning against a tree, watching, listening. They were a lot alike, his grandmother and the young woman who so devotedly doted on her. Willful and intelligent, neither would so much as consider shying away from an argument. Both possessed physical strength that belied their small statures. Mee-Maw had always been fiercely defensive of her loved ones, and Josh sensed that the same, stubborn protectiveness beat in Dinah's heart, too. How else could he explain the way she hovered over Mee-Maw, determined to disprove the doctor's theories?

By the same token, the contrasts between Dinah and his late wife were monumental. Where Sadie had been tall and big-boned, Dinah reminded him of the Lilliputians described by Jonathan Swift in *Gulliver's Travels*. Soft-spoken and shy, Sadie had never been overly talkative, whereas Dinah could probably strike up a dialogue with a field mouse and keep it happily engaged. Sadie's kitchen specialties had been robust soups and stews, and it was Dinah's biscuits and pies and cobblers that made his mouth water. But the biggest difference of all? Dinah's way of putting everything she had into everything she did.

Like that kiss. *Especially* that kiss.

He shook his head. This was neither the time nor the place for such thoughts! Besides, Dinah had started reading aloud from the Good Book, and her lovely voice sounded like the warble of a songbird.

"S-sing?" Mee-Maw stammered.

"Any particular song?"

"M-may-zng—"

"'Amazing Grace' it is, then."

And so Dinah sang, making him wonder why there wasn't a halo over her head and gossamer wings fluttering on her narrow back.

Mee-Maw was doing her best to tap a toe in time to the tune, but the effects of the apoplexy made it next to impossible. As much as he was enjoying the beautiful melody, Josh was tempted to ask Dinah to stop singing, because then, at least, there'd be one less thing to upset his grandmother. But he noticed that Mee-Maw was far from upset. In fact, a peaceful, contented expression had smoothed the furrow of frustrated on her brow.

After Dinah sang the hymn, she slid into a sad, Scottish ballad, then broke into a lively nursery rhyme that spoke of silver bells and cockle shells. Mee-Maw's eyelids fluttered shut during the first verse of "The Yellow Rose of Texas," but Dinah crooned on.

The song could have been written just for Dinah. Garbed in yellow, from the bow in her glistening hair to the hem of her lace-trimmed dress, she was every bit as beautiful as a delicate rose.

"Her eyes are bright as diamonds, they sparkle like the dew...."

More beautiful than a rose, Josh thought, nodding to himself, because her eyes were as bright as diamonds—*especially in the moonlight, when she's looking up, waiting for your kiss.*

He watched as Dinah rested her chin on the arm of the chair and, smiling softly, tapped out the tempo on the back of Mee-Maw's hand.

"Oh, now I'm going to find her, for my heart is full of woe...."

Woe. Now, that seemed like the perfect word to describe how he'd feel once Dinah left him. He leaned his head against the tree and closed his eyes, hoping to etch the image of Dinah's face and this magical moment in his mind, because, if she wanted to go, he couldn't very well stop her.

Or could he?

"And the Yellow Rose of Texas shall be mine forevermore."

His? Forever? If only! Why, his whole life would take on a new and wonderful meaning if—

"What are you grinning about?"

Even before he opened his eyes, Josh knew that Dinah was smiling, for he could hear it in her voice. "Just enjoying the pretty music, that's all."

The rustle of material told him she'd gotten to her feet, and the crunch of sun-dried grass meant she had left his grandmother's side to move closer to him. "Bet you didn't know a woman could snore like that," he said, sitting up taller.

Dinah glanced back at Mee-Maw, whose chin had dropped to her chest as she slept. "Dr. Lane says it's to be expected." She knelt beside him. "Because of the apoplexy."

"Nonsense."

She looked surprised, but only mildly so. "I'd hardly call her condition 'nonsense.'"

The breeze had mussed her hair, loosing several tendrils, which fluttered around her face. Josh resisted the urge to smooth them back into place. "Snoring might be a symptom in other patients, but it's nothing new for Mee-Maw."

Dinah tidied her skirt. "I know. She told me that one evening after Dr. Lane left." She giggled, then said, "I realize that you have chores to do, so, really, I hope you don't feel that you have to stay. I promise to watch over her as if she were my own grandmother. And, when she wakes up, I'm sure I can find someone to help get her back inside."

Frowning, Josh sat up and rested his arms on his knees. "Is that why you think I'm here? To keep an eye on you, make sure you'll take proper care of her?"

Dinah shrugged, as if to say, "Why else?" Instead, she said, "It's perfectly understandable. She means so much to you, to your whole family, so, of course, you want to ensure that—"

"She couldn't be in better hands. I know that as well as I know my own name."

She muttered something unintelligible under her breath, then fiddled with her hair ribbon. Long, flowing tresses poured down her back as she attempted to repair the damage done by the wind. Just as she prepared to twist it up again, he caught her wrist. "Please don't," he said. "It's too beautiful to bind up in a matronly bun."

"Then how, exactly, do you propose I keep this mess out of my face?"

"The last thing I'd call it is a mess." Josh combed his fingers through her curls to hold them in place, then rested both thumbs on her cheekbones. "There. It's out of your face now."

She laughed and clasped both his wrists with her hands. "Well, now, isn't this just as silly as silly can be? You can't sit here all day, holding my hair in place."

If only I could, he thought.

Mee-Maw snorted, and Dinah used the interruption as her excuse to scramble to her feet and run to her side. "Her tea is cold," she called softly to Josh, lifting the cup and saucer. "If you can spare just a few minutes more to stay with her while I fix another cup—"

"Mee-Maw is off in dreamland," he said as he relieved her of the china. "If she wants more tea, you can get it for her when she wakes up."

Cupping her elbows, Dinah took one step backward. Did it mean she thought he intended to repeat the moonlight kiss? Or that she was still bristling over the clumsy apology it had prompted?

He returned the cup and saucer to the table beside Mee-Maw's chair. Dinah hadn't elaborated on her past, and Josh hadn't asked about it, partly because he didn't like poking his nose into other people's affairs and partly because he didn't know what he might be tempted to do if she named the thug who had used her as a punching bag.

He pretended that his grandmother's blanket needed tidying, frowning as he tucked it into the cushions that supported her frail body. Thanks to that wanted poster, he had a pretty good idea where Dinah had been before appearing from out of nowhere with nothing but the clothes on her back. If Dinah Theodore and Kate Wellington were one in the same person, it only proved one thing in his mind: she'd gotten tangled up in something beyond her control. It was as simple—and as complicated—as that. But he refused to believe anything else, because her heart was just too big, her soul too pure, to have committed robbery—or worse. He couldn't afford to be wrong, for in bringing her here, he'd bet his life—and the lives of everyone at the Lazy N—on that.

Dinah licked her lips, reminding him yet again of that glorious, mesmerizing, life-changing kiss. He had meant it to convey all he'd come to feel for her, and what he'd talked himself into believing about her, since he didn't have the faculty to put it into words. But when he'd wrapped his arms around her and felt her heart beating fiercely against his ribs, when he'd tasted the sweetness and goodness that he'd known were in her, passion had pretty much drowned out his intended message. That's why he'd apologized, because the good Lord knew he wasn't sorry for kissing her!

And, lovesick fool that he was, Josh couldn't find the words to admit that, either.

He watched Dinah as she stared off toward the horizon, wearing that same expression he'd seen so many times before. "What's out there that frightens you so?"

She turned to him so quickly that another curl popped free from her yellow ribbon. "What? Oh, nothing." Giggling nervously, she tucked the curl behind her ear. "Afraid? What a silly thing to say!" Straightening her back, she added, "I'm worried about Esther, same as everyone who cares about her. But afraid?" Another giggle. "What could I possibly be afraid of?"

"Me."

It was a simple, one-syllable word. If he'd known it would put tears in her eyes and make her tremble from head to toe, he never would have uttered it. Three long strides put him in front of her, and, gathering her close, Josh whispered into her hair. "Dinah, oh, Dinah, Dinah, Dinah. It just breaks my heart to know you're afraid of me." He held her at arm's length, searching her face. "Why? What have I done to make you—"

"I'm not afraid of *you*; it's—it's—"

She looked toward the horizon again, and, with every blink, a fresh, silvery tear trickled down her cheek. Josh caught one with the pad of his thumb. "If not me, then what?" Or, more accurately, whom?

One sigh, deep and shuddering, escaped her lungs as she wiped her eyes with her knuckles. "Myself, mostly."

Despair emanated from her pretty face, along with hopelessness and regret and a muddle of other things Josh couldn't put a name to. He hated seeing her so unhappy and prayed that the good Lord would put the right words into his mouth, give him the wisdom to articulate them in a way that would ease her misery. "I can name a thousand things in this old world you might be afraid of, but a little slip of a thing like you?" He forced a chuckle. "Hardly something to fear!"

Her chin was practically touching her chest when she said, "You're only trying to help, and I appreciate that. More than you know. But—you don't know me."

"I want to," he insisted. "I want to know everything about you."

She put her back to him and hugged herself again. "Please, no, Josh. I—I couldn't bear that."

Now didn't seem like the right time to admit that he already knew who she was and what she'd been accused of doing—and that it didn't matter a whit to him, because he didn't believe a word of it. *All in good time*, he told himself. *All in good time.*

Josh would settle for the next best thing. At least, for now. Embracing her from behind, he rested his chin on her head and hoped with all his might that everything he'd come to feel for her would seep from his being into hers.

That would simply have to do—for now.

*T*here," Kate said, fluffing Esther's pillow. "Is that any better?"

The woman's eyes drooped sleepily, but she managed a crooked smile.

"And how would you like a little more tea before I turn down your lamp for the night?"

Esther held up one hand. "No. You...did...enough." Her smile widened a tad. "You rest...too?"

"Yes, ma'am, I'm going to rest now, too." Though "rest" was hardly the word. Since the night of the apoplectic attack, Kate had been sleeping in Esther's room on a cot Josh had brought in from the bunkhouse. Every sound that broke the silence had her wide awake, and she'd spent far more time checking on her patient than she had sleeping. Eva Neville, Susan, Sarah, and even Lucinda had offered to take her place, but Esther's imploring expression was all it took to keep her here almost round the clock.

And she wouldn't have had it any other way.

Bending down, she folded the hem of a hand-embroidered sheet over the colorful quilt on Esther's bed. "Are you warm enough? I can fetch the quilt from my cot and—"

The older woman shook her head and grabbed Kate's hand. "No, but...you can fetch Josh...."

"Certainly," she said, pressing a kiss to Esther's forehead. "I believe I heard him in the parlor, talking with Daniel and Micah and Paul." She headed for the door, then turned around with a smile. "Say, would you like me to have all of them come up?"

"Just Josh...th-this time."

As Kate was about to close the door behind her, Esther added, "Y-you...will you come...back...w-with him?"

"Of course," she assured her.

In the hall, Kate pressed her forehead against the closed bedroom door. If only she were smarter, wiser, more thoughtful, maybe she could anticipate some of the woman's needs and spare her the ordeal of trying to verbalize everything.

"I didn't realize Miss Taylor was here—"

"Josh!" Kate said, a little louder than intended. "You startled me—again!"

He grinned. "Sorry."

"Every time you sneak up on me that way, I'm more and more convinced I ought to put a bell around your neck."

Extending his arms in halfhearted supplication, he shrugged.

"Who's Miss Taylor?"

"Schoolmarm. The way you were standing there just now reminded me of the countless hours she made me stand against the wall when I was a boy."

"Goodness! She must have been a heartless old hag, because I can't imagine Joshua Neville doing anything to deserve such punishment."

"As much as I appreciate your confidence, I have to admit that Miss Taylor was a sweet-tempered young thing. I earned every minute I spent standing with my nose to the wall in that schoolhouse. Fact is, I earned about ten times more than I got."

"Oh, the questions *that* confession arouses!" Kate exclaimed with a smile. "But I'll have to save them for later." With one hand on the doorknob, she said, "I was just on my way downstairs."

"Why?"

"Because your grandmother sent me to find you."

His grin vanished, and in its place came a troubled expression. "What's wrong? She's not worse, is she? Because—"

"Shhh," Kate said, pressing a finger to her lips. "She's awake, and you know better than I do that she can hear through walls and floors and doors! Relax—she's no better, but she's no worse, either."

"Then why does she want to talk to me? Why not Pa or Ma, or one of the girls, or—"

"C-come..." Esther called through the door, "and...I'll t-tell you!"

Josh's gaze slid from the closed door to Kate's face. "Told you she could hear you," she whispered before pushing the door open. "Look what I found in the hall," she announced as she entered the room, trailed by Josh.

"Y-young w-whelp," Esther said, a slanted grin brightening half of her face. Her right hand gave the mattress three clumsy thumps. "S-sit, b-boy."

As Josh balanced on the edge of the bed, Kate moved toward the door to give them some time alone, but Esther's growling "Stay!" stopped her. She perched on the bed across from Josh and fussed with the bow at the collar of her dress.

"So, tell me, Mee-Maw, how are you today?" Josh asked.

Esther frowned. "O-o-old," she mumbled. "Weak...as a newborn kitten."

She signaled them both to come closer, so they leaned in. "T-tell...tell her."

With a baffled expression, Josh sat up straighter. "Tell her...?"

Esther pointed at Kate. "Don't...be stubborn!" With eyes narrowed, she tried to sit up. "You...know what. So, t-tell her!"

"Now, now," Kate said, a gentle hand guiding the woman to her pillows again, "please lie back and relax, Esther. You know what Dr. Lane said about getting riled—"

"What?" Josh interrupted her. "What did Lane say? And why was she riled up in the first place?"

Kate closed her eyes and hung her head. If she hadn't been such a clumsy little idiot, she wouldn't have twisted her ankle. And if she hadn't twisted her ankle, she wouldn't have been forced to follow him here to heal. She'd be in Mexico now instead of trying to figure out how to keep grandmother *and* grandson calm in the midst of a family tragedy. "The other evening," she began, straightening covers that didn't need straightening, "when the doctor tried to explain about apoplexy, well, let's just say Esther's reaction was...noisy." She shared a grin with her patient. "And that's when Dr. Lane emphasized how important it is to stay calm. Isn't that right, Esther?"

Esther loosed a harrumph and shook her head.

"What? *What* did he tell her?"

Josh had been right there at the foot of her bed, same as the rest of the Nevilles, when the doctor had delivered his prognosis. He'd heard the list of symptoms and what they meant, hadn't he? Well, that didn't matter now. She could fill him in on the details later. Right now, Kate needed to find a way to humor him, and carefully. Because, if Josh got upset, Esther would get upset, and he'd never forgive himself if his overwrought behavior played even a small part in the possible outcome.

Kate aimed a warning finger at Esther, then said, "He simply made it clear that the less stress she experiences, the sooner we could see some improvement." Kate gave Esther's hand a gentle squeeze. "Isn't that right, Mrs. I-Don't-Like-Lying-Around?"

The woman's chuckle sounded more like a snarl, but it was music to Kate's ears.

"I am…calm." To Josh, she said, "N-now…*tell* her."

Pressing the fingers of his grandmother's other hand between his own, Josh spoke in a voice that was scarcely above a whisper. "Mee-Maw, I honestly don't have a clue what you're talking about. Can you give me a hint what you want me to tell her—without getting yourself worked up about it?"

"W-worked up," Esther scoffed, grinning again. She looked at Kate. "M-my big…strong…cowboy…." She gave another chuckle, then puffed out a sigh, and her grin evaporated. Closing her eyes, she slowly rolled her head left, right, then left again. "Life…too short." Fixing her blue-eyed gaze on Josh, she puckered her brow. "Stop…wasting…time. *Tell* her!"

Kate tried to read Josh's face but found it impossible in the semidarkness of Esther's room. Had he talked with her about personal, private things, like matters of the heart, and his feelings for her?

Dare she hope?

Then, at the thought, she covered her face with her hands. Every day that passed put Frank a day closer to destroying them. And she knew that as surely as she knew her name was not Dinah Theodore.

And yet she stayed.

Earlier that day, Josh had asked her what she was afraid of, and she'd answered truthfully. Kate *was* afraid of herself—and the devastation that seemed destined to shadow her.

This madness needed to stop.

Her selfishness had to end.

The sooner, the better.

Kate got to her feet and folded both arms over her chest. "I'm going down to the kitchen to fix myself a cup of tea. Would you like one, Esther?"

When the woman started to protest, Kate stopped her. "You've been up and about far too much today, and I, for one, don't want to answer to Dr. Lane if you have a relapse." She pointed at the door and gestured for Josh to follow her. "So, shall I bring you some tea?"

Glowering, Esther blurted out, "No!" With a wave of one hand, she dismissed them both. "F-fine, then. Go," she said, and promptly closed her eyes.

Kate pulled the door shut behind them and hurried toward the staircase, Josh close on her heels.

"Would you mind making me a cup of tea while you're at it?" she heard him say.

She started down the steps. "You don't even like tea."

"Is that so?"

"I've never seen you drink it. Never heard you ask for a cup, as a matter of fact." Their dialogue was ridiculous, almost laughable, but it was better than the alternative!

"Did you ever stop to think maybe that's the problem?" he said when they reached the landing.

"What's the problem?"

"You don't see me drinking the stuff because nobody has ever bothered to fix me a—"

"Do you really expect me to believe that a man who can move thousands of cows from Texas to Kansas can't brew himself a cup of tea? Please." With that, she dashed down the remaining stairs and half ran down the hall.

In the kitchen, she stood at the cupboard and reached up for two cups hanging from hooks beneath a high shelf.

Josh had stopped in the doorway, standing with one booted foot crossed over the other. "Never said I *couldn't*. I only pointed out that it's never offered to me."

"And why would anyone offer you tea, since you're of the opinion that the beverage is strictly for old women and sick people?" She cut him a quick glance and, seeing that her remark had made its intended result, resisted the impulse to grin. Oh, how she loved that slanting smile and those twinkling, blue eyes!

Kate busied herself preparing the tea, thinking that what she really needed at that moment was a good, solid reason *not* to like Josh. But, try as she might, she couldn't think of one negative aspect of his character or his personality. She would compile a list of reasons to dislike Josh Neville later, when sleep eluded her, as she knew it would. But something told her it would be a very short list, indeed.

She grabbed a spoon and picked up Esther's cup. "I'm almost certain I can talk her into swallowing just a few more drops before she goes to sleep. Dr. Lane said it's important not to let her get dehydrated, so…." Josh said nothing more, so she shrugged and squeezed past him, then walked briskly down the hall and climbed the stairs.

Esther didn't look nearly as surprised to see her as Josh had when she'd made her hasty getaway. "Thought you might have changed your mind about that tea," Kate said, setting the cup and saucer on the night table. She helped Esther sit up. "If only I knew how to pray...."

"W-why?"

Kate forced a cheeriness into her voice. "Because then I'd ask God to just—to just fix you right up, good as new, that's why!"

"Ask, an'...ask, an' ye shall...."

She put a stop to the woman's struggling by saying, "'Ask, and ye shall receive.' Yes, I've heard that one many times." She scooped a spoonful of tea and held it to Esther's lips. "But that's yet another verse intended for good Christian folk, not someone like me."

Even as the words tumbled from her lips, Kate wondered what had possessed her to say such a thing. What was poor, sick Esther to think, except that her history had either been positively wicked, or that she craved attention? "I haven't attended church since I was a very little girl, you see," she quickly inserted, "so my knowledge of the Bible and such things is—well, it's virtually nonexistent, that's what." She paused, then added, "The good Lord has better things to do than listen to the prayers of a woman like me!"

Good grief, Kate, will you just hush already!

Esther held up a hand to stop the next spoonful of tea. "You are...good, good girl...."

Oh, Esther, she wanted to say, *if only that were true.* "Come now," she said instead. "The tea isn't nearly as tasty when it's lukewarm. Besides, you know what Dr. Lane said about staying hydrated—"

"God l-loves you. He *will* hear...your...p-prayers!"

Kate put the teacup on the bedside table, rested the spoon on the saucer, and folded both hands in her lap. "I hate to admit it, Esther, but, the truth is, I don't know how to pray."

Esther harrumphed.

"I wouldn't even know where to begin reciting beautiful, poetic prayers like Matthew does before meals."

The woman waved away her remark. "Prayer is...talk. Just *talk*...to Him."

Oh, but praying was so much more than that! Kate knew this as fact because she'd *talked* to God a thousand times as a little girl—when her father was beating her mama bloody, when her stepfather picked up where her father had left off, and when the horrible man lit into her and then made arrangements to trade her like a sack of flour to pay off his gambling debts. After her mama took her own life, she had talked to Him. *Show me the way,* she had pleaded, *so I won't get lost, like Mama did....*

But He had chosen not to answer, and the only thing she'd been able to draw from that was that she hadn't been worthy of an answer.

"I have...heard you," Esther managed to say. "Y-you pray...often!"

If God truly loves His dear child, Esther, Kate thought, *He'll send an angel to earth to flog me, right this instant, for putting the poor woman in the position of trying to comfort me, when it should be the other way around!* Because what had she done in her miserable life to merit consolation from this good, long-suffering woman?

Nothing.

She crossed the room, intending to close the curtains, and paused near the hand-hewn cradle near the windows. "This cradle is just lovely, Esther. Has it been in your family long?"

"Ezz-ra...."

"Your husband made it? I might have known." Smiling, Kate knelt, gave the cradle a gentle push, and watched it rock slowly back and forth. If she closed her eyes, she could picture a tiny infant nestled inside, amid a tangle of soft blankets. She ran one hand over the well-worn wood, tracing the big, bold letter N carved into the headboard.

A peaceful smile settled upon Esther's face, and she nodded.

The cradle had likely embraced all four of her boys, each of their children, and little Willie, too, from the looks of it, and yet, it was probably just as sturdy now as when Ezra had lovingly crafted it all those years ago. When it dawned on her that Josh had likely slept in this cradle, too, Kate met his grandmother's eyes. "It's so beautiful. So precious and priceless." Oh, to lay a child of her own in this lovely bed one day, a baby born to her and Josh....

The thought put her on her feet so quickly, she nearly lost her balance. *Foolish little ninny!* she scolded herself. *Dreams like that are for other young women, not those who stupidly link themselves to killers and robbers and—*

"S-someday," Esther rasped. "You will...you will see...."

Thankfully, the poor dear drifted into peaceful slumber, sparing Kate the hard task of explaining the tears of regret and remorse that began rolling hot and fast down her cheeks.

*O*n his way to town, Josh stopped by the small parcel of land where his wife and infant twins were buried. Griffen, true to his word, had constructed a crude fence around the plot, and as he dismounted, Josh asked God to forgive him for the impatient, unfriendly thoughts he'd harbored about his neighbor.

Holding Callie's reins in one hand, his Stetson in the other, he read the simple inscription carved into the lone headstone. There should have been three names listed, not one. "Why'd you have to be so confounded stubborn, Sadie?" he grumbled.

SADIE NEVILLE
BELOVED WIFE AND MOTHER
JULY 29, 1864–MAY 5, 1885

He had wanted to continue the Neville tradition of choosing baby names from the Bible, but Sadie had refused to discuss it. "Let's wait until they're born," she'd insisted, "so we can pick names that fit their personalities." Thinking he had months to change her mind, Josh hadn't pressed her to reconsider.

However, she'd gone into labor far earlier than expected, and, after hours of struggling, she'd barely found the strength to deliver her lecture about Josh welcoming love if it ever found him again. Then, she'd lapsed into unconsciousness and had never come to, leaving him to make the difficult decision alone regarding the inscription.

Even the smallest coffin available had looked a hundred times too large for his tiny baby boys, and he hadn't been able to bear separating them, so he'd instructed the undertaker to tuck one baby under each of Sadie's arms.

The wind whispered through the grass and mingled with the peaceful lowing of cattle. He hadn't known what lesson God was trying to teach by making him a widower at the age of twenty-four, and, three years later, he still hadn't figured it out. "Don't rightly know why I'm here," he said, his hat over his heart. But that wasn't the whole truth, and Josh knew it. He'd come to say good-bye, once and for all.

As the pallbearers had lowered the casket into the earth, he'd walked away, and, even now, if he closed his eyes, Josh could still hear the dry, Texas dirt being dumped onto the coffin.

"Did you name our boys when you arrived in paradise?" he whispered. Maybe she would have called them Gabriel and Michael, since she'd always claimed each star in the sky represented an angel in heaven.

But the stone stood cold and silent against the blue sky, so he put on his hat and climbed into the saddle. "Well," he drawled, "I suppose I'll have to be satisfied, knowing the three of you are with God."

He gave the marker and the fence and the little plot one last glance, then urged Callie forward and headed west.

For the first quarter mile, he pulled gently on the reins. "What's your hurry?" he muttered to the mare. But even as he asked, Josh knew the answer. The only running Callie had done in the past week had been from the barn to the corral, then in figure eights and circles inside the enclosure. As much as she liked frolicking with the other saddle horses, Callie had been born to run, had lived her first years wild and free. She could clear a six-foot fence without even trying, so, near as he could figure, she stayed at the Lazy N because she liked the work—and her master.

Callie could pick him out of a crowd of cowboys, even when he tied her clear at one end of town while he did his business at the other. There was nothing particularly special about that, since most horses that received proper care knew their owners by sight and scent. But Callie? Josh grinned, picturing that way she had of prancing, bobbing her head, and whinnying until he waved or whistled to acknowledge her. If he had a nickel for every time he heard "If I didn't know better, I'd say that filly has a crush on you, Neville," Josh would have a pocketful of them. He understood that the good-natured taunt was rooted in respect and admiration, for the relationship between horse and cowboy was an important one—one that could mean the difference between life and death for rider and pony. If Dan had been on his own horse instead of the first one picked from the pony line the day those rustlers had showed up, he might not have ended up in the middle of a stampede.

Callie could sense his moods and knew what he needed from her, sometimes even before he identified it himself. She loved the feel of the wind in her mane almost as much as he enjoyed watching the earth speed by under her belly and disappear behind them. Clearly, Callie would have been happier with a trot this day, but earlier, when he'd measured her girth, he was more certain than ever that she was carrying twins. "Plenty of time to gallop later," he said, patting her shoulder, "after you've weaned your young'uns." She wouldn't like it, and neither would he, but until then, ambling would have to do.

If he'd chosen another horse today, he could have made it to town and back in half the time. But Callie needed the exercise, and he needed to keep a close eye on her. If he didn't run into the mayor and the sheriff and the rest of the men who enjoyed jawing on the grocer's steps, he might get home in time for supper. Plenty of time for a bite to eat and a visit with Mee-Maw. And, maybe, if the good Lord saw fit to answer his prayers, a few minutes with Dinah before turning in for the night.

"How goes it, Neville?"

He looked toward the voice and groaned inwardly. *Griffen.* "It goes."

Josh dismounted and tethered Callie. He'd never been the envious type, but it was difficult to swallow the lump of resentment forming in his throat. He reminded himself that it wasn't Griffen's fault that anthrax had necessitated the sale that had brought him to Eagle Pass. In time and with prayer, he expected the sting of bitterness to ease. So far, unfortunately, it had not.

"And what brings you to town today, neighbor?"

If it had been any other man, Josh might not have noticed. But this was the fellow who'd gobbled up those Lazy N acres like a greedy railroad man. He wore black trousers and a blue shirt—just like Josh's. He'd bought himself a Stetson, too—a duplicate of Josh's—and now stood, adjusting the knot of the black neckerchief at his throat.

Lots of time and lots of prayer, he thought, doing his best to match Griffen's grin, tooth for tooth. "I'm here to fetch the mail. You?"

"The buyer of my printing business back in Boston finally came through with the payment." He laughed. "Brockman, the builder, will be glad to hear it. I'm sure he thinks he's working for a deadbeat, because I've been promising for weeks to pay for labor and materials."

Griffen was a lot of things, but deadbeat wasn't among them. He'd paid for those acres sight unseen and no questions asked, other than price. "Should've sent him to me. I would have set him straight," Josh said.

"That's high praise, coming from you." Griffen frowned. "Hasn't been easy, earning folks' respect. I'm not just a newcomer to Texas, you know, but a newcomer to this country." He tipped his hat. "So I am humbled, and I thank you."

Josh felt the heat of a blush in his cheeks but couldn't say if shame or guilt had brought it on. He hadn't tried to make conversations with Griffen difficult. But then, he hadn't exactly made them easy, either. "Aw, now, no need to get all sappy and sentimental on me." He chuckled. "Just tellin' it like it is, that's all." He took a step back, adjusting his hat. "Guess I'd best be moving if I hope to be home before dark."

Griffen stared hard at Callie's belly. "She's got herself quite a load there. Hope she hasn't got into any meadow saffron or moldy hay—"

"Nah. She's pregnant."

As he met Josh's eyes, Griffen's frown deepened. "I'm no rancher yet, but I've studied on it some." He stroked Callie's belly. "Not the right season for her to be so far along, is it?"

Josh had to hand it to the man, for it appeared he really *had* studied on it. "No, it isn't. And I fear the reason she looks like she does is that she's carrying twins."

His eyes wide with shock and dread, Griffen said, "Not a common thing, ya?"

"Right." Less common? Twins born alive. Rarer still—keeping them alive to become yearlings.

"She's a good horse."

Josh nodded.

"I can see the bond between you."

Another nod.

"I will pray."

And with that, Griffen walked away, his head down and his hands in his pockets, looking every bit as forlorn as Josh felt.

Just then, a stranger approached. "You one of the Nevilles from the Lazy N Ranch?"

Josh gave the man a quick appraisal. Not a working man, as evidenced by his domed hat, short-breasted suit coat, and polished boots.

"Name's Gardiner. Collin Gardiner. I work for the *Philadelphia Inquirer*. I understand your ranch had an outbreak of anthrax."

Josh felt every muscle tense. "Where'd you hear that?"

"My brother-in-law is Thomas Schaeffer, of San Antonio."

With his eyes narrowed, Josh pictured the uppity, bulbous-nosed banker, who'd almost smoked him like a hothouse ham in that stuffy little office of his rather than risk sending their papers flying "hither and yon."

From his pocket, the man pulled out a small writing tablet and a pencil stub. "So, it's true, then?"

If Josh admitted the truth, word would spread like wildfire, making the healthy Lazy N cattle worthless. "Always has amazed me how ignorant city folk can be," he said slowly.

Gardiner's beady eyes narrowed as the bushy brows above them inched closer together. "Ignorant! Why, I'll have you know I attended Harvard!"

"You don't say." If he hoped to talk the man out of writing his anthrax story, Josh realized he'd better try a different approach. "This sham anthrax story is just a cover, right? You're really here to write about the outlaw gang that's holed up in the area."

Gardiner's eyes flashed like black diamonds. "Outlaw gang? Which one?"

He'd heard that people back East were hungry for stories about showdowns and train robberies, but Josh had never witnessed proof of it before. He did his best to hide his amusement. And his disrespect. "Frank Michaels, if the rumor mill is right. But I'm sure the sheriff or his deputy could set the record straight and give you all the information you need."

"Just got into town on the morning train," the reporter said. "Got me a room at the hotel and haven't even unpacked yet. Mind telling me which way to the sheriff's office?"

Josh tilted his head toward the courthouse. "You write novels and stories, too, or just newspaper articles?"

Smiling, Gardiner revealed two gold teeth, one up top, the other in the center of his lower jaw. "Matter of fact, I sent one off just before boarding the train."

"I'm sure the missus will let you know if a publisher shows interest."

The statement wiped away Gardiner's grin as quickly as a schoolmarm erasing the alphabet from her blackboard. "Never married," he said. "Probably never will. Nothin' against women, mind you, except they talk too much and work too little."

Josh pretended the joke was funny. "I hear ya."

The man stared toward the courthouse. "If I could get an interview with a real, live outlaw," he said, more to himself than to Josh. His eyes glassed over as he tucked the tablet and pencil back into his pocket.

"How long will you be in Eagle Pass?" Josh asked.

"Long as it takes to get a good story." Walking backwards down the street, he added, "Pleasure to make your acquaintance, Neville."

"Believe me, the pleasure's all mine." But Gardiner hadn't even made it halfway to the sheriff's office when Josh began to worry what his family would do if the reporter didn't find a better story than anthrax to write about. He could almost hear Mee-Maw saying, "Lay it at the foot of the cross." So, he shrugged and glanced skyward. "I reckon it's in Your hands, Lord."

He'd barely uttered the sentence when Jame Windel rode up. "You hear about the widow woman down in Laredo what's sellin' off her man's herd, one cow at a time?"

Chuckling, Josh doffed his hat and used it to shade his eyes from the bright sun. Looking up at the man in the saddle, he said, "Jame, you take longer getting to the point of a joke than any man I can name."

"Ain't no joke!" Windel said. "Heard about it from that infuriatin' reporter who got off the train this mornin'."

Josh didn't ask how the men had happened upon the topic of cattle, for fear it might reawaken Gardiner's interest in anthrax, but he *was* interested in the rest of the story. "Any bulls for sale?"

"I'll say!" Windel dismounted and gave Callie a cursory glance. "Way the feller told it, this woman's got two stud bulls on the market."

"You fixin' to buy one?"

He combed his fingers through his shaggy beard. "Wish I could, but I can't spare the cash right now. Mable's all crippled up with the arthritis, and it's costin' me every spare penny for ointments and salves to ease her pain."

So that's why Windel and his wife hadn't attended the annual Neville gathering. "Sorry to hear it, Jame."

"Your mare get into some yeasty hay?"

Josh groaned. It should have been easier reciting the same facts he'd just delivered to Griffen, but it wasn't. Maybe he ought to just paint a sign to hold up for everybody to read when they are about to ask about Callie's swollen belly.

"Well, you need any help with her, should she go breach on you, give a holler. I've one-armed many a foal birth in my day."

He'd be hard-pressed to name a rancher who hadn't aided a horse or cow in the same way. But "Give Mable my best" is what he said before hustling to the sheriff's office to pick Gardiner's brain.

Fifteen minutes later, armed with the name of the widow and her Laredo ranch, Josh sent her a telegram, picked up his mail, and headed home. There'd be a family meeting to discuss the cost of purchasing the bull, and if he could talk the other Neville men into it, he would suggest that they offer the widow seven hundred dollars and let him make the trip to cut the deal. He sure could use the time it'd take to get there and back to puzzle out what he should do about "Dinah Theodore"—if she were still there when he returned.

I't's a good deal, I tell you."

Matthew Neville rested his chin atop steepled hands. "I'm not quibbling about the bull's value, son. It's the price that concerns me." He looked to his younger brothers for support.

Mark, perched on one corner of the big mahogany desk, spoke up first. "I'm of the same mind as your boy. We need insurance, and a strong line of Angus will give it to us."

John nodded. "And going in there blind, Josh has to be prepared to top all offers."

Then it was Luke's turn. "We could get lucky. Maybe Josh will get there and discover the top offer is just a couple hundred dollars."

"But we want to be fair," Dan pointed out. "Wouldn't do to cheat a widow."

Micah started to pace. "Dan's right," he said. "The lady has a right to get what the stud is worth. But Uncle Matthew is right, too—seven hundred dollars is a lot of money."

"Not if he's a quality animal," Paul put in.

"A lot to gamble for an *if*," said Matthew.

Josh sat back and surveyed the seven other men gathered in his father's study, each of them smart, tough, and capable to a fault, whether born into the second generation of Nevilles or the third. Yet not one could make a decision without the approval of the rest. "I'll find a way to repay y'all, if this beast doesn't earn his keep," he offered. "You've got my word."

"And deprive us of taking it out of your hide?" Dan joked.

A quiet ripple of laughter rolled around the room, and then Matthew cleared his throat, effectively silencing it. "There's work to be done around here," he reminded them, "so let's nail down a decision, boys, and get to supper. I'm starved."

It was times like this when Josh wished he'd given in to the urge to strike out on his own after Sadie's death, because then he wouldn't need the consent of seven other strong-minded men before making important decisions. "I wasn't fooling earlier," he said. "I say, let's do this thing, and if it turns out poorly, I'll take the hit."

"You'll do no such thing," Uncle Luke growled.

"What affects one of us..." Uncle John started.

"...affects us all," Uncle Mark finished for him.

In the ensuing silence, Josh reminded himself that the real decision—go or stay, buy or not—was God's.

"So, when will you leave, son?"

He sat up straighter at his father's inquiry. "First light, I reckon."

"Take my wagon," Dan offered. "It's built for hauling livestock, plus it's brand-new, so you won't have to fret about losing a wheel on the way home."

That's all we need, Josh thought as Uncle Mark volunteered his team—*to lose a seven-hundred-dollar bull in a freak wagon accident.*

But they'd finally come to a decision, and for that, he sent a silent prayer of thanks heavenward.

He made a point of visiting his grandmother before turning in that night, and she insisted that he pull a chair up close to her bedside. It broke his heart to watch her struggle with every word, and he prayed for the ability to comprehend what she was trying to communicate before she had to wear herself out with repetitions.

"Watch for s-snakes," she said. "And d-drive s-slow, you hear, es-espesh…coming home."

She wanted to know which route he'd take and how long he thought he would be gone and also made him promise to come see her the minute he returned.

Josh secured a promise from her, too. "I know how anxious you are to get back to doing things the way you did them before, but promise me you'll take it easy, all right?" When she answered with a jerky nod, he kissed her good night. And because Callie had worked hard, taking him to Eagle Pass and back, he decided to walk back to his place.

Looking down as he sauntered along the well-worn path, he didn't see Dinah step out of the shadows, and he nearly leaped out of his boots when she said, "I wish I could ride to Laredo with you, Josh."

He masked his surprise with a hearty chuckle. "You must be taking walk-like-a-cat lessons from Daniel."

But she ignored the joke. "It's a long, dangerous ride, and even if you don't count bandits and outlaws, I can think of a hundred reasons why it's just plain crazy for you to make this trip alone."

Her skin glowed like alabaster in the light of the moon, making him want to reach out and touch her, just to remind himself how warm and soft it was. "I'll be fine," he said, flattered by her concern.

"Oh, and now I suppose you're going to tell me that you've made the trip a thousand times and never encountered so much as a big ol' spider along the way."

He chuckled. "Well, not a thousand times, but...."

She propped her fists on her curvy hips. "Very funny. But, rest assured, *this* is no joke: if Esther didn't need me, I'd ride with you, no matter what you said. No doubt about it."

Josh believed every word, and if his grandmother hadn't needed her, he wouldn't have fought her on it. "I won't be gone all that long."

Her eyes glittered like the stars in the sky as she looked up at him. "How long?"

"A week, give or take a day."

A certain sadness replaced her former spunky expression. "Why can't Dan or Micah or Paul go with you? They don't have wives or children depending on them."

"Their pas and mine depend on them, though."

Dinah exhaled a frustrated groan. "Well, it just doesn't seem right!"

He took a step closer. "What doesn't?"

"That you're obliged to bear the whole burden of risk all by yourself, when the results will benefit everyone at the Lazy N."

Not even Sadie had shown this sort of protectiveness toward him, and it touched him deeply. "I'm not obliged."

When she looked away, it seemed as though a cloud had slid in front of the moon, dimming the light in his world. He lifted her chin on a curved forefinger. "This whole thing was my idea."

"And why doesn't that surprise me, Mr. I-Must-Save-the-Whole-World-All-by-Myself?"

With one hand on either side of her face, he held her gaze. "I don't want to save the whole world," he whispered. "Only the part with you in it."

Her mouth formed an O, as if she had something to say, something to admit. But, as quick as a blink, she bit her lower lip. "I probably won't be there to see you off in the morning," she said, stepping away from him. "So, I want you to know, I'll be...I'll pray for your safe return, that's what."

And with that, Dinah lifted her skirts and raced back toward the house. If the screen door hadn't banged shut behind her, who knows how long he might have stood on the walk, staring into space, like an empty-headed scarecrow?

It took him an unusually long time to fall asleep because he couldn't get that look out of his mind. Couldn't figure out what it was she'd stopped herself from saying, either. The next morning, Josh woke up feeling groggy and grumpy, and not even Lucinda's hearty breakfast could lift his spirits. Not the best way to start a grueling trip.

The Neville men were there to see him off, just as they'd promised. And, just as she'd promised, Dinah was not, a fact that disappointed him far more than it should have, far more than he cared to admit.

As the others headed out to perform their chores, Matthew hung back. With one hand resting on Josh's shoulder, he said, "I'm trusting you to take care of things, son, you hear?"

Josh knew by the loving look on his father's face that the advice was more than just an exhortation to protect the emergency funds taken from the safe earlier that morning. The last time Matthew had traveled the same road, he'd encountered bandits, who had left him penniless and horseless, forcing him to make a long, solitary walk home. Josh was well aware that the farther south he traveled, the more likely he was to encounter predators of the four-legged variety—and the no-legged variety, as well. "I've got my Winchester," he assured his father.

"Well, let's just pray you won't have cause to use it."

The men exchanged a clumsy hug, and as Josh prepared to climb onto the wagon seat, his mother came running across the yard. "Josh, wait—I made you some fried chicken and packed a few pieces of fruit," she said, thrusting a sack into his gloved hands. "Do you have plenty of water for the horses?"

"Yes'm," he said. How like her to pretend that her concern was for the animals instead of her only son. It reminded him that not all women were cut out for ranch life—and that fewer still made good ranchers' wives. "Thanks for the grub." He hugged her tight. "And I love you, too."

Tears glistened in her eyes when she said, "God go with you, son."

Josh hoisted himself into the wagon. "Maybe you can roast a fat hen to welcome me home," he suggested. Then, with a wink, he urged the horses forward.

He'd gone only a few yards when he saw Daniel limping across the lawn. He knew it was a rugged, possibly dangerous, trip, but he hoped the rest of his cousins wouldn't show up, one by one, to wish him well. At this rate, he'd never get on the road!

"Hold up, Josh! I'm going with you."

"But, Dan, I thought you—"

"I have nothing to do that can't wait a week. Now, slide over and make room for me up there. With this bum leg, once I commit myself, I could very well land in your lap. And wouldn't that be a nice mental picture for your sweet mama to hold on to while we're gone!"

Chuckling, Josh did as instructed. As the wagon rolled forward, Dan called over his shoulder, "Don't you worry, Aunt Eva—I'll take good care of him!"

It would be good having Dan's company. Not only was his cousin a better shot, but his constant joke-telling would keep his mind off Dinah and the sad-eyed look she'd left him with.

Was that her way of letting him know she wouldn't be at the Lazy N when he got back?

With a bit of luck, Dan would distract him from that dreary notion, too.

32

*D*uring the first few days after the apoplexy attack, Esther had fought slumber the way a toddler fights naptime. It seemed to Kate that the poor woman feared falling asleep might mean she'd never wake up again. But, as the days passed, Josh's grandmother spent more time asleep than awake—which became a source of worry and concern for her nurse.

This morning was worse than most.

Kate tried keeping Esther awake by chattering on and on about how Lucinda's broth was filled with vital nutrients and ingredients, but the woman only moaned, shook her head, and waved the spoon away.

"If you don't eat something, I'll have no choice but to call your son and his wife," Kate warned her gently. "Maybe *they'll* be able to talk some sense into you!"

The threat inspired a little pout—and a little cooperation. But, after just a few spoonfuls, Esther shooed her away again.

"Half a teacup of weak broth isn't enough to sustain you, Esther Neville. You have to eat more than that, or you won't be strong enough to welcome Josh back from Laredo."

"L-Laredo?"

Kate reminded her that Josh was headed south to buy a stud bull, one that they hoped would revitalize the herd. But her mind wasn't on the conversation. Rather, Kate recalled the discussion she'd overheard from the pantry last evening, when Josh had told Lucinda that, when he'd said good night to his grandmother, she'd looked weaker and paler than usual. "Maybe you can talk her into eating something other than clear broth?"

During supper, the men had discussed the potential dangers Josh would face along the way, each sharing suggestions for preventing those he could avoid and methods for handling those he couldn't. Their conversation had made it blatantly clear that, to remain safe, Josh first had to remain alert. And how could he do that if his head was filled with worries about his grandmother?

Her intent, when Kate had gone looking for him, had been to promise that she'd remain at Esther's side every minute until he came home again. If she'd known he would look at her so tenderly, that he'd touch her with such gentleness, she would have written her reassuring words in a note to be delivered by George. Because, now, every time she closed her eyes, she'd picture the confused, wounded stare inspired by her hasty departure.

She hadn't meant to run off like a spoiled, frightened child, but in those warm and wonderful moments, she'd come dangerously close to confessing everything to Josh, right there on the path. In a blinding flash of clarity, she'd realized that blurting out the truth could do more than just end their warm and wonderful interlude. It could distract him out there on the trail. And if, God forbid, something happened to him because of it, she'd never forgive herself.

She'd made a lot of mistakes in her life, but one of the biggest had been accepting his kindness. From the moment she'd stumbled upon Josh's camp, she had tainted his life, just as surely as Frank had tainted hers.

When he was home, safe and sound, Kate would reveal the truth. And, just as soon as Esther was better.... *Oh, who are you kidding?* As much as it pained her to admit it to herself, Esther wouldn't get better. The best Kate could hope for was to keep the poor dear as comfortable as possible until the end came. And something told her that would be soon— very soon—if she couldn't talk Esther into staying awake long enough to eat and exercise her rapidly deteriorating muscles.

"Esther," she said, settling onto the edge of her bed, "let's sit you up a little, all right?" Sliding an arm behind her back, Kate tried to prop her up against the headboard, but the poor old woman was as limp as a rag doll.

"Not to worry," she announced, settling Esther back onto the pillows. "I know how to remedy this!" Kate darted to her makeshift bed against the wall and grabbed her pillow, then flung open the wardrobe and gathered the extra pillows stored on a shelf inside. One by one, she positioned them beside her patient, under her arms, next to her hips. "There!" she said when at last Esther sat upright. "Maybe now you can stay awake long enough to eat something!"

Esther clamped her teeth together and squeezed her eyes shut, a silent but obvious refusal to cooperate. Kate began to pace at the foot of the bed, muttering to herself as she tried to come up with something—*anything*—that would rekindle Esther's desire to live. She knew the dear woman was tired and beyond discouraged by her own helplessness. And how many times during their many hours alone together had

Esther said she wanted to go to heaven, where she could see Jesus and reunite with Ezra?

Exasperated, Kate knelt beside the bed and held Esther's hand. "Now, you listen to me, Esther," she began. "You can't just give up this way, especially not while Josh is away on family business. It would break his heart if something happened to you while he was gone. Just think how disappointed he'd be to know you didn't fight this thing right to the end!"

The woman's left eyebrow rose ever so slightly. "D-don' tell him that...that I gave up."

Don't tell him! The notion put Kate on her feet so fast, she nearly overturned the bedside table. "How can I make you understand—"

"*You* don'...under...stand!"

On her knees again, she kissed Esther's bony knuckles. "What don't I understand? Oh, dear, sweet Esther, tell me, please, because I'll do anything to help you."

"Don'...wan' help."

For the first time since volunteering to care for the woman, Kate was angry with her. "Well, if you're bound and determined to give up, just like that, then I hope you'll help me figure out how I'm supposed to explain a thing like that to Josh!"

A single, perfectly pronounced and enunciated word sighed past her parched lips: "Tired."

"Of course, you're tired. But if you'll let me feed you something, I'm sure—"

"I wan'...to be with Ezz-ra." Tears shimmered in her eyes, and her lips trembled. "I m-miss him." She nodded slowly. "It's *time*."

Kate considered keeping the pressure on, but the agony in Esther's eyes silenced her. If she missed Josh this much after sharing such a short parcel of his life, how much more must Esther miss Ezra, when they'd been together for decades before his death?

"You get some sleep, dear Esther." Maybe she'd eat after a refreshing nap. Perhaps the nourishment would rejuvenate her love of life. And, if it didn't, Kate would seek the guidance of Josh's mother and father. Hopefully, they would talk some sense into the stubborn woman!

One by one, Kate carefully removed the pillows she'd positioned around Esther, leaving a few in place to keep her up in order to ease her ragged breathing. She tidied the covers and tiptoed from the room, and then, closing the door quietly behind her, pressed her forehead against the cool, plaster wall. It wasn't until she attempted to fold her hands in prayer that she realized how tightly she'd been clenching her fists.

She dropped to her knees outside Esther's room and bowed her head. "I'm not asking for myself, but for these good people and that good woman. Enlighten me, Lord. Help me find the words that will restore Esther's will to live."

Because it would break Josh's heart to learn she had joined Him in heaven while he was so far from home.

33

*T*heir first day on the trail, Josh and Dan talked about little else than the promising potential a fresh, new bloodline would bring to the Lazy N. The family had already earned a reputation for sturdy, weighty cows, but they couldn't take the chance that news of the anthrax outbreak hadn't spread east and north, where their regular buyers were. Folks feared the disease, and that alone threatened the ranch's solvency.

"Hard to believe something you can't see or smell could cause such mayhem," Dan said. "If I live to be a hundred, I don't think I'll ever forget how those poor animals looked, lying there."

The comment roused ugly images in Josh's mind, too, starting with the blood oozing from every possible orifice of the wide-eyed bovines to their struggle to breathe during their last agonizing moments. George had been the one to identify the problem; his father and grandfather had experienced the same thing in Mexico. Whether or not it was mere superstition, his advice to let the land go fallow indefinitely was not ignored by the Nevilles.

Dan peered through the scope of his rifle. "Seems a shame we can't use those acres for fifty years."

"Everything I've read indicates it should be even longer," Josh said glumly.

Laying the weapon across his knees, Dan shook his head. "Meaning our young'uns will inherit the problem along with the land."

"'Fraid so." *If either of us ever has young'uns.* But, even if neither of them did, there was Willie to consider, and the children Susan and Sarah and the other cousins might have in the future. "Makes a body wonder if we did all we could to kill it."

"Don't see how we could have done more," was Dan's somber reply.

Under George's tutelage, they'd worn damp neckerchiefs over their mouths and noses, and wrapped their horses' faces with wet rags, too, a feeble precaution they'd hoped would keep the germs from invading, as they'd set fire to the cow corpses, one by one, and let them burn where they lay. The odor had attracted predators from the air and the land, which had necessitated constant patrols to chase them off, lest they feast on the fire-roasted meat and perhaps spread the contaminant far and wide. "True enough, but the question keeps me up nights, all the same," Josh finally said.

Dan elbowed him playfully. "Something tells me there's more keeping you awake these days besides dead cows and empty acres."

Josh gave him a sideways glance, and before he could ask what in the world his cousin was yammering about, Dan said, "That pretty li'l gal you brought home, for starters."

He stared hard at the horizon, knowing full well that if he gave Dan the chance to read his expression, he could forget about denying his feelings for Dinah. "She was in trouble. I helped her out. End of story."

"So says you," Dan said, giving him another playful jab in the ribs.

Squinting, Josh used his chin as a pointer. "That a rattler I see out there?"

Dan attempted to follow Josh's gaze. "Where?"

"Sunning itself on that rock, yonder."

Dan squinted, too, then said, "Why, I do believe it is." Lifting the weapon, he zeroed in on his target. "Say 'Goodbye, cruel world,'" he whispered before squeezing the trigger. The bullet exploded from the barrel, then whistled through the air and embedded itself in the serpent's flesh. The diamondback spiraled upward and turned end over end before landing in the powdery dirt. "Well, sir, there's one less snakebite waiting to happen," Dan said, calmly returning the gun to his knees. "Now then, as I was saying, when are you planning to propose, if I may ask?"

Maybe if Josh played dumb, Dan would take the hint and change the subject. If he knew what was good for him, he'd come up with an answer that would satisfy his curious cousin—or prepare to hear the question a dozen times between now and their arrival in Laredo.

"Haven't prayed on it enough yet," he said truthfully.

"So, you've considered it, then." Dan paused for a quick breath, then exclaimed, "I knew it!"

Yes, Josh had considered it, pictured it, and prayed for it. But he wasn't foolish enough to admit any of that to Dan. "Hungry?"

"It'll be dark soon. We can eat when we bunk down for the night." He took a sip from his canteen and then held it out to Josh. "So, when do you suppose—"

"Tell me, Dan, when was the last time you remember me prying into *your* personal, private life?"

Dan pretended to count on his fingers, then chuckled. "Never. At least, not that I can recall, at the moment. Let me sleep on it and get back to you in the morning."

That would do, Josh thought, because soon they'd be far too busy setting up camp to talk about Dinah and his feelings for her, or hers for him. Yet Josh knew that the subject would come up again, as sure as the sun would rise in the morning. "All right, look. I'll make a deal with you. If you can think of one time when I poked my nose where it didn't belong, I'll tolerate one last personal question. *One*, and that's it. Do I have your word?"

Dan sat erect and saluted. "Yes, sir. Understood, sir." He went back to slouching. "Sounds to me like you're fairly certain I'll think of a time when you snooped."

"We've known each other all our lives, were raised practically like brothers. I'm sure, if you put your mind to it, you'll come up with something. In the meantime, can we drop the subject?"

"Like a hot potato."

And, to give him his due, Dan kept his word. He didn't mention Dinah as they set up camp, or while they chomped on hard-boiled eggs, or even as they lay in their bedrolls, staring up at the stars. If he had to, Josh would remind Dan about Trisha Storm, the pretty young thing who'd stolen his heart and then ridden off on a train bound for California with a gambling man. Dan had moped around for months, hoping she'd come back to him. When she didn't, he'd sworn off women forever, using his bum leg as an excuse. On second thought, even if Dan persisted with his inquisition, Josh wouldn't stoop that low.

"Speaking of eggs...."

Josh groaned inwardly, wondering how in the world his jokester cousin aimed to draw a parallel between eggs, of all things, and his relationship with Dinah. With a mind like Dan's, the possibilities were endless. *Just bide your time*, he thought, *and you'll find out soon enough.*

"Seems to me we'll be wise to hatch a plan."

Josh was almost afraid to ask what he meant. "What sort of plan?"

"What we'll do on the way back to Eagle Pass, when there's a full load of bull in the wagon. I mean, what if rustlers decide to jump us, or a wildcat sneaks up to make a meal of beef and boiled eggs?"

"I don't mind admitting, the thought has been tumbling in my head all day, too." When he wasn't thinking about Dinah, that is. "Any suggestions?"

"We'll swap out driving the team, just like we've been doing. And whichever one of us is on guard duty will sit facing backward. That way, between us, we'll have a panoramic view."

"Guard duty?" Josh chuckled softly. "You talk like we're Jim Bowie and Dan'l Boone, defending the Alamo."

"Let's hope we do a mite better at surviving than those poor fellows did. Besides, you'll be laughin' out of the other side of your mouth if either of us spots something that doesn't belong out there on the horizon."

"True enough," Josh conceded.

"There's a lot of territory between here and Laredo, between Laredo and home. I'd hate to get halfway back to the Lazy N, only to have some outlaw take what's rightfully ours."

Josh nodded. "We won't give it up without a fight, that's for sure."

"Amen."

"So, if we spot somebody, then what?"

"We shoot first and ask questions later. I can blow the wick off a candle at four hundred yards with this thing." Dan patted his rifle stock. "I'll aim for their gun hands, and if that doesn't stop 'em, let's see how effective they are at stealin' with a round in their shoulders."

Josh gave the .44-40 Winchester an admiring glance. "Well, like my pa said as we lit out, let's pray we don't have cause to use it."

"Amen," Dan said again. He crawled out of his bedroll, pulled his Stetson low on his forehead, and, pivoting on his good foot, scanned the area. Then, just for good measure, he cocked the rifle. "I'll take first watch," he said, limping to the nearest tree. "You've got three hours. If I were you, I'd make the most of 'em."

It turned out to be a long, restless night. Josh tried sleeping on his left side, but Dan's pacing drove him to distraction. He tried his right side, but the heat of the fire only made him empathize with the pig George had roasted for the Fourth of July shindig. He tried counting stars, but they reminded him of Dinah's twinkling, green eyes, which didn't help him to settle down. And reciting the Lord's Prayer didn't work, either, because he kept getting stuck on the "forgive us our debts" line.

Would Dinah ever trust him enough to come clean about her past?

And, if she did, would he be able to cope with the truth? "A man can hope and pray," he muttered.

"What's that?"

"Nothin'. And if you want my advice, you'll quit walking back and forth like a zoo lion. Rest your poor ol' leg, or it'll never last three whole hours."

"Says you."

"Says me."

It was a game they'd played since childhood, but instead of smiling the good-natured grin it usually inspired, Josh felt annoyed. Surly. Old and grumpy. When Dan didn't counter with a teasing barb, as he usually did, Josh closed his eyes and prayed for an hour of slumber, even if it was fitful and interrupted.

34

O h, yes, I most certainly did receive your telegram." The widow grabbed Josh's hand and pumped his arm as if she expected water to trickle from his fingertips. "You're the answer to an old woman's prayer, I tell you! Would you believe you're the one and only offer I've had on Charlie?"

Over her shoulder, Josh eyed the big Angus in a pen.

"Is that Charlie?" Dan asked.

The bull lowered his head and snorted menacingly. "Yes, and isn't he just the biggest, most spirited animal you've had the pleasure of laying your eyes on?"

Beulah Reynolds's laughter was more a grating cackle, but it was contagious, and the cousins couldn't help but smile.

"How many calves has he sired?" Josh wanted to know.

"Only a few dozen. But he's barely three, so he has a long life ahead of him."

"How much do you want for him?"

Beulah blushed. "Oh, I couldn't possibly let you take him for less than four hundred dollars."

Josh and Dan exchanged a surprised glance, and she evidently took it to mean the price was too high. "I know that's steep, times being hard these days and all, but I have outstanding bills all over town, and that's how much it'll take to clear them up."

"Four hundred is more than fair, Mrs. Reynolds. And we've got cash."

"Oh, you really *are* the answer to my prayers!" she gushed. "Can I get you anything before you load him up?"

Dan nodded. "Just a bill of sale."

Her eyes filled with tears. "Oh dear, oh dear, oh dear," she chanted. "I'm afraid I never learned to read or write. My Gideon, he used to handle things like this, you see—"

Josh held up a hand. "It's not a problem. Dan, here, can write it up for you while your men help me load Charlie onto the wagon. Then, we'll find somebody you trust to read and witness the document."

"Well, aren't you just the sweetest boys ever? Makes me wish Gideon and I had a couple of sons of our own. The Lord never saw fit to bless us with children, I'm afraid."

So, she was totally alone, now that her husband had passed. Josh found himself wondering what Dinah would have to say about that. Instantly, he pictured the look of pity that would no doubt flicker across her pretty face as she eyed the widow's faded dress and tattered apron, and he decided to add fifty dollars to the pot. His family had been hit hard by recent events, but they were a long sight better off than this poor old widow. And besides, they'd still have two hundred and fifty more than they'd expected to take home after this deal had been cut. What would Dinah think of that?

It was a good thing they'd had the foresight to bring along plenty of sturdy rope. Dan had used thick boards to build the wagon's tall, narrow sides, but if they didn't tie Charlie up inside them good and tight, he'd blast through the barrier as easily as a knife slices through butter. It would be a long trek back to Eagle Pass, and their mules weren't suited to chasing an angry bull across the prairie.

Charlie was none too happy about his cart-and-buggy confinement, and he made his feelings known with discontented snorts and grunts. Beulah brought out a burlap sack to put over his head, saying, "He'll be safer—and so will you handsome cowboys—if he can't see what's going on." She stood on a rail and deftly slid it over his horns. "You can take it off when you stop for the night, but I don't advise traveling without it."

"Thanks," Josh said. "Now then, soon as we get that bill of sale signed, we can pay you and be on our way. Any suggestions who might witness it for you?"

"The sheriff is a right nice young fellow," she said. "The jailhouse is just over that next rise. I'll follow you in the buckboard."

Half an hour later, they were standing in the office of Sheriff Arthur Tate, who sat at his big, walnut desk and squinted through his tiny spectacles. "On this thirtieth day of July, 1888," he read aloud, "Beulah Reynolds of Laredo sold an Angus bull named Charlie to Josh and Daniel Neville of Eagle Pass for the sum of four hundred and fifty dollars. Witnessed by...." He peered over his glasses. "They's four blank lines drawed here."

"One for Mrs. Reynolds," Josh explained, "one each for Dan and me, and one for you."

"But, young man," Beulah spoke up, "you've made a mistake. We agreed on four hundred, not four fifty."

"Charlie's worth the price," Josh said, signing on the line. He handed the pen to Dan, who scribbled his name under

Josh's. "Your mark goes here, Mrs. Reynolds," he added, pointing to the appropriate line.

Once she'd drawn her X, the sheriff wrote "Arthur B. Tate" with more curlicues and squiggles than Josh had ever seen in a signature.

While the sheriff blew the ink dry, Josh handed the widow her money. "It's been a pleasure doing business with you, ma'am."

"Oh, Josh Neville," she said, counting the bills, "I assure you, the pleasure's all mine."

"What's that?" growled a gruff voice from the back room. "Did I hear right? Is there a Josh Neville out there?"

Frowning, Dan whispered to Tate, "Who's that?"

"Leo Broderick," the sheriff said, shaking his head. "Man rode into town leading a whole circus of charlatans and thieves, tryin' to pawn off liniments and potions and some bogus concoction called 'Lydia E. Pinkham's Herb Medicine.'"

"Since when is it against the law to sell herbal remedies?" shouted Leo.

"When it makes people sick enough to almost kill 'em, that's when," Tate retorted.

"Josh," Leo yelled, "vouch for me, old friend. Tell him how we shared a dormitory room at the Yale School of Law!"

Josh couldn't believe his ears. Not *that* Leo Broderick, sitting in the Laredo jail for selling…potions? "Mind if I go back there, see if he really is who he claims to be?"

"Well, all right, but take care to stand clear of the bars, or he'll have your watch and your wallet and whatever else you might've stowed in your pockets, all before you can say howdy." Tate narrowed his eyes to add, "The man's a quack. Slipperiest snake-oil salesman I've ever come across, and I've seen my share, especially since the confounded Missouri-Pacific laid down tracks."

"Speaking of tracks," Dan said, walking alongside Josh, "we really ought to make some. We can't keep Charlie tied up with his head in a sack any longer than necessary. It just ain't right."

"If that really is the Leo Broderick I went to school with, this won't take long," Josh said, frowning at the memory. "I'll just have a word with the man, and then we'll be on our way."

He left his concerned cousin in the sheriff's office and headed for the back room, where he found Leo in the middle cell, clinging to the bars like a monkey at the zoo. "Well, if this don't beat all," Leo said, grinning. "Josh Owns-Half-of-Texas Neville, in the flesh."

Josh ignored the loathsome taunt, just as he had done during their college days. "Leo. What sort of mischief put you in a Texas jail cell?"

"Trumped up charges, that's what, made by that Wish-I-Was-a-Sheriff boor out there." Leo poked his right hand through the bars. "So, how've you been, friend?"

"Well, since I'm the one standing on this side of the bars," he teased, shaking Leo's hand, "I'd have to say I'm a good sight better than you." It surprised Josh to see how much Leo had aged, and a surge of guilt coursed through him. "What's Tate charging you with?"

"My memorization skills are as bad now as they were in school, so I couldn't recite the list if I tried, but I'm happy to give it a try." Squinting up at the ceiling, he began counting on his fingers. "Operating a flea circus without a license, selling medicine without a medical degree, charging the good folks of Laredo to step up and take a peek at my freak show...."

If he didn't know better, Josh would have said Leo sounded proud of himself! "Flea circus? Leo, you were top of our class, before—" He couldn't bring himself to admit that he'd been a big part of the reason Leo had left Yale without graduating.

"Why work hard when you can work smart?" Leo said with a shrug. He nodded, indicating Josh's hands, then held up his own, as if to prove his point. "See? No calluses here."

Josh saw no point in saying that in his book, blisters and calluses topped sitting in a jail cell any day. "How long have you been in custody?"

"Three days. The judge was out of town. Or so I was told. So much for my right to a speedy trial, eh?"

"Have they set a date?"

"Tomorrow morning, nine o'clock sharp. Provided they can round up six sober men in this fine community of upstanding citizens, that is." Leo's dark eyes narrowed. "So, did you stick it out? Did you get your law degree?"

It hadn't been easy, attending classes eight hours a day, working another six at the lumber mill, studying, and trying to sleep in that crowded dormitory, but Josh had done it. He'd graduated with full honors and in record time, because every minute away from the ranch and those he loved had seemed like torture. "Yeah," he said, "I finished." And he remembered Dinah's delighted surprise when she'd noticed the framed certificate hanging on the wall of his parlor.

"Praise the Lord, hallelujah, it's my lucky day!" Leo did a little dance in the small space between his cot and the stone wall of his cell, and, when it ended, he stuck his face between two bars. "So, what'll it take to talk you into representing me? I've got money. And a girl...."

Those last words echoed in Josh's head like a Chinese gong and caught him off guard. He tried to concentrate on present facts: Charlie and Dan were outside; he'd promised not to keep them waiting; his frail grandmother was laid up at home with apoplexy; he missed Dinah more than words could explain. "I'm in town just for the day," he began. "Came to buy a stud bull for the ranch, and—"

"Tell me," Leo interrupted him, "how's my little Sadie?"

Josh stifled a nervous snort, because there wasn't anything amusing about what came to mind. The only child of elderly parents, Sadie had been a waitress at the restaurant in New Haven where Leo would take most of his meals, leaving generous tips and plying her with compliments. Eventually, she'd accepted his invitation to a Shakespearean stage production. Leo had showed up too intoxicated to watch the play, and Sadie had spent the next several months trying to sober him up. Lonely, confused, and brokenhearted, she'd turned to Josh for help, but even working together, his girl and his friend hadn't been able to fix whatever was wrong with Leo Broderick.

Those hours with Sadie were Josh's best memories of his Yale days. She'd made him feel smart and heroic, and, by the grace of God, he'd managed to convince her that she deserved better than a drunken gambler. Then, one day, when Leo saw them walking hand in hand, he knew they'd fallen in love—and he never spoke to either of them again. A few months later, when he dropped out of school and disappeared, they blamed themselves. After the wedding, cuddled in their dark bedroom, they'd wondered whatever had become of Leo

Broderick. With time and maturity comes wisdom, however, and, before long, they'd stopped feeling responsible for Leo's actions.

"Sadie died giving birth," he blurted out.

Leo's face blanched, and he drove a hand through his hair. "I'm sorry, my friend. Sorry as can be."

Josh felt a little guilty for delivering the news so tactlessly. "Happened three years ago." He could have added that the pain of his loss had lifted significantly, thanks to a diminutive, green-eyed beauty who called herself Dinah. But he chose not to.

"So then, maybe you'll take my case—for old times' sake?"

"Like I said, we've got a bull tied up out there, and we need to get on the road, so that—"

"Do just this one thing for me, and we'll call it even. No hard feelings."

How many times had he heard that line before? It had taken less than a week at Yale to figure out there was no such thing as "just this one thing" with Leo. Josh pictured Charlie in his makeshift pen on wheels, straining at his ropes to get free. He pictured Dan, pacing impatiently as he checked and rechecked the knots.

"It'll all be over in a matter of hours," Leo pressed. "You'll be on the road by lunchtime tomorrow."

Would Leo have stayed at Yale and earned his law degree if Josh hadn't stolen Sadie's heart? Josh gritted his teeth. He'd never been able to come up with a suitable answer to the question before, so what made him think he'd find one now? Could he really hope to erase years of guilt, once and for all, by helping him now? Probably not, Josh thought, but it sure was worth a try. "Give me a few minutes to make some arrangements and I'll be back to discuss strategy."

As he headed outside, Josh relied on the grateful look on Leo's face to give him the courage to face Dan with the change of plans.

35

"Mrs. Neville," Kate began, "I hate to bother you with everything else that's on your mind, but it's your mother-in-law...."

Eva's face paled as she put down her fountain pen and looked up from her desk. "Is she—is she all right?"

"She's still with us, if that's what you're asking, but I can't get her to eat. All she wants to do is sleep." Kate clasped and unclasped her hands. "I thought—I hoped, maybe, you and Mr. Neville, and his brothers and their wives—if each of you visited her—she loves you all so much that—well, maybe, you'll be able to convince her to eat something."

Nodding, Eva slumped in her high-backed chair. "I'm glad you came to me, Dinah." With a wave of her hand, she invited her to sit down in the seat across from her. "You've been such a help to us, a real blessing." She leaned forward, folding her hands on the blotter. "So thank you. I know you wanted to leave here long before now. And everyone at the Lazy N knows that, if it weren't for you, we'd probably have lost Esther on that awful Sunday...."

The image of Esther, gray-faced and limp in the church pew, flashed in Kate's mind. Then, Eva's chair squeaked, rousing her from the unpleasant memory. "I'm the one who should be thanking you," she admitted. "You didn't know me from Adam, and yet you took me in and gave me a safe place to rest and heal. I'll be indebted to everyone at the Lazy N for the rest of my days."

Josh's mother laughed softly. "The gratitude is mutual, believe me."

Kate smiled and stood up again. "I'd best get back to Esther, and let you get back to your work."

Eva heaved a huge sigh, "Keeping the books for this place is quite a job, I tell you. I don't know how I'd have done it and cared for Esther, too. You've been such a help!" She got to her feet and walked around to Kate's side of the desk. "Esther turned eighty-two on her last birthday. Did you know that?"

"No, ma'am."

"She has talked about Ezra more often than usual these past few years. It's been a source of concern to Matthew, in particular, since he's the eldest son." She bit her lower lip, then continued, "He told me on the night she fell ill that he fully expected to pay a visit to the undertaker. And that you're the reason we've all had this time, this opportunity to tell her how much she means to us."

She gave Kate a hug, then slid an arm around her shoulders and walked her to the door. "Tell me, Dinah, have you ever played bridge?"

Kate pictured Etta Mae and her dancing girls, giggling from behind fans made of playing cards. "No, but I've watched many a game."

"Well, what you've done for us trumps anything we could have done for you. I'm ever so sorry about your ankle, but I can't help thinking the injury was divine providence, since it resulted in Josh's bringing you home." She walked back to her desk. "Just between you and me, I won't be the least bit disappointed if Josh insists that you make this your permanent home."

There was no mistaking the woman's meaning, and Kate felt helplessly silly as she stood there, smiling and nodding, trying to come up with a proper response.

"Rest assured, I'll corral the family," Eva said, preparing to go back to her work. "I like your idea of each of us going in, one at a time, in hopes that, while we're there, she'll stay awake long enough to take some nourishment."

It pleased Kate that Josh's mother approved of her plan. "I'm on my way to the kitchen now to see about bringing her some soup. Can I bring you anything?"

"Why, thank you, Dinah. A cup of tea would be lovely."

Kate headed straight for the kitchen to fix two trays—one for Esther, one for Eva. Oh, if only Josh were here so she could tell him about their lovely chat! He'd been gone only a few days, but it felt more like weeks. She thought about him almost constantly and wondered if she'd been on his mind, too. *Not likely*, she decided, grinning, *what with Daniel to keep him company and ranch business to occupy his mind.*

An hour later, after yet another failed attempt to feed Esther, Kate sat in the window seat and gave the cradle a gentle nudge with the toe of her shoe. As it rocked to and fro, a sob ached in her throat. And here, she'd thought she'd come to grips with knowing there wouldn't be babies in her future, thanks to Frank! Evidently, what she really needed to accept was that she'd never get used to the idea of being barren.

She held the curtains aside to peer out at the backyard, where little Willie squealed and giggled as Susan chased after him with a washcloth, evidently intent on wiping jam and cookie crumbs from his mouth.

Beyond the yard, mountainous clouds hung dark and heavy in the vast sky. Thankfully, Josh and Dan had traveled south; with any luck, they'd be home before the storm hit.

"I—I w-want...."

Kate leaped up and rushed to Esther's side. "Well, hello there, sleepyhead!" She tidied the covers and fluffed her pillow. "Are you hungry?"

"No." She focused on something near the window.

Kate followed the line of her gaze, then met her eyes. "The cradle?"

Esther nodded, and the left side of her face broke into a smile. "You...will be...next."

Even if Frank's attacks hadn't left her too battered to carry a child to term, what man would want a woman like she to be the mother of his children?

"B-boring."

"Boring?" Kate echoed. *Lord,* she found herself praying, *don't let this be a sign that the end is near—not when the family hasn't had a chance to say good-bye. Not with Josh and Dan so far from home....*

She took Esther's hand in her own and sat down beside her. "What's boring, Esther?"

"You are," she replied, as clear as day.

Blinking, Kate heard a nervous laugh escape her lungs. "I'm boring?" *Oh, Esther. If you only knew the awful truth about me, you wouldn't say that!*

"You're not fooling me." She gave Kate's hand a squeeze, the strength of which belied her frail condition.

All right, Kate silently conceded, *that much is true.* Esther had seen that wanted poster in Amarillo. "You think the life

I've lived is *boring?*" The question inspired a giggle, and it made Esther chuckle, too. But she sobered in a heartbeat to say, "I...know...you."

Kate squeezed the woman's hand. "And you're probably the only person in this whole wide world who can say that—and mean it."

"Josh...knows."

Kate pressed a kiss to the withered hand in her own. "No, like everyone else, he *thinks* he knows me. But I'm happy—relieved, even—that he doesn't."

Esther frowned.

"If he knew the truth, he'd hate me."

"No!"

She said it with such conviction that Kate was almost inclined to believe her. "The trouble with you, Esther Neville, is that your heart is bigger than your head." On her feet now, she went back to plumping pillows and tidying covers. "You need to rest while I get some soup, and—"

"Boring."

Laughing softly, Kate kissed Esther's forehead. "All right, then, so I'm boring. But that's a lot better than having Josh know the truth about—"

"No!" his grandmother interrupted her. "Stop." With a clumsy wave of her hand, she added, "Stop feel...sorry for... y'rself. Then you can see...truth...."

Kate wasn't sure which surprised her more, the clarity of Esther's lecture or the meaning behind each painstakingly uttered word.

"Go. Now. Fetch sons, gran'chil'ren." And with that, she closed her eyes.

"I'll bring them to you, on one condition."

The clock ticked once, twice, three times, before Esther opened her eyes. "Well…?"

"You must eat something while they're visiting."

She gave a great harrumph, then said, "Fine. Now, fetch them." A mischievous grin lit her eyes. "Please?"

"I'll be back in two shakes of a lamb's tail with sons and daughters-in-law and grandchildren—and soup!" Before Esther could change her mind, Kate exited the room and closed the door.

Two hours later, after getting nearly an entire cup of broth into her patient, Kate sat in a straight-backed chair just outside Esther's room, pretending to read a book. One by one, the elderly woman's loved ones paraded into the room, visited with her, and left, red-eyed and sniffling, each stopping to thank her for her tender, loving care, which had given them weeks of extra time with Esther. "If not for you," Matthew said, "we might not have had this chance to say good-bye."

Good-bye? *But this isn't a good-bye visit!* she wanted to say. Esther had seemed better, almost as good as new. Seeing her family, Kate believed, would be the medicine to keep Esther going strong, to hang on long after Josh and Dan's return.

She remembered how Josh had paid a visit to Esther the night before he and his cousin had left for Laredo, and how Esther had promised to try to hold on until he was home again, safe and sound. It would break his heart to learn that she'd joined Ezra while he'd been gone.

That shouldn't happen. Couldn't happen. And Kate would move heaven and earth to make sure it didn't.

She owed him that—and so much more.

36

"I can't tell you what a privilege it is," the reporter said, "to be sitting in a Fort Worth, Texas, saloon, talking to the great Frank Michaels."

Frank lit a match and held the flame to the tip of his cigar. "What are you planning to call this novel of yours, if you don't mind my asking?" he said through the smoke.

Gardiner's eyes widened. "Oh, but I don't mind at all! I'm thinking something like *The Guns of Frank Michaels: An Outlaw's Story*." He grinned at Frank. "If *that* doesn't sell half a million copies, I don't know what will."

"Seems a pitiful shame *you'll* make out like a bandit, telling my tale." He inspected the ashes before flicking them to the floor. "I think it's only right that I get a cut of the profits."

All color drained from the writer's face, and, after several false starts, he managed to squeak out, "Nothing happens fast in publishing, Mr. Michaels. Why, it could be a year before I see any money from the sale of this story. And, even then, it'll come in dribs and drabs as the book sells." He coughed nervously. "*If* it sells! And then, I'd have to find you to deliver your—uh, your share—"

"So, you're saying my life's work won't be of interest to a big-shot editor in New York?"

While Tom and Amos snickered, Frank wondered if it was possible for the man's face to go any whiter.

"No, of course, that isn't what I'm saying. It's just—well, I've never had a book published before, so it might take a while for them to research my background. You know, to decide if I'm worth their investment of paper and ink."

"So, tell me, Collin, if *they* don't think you're worth the gamble," Frank said, resting both elbows on the table, "why should *I*? There must be hundreds of would-be writers like you out there who'd jump at the chance to tell my story— writers with books already published, who won't need to be 'checked out.' What if I just ask one of *them* to write the book, instead?"

"Well, I hadn't thought of it in quite those terms." Gardiner pushed back from the table and started to rise. "I'm sorry to have wasted your time, Mr. Michaels. I'll just be—"

"Sit down, boy. Can't you tell when someone's funnin' with you?" Once Gardiner returned to his seat, Frank said, "Now, where is your paper and pencil?"

"Lookit his hands a-shakin'," Frank heard Tom whisper.

"Yeah, Frank. Ease up on the poor fool," Amos said. "How do you expect him to write if you're gonna scare him so bad he can't hold his pencil?"

The two men shared a round of boisterous laughter, and the one good thing to come of the commotion, in Frank's mind, was that being the butt of their joke had put the color back into the man's cheeks. Frank slammed a fist onto the table, rattling beer steins and shot glasses. "You two have a choice to make, boys."

Their startled expressions made it clear that he had their attention.

"You can sit there quietly and pretend you have some manners, or you can leave."

Amos upended his shot glass and set it down with a thud. "Think I'll see what-all they call a bathhouse in these parts," he said, getting to his feet. He tossed a silver dollar onto the table and was out the door before the coin stopped spinning.

Tom stared after him, clearly undecided about whether he should stay or follow. Then, he added a dollar of his own to the table and swallowed the last of his beer. "Bath sounds mighty good," he said, and with that, he was gone.

Frank had won more than his fair share of poker hands—some, not quite so fairly—and took great pride in the fact that he knew how to read a man. And if Gardiner wasn't sitting there, wishing he could join Amos and Tom, Frank would eat his pistol. He decided to soften his approach—at least, until the fool had finished the book. *The Guns of Frank Michaels* had a nice ring to it, and the more he repeated the title in his mind, the more he wanted to see it in print.

"Barkeep, bring my friend here a bottle of your best," he said to the man in an apron who came to collect their empty glasses.

When the bartender left them, Frank leaned back and propped his feet on the table, one boot atop the other. "So, tell me, Collin, where do we start?"

Gardiner picked up his pencil and said, "Why don't you tell me where you were born, Mr. Michaels?"

"Frank," he corrected him. "Please, call me Frank."

During that first hour, the piano player and the dancing girls continued entertaining the men at the bar. But by the end of the second hour, Frank was the entertainment. He told Gardiner that, despite his reputation for being a cold-blooded killer, he had a heart. "And I gave it to a pretty young thing in San Antonio. Fell head over heels for her, but she ran off with a cowboy and broke my heart."

Gardiner's brow furrowed, and, with his pencil hovering above his tablet, he said, "Don't tell me. You broke the cowboy's heart—with a bullet?"

Frank smiled, thinking about how, very soon, he'd be reunited with the only woman he'd ever really loved.

On second thought, might be best to keep that part to yourself, Frank, old boy.

37

*W*hen Kate returned to Esther's room following the rounds of family visits, she found the woman sitting up in bed, smiling.

"Goodness gracious, sakes alive!" Kate exclaimed, hugging her. "What a wonderful welcome home this will be for Josh!"

"S-sit." Esther patted the mattress. "I h-have some-something to t-tell you."

"All right, but I hope it's something simple and brief. I'm much too happy and excited about the improvement in your condition to pay attention for long."

"How long…how long we know…?"

Kate gave it a moment's thought. "A month or so?"

"You come…'n May, w-when I was…I was in Amarillo." Esther took a ragged breath. "Today…August second."

It hardly seemed possible she'd been with the Nevilles that long.

"L-long enough to love you."

Kate's eyes misted. "I love you, too," she said, patting Esther's hand.

"When Josh…comes home, you t-tell him…s-something for me."

"Oh, don't be silly! You're almost your old self. *You* can tell him!"

But Esther shook her head. "No. This…miracle."

Kate didn't understand, and said so.

"W-when you thought I w-was sleeping? W-when you w-worried because I w-wasn't eating?"

Kate nodded.

"Praying. Praying *hard*."

Before Kate could say how thrilled she was that God had answered those prayers, the woman continued.

"I l-lived good life. Lots of sadness, disappointment. Lots of joy, too. But, but I miss Ezra. W-want to be with him."

That's what Esther had prayed for? To die, so that she could join her husband in heaven?

"First, I t-tell you something."

"As long as it isn't good-bye—"

"Please, hush. You test my p-patience."

Kate shrugged. "Sorry."

"S-soon, your name will be cleared."

She didn't understand, and opened her mouth to say so.

But Esther held up a hand, silencing her. "You can t-talk when I finish…if you let me."

"Sorry," she said again.

"Josh, he love y-you, and when he get back, he need to know y-you love him, too."

He loves me? Kate thought. But how could Esther be so sure, unless he'd told her before his trip to Laredo?

"T-tell him…everything. S-so, when y-your name is cleared, he w-will know he can trust you."

But what if he decided he didn't want a tainted, barren outlaw?

Esther frowned. "C-consider it my d-dying r-request."

"But Esther, you aren't dying. Just look at you, sitting up, all rosy-cheeked and smiling!"

"It…mmmiracle. I w-wanted to spend last moments…w-with you."

If it was true—and Kate hoped it was *not*—why would this wonderful woman want to spend her last moments with the likes of her?

Esther pointed at her night table. "P-pencil and paper in th' d-drawer…."

Kate found them and held them out to Esther.

"N-not for me. For *you*. Write this: 'I s-solemnly swear….'"

Esther waited while Kate put pencil to paper, then gave a satisfied nod. "…'t-to love and ch-cherish J-Josh, all the days of his l-life.' Th-then, sign 'Dinah K-Kate Th-Theodore.'"

Kate got as far as "life" and nearly dropped the pencil. How could she sign something so important with a fake name?

"Y-you love him?"

"With all my heart."

"Then admit it! Wr-rite. S-sign. S-so I can go to Jesus, knowing I d-did w-what I could to ensure my grandson w-won't pine away f-for you."

Even in the waning light of evening, Kate could see the gray pallor returning to Esther's cheeks. Noticed that she'd sunk deeper into her pillows, too. As quick as she could, Kate wrote down the rest of what Esther had dictated, word for word, hoping to appease the woman and encourage her to revive. When she finished, she held out the paper like a schoolgirl seeking her teacher's approval.

"S-sign."

"But Esther," she whispered, "we both know that Dinah Theodore isn't my real name. What's the point of—"

"Who you are is there," she said, poking a finger at Kate's chest. "K-Kate. D-Dinah. J-just *names*." Gasping, she slid further under the covers. Her teeth started to chatter. "C-cold... so c-cold...."

Kate grabbed the quilt from the chair beside the bed and draped it over Esther. She then retrieved several more from the wardrobe, the window seat, and her cot, and added them to the pile.

"H-hold me...."

Without hesitating, Kate climbed onto the bed and drew Esther close. "There," she whispered, fighting back tears. "Is that better?"

Nodding, the woman said, "W-when th' time is right, t-take Josh aside. T-tell him he w-was my favorite. B-because...."

Unable to trust her voice, Kate remained silent.

"B-because he is Ezra, inside...and out."

Kate held her at arm's length. "All the more reason to hold on, so you can tell him these things, yourself."

Esther patted her hand. "No. D-don' want him...to rr-remember me this way." A rattling breath escaped her lungs. "Y-you and Josh will share love like ours. K-kind that w-won't be doused or dimmed, n-not even by death."

Esther's words were coming more slowly now, and each syllable seemed to sap her strength. "Shh," Kate whispered. "You need to rest."

Esther chuckled quietly. "H-have eternity for th-that."

Now, no matter how high she pulled the covers up or how tightly she hugged her, Kate couldn't seem to warm the poor, frail woman, and she knew with certainty that Esther hadn't been kidding when she'd said she would leave them. *Today.*

"Please, Esther," she choked past the sob in her throat, "won't you wait for Josh—"

"No."

The cold monosyllable that passed her lips cut Kate to the quick, and tears began rolling down her cheeks. "But think how brokenhearted he'll be, hearing secondhand what everyone else got to hear directly from you."

"Th-that's why he needs you. N-now, *sign*. I w-want Ezra."

Kate reached for the pencil and paper, then scribbled her alias across the bottom.

"G-good girl." Esther nodded, then said, "B-burn it."

"Burn it?"

"M-must be closer to heaven th-than I thought," she said, grinning. "I s-seem to hear an echo...."

Kate wanted to shake her, scold her, tell her it wasn't fair, leaving this way. That it was downright mean to go without saying good-bye to Josh and Dan. Instead, she crumpled the paper and dropped it into the metal wastebasket beside the bed, and then, taking one of the matches used for lighting Esther's oil lantern, set the note afire. When the tiny flames diminished and the small plume of smoke cleared, Kate stared at the charred bits of paper that fluttered in the bin with her every breath. She had no idea how she'd provide the comfort and support Josh would need, but she would.

"Y-you will comfort Josh. I know th-that." Then, "Get my Bible, p-please?"

By now, Kate was beyond wondering how this dear lady always seemed able to read her heart and mind. Some things, she decided, must simply be accepted on faith. As she lifted the Good Book from the night table, Esther said, "Open. F-First Corinthians. R-read ch-chapter fifteen. V-verse fifty-two."

"*In a moment, in the twinkling of an eye, at the last trump: for the trumpet shall sound, and the dead shall be raised incorruptible, and we shall be changed.*"

A peaceful smile crossed Esther's face as she reached for Kate's hand. "Every wife, every m-mother, needs a B-Bible of her own. I w-want…I w-want you…t' have mine."

"But—but, Esther, you have daughters-in-law and granddaughters who would cherish this!"

"Th-they have B-Bibles. Ezra gave me this…w-wedding day." Her smile became a mischievous grin. "S-something inside…."

Kate made a move to find it when Esther clutched her wrist. "No. S-save it. Read…w-when you're with Josh, when you t-tell him…."

It was happening, right before her eyes, and Kate was powerless to stop it. She regretted now more than ever that she'd strayed so far from God's love, because, if she'd stayed closer, she could call out to Him now and trust that He'd answer.

"A s-surprise waiting for y-you. W-when it arrives, y-you'll know…."

"No," Kate said around a sob. "Please, Esther, no. I've come to think of you as my own family. I'll miss you so, and—"

"I know," she said again. "I l-love you, t-too. Y-you'll grieve, and s-so will Josh. You'll b-both heal, b-because you have each other."

Esther's serene smile glowed brighter than the burning note had just moments ago, and, as quick as a flash of lightning, she was gone.

38

*J*osh stood beside Dan's wagon and shook Leo's hand. "Consider yourself lucky."

"Lucky," Leo echoed, "to be run out of town *and* made to pay a fine?"

"Judge Williams went easy on you. He could have sentenced you to sixty days and five hundred dollars."

Leo shrugged. "I suppose. It's just that I had hoped to settle in here for a few weeks, give my people a break. We've been on the road for months."

"Maybe in the next town."

"Yeah, maybe. So, how much do I owe you?"

Josh hoisted himself up into the wagon seat. "Nothing," he said, taking the reins from Dan. "I did this to even the score, remember?"

Chuckling, Leo took off his hat and bowed low. "To old times, then," he said, and walked away.

"I have to admit," Dan said as the wagon lurched forward, "if we had the time, I wouldn't have minded browsing that menagerie of his."

"Same here. Sad how he ended up, though."

"Aw, he didn't seem so sad to me."

"Can't feel good, being pushed from one town to the next because you've worn out your welcome."

"Where do you suppose 'Dr. Leo' found those oddities that make up his freak show?"

Josh could only shake his head.

"One-eyed pigs and three-horned goats are rare, I'll give Leo that much, but any farmer can say he's seen stranger things."

Josh chuckled. "A mouse-eating spider and fleas hitched to wagons and such? I'd pay a dollar to have a peek at that."

The cousins laughed good-naturedly as they headed north. They were nearly four days behind schedule, thanks to Josh's decision to help get Leo out of jail.

Two days later, their bull-laden wagon rolled under the Lazy N arch.

"Well, ain't that a sight for sore eyes," Dan said as they pulled up in front of the barn.

"You can say that again."

They off-loaded Charlie in the nearest corral and took care of the mule team, then headed for the house, laughing about the two-headed snake pictured on Leo's publicity pamphlet. Their smiles faded the instant they walked into the kitchen and found Lucinda at the table, crying into her apron.

"No," Dan whispered, "not Mee-Maw...."

George nodded somberly. "Sí. She die six nights ago."

Josh felt as though he'd been sucker-punched as George explained that, because of the blistering heat, the family had been forced to bury their beloved *abuela* immediately. "Was Dinah with her?" he asked.

"*Sí,*" George said again. "That girl, she never leave her side."

"We try to get Dinah out of that room to rest," Lucinda said, dabbing at her eyes, "but that girl, she is *muy testaruda!*"

For once, stubbornness seemed a very good quality in a woman. Josh needed to see her, make sure she was all right, and find out if his grandmother had suffered in the end. "Where is she?"

"Have not seen her since the morning," George said.

His wife nodded. "I have seen her walking, alone. She likes to talk to the horses...."

So, he'd find her with Callie. Josh was as certain of that as he was of the ache in his heart. "Where's Pa?"

"Eagle Pass," George offered, lowering his head. "Picking up the headstone. Your mama, she ride with him."

"I'll be back," Dan said, "after I talk with my folks."

"I'll walk with you as far as the barn," Josh said, placing a hand on Dan's shoulder. There would be time enough later to express his grief. For now, he'd hold it together, as he always had—the eldest cousin, setting an example for the rest.

Together, they saddled Dan's horse, then bid each other a sad and silent good-bye. Josh watched until his cousin disappeared over the horizon, then headed for the corral to see if he could find Dinah. But a strangely familiar hum captured his attention, and it stopped him cold. It was identical to the sound he'd heard many weeks ago in the middle of the prairie. Craning his neck, he followed it to the source—and found Dinah, curled up in the corner of Callie's stall.

"Are you out of your mind?" he said, pulling her to her feet. "She's an easygoing mare, but if something had startled her, you could have been trampled." Didn't she realize how much she'd come to mean to him? Wasn't she aware that if he lost her now, he'd be lost?

Dinah dabbed her teary eyes with the hem of her apron. "Have you been to the house yet?"

With his jaw clenched, he nodded.

"So, you know about your grandmother."

Another nod. "George and Lucinda said you refused to leave her side. Thank you for that. It's a relief to know she wasn't alone when—"

She turned her back to him, folded her arms across her chest, and cupped her elbows. "Oh, Josh," she said through her tears, "if only she could have held on, just for a few more days, to say good-bye to you."

"I have only one question." Gently, he turned her around. "She didn't suffer, did she?"

Dinah shook her head. "No," she rasped. "It was a very peaceful passing. She...she smiled at the end."

"Smiled?"

She met his eyes. "She had asked me to read to her from the Bible, and we talked about how much she missed your grandfather."

That didn't surprise him, for folks had often remarked about how in love they were, right up until the moment when his grandfather had died. He and Dinah would have a love like that—if he could convince her to stay.

She sighed. "I'm going to miss her so much." A sad giggle passed her lips. "What am I saying? I miss her already."

He gathered her close. "I know. Me, too."

"She was a wonderful woman. And she loved you so very much."

"I know." He buried his chin in her soft, sweet-smelling hair. "But only about half as much as I loved her." Josh would have said more, might have shared stories about Mee-Maw, if he thought he could do it without blubbering like a baby.

"Did you know that you were always her fav—"

"Ah, *there* you two are."

"Pa," Josh said. He couldn't believe how much it hurt to turn Dinah loose right then, but he did, then walked to meet his father. "George said you and Ma went to town to pick up Mee-Maw's tombstone."

"Yeah. Good thing your mother was there. Don't know how I'd have chosen a proper inscription on my own."

Josh remembered all too well how tough it had been doing the same thing for Sadie and their sons.

"Glad you're home, son."

"Glad to *be* home." And he meant it for a few dozen reasons—one of which stood, crying quietly, outside Callie's stall.

*W*ell, if this don't beat all!"

At the loud, gravelly greeting, Josh hooked the hammer over the top rail of the fence and looked up as five riders approached. He recognized three as the Texas Rangers who'd bunked in the field cabin with him and Dinah.

"Well, well! What brings you boys all the way out here?"

"We've got a beat on that weasel, Frank Michaels," Gus said, dismounting. "You haven't seen him by any chance, have you?"

Josh shook the offered hand. "Wouldn't know him if I tripped over him."

"Not to worry," Stretch said, joining them. "Got us a pi'ture of the varmint now."

He handed the wanted poster to Josh. "Purty, ain't he?"

Josh shook his head. "Not my type," he said, grinning.

"So, how's that li'l woman of yours?" Shorty wanted to know.

"Fine." Josh returned the poster.

"And, speakin' of posters and such," Stretch said, "I've got good news."

"News?" Josh ran his shirtsleeve across his sweaty brow.

"Well, you remember how Shorty, there, thought your woman looked familiar, then decided it was 'cause she looked like my sister?"

Shorty groaned while the rest of the Rangers laughed, their boots stamping the dust in rapid succession.

"Yeah," he said, somewhat uneasily. "I remember." And he remembered how red-faced and uncomfortable the whole scene had made Dinah, and how she'd fainted dead away.

"Well, turns out she was the spittin' image of a lady outlaw," Gus said.

Stretch whistled. "One beautiful bandit, that one."

Josh's heart pounded so hard, he wondered if the Rangers could hear it. "So, you caught her?"

"Turns out she weren't a bandit after all," Gus said, then proceeded to explain how, on the day of the bank robbery in San Antonio, a teller had spoken the name "Kate Wellington" half a dozen times before slipping into a coma. "Poor woman finally come to," he continued, "gave us all a good tongue-lashing for not paying closer attention. Because what she'd *said* was that Kate had been a hostage of Frank Michaels, not a member of his gang."

Well, that sure cleared up the matter of where she'd acquired the cuts and bruises....

"Miss Claribel Carter gave an official statement, saying she heard one of the gunmen call him Frank, and that he had a gun pressed to the girl's ribs when she'd asked for the money. Described the rest of 'em, too." A proud grin threatened to split his face in two. "Never had an eyewitness survive his crimes before, so this is the first wanted poster with Frank Michaels's picture on it."

"Well, I'll be," Josh heard himself say.

But if Michaels was this close, it could mean only one thing. He aimed to find his pretty captive and finish what he'd started months ago.

"Well, we'd best be headin' out," Gus said. The big man heaved himself up into the saddle with a great grunt, and the others followed suit. "Somebody give this feller one of them wanted posters."

Shorty handed a folded-up placard down to Josh, who took it with a grateful nod.

"Maybe you can show that around among your hired hands and see if any of your neighbors recognize that skunk."

"If nothing else," Josh said, tucking the poster into his shirt pocket, "it'll let 'em know who to look out for."

Shorty took a moment to roll a cigarette. Lighting it, he said, "You want my advice? If you see that low-down, murderin' thief, shoot first and ask questions later."

"For your sake," Stretch said, "let's hope it doesn't come to that."

"We'll follow the Rio Grande north for a spell, in case you have cause to send for us." Pointing skyward, Gus signaled his men forward.

Josh went back to work on the rail, thinking that, once he finished up the job, he'd ride back to the house to find Dinah and deliver the good news. If he'd guessed right—and he believed he had—and she was Kate Wellington, the news about the bank teller's story might just be enough to change her mind about going to Mexico. It was a thread of hope to hold on to in the midst of his despair at losing Mee-Maw.

"Thank You, Lord," he whispered as hammer hit nail.

He prayed that it was a strong thread, because Shorty's parting words made him feel a bit like a fly tangled up in a web, just waiting for the spider's appetite to lure it out of hiding.

The music of the first dinner bell roused Josh from his gloom. Lucinda would ring it again in a few minutes to signal that the meal was on the table. The in-between time gave everyone ample time to come in and clean up, for they'd all learned what would happen if Lucinda saw grimy hands at her table.

Hopefully, after unsaddling Callie, he'd have time to pull Dinah aside and deliver the good news. Here it was, just the middle of August, yet that old anticipation he'd felt as a boy every Christmas Eve bubbled in his mind.

He'd just poured a scoop of oats into Callie's manger when he heard a familiar voice say, "I was hoping I'd find you here."

Dinah stood in the stall's opening, hands clasped behind her back as the wind, blowing in through the open door, riffled her hair. *Not half as much as I was hoping to see you*, he thought.

She was wearing that yellow dress he liked so much, and the possibility that she'd chosen it just for him made him smile. "Come to warn me that the first bell has rung, have you?"

"No. But I do have something to tell you."

He'd come to love the music of her voice, and its absence hit him hard. Shoving the scoop back into the sack of oats, he faced her. With any luck, her ragged tone was nothing more than a signal that she was missing Esther. Because, if she'd come to say good-bye…. Josh couldn't bring himself to finish the thought. He was about to ask her what was wrong when she said, "Your grandmother gave me her Bible."

That should have pleased her, so why the long face? "Doesn't surprise me," he said. "How many times did she say you needed one of your own?"

Dinah nodded. "I read what you wrote on the back page."

He breathed a sigh of relief because she was finally smiling. He smiled, too, as he remembered his grandmother's reaction to his childish scribblings. "Did she tell you the story behind that inscription?"

"No."

"Happened one Sunday when I was about eight," he began, leaning his forearms on the stall gate. "I'd left my Bible home. Again. And she scolded me all the way back from church, saying how the Good Book was God's gift to me, and I ought to be more mindful, and such." The picture of Esther, turned sideways on the buckboard so she could shake a finger at him in the backseat, made him chuckle. "So, after dinner, I sneaked up to her room, found her Bible, and wrote down the truth as I saw it back then."

"I love the Word, but *you* are God's gift to me," Dinah recited.

If she hadn't looked so sad and scared, he might have kissed her for putting the emphasis on "you." "I was just old enough to have figured out the special bond between us that grew stronger every time she baked my favorite cookies when Pa handed down a punishment, or when she wrote sweet notes and tucked them into my lunch bucket. Powerful stuff," he acknowledged, "and almost as healing as God's Word."

Oh, to get inside her head and read the thought that painted the I'm-in-no-mood-for-nonsense expression on Dinah's face! Did it mean she hadn't come here for idle chit-chat, or that, in her opinion, God's Word *wasn't* powerful and healing? He'd never been overly fond of useless conversation, himself, so he said, "You came to tell me something?"

With her eyes closed, she tilted her face toward the ceiling and inhaled a great gulp of air. "I'm not who you think I am."

"Oh?" Had she decided, finally, that he could be trusted with the truth? *A man can hope.*

"My real name is Kate Wellington."

She proceeded to tell him an unabridged version of the Rangers' story, and, when she finished, she held out her hands, palms up. "So, now you know why I have to go to Mexico. The sooner, the better."

There was so much he wanted to tell her, starting with the fact that the Rangers believed they were close to capturing Frank Michaels. That she'd been exonerated of any crimes. That he loved her more than life itself. But he couldn't get a word in edgewise, what with her babbling about how she owed him for clothes and a hat and a horse, and how she'd repay him once she got herself a job singing in some Mexican cantina. He wanted to tell her that none of that mattered now but couldn't figure out whether to say "Dinah, hush!" or "Kate, be quiet!"

"I have something to tell you, too," he said when she finally paused.

When he took her in his arms, she stiffened at his touch. That was to be expected under the circumstances, he supposed, but it cut him to the quick all the same.

"I was out repairing the fence along the old post road just now."

Dinah tucked a loose curl behind her ear, then fiddled with the black, velvet bow at the collar of her dress. She absently traced the outline of the top button on his shirt. "That's what Lucinda said when I asked if she'd seen you."

Josh gently grasped her wrist with one hand and lifted her chin with the other. Tears shimmered in her eyes when she blinked up at him. He hadn't expected that—what was there to cry about, now that the truth had been told? Gathering her close, Josh pressed a kiss to her forehead. "It doesn't matter," he assured her. "You're just going to have to face facts."

"What facts?"

"That you're just not cut out for a life of crime." Chuckling, he kissed her cheek. "I mean, if you can't even pull off a phony name."

When she attempted to step back, her palm brushed his shirt pocket. "What's this?" she asked, pulling out the folded poster.

He didn't see the point in telling her, when the information was there for her to read in black and white.

"Where—where did you get this?"

Josh had never seen such white-hot fright on a face before, and it confirmed his belief that the outlaw had done far more than hold her as his hostage.

"*Where?*" she repeated, rattling the paper.

"The Rangers gave it to me."

Dinah scanned the poster with a nervous look on her face before shifting her gaze past Josh, toward the door. And then, like a wounded dove, the wanted poster fluttered to the floor as Dinah whispered a hoarse and terrified, "Frank!"

40

I wouldn't if I were you."

Josh froze, but his fingers never loosed their hold on the handle of the pitchfork.

"I've heard stories about cowboys being dumber than a box of rocks," Frank said, grinning, "but I never believed them until now." An evil laugh erupted from his chest. "This one thinks he can stop three bullets—with a pitchfork."

Amos said, "Maybe he's lookin' to die a hero."

"Then he ain't just dumb," Tom put in, snickering. "He's a dumb hero."

Frank shot a look of disdain at the man to his left. "Every time you open your mouth, Tom, I'm reminded of your lack of intelligence. And since a man is judged by the company he keeps, I'll thank you to *shut up*."

Tom's eyes narrowed with resentment, but he did as he was told.

"You two, tie him up and gag him. And make sure he can't get loose."

He let a moment pass, watching the three men struggle. Then, he grabbed Kate by the hair and jerked her close, securing her with an arm around her neck. "I rather thought that might get your attention," he said when Josh froze. Pressing his gun barrel to Kate's temple, he breathed into her ear, "What's your boyfriend's name?"

She had no idea what Frank might do with the information, but something told her that if she didn't answer, Josh would pay the price.

He turned his attention back to Josh, whose eyes bulged with fury as Tom's greasy hand pulled a cloth over his mouth and Amos pinned his arms behind him. "I have no quarrel with you or your family, *Josh*, but make no mistake: unless you cooperate, I'll kill her, and I'll make sure you see me do it."

She met Josh's gaze. "Do what he says," she told him. "*Please*, do what he says."

Frank's threat and Kate's plea had the intended reaction, and Josh allowed Tom and Amos to tie him up, using his own bandanna to gag him.

"Who's up at the house?"

Kate's fear was supplanted by rage, and when she tightened her fists at her sides, Frank tightened his hold, nearly strangling her. "Josh's father and his uncles," she choked out, "and their sons, and sons-in-law, and—"

"—and they'll all come running when the first shot is fired, is that what you're trying to tell me?"

She tried prying his grip loose, but it was no use. Tears filled her eyes, and she nodded weakly.

"And the boys and I? We'll pick them off, one at a time."

She'd spent enough time with this madman to know he wasn't bluffing, and that those sorry excuses for men who rode with him would do anything he told them to. It was bad enough they'd come here because of her. Kate wouldn't put the Nevilles in further danger by agitating Frank.

She glanced at Josh's revolver, holstered and hanging from the hook in Callie's stall. If she stomped on his instep, chances were good he'd release her. But, even if she managed to reach the sidearm before Frank or one of his cohorts got off a shot, did she have what it took to kill him?

"Don't be a fool, Kate."

She hadn't thought it possible to hate him more, but she'd been wrong. Yes, she did have it in her to kill him. Now, the question was, how good was her aim?

"If your pretty little fingers so much as touch that gun," he said, "I'll kill him, and then I'll let you watch as I kill off his precious family members, one by one."

Kate didn't much care what happened to her, but she wouldn't risk Josh's life, or the life of anyone else at the Lazy N. She had one chance to save them, and she took it.

"Leave them alone," she said through clenched teeth, "and I'll go with you."

Frank eased his grip on her and turned her to face him. "Oh, make no mistake, you're going with me."

She pointed to the wanted poster. "A group of Texas Rangers gave that to Josh just this morning. They're close, Frank, and while I have no doubt you could kill everyone on this ranch, the gunshots would put the Rangers right on your heels."

"Close, you say? *How* close?"

"Five, ten miles, if that. And you know how far and fast the sounds of gunfire can travel over the flatlands, especially considering the wind is blowing in the same direction they're headed. "

Eyes narrowed, he gave her warning a moment's thought. A slow smile spread across his face. "It seems Lady Luck is riding with me today, because I was planning to ride south. Thanks to your little tidbit, we'll head north, instead."

Kate stared hard at the floor. She couldn't risk even the briefest glance at Josh, for fear Frank would see it and understand that she'd deliberately misled him. He told Tom and Amos to fetch the horses, and when they left the barn, he slid a hand behind Kate's neck, grabbing a handful of hair. "I'm not going to have to tie you up, too, am I?"

"No."

"You won't leave me again?"

Something in his voice—an almost gentle softness she'd never heard before—strengthened her resolve. "If you leave them alone, I'll go with you, willingly." He pulled her closer, and if Tom hadn't shown up when he did, Kate believed Frank might have kissed her.

"All set, Frank."

"You want me to shoot him?" Amos wanted to know.

In the time it took him to blink, the warmth in Frank's eyes died, replaced by icy contempt. "I swear, Amos, I can't decide if you're half crazy or just plain stupid. What have we just spent the last five minutes discussing?"

Amos scowled as Tom unsheathed his knife. "I could cut his throat. That wouldn't make no noise."

Kate gasped when she realized Frank was seriously considering the idea. "If you do, you'll have to kill me, too," she spoke up.

Frank chuckled and held up his free hand. "All right, you win." And, with a gentlemanly bow, he said, "After you, m'lady." He stopped in the doorway and faced Josh. "I have no doubt that you'll work yourself loose in an hour or two, after which you'll round up every man on the Lazy N. Let me assure you that following us would be a mistake." He narrowed his eyes to add, "A deadly mistake."

Kate walked purposefully toward the door and climbed onto the spare horse he'd brought. She glanced over her shoulder just long enough to read the helpless expression on Josh's handsome face. When he didn't show up for dinner, someone would come looking for him. They'd find him tied to the barn's support beam and set him free. Hopefully, he wouldn't do as Frank predicted, because she knew he'd set the Rangers on Frank's trail. *Please,* she silently begged Josh, *don't ride with them!*

Then, as quick as you please, she faced front again, her yellow gingham skirt flapping like a tattered sail as she, Frank, Tom, and Amos were swallowed up by a thick cloud of dust.

*J*osh rubbed the welts on his wrists the rope had made. "If I hadn't taken my gun belt off like a blamed fool—"

"—you'd be dead, and so would Dinah," Dan said.

"The boy's right," Matthew agreed, jamming a shell into his shotgun. "Wasn't as if you could reason with a man like that."

The image of her riding off with that bunch flashed in his mind. Wincing, Josh said, "She sacrificed herself for us. I'm going after her."

"I had a notion you'd say that." Micah squinted one eye and peered down the barrel of his Winchester. "Well, you're not going anywhere without me."

Paul spun the chamber of his Colt, then nodded. "Me, too," he said, holstering it.

Josh's uncles agreed, one by one.

"Who's gonna fetch the Rangers?" Sam asked.

"You thought of it," his father-in-law said. He held up a hand to avert the younger man's objections. "Eva threatened to tan my hide if I let on, but this situation takes precedence over keeping Susan's secret." He aimed a finger at Sam. "Your duty is to your wife and young'uns."

"Young'uns?" Dan echoed. "You mean—?"

Sam nodded, but it was clear by the uncertain look on his face that he was torn between happiness about the baby his wife carried and disappointment that he couldn't ride with the rest of the Neville men. "I guess you're right. Susan isn't having as easy a time of this one as she did with Willie."

Dan grinned. "Aw, don't worry. She's strong and healthy."

"Sam, once you've told the Rangers where we're headed, I want you to head straight home," Josh said. Sam was the youngest, and the only man in the bunch who wasn't blood kin, and his heart went out to him. "Somebody needs to hold down the fort," he added, "in case Michaels and his bunch decide to double back. And I wouldn't put it past him."

Sam's face brightened. "You can count on me," he said, standing taller.

"Now, there's just the matter of alerting the womenfolk."

A chorus of moans and groans floated around the barn. "You're the oldest, Matthew," said his youngest brother, John. "Seems only fitting that dubious duty fall to you."

He harrumphed. "As the oldest, I could insist that you do it, John."

The men snickered and chuckled, and then Matthew said, "You boys saddle up while I let the women know what's going on."

Half an hour later, they rode two by two in somber silence, eyes on the horizon, their minds on the dangerous task ahead of them. A man as arrogant as Frank Michaels— who considered himself above the law and smarter than anyone—would probably have no qualms about lighting a fire. He and his men would alternate as lookouts, of course, but not even the most alert man could watch his front *and* his back. So, the plan was simple. The gang was outnumbered by five guns. They figured that this fact, combined with the element of surprise, should guarantee a successful raid on the outlaws' camp.

It was just past midnight when Josh spied an orange glow due north on the horizon. The makeshift posse dismounted to discuss strategy. Luke and Mark reminded the others that they'd served with Hood's Texas Brigade at Gaines's Mill, and their bayonet charge had stopped the Federals from taking Richmond. The rest readily went along with their battle plan: Josh would go in on foot and report back on the precise position of each man—and Kate. And then they'd decide how and when to attack.

Josh tossed his Stetson aside and, ducking low, moved stealthily across the grassland, darting left, then right, until the outline of a man crouching over the fire came into view. He crawled on his belly from that point on, taking care to stay low to the ground so that he could watch, unnoticed, from the cover of the gall grass, which whispered in the wind. Clumps like this were favorite hiding places for quail, and he prayed he wouldn't disturb a nest, for their frightened flapping and squawking would surely signal his presence and pinpoint his location.

Thankfully, the thicket he'd chosen housed no birds. He said a second prayer that it didn't provide cover for any scorpions.

It appeared Frank and his gang had come well-equipped to enjoy the most rudimentary pleasures of camp life, right down to the iron Y-supports for the rod that held their coffeepot above the fire. When Josh was close enough to smell the biscuits they'd cooked up for supper, he slowly raised his head and scrutinized the scene.

Frank must have assigned Amos to the first watch, for it was his silhouette Josh had seen earlier. That was a bonus for the Nevilles, and not so good for the outlaws, because, of the three, Amos seemed the least clever. But Josh had been a rancher long enough to know that, sometimes, what a man lacked in intelligence, he more than made up for in other ways. Perhaps, in place of brains, Amos could hear better than most of his contemporaries.

Tom lay with his back to the fire, snoring softly. Frank, his face hidden by his hat, lay on his back with his fingers linked behind his head. And Kate sat, her shoulders hunched, wide awake and staring into the fire. As much as he would have liked to let her know help had arrived, Josh couldn't risk calling attention to himself, because all three men still wore holsters and were within inches of palming their six-shooters.

As he made a slow turn in preparation to retreat and report back to the others, the grit and gravel beneath him crunched—a sound barely audible but enough to alert Amos. The man was on his feet in a whipstitch, his gun in hand, his thumb on the hammer. "What was that?" Josh heard him hiss.

Kate raised her head. Oh, what he'd give to comfort her! He'd no sooner finished thinking that when he saw Frank raise his head and thumb his hat higher on his forehead. "What's got you caterwaulin' like a woman?"

"Thought I heard somethin' over yonder." And Amos pointed to a spot dangerously close to Josh's hiding place.

Propping himself up on one elbow, Frank squinted into the darkness.

Josh froze, held his breath, and prayed the moment would pass quickly. Prayed, too, that his uncle John, who'd probably seen the whole thing through his binoculars, hadn't gone off half-cocked and got the others riled and ready to ride.

A jackrabbit chose that moment to jump from the brush beside him. It skittered along the edge of their camp as Amos took aim and fired a single, earsplitting shot. He missed it, but just barely, and set off a cacophony of coyote howls to the east. Josh glanced over his shoulder and prayed his battle-savvy uncles could keep their cool long enough to control the rest of them.

Tom, half asleep yet on his feet, turned round and round, muttering to himself, looking ready to shoot the next thing that moved. "Put that thing down," Frank snarled, "before you hurt somebody."

Then, Frank got on his feet and began to pace around the fire. "What's *wrong* with you?" he demanded, hitting Amos hard with the back of his hand.

The slap echoed across the prairie as Amos touched his lip, then stared down at his bloody fingertips. "Land sakes," he said. "You had no call to do that, Frank."

But Frank stood toe-to-toe with the smaller man and jabbed a forefinger into his chest. "No call? *No call?* If the Rangers aren't breathing down our throats in ten minutes…." Frank ran both hands through his hair. "I ought to shoot the lot of you and go to Costa Rica alone. I'll live longer without your constant aggravation."

And, like a nightmare, it began—the thunder of horses' hooves, the distinctive *snick* of gun hammers clicking into place.

In the seconds that had passed since Frank's idle threat, Josh had remembered Shorty's advice: "Shoot first and ask questions later." But what if, in the fracas, Kate was hit by a stray bullet? *Why didn't they wait for my signal?*

In the next second, a quick glance was enough to tell Josh that his pa had assumed the lead position. Josh could faintly hear him holler, "Firstborn, first to fall!" as he led the charge.

"Not if I have anything to say about it," he muttered, and, in one swift motion, Josh was on his feet. He had six rounds in the chamber, and he aimed to make every one count.

"Kate," he bellowed, "get down! Behind the horses!"

In the second it took Josh to issue his order, Frank got behind her and, with one hand on her throat, fired a shot over her shoulder. Its blinding, orange glare sliced through the darkness and whistled past Josh's left ear; an inch down and to the right, and he'd have been a goner, for sure.

Matthew and John drove their horses right into the center of the camp and brought them up short. "Guns on the ground!" John shouted.

"Do it, slow and easy!" Matthew ordered. "Make one wrong move, and we'll cut you in half, one at a time."

The rest of the Neville men rode up from the other side, their weapons at the ready, but Frank's men barely noticed. Tom stared down the barrel of a Henry rifle while Amos gaped at a Ward and Sons over-under shotgun. The outlaws exchanged a worried glance, dropped their Colts, and slowly raised their hands.

Josh took advantage of the flurry to advance on Frank. "It's over," he growled. "You're outgunned and outnumbered."

Frank's sly grin never reached his eyes. "Fortunately," was his calm reply, "I'm not outwitted." For the second time that day, he pressed the barrel of his pistol into Kate's temple.

"You're a coward," Josh snarled, "to hide behind a woman's skirts."

Frank chuckled and put his lips close to Kate's ear. "He thinks I care about his opinion of me." He gave her a rough jerk. "Tell him, Kate, that the opinions of others have never mattered to me."

"The opinions of others have never mattered to him," she echoed obediently.

The tremor in her voice and the fear in her eyes stirred something in Josh, something primal and baleful, which made him forget he'd been raised by a God-fearing mother, who'd taught him to practice civility and good manners, who'd insisted that he live by the Golden Rule. The only rule Frank Michaels lived by was survival of the fittest. Knowing that, Josh snarled, "Turn her lose."

"Do I detect an 'or else' implied in that sentence?"

By now, his cousins had bound and gagged Tom and Amos, and the remaining Neville men had formed a circle around Josh, Frank, and his prisoner.

Frank searched the men's faces and nodded with resignation as he counted the weapons aimed at his heart. "Give us two horses and an hour's head start. I'll leave her along the trail."

"Dead, no doubt." Josh shook his head. "I don't think so."

"You don't trust me? I'm hurt." Frank feigned a pout, then gave Kate another forceful tug, as if to remind them that if they fired, she'd die, too. In the ensuing silence, all eight gun barrels raised slightly, this time aiming at an invisible spot between Frank's eyebrows. He worked his jaw back and forth, making a thin line of his lips. "All right, gentlemen, so you've made your point. Now, let me make mine: I have no desire to die on this godforsaken Texas prairie tonight. You have my word that I won't kill her. Give me *one* horse and thirty minutes, and—"

"Don't listen to him," Kate said. "You have loved ones waiting for you back at the ranch. I couldn't live with myself if every last one of you didn't go home to them, safe and sound."

"One bullet to the brain, and he'll drop like a rock," Dan said.

"Maybe," Frank spat, "but I bought this piece because of its hair trigger. Shoot me, and we'll both be dead before we hit the ground."

For the second time in minutes, the sound of horses' hooves thundered across the prairie, this time mingling with gunshots, which sparked into the dark sky like red and yellow fireworks. The fleeting disruption gave Josh just enough time to dart behind Frank and throw him off balance, and he lost his grip on Kate.

⌒

Kate ran to the edge of the campfire, where the outlaws had tethered their horses. The animals' terrified trumpeting made eerie music as their hooves pounded the dust.

Then, a single blast cracked the night, followed by complete, utter silence.

An excruciating moment passed, and everyone seemed to notice at once the slowly spreading bloodstain an inch above the pocket flap of Josh's shirt.

Josh!

His gun slid from his hand and hit the dirt with a quiet thump. With his arm hanging limp at his side, he crumpled slowly to the ground as the Rangers reached the outskirts of the camp, riding low in their saddles.

For the first time since meeting him, Kate saw fear on Frank's face. Clearly, he knew he wasn't just outnumbered, but surrounded, as well. She took full advantage of his distracted state and crawled on her belly toward Josh's pistol. Frank's eyes glittered in the firelight as she pulled back on the hammer, prepared to force him to surrender. They narrowed to mere slits as he raised his gun arm and took aim. *Shoot or be shot*, she told herself. *Shoot or be shot!*

In less time than it took to blink, Kate realized Frank's six-shooter wasn't aimed at her but at Josh. The deafening discharge captured every man's attention, and, for the second time in less than a minute, the prairie fell silent.

Frank looked down at the growing red stain in the middle of his own shirt. His eyes were wide and unblinking, and one corner of his mouth lifted in a wry grin. "Why, I do believe you've killed me, darlin'," he said before toppling like a freshly hewn tree.

42

*D*r. Lane wiped his hands on a white towel. "He's lost a lot of blood, but I think I've got him patched up. Main worry now is infection, so we need to watch for signs of fever." He tossed the towel onto the foot of Josh's bed and focused on Kate. "He's young and strong. If you can get plenty of liquids into him and keep him from moving around and tearing those stitches, he'll come round."

Kate held her breath, waiting for one of Josh's relatives to take her to task for putting him in this situation. For putting them all in this situation. "I'll stay with him night and day."

"Won't be easy," Matthew said. "That boy's as stubborn as—"

"—you?"

The others chuckled at John's remark.

Eva stepped away from her only son and put her hands on Kate's shoulders. "It's a mother's place to see him through this."

Kate took a breath, intent on asking her, *pleading* with her, to let her stay with him. The family had been so good to her, and, besides, Josh had saved her life—more than once. It was the least she could do. But the sob in her throat stalled her speech long enough for Eva to deliver one of her own.

"You've already done so much for us, dear girl, caring for Esther the way you did." She tucked several wisps of Kate's hair behind her ears. "We know you never intended to stay this long." Tears filled her eyes when she pressed her fingertips to Kate's cheeks. "It's a mother's place to be with her son at a time like this, but...."

Kate's heart ached, and her gaze shifted to Josh. *But I love him*, she wanted to shout, *so it is my place to see him through this!* But she was stopped by the ugly fact that she was the reason he lay still and pale, fighting for his life.

"But I can't be in two places at once," Eva spoke again. "Susan needs me, too."

"Susan?" Matthew said. "Has something happened to the baby?"

Eva tucked her lips inward in an effort to stanch her tears, and the men murmured and muttered. Clasping both hands under her chin, she said, "We could tell this would be a difficult pregnancy. That's why we didn't want to make an announcement, in case...." She shook her head. "So much blood," she whispered. "I'm afraid that...."

As Dr. Lane filled the momentary gap with a brief explanation about the complications with Susan's miscarriage, Kate drew Eva close and held her tight. How horrible for the woman to have two of her three children so close to death at the same time! "Don't you worry," she said when the doctor finished. "I'm not going anywhere."

"Thank you, Kate," Matthew said. "You've been a blessing to this family." With that, he led his wife from the room, murmuring comforting words, as Dan stepped up to Kate's side. "If you're serious about staying with Josh," he said softly, "you really ought to clean yourself up."

It had been Dan and Kate who'd stayed behind while half of the Neville men had gone to fetch the doctor and the other half, including Matthew, had gone for the wagon. And it had been Dan and Kate who'd tried to hold the compress in place during the rough and seemingly endless ride back to the Lazy N. She looked from her own bloody clothes to Dan's, then fixed her gaze on Josh. "I know I should, but—but I can't leave him."

Dan slid a brotherly arm across her shoulders and led her into the hallway, where the doctor stood, shrugging into his coat. "You don't want that stale, old blood to contaminate him, now, do you?" Dr. Lane asked her.

"Of course not."

"Then, clean yourself up. Dan will stay with Josh until you get back." He picked up his medical bag and started down the steps. When he reached the bottom, he looked up. "Get lots of liquids into him, and keep him cool. I've left a bottle on his bedside table. If it seems he's in pain, give him a spoonful every few hours." And then, he was at the door. "I'll be back tomorrow to check his dressing and to look in on Susan."

Kate gripped the banister so tightly that her fingers ached. She wanted to call after him, plead with him to stay. Lucinda appeared at the bottom of the landing and came up to her. "The poor man needs to rest now," she said gently. "He been here since George got him to take care of Susan. Thank the Lord he had not left when Josh come back hurt."

From where she stood at the top of the stairs, Kate could see him, lying still and pale, in his room. She could hear Willie down the hall, asking why his mommy was crying, as Sam quietly assured his son that in no time, God would make things right.

One by one, the Neville men filed from Josh's room. Luke said, "Thank you," Mark offered a word of encouragement, and both sentiments were echoed by the others as they walked past her. Only Dan remained, and when the rest had left the house, he echoed the doctor's words, adding, "If you'll fix me something to eat after you've cleaned yourself up, I promise to sit with him."

Not trusting herself to speak without breaking into tears, Kate smiled and touched his forearm, then hurried down the hall to wash up and slip into one of Sarah's dresses, hanging in her wardrobe. "Wait," she said, whirling around to face Dan again. "Where's Sarah?"

"Took the morning train to Amarillo to visit with Mee-Maw's sister, remember?"

No, she didn't remember. In fact, this was the first she'd heard of Sarah's trip. Still, Kate expelled a sigh of relief. *The family must have made those plans while you were busy feeling sorry for yourself, making plans to confess your sins to Josh and then run off to Mexico like the spoiled, self-centered brat you are.* What a horrible human being she'd become! How ironic that these good, Christian people considered her a hero and a helpmate all rolled into one. So much for faith in their all-knowing, all-powerful God! Where had He been as one tragedy after another fell upon their devout shoulders? And why hadn't He lifted the veils from their eyes so they could see her for what she was?

She was angry at God on the Nevilles' behalf. They worked hard, from the oldest to the youngest of them, to live lives of faith. Worked hard turning what had been barren wasteland into a place where even the livestock flourished. And how had He repaid them for their devotion? With death and loss and heartache. She couldn't worship a God like that. *Wouldn't* worship a God like that.

Instead, she'd dedicate herself to the family that had welcomed a stranger as if she were one of their own. She'd tend to Josh until he was on his feet, hale and hardy, and keep right on doing it for as long as they'd let her—or until the Rangers came to collect her for the sins of her past.

43

*K*ate wasn't in the mood for tea, but she brewed some, just in case Dan needed something to wash down the thick slabs of cold roast beef, left over from supper, which she'd arranged on his plate. With the additions of a small sliced apple and one heaping spoonful of Lucinda's rice pudding, the meal was ready to carry upstairs.

Leaning stiff-armed against the sideboard, Kate planted a palm on either side of the tray and hung her head as hot tears filled her eyes. *Don't give in to them,* she urged herself. *Be strong, for Josh's sake!*

"Kate?"

The quiet baritone startled her so much that she nearly upset the mug of hot tea. "Daniel!" she said, putting one hand over her pounding heart. "Who's with Josh?"

He slid Lucinda's kitchen stool closer to the sideboard. "Easy," he said, perching on it. "Uncle Matthew is with him. Said he was only getting in the way in Susan's room."

A wavering sigh escaped her lungs. "The poor man. What a horrible welcome home from all that mayhem." There wasn't a blessed thing she could do about Susan's condition, but what had happened to Josh on the prairie had certainly been her fault.

"Were you crying just now?"

"No. Of course not." If her words sounded hollow in her own ears, surely Dan had heard the falseness in them, too. Kate tried covering the fib with a too-loud, too-long giggle. "What in the world do I have to cry about?" Frowning, she cupped her elbows. "I'm not the one who lost a baby tonight. It isn't my son hovering near death's door, and I didn't just bury a beloved relative. And—"

Dan stood up again and placed a firm hand on her shoulder. "Kate. In the short while you've been with us, you've become one of us. So, the losses you just listed? They hurt you, too."

She looked up into eyes as clear and blue as the Texas sky. Eyes that, if framed by thick, blond lashes, could have been Josh's. The thought conjured a mental picture of him, lying silent and still, with a bullet wound in his chest—because of her.

"I know what you're thinking, but it isn't your fault," Dan continued.

"Oh, isn't it?" She didn't feel deserving of the comfort of his touch and took a step back from him. "Then whose fault is it? If Frank hadn't followed me to your doorstep, if Josh hadn't insisted that all of you come after me, if I hadn't come here in the first place—"

"If," Dan interrupted her. "The biggest little word in the dictionary."

"Maybe, but that doesn't change the facts."

His smile vanished, replaced by a hardened glare that made him look far older than his twenty-six years. "You're a wonderful woman with an amazing spirit, and your nurturing did wonders for Mee-Maw. But the *fact* is, you're just an ordinary human being, nowhere near powerful enough to have prevented the things that have happened."

"And I suppose you're going to tell me that your precious Lord *is* in control."

The blue of his eyes darkened as both brows dipped low in the center of his forehead. "I don't know what has made you so bitter and angry with God. Don't know what sort of childhood you had, or what your life was like before Josh brought you home. But, based on what I've seen, you were a follower—once."

Dozens of Sunday-go-to-meetings flashed through her mind as quickly as a card shark shuffles his deck. She remembered sharing the hymnal with her mama as they stood, side by side, praising the Lord in song. Remembered standing at the altar, singing solos that made the good ladies of the church cry. There had been picnics and weddings and funerals, and, on her twelfth birthday, after Pastor Anderson had dunked her in the murky waters of Flintstone Creek, she'd gasped for air and dried herself with the towel he'd offered, feeling clean and holy and every bit a baptized-in-the-blood Christian.

"Yes," she whispered, "I was a follower once. But that was a long, long time ago." *A lifetime ago*, she thought, before her father was killed and her mama died and her stepfather tried to use her as payment for a gambling debt and—

"I'm sure you believe you have solid reasons for abandoning God, but it's never too late to come back to Him, you know."

He'd spoken softly, and yet his words sliced into her soul like the wail of a banshee. Daniel had lived his whole life on this ranch, surrounded by beautiful vistas and wondrous things and a loving family. What could he possibly know about near starvation and homelessness and the fear and desperation that drive young girls to leave the only home they've ever known to search for food and shelter? How would she ever explain to this devout man, who spent countless hours poring over Bible passages, that God had abandoned her, not the other way around?

"You sacrificed yourself to save us."

Kate shook her head. "I'm the one who put you all in danger in the first place. There was nothing self-sacrificing about what I did."

"Say what you will, but love like that is described in the Good Book! You were willing to die at the hands of that madman to protect us." The kitchen mantel clock ticked three times, then four, before he added, "You're the stuff heroines are made of."

She stood there, blinking in silence, because he'd meant every word, as evidenced by his earnest expression. Her cheeks grew warm, and Kate knew the blush had been brought on by shame, not Dan's compliment. When he'd called "if" the biggest little word in the dictionary, oh, how right he'd been! *If* she'd taken a different path in life, *if* she hadn't been so naïve and gullible, *if*....

There was little point in dwelling on what might have been. Especially since she could see in Dan's gentle face that her silence had led him to believe he'd insulted rather than flattered her. "I know you mean well," she admitted, "and I appreciate it."

Dan only shrugged.

"Your tea is getting cold," she said, sliding the tray closer to him.

He took a sip, then took a bite of meat. "Didn't realize just how hungry I was," he said, taking another bite.

It seemed her tactic to distract him had been successful. But, just in case Dan was merely being polite—again—Kate decided to add to it. "Think I'll fix a little something for Josh's father. I'm sure he must be famished, too."

Dan stopped chewing and studied her face for a moment. "See what I mean?"

"I—I'm afraid not."

"Your every thought is for the well-being of others. A person with a heart and a nature and a spirit like that? You can't tell me you don't love the Lord!"

"I never said I didn't love Him. It's the Lord who doesn't love *me*," she blurted out.

"Nonsense. He loves all His children."

"Oh, does He, now? Then maybe you can explain to me why He has never seen fit to answer my prayers!" As she prepared the tray for Matthew, she recited her list of grievances, from the grisly way her father had died, to her stepfather's abuse and her mama's death, to Esther's passing. "And now, poor Susan has lost her baby, on the very night Josh was shot by an outlaw who followed me right to your doorstep!"

"Feeling mighty important, aren't you?"

Important? If anything, she felt quite the opposite! But she wasn't about to get into a battle of wits or wills with Dan. She'd done enough damage to this family without spewing ungrateful, hurtful words. "Well, then," she said, hoisting Matthew's tray, "I'll just take my important self upstairs and deliver this to Matthew. If you need me"—*and I certainly hope you don't*—"I'll be—"

"Will you pray with me, Kate?"

Of all the ways he might have responded to her little tirade, Kate certainly hadn't expected that! "I'll tell you the same thing I told your grandmother when she asked me to pray with her: I'm very much out of practice. And not very good at it, either."

Daniel grinned. "I can only imagine what Mee-Maw said to *that!*"

In spite of herself, the memory of those precious moments inspired a fond smile. Dare she admit that his grandmother had talked her into saying an impromptu prayer? But Esther was gone, and so was Kate's desire to pray. Her smile faded as she shook her head.

He relieved her of the tray, clasped her hands between his, and bowed his head. "O Lord in heaven," Daniel began, "You have promised to be with us, always, whether we rejoice or weep, when we're strong and when we're weak. When the leper turned to You in his time of need, You healed him. I ask that You look at Your daughter, Father. Read her broken heart and see her crushed spirit. Doesn't she remind You of the blind man, Father, who walked by faith, not by sight? Remind Kate that she, too, can come to you, trusting and untroubled, unafraid and—"

Kate jerked her hands free. "I appreciate your sentiments—really, I do—but you should be praying for your cousins Josh and Susan, and for Sam and Willie." She picked up the tray and hurried toward the hallway, stopping in the doorway to add, "Pray for your aunt and uncle, who lost a grandchild and nearly lost a son tonight. But please, Daniel, do us all a favor—*especially* your dear Lord—and stop wasting your breath on the likes of me."

His surprised expression stayed with her all the way up the stairs and into Josh's room, where she found Matthew dozing in the big chair against the wall. After quietly depositing the simple meal of meat and biscuits on the bedside table and checking on Josh's condition, she tiptoed to her own room and, the instant the door clicked shut behind her, fell to her knees. Pressing her eyes with the palms of her hands, she willed herself not to weep.

Yet the tears came—tears she hadn't been able to shed at her father's grave, or when she'd found her mama's lifeless body, or when fear of her stepfather had driven her into the dark, rainy night, never to return to the house she'd shared with her mama. And because she'd refused to allow Frank the satisfaction of knowing his abuse had caused her pain and despair at all he'd taken from her, she hadn't let him see her tears, either.

Well, you're more than making up for it now, you sniveling little weakling! she thought. Muffling her moans with an overstuffed feather pillow, she saw images of Esther, Susan, Sam, little Willie, and Josh flit through her mind. Daniel had accused her of believing she was important enough to change things, to keep them from happening. If only she did have the power to spare them from fear and pain and loss!

It felt as though her sobs originated deep in her soul, and, as they pulsed throughout her being, the awareness surprised her. Until now, Kate had had no proof that she'd been blessed with a soul. Daniel's prayer echoed in her mind, and, at the moment, she thought it just might be possible to have a broken heart and a crushed spirit. Was it possible he'd been right when he'd hinted that God might have answered her prayers if she'd had faith in His love, if she'd trusted His mercy?

Just as quickly as they'd started, the tears stopped, and the sobs subsided. Using her apron, she dried her eyes and sat back on her heels, depleted and dog-tired. "Should have eaten a bite of that beef," she chided herself through clenched teeth. Then, an idea flared in her head: Just as food would deliver nourishment to her weary mind and body, God's Word would feed her hungry soul.

She looked over at the window seat, where Esther's Bible sat, right where it had been since the day her dear friend had died. Kate had picked it up several times since then, but only to move it so she'd have room to kneel on the padded bench and peer through the wide window. It called to her now, and, rising slowly, she moved toward it.

Sitting with her back to the bleak black night on the other side of the glass, Kate picked up the Good Book, one trembling fingertip tracing the worn gold letters on its cover. If only Esther were here to suggest a comforting verse to bring healing!

She'd no sooner completed the wish than the elderly woman's bright eyes and playful smile flashed in her mind. Kate could almost hear her gravelly voice saying, "You don't need me to point to a passage, silly girl. Open the book and let the good Lord tell you what He wants you to hear!"

And so she opened the Bible haphazardly and read Romans 8:35–39:

> *Who shall separate us from the love of Christ? shall tribulation, or distress, or persecution, or famine, or nakedness, or peril, or sword? As it is written, For thy sake we are killed all the day long; we are accounted as sheep for the slaughter. Nay, in all these things we are more than conquerors through him that loved us. For I*

am persuaded, that neither death, nor life, nor angels, nor principalities, nor powers, nor things present, nor things to come, nor height, nor depth, nor any other creature, shall be able to separate us from the love of God, which is in Christ Jesus our Lord.

Could she believe that the almighty Father loved her, in spite of all the years that had passed since she'd first come to Christ, and through all the suffering she'd endured?

Warmth flooded her being, and Kate trembled from her hair bow to her boots. New tears filled her eyes—this time, not tears of anguish and loneliness, but tears of hope and joy, because, for the first time in many years, she believed—*really believed*—in the power of God's mercy and love.

Hugging the Bible to her chest, Kate bowed her head. "Thank You," she whispered. "Oh, thank You." She'd never meant the words more. He'd shown her, in the twinkling of an eye, that He *had* answered her prayers. She'd survived conditions that would have destroyed other young women without the Lord in their hearts to strengthen and sustain them.

How silly she felt, how humbled she was, admitting that He'd been there all along, loving her, guiding her, protecting her, even as she'd voiced angry words, even when she'd turned her back on Him.

Starting now, when doubt whispered doom into her heart, she'd pray it away, knowing even as she uttered her pleas that God above would hear and answer.

She gently placed the Bible on her night table, where it would be easy to reach if she awoke in the night. Then, she peered into the mirror, and, as she tidied her hair and dried her eyes, she couldn't help but be astonished by the joy written on the face looking back at her.

As she made her way down the hall toward Josh's room, she took a deep breath. "You know my heart, Lord," she whispered, "so You know how much I love him. Bring him back to us, as hale and hardy as before the gunshot wound."

Just outside his door, she paused, placed one hand over her fluttering heart, closed her eyes, and silently added, *And if You see fit to let him love me, too, I'd be forever grateful. But I'll do Your will, even if it means living without him. Amen.*

*J*osh had heard her for quite a while now, muttering about the unfairness of it all as she tidied his covers and plumped his pillows, as she pinched the sides of his mouth to help him swallow spoonfuls of broth, as she laid cool compresses on his forehead. If he could have found the strength, Josh would have told her life wasn't about fairness or the lack thereof. It was about putting one boot in front of the other, no matter what, and thanking God for handing down the strength to make it from day to day.

The Neville women had always been religious, and they could quote the Scriptures as well as any preacher. But the men—with the exception of his cousin Dan—lived more by the Bible's overall message than by memorized verses. Josh understood that Kate's lack of faith was the result of her having lived on the fringes of the Christian community most of her life. Orphaned as a girl, she'd grown up by dint of her own will and drive to survive. How she'd done it without the Lord in her life, he couldn't say, but he respected her for what she'd become, all the same. As soon as he was able, he'd tell her so. And he'd find a way to prove that her Father in heaven loved her every bit as much as He loved those who'd been attending services since they were in diapers!

And, speaking of diapers, the fact that Kate had changed his grandmother's just as willingly as she'd read her stories and sung her songs proved she was a woman with the heart of an angel and the soul of a saint. He'd point that out, too.

But why hadn't she sung for him? Oh, what he'd give to hear the music of her lovely voice, floating softly around his sickroom.

Then, it dawned on him that he'd never gotten around to telling her what the Rangers had said. Now that the pieces of the Dinah/Kate puzzle had come together, he admired her all the more. Somehow, he had to find the strength to let her know she was completely safe and considered blameless. Maybe once she knew that she had nothing to fear, she'd give up her cockeyed notions about going to Mexico. At least, that was his prayer. But if he caught so much as the glimmer of a sign that she still aimed to leave, well, he'd just have to ask her to marry him. And how could she say no, once he admitted that he'd loved her almost from the start?

Hearing the bed linens rustle, he held his breath, waiting, waiting, for the other signal that she was near.

And there it was: Kate pressed her lips to his forehead, the same fever test his ma had used on him in his childhood. He heard the joy in her voice when she quietly exclaimed, "Your fever is gone!"

She followed it up with, "All right, Rip van Winkle, you can wake up any time now."

Josh wanted to smile, because she'd been calling him by that name for who knows how long; she'd even told him about the story she'd read as a girl about a man who'd slept for years and years just to escape his wife and his humdrum life.

He felt the mattress dip as she sat beside him. "Oh, Josh," she whispered, resting her head on his chest, "what have I done to you?"

Even in her misery, she'd taken care not to touch his wound. Warmth and affection surged through him, giving him the strength to wrap his good arm around her. "You've made me love you, that's what you've done to me," he croaked.

Kate gasped and made a move to sit up, but he held tight. "Stay, please."

He said a silent prayer of thanks that she complied.

"You haven't talked in so long that you sound like the bullfrog that used to live in my grandmother's pond," Kate said. "Now, at least turn me loose long enough to get you something to drink."

The need to see her smiling face was greater than the desire to hold her close, so he did as she asked. It seemed to take her forever to get the water glass from the bedside table and carefully serve him a spoonful, but he used the time to drink in her loveliness.

"I'm so relieved that you're finally awake," she said, putting the spoon into the glass, which she set back on the table.

He didn't have the heart to tell her that he'd been awake for quite some time, for then, he'd have to explain he'd been too weak to speak, and that would only worry her more. "How long was I out?"

"Three days."

"Three!" Josh tried to sit up, but a white-hot bolt of pain stopped him.

Comfortably, naturally, Kate slid her arms around him and rearranged his pillows. "There," she said, folding his sheet neatly over the blanket, "is that better?"

He'd just admitted that he loved her. Why hadn't she echoed the words? Everything she'd said and done, almost from the instant they'd met, told him that she cared deeply for him, that she loved him, too. But Josh needed to *hear* it, needed to watch those beautiful lips form the words and see the truth of them sparkling in her amazing, green eyes.

Josh grabbed her hand. "All that gunfire on the prairie the other night—did it affect your hearing?"

A look of bewilderment furrowed her brow. "My hearing? I—I don't—"

"It got pretty loud out there, and I've learned from painful experience that it sometimes takes a while to recover from all the noise."

She leaned forward and pressed another kiss to his forehead, then leaned back again. "No, the fever hasn't returned, so I don't understand why you're rambling on and on about my hearing—"

He slid his arm around her, just as he had just moments ago. Her lips were a mere fraction of an inch from his when he said, "Didn't you hear what I said just now?"

When she blinked, he could have sworn those long, lush lashes stirred the very air between them. "When you asked what you'd done to me," he coaxed her.

Now she understood, as evidenced by the way her perfectly arched brows disappeared into her bangs as she attempted to withdraw. "Is this just your way, running off every time something seems the least bit uncomfortable or challenging?"

Tears filled her eyes, and her lower lip trembled when she said, "I don't want to run, Josh. Not ever, ever again." She blinked, and a tear plopped from her eye onto his cheek. "It's just— You're so— And I'm—I'm—"

He half expected her to say that he was too weak for all this carrying on. That he had a big, loving family, and she was alone in the world. The last thing he'd expected her to say was, "I'm tainted."

There were tears in his eyes, too, when it dawned on him what she meant. What she'd gone through at the hands of Frank Michaels made him ache to the marrow of his bones. If he hadn't heard his father telling someone she'd already killed the sorry excuse of a man, Josh would do it himself!

"Aw, darlin'," he crooned, "what happened to you... it doesn't matter. Can't you see that?" He gave her a gentle shake. "None of it matters! You sacrificed yourself for us, and then you saved my life. And, just so you know, you don't need to worry about the Rangers anymore; they know all about what happened, and they've cleared you of any guilt." With one hand on each of her cheeks, he said, slowly and deliberately, "I love you."

It felt like ten full minutes passed as her beautiful eyes scanned his face, as her fingertips combed through his hair. "I know," she whispered at last, "and it breaks my heart, because you deserve more, so much more, than someone like me, who can't even give you children."

Josh was confused. Of all the things swirling in his head, children were not among them. "Why can't you give me children?"

"Because, when he—" She bit her lip. "When Frank— There was blood, and—" Now, she heaved a ragged sigh. "It probably means I'm barren."

He would have laughed if she hadn't looked so forlorn. "Kate, sweetheart," he said, kissing the tip of her nose, "we don't know what the—" He couldn't bring himself to say "blood," because it only reminded him of all she'd been through. "It might not mean anything of the kind."

She studied his face for a moment, and, as she did, he watched her worries and fears fade. In their place, he saw a certain serenity, which told him she believed it when he said he loved her—despite her past and because of it.

"Oh," she said, "so now you're a lawyer *and* a doctor, are you?"

After seeing her go from terrified to relatively composed, he felt like a cad and a heel for having heard about the blood, but it was a blessed relief to know she'd been chaste when Michaels had brutalized her. "Let's talk to Dr. Lane about it. Maybe we'll have babies, and maybe we won't. As long as I have *you*, I'll be a happy man."

She sighed, and her expression said, "Are you sure?" But in place of the question, Kate chewed her lower lip.

"I'm as sure of that as I am that your name will soon be Kate Neville."

He tried to wipe a wayward tear from her cheek and cringed at the pain caused by even such a small movement.

"Let go of me, you fool man," she said, smiling sweetly. "You have a long, long way to go before you've recuperated enough to talk of such frivolous matters as marriage."

"Well, think about this—I'll have a whole lot more incentive to get better fast if you'll agree to marry me."

Another agonizing moment of silence passed, and Josh groaned inwardly. "For the love of God and all that's holy," he said, "just say yes!"

She grinned and pressed a gentle kiss to his cheek. "I love you, Josh. But that isn't the only reason I'm going to marry you."

He waited patiently as she adjusted his pillows and smoothed his sheets.

"It'll take me *years* to pay you back for the horse, and the boots, and that big, floppy hat, and—"

"Kate," Josh whispered, pulling her close again.

"Hmm?"

"Shut up and kiss me."

*K*ate stood at the back of the church, hiding behind her bouquet of bluebonnets and smiling, because, even through her veil, she could see Josh tugging at the collar of his shirt. How good it was to see him looking so strapping in his dark suit. A far stretch from the haggard man he'd been just weeks ago.

With determination, Kate pushed the memory of the gunfight—and everything that had led up to and followed it—from her mind. For the first time in her life, she was happy, truly and completely content, and she refused to let the haunting memories of Frank Michaels ruin her wedding day.

She glanced around the church, seeing Eagle Pass residents and folks who worked at the Lazy N; seeing the Nevilles, who had welcomed her so warmly into their home when she'd arrived, bruised and limping and frightened. How blessed she was that, after learning about her past—a past that nearly cost them one of their own—they'd still seen fit to shower her with love and affection, making sure she knew without a doubt that they considered her *family*.

She waved at Dinah, Theodore, and Etta Mae, who sat there in their Sunday finest, smiling like proud parents. Yes, she was blessed, indeed, for they'd made the long trek from San Antonio to be a part of her happy day.

Kate bit her lip to stanch the tears that threatened to puddle in her eyes, because, oh, how blessed she was! How she'd merited any of this—the warmth of the Neville family, the acceptance of the church parishioners, the strong, sure love of a man like Josh—Kate couldn't say. But she would never take it for granted from this day forward. *And I'll never take You or Your provision for granted again, Lord, after doubting You for so many years.*

The thought reminded her of the gentle scolding Josh had given her when she'd shared all the reasons why she'd felt justified in blaming the Almighty for the misfortune and hardship He'd rained upon the Nevilles and her. She'd followed it by telling him that if he could accept the Lord's tender mercies as fact, despite all his family had gone through, she owed it to him to try faith on for size. "Trust in God is something you owe *yourself,* beautiful Kate," he'd said.

Thank You, she silently prayed, *for every blessing You've bestowed on this unworthy servant.*

A flash of white up ahead captured her attention, and it was all she could do to keep from running to the altar to help Josh adjust his sling. He seemed to sense her concern and, smiling, slowly shook his head, forefinger ticking left and right. "I'm fine," he mouthed. Then, he pointed at the floor, a silent signal that she should get up there and take her vows so that she could become his wife, once and for all.

Once and for all....

The concept made her heave a wistful sigh, because in no time, the handsome cowboy standing at the front of the church would be her husband. *Her husband!*

He'd polished his boots, and the silver studs on his string tie matched the slide nestled under his Adam's apple. It rose and fell as he swallowed, proof that he was as anxious as she to get the ceremony under way.

Yes, any minute now, the pastor's wife would pound out those first rib-racking chords of "Amazing Grace"—Esther's favorite hymn—and those gathered there would stand to watch her walk down the aisle in the gown Sarah had worked on, day and night, for the past several weeks. The simple dress of silk was unadorned, save for the shimmering train that trailed behind. Yards of hazy lace cloaked her from the circlet of flowers on her head to the satin slippers on her feet. In the weeks since he'd asked her to marry him, Josh had called her pretty and beautiful, lovely and stunning, and, today, she felt all of those things, because the glow of his love had shined its way right into her lonely heart.

The organ music swelled, and she moved forward, feeling more like a tuft of cottonwood floating on a breeze than a bride, on her way to join her groom. Josh held out his hand as she ascended the front stairs to the altar, and she slipped hers into it. Side by side, they faced Reverend Peterson, who opened his Bible and instructed them to join their other hands, as well.

To Josh, he began, "Wilt thou have this woman to be thy wedded wife, to live together after God's ordinance in the holy estate of matrimony? Wilt thou love her, comfort her, honor and keep her, in sickness and in health; and, forsaking all others, keep thee only unto her, so long as ye both shall live?"

Kate knew that look, and when the preacher finished talking, she half expected Josh to say, "Finally!" But he gave her hand another squeeze and, smiling, said, "I will."

Then it was her turn to listen as the pastor repeated the vow, and when she said, "I will," Josh squeezed her hand yet again.

"What token of your love do you offer?"

Josh let go of her hands long enough to produce a gleaming, gold band from his jacket pocket. When had he found time to buy it? Then, his lips formed the name "Mee-Maw," and Kate understood in a heart-swelling flash that this must be the surprise Esther had mentioned on the day of her death.

Reverend Peterson handed Josh back the ring and said, "Place this ring on Kate's finger and repeat after me."

Josh's hand trembled slightly as he slid the band onto the third finger of her left hand and repeated after Reverend Peterson, "With this ring, I thee wed, in the name of the Father, and of the Son, and of the Holy Ghost. Amen."

Kate felt Josh shift restlessly as Reverend Peterson prayed, "Bless, O Lord, this ring, that he who gives it and she who wears it may abide in Thy peace, and continue in Thy favor, unto their life's end; through Jesus Christ our Lord. Amen."

Kate felt a little sorry for the reverend, but only a little, for she was just as eager to become Josh's wife as he was to become her husband.

After the final prayer, Josh unceremoniously lifted her veil. Slipping his right arm around her waist, he pulled her close and pressed his lips to hers in a long, lingering kiss. When at last he stood back, he looked at Reverend Peterson. "Well," he said, grinning, "what are you waiting for, man? Get on with the 'I now pronounce you' part, why don't you?"

Matching his grin tooth for tooth, Reverend Peterson chuckled. "Forasmuch as Joshua and Kate have consented together in holy wedlock, and have witnessed the same before God and this company, and thereto have given and pledged their troth, each to the other, and have declared the same by giving and receiving a ring, and by joining hands, I pronounce that they are man and wife, in the name of the Father, and of the Son, and of the Holy Ghost. Amen."

Josh kissed her again, and as they walked slowly toward the back of the church, he leaned close. "Are you happy, Kate?"

Smiling through tears of joy, she said, "Absolutely. Completely. Totally. Wholly." She stepped in front of him and blocked his path. "And you, Josh? Are you happy?"

"You bet I am," he whispered, pulling her into another embrace, "now that finally I've made an honest woman of my beautiful bandit."

She stood, slack-jawed and staring, for a moment, which set off a chain reaction of whispers that drifted from pew to pew. And when Kate's merry giggle echoed throughout the church, he silenced it with another sweetly satisfying kiss.

An Excerpt from *Maverick Heart,*
Book Two in the Lone Star Legends Series

Coming in Winter 2011

CHAPTER ONE

May 1888 • Somewhere along the San Antonio Road

*L*evee huddled in the corner of the stagecoach and prayed that Liam wouldn't notice her tears. "You behave as though you're the first woman to have a miscarriage!" he'd scolded her. "Pull yourself together. Can't you see you're making *everyone* miserable?"

That had been three days ago, but the memory of it still stung like gritty, windblown Texas dust. She'd never been the type to wallow in self-pity, but was it too much to ask her husband to show some warmth and compassion? As a doctor, he should have realized her reaction to losing the baby was perfectly normal, especially if a mere nurse, such as Levee, understood it.

Frowning, she tucked her lace-trimmed handkerchief back into her purse—a mistake, for Liam saw and correctly guessed that she'd been crying. Again.

"You'll never get over it if you don't at least *try* to put it out of your mind."

Impatience and disappointment echoed in his voice, which hurt almost as much as his earlier reprimand. Levee heaved a sigh. Oh, if only she *could* forget!

Maybe, he had a point, and thirty-four days was long enough to grieve for her lost child. As one of the first women to earn a nursing degree, Levee understood the mental and physical aftereffects of a failed pregnancy. But could melancholia explain why she believed her husband couldn't mourn the loss of his firstborn because he was too excited about opening his clinic?

Another sigh. Like it or not, they'd arrive in Mexico in a matter of days. Chihuahua, of all places, where she didn't know a soul, and the people spoke a language she didn't understand. Where, according to Boston newspapers, gangs of outlaws roamed the—

"Hold on to your hats, folks!" the driver bellowed. "Bandits, ridin' in hard and fast!"

Amid the thunder of horses' hooves and the percussion of gunfire, their fellow passenger—who'd introduced himself only as Mack—calmly unholstered one of two six-shooters. "You got a gun, Doc?" he asked Liam, peeking through the leather window covering.

Liam clutched his medical bag tight to his chest. "Yes, but—"

"Then you'd best get 'er loaded and cocked. There're three of them and five of us. We might just have us a fightin' chance"— he fixed his brown eyes on Levee—"if you can shoot."

Just as she opened her mouth to confess that she couldn't, one of the stagecoach drivers cut loose a bloodcurdling scream. As quick as a blink, his body hurtled past the window and hit the ground with a sickening thump.

Levee clutched a trembling hand to her throat as Mack groaned. "Make that four of us." He spun the chamber of his second revolver and, after pulling back the hammer with a *snick*, leaned over and wrapped her fingers around the grip. "Just aim and pull the trigger, and keep on doing that until you're out of bullets."

"B-but, how will I know when I'm out of—"

"Are you two God-fearin' Christians?"

She heard Liam swallow before saying, "I don't see what that has to do with anything."

Mack aimed a dark glare at him. "If you want to get out of this alive, you'd best pray. Pray like you've never prayed—"

His warning was cut short by the shouts of men and the terrified trumpeting of horses and the grinding of gears as the coach came to a jolting halt.

Then, a deadly hush rode in on a cloud of dust.

The door nearest Levee flew open with a bang. "Throw them guns in the dirt," growled a masked gunman.

When Liam slid his revolver back into his medical bag, Mack gave a slight nod, then tossed his pistol out the door. Uncocking Levee's gun, he flung it to the ground, too.

The bandit raised his rifle barrel higher. "Now, get on outta there. One at a time—and don't try no funny stuff, neither."

Levee climbed down first, followed by Liam. *So much for Mack coming up with a last-minute scheme to save us*, she thought as he joined them in the shade of the coach.

A few yards away, two more bandits sat in their saddles. The smooth baritone and well-enunciated syllables of the tallest didn't fit with the rudeness of his words: "Gather anything of value you find on their persons or in their valises," he told the rifleman. And, nodding to the man on his left, he said, "You. Get the money."

Their immediate obedience made it clear that this was a man to be reckoned with. Levee's heart beat harder as his cohorts carried out his orders, but it wasn't until the strongbox hit the ground with a loud clang that she noticed the other driver, hanging like a half-empty flour sack from his seat. She could almost hear Mack thinking, *And now, we're down to three.* Their only hope was the tiny pistol hidden in Liam's bag. But, even if, by some miracle, the cowboy managed to retrieve it, could he disarm all three thieves?

The second bandit fired one round, demolishing the heavy, iron lock on the strongbox. If he noticed Levee's tiny squeal of fright or Liam's shocked gasp, he didn't show it. "Must be fifty thousand dollars in here!" he said, pawing through the contents. He loosed a rousing "Yee-haw!" and saluted his leader. "All's I can say is, you sure know how to pick 'em, Frank!"

"Shut up, fool!" bellowed the rifle-toting robber. "Now we'll hafta kill 'em, so's they won't be able to tell the Rangers they was robbed by the Frank Michaels Gang!"

The Frank Michaels Gang? Why did the name sound so familiar? But the question was quickly swallowed by a sickening realization: the outlaws had killed two men in less than two minutes. In all her twenty-one years, Levee had never given a thought to how she might leave this earth—until now.

"No need to get your dander up," Mack drawled. "Y'all just keep right on helpin' yourselves to everything we've got. Think of us as the three monkeys—we didn't see or hear a thing."

"That's right," Liam agreed. "And if the Texas Rangers ask questions—an unlikely event, since we don't plan to seek them out—we won't *speak* a thing, either."

Levee looked up at her husband, unable to decide which surprised her more, the fact that he'd opened his mouth, or that he'd opened his medical bag. In one beat of her hammering heart, his hand disappeared inside the bag. In the next, his puny revolver was dangling from his fingertips. "I think you boys should—"

One shot rang out, and even before its echo fell silent, Liam fell to the ground in a heap. "No-o-o!" Levee wailed. "Why-y-y?" Dropping to her knees, she cradled his head in her lap, wishing for the first time since graduating from the New England Hospital for Women that she *hadn't* earned a degree in nursing, because one look at the bloody wound in the middle of his chest told her that, although he wasn't dead yet, he soon would be.

"I—I wanted to—give them—the gun," he sputtered, "to prove we—could be trusted—"

"Hush, now," she whispered, kissing his cheeks and combing the dark curls from his forehead with her fingers. "Shh."

Mack threw his Stetson to the ground. "Of all the...." He kicked the hat. "Did you hear what the man said? He's from *Boston*, for the luvva Pete. He meant you no harm. Why, I doubt he could've hit the broad side of a barn with that peashooter of his, even if he'd tried!"

"Looked to *me* like he was aimin' to shoot," one of the men said in his defense, "an' nobody takes aim at Frank Michaels."

The rifleman cursed under his breath. "Thought I tol' you to shut up, Tom."

"*Both* of you shut up," Frank snarled. He touched a finger to his hat brim and aimed a steely stare at Levee. "My apologies, ma'am. And, to prove my sincerity, we aren't going to kill you. You have my word on that." A grating chuckle passed through the red and black fabric of his bandanna. "At least, not today."

His implied threat hung on the parched air as Levee looked into her husband's ashy face. "Fight, Liam," she urged him. "Hang on—stay with me! You promised that, as soon as we were settled, we'd—"

His eyelids fluttered open, and an enormous, silvery tear leaked out of the corner of one eye. "S-sorry, Levee," he rasped, grabbing her hand. "S-sorry...."

"There's nothing to be sorry for, Liam. You're going to be fine." *Oh, please, God, let it be true!* "Just fine, do you hear me?" No sooner had the words passed her lips than his body shuddered once, and the fingers that had been squeezing hers went limp. A trickle of blood crept from the corner of his mouth to his chin. Then, with one ragged breath, he was gone.

A swirl of raw emotions roiled inside her, and, like a cyclone, lifted her to her feet. These horrible men had murdered her husband, but she acknowledged the part she had played in his death. If she hadn't put her graduation ahead of their wedding plans, they would have had a house, and maybe a child or two, to keep Liam's boredom at bay. Maybe with a family to occupy his time and fill his heart, he wouldn't have reacted with such enthusiasm to that article in the *Boston Globe* bemoaning the lack of medical professionals in Mexico. She'd agreed to travel through this godforsaken country to help him achieve his dream because the Good Book and the dictates of society told her that her place was beside her husband. Well, she had no husband now, thanks to her own self-centeredness and these heartless killers. She watched, helpless, as the thugs helped themselves to Liam's hard-earned savings, as Frank tucked Grandpa O'Reilly's gold pocket watch into his vest, as his men carelessly poked through her small suitcase in search of jewelry.

Almost from the moment they'd left Boston, Levee had been afraid. Afraid of ghastly-looking bugs and wild animals, afraid of the unrelenting wind and the dry, desolate land that seemed to stretch on forever. Afraid of outlaws and bandits she'd read about. Distraught and anguished, she was beyond fear now. With her fists balled at her sides, Levee marched up to the leader's horse.

"You killed my husband for no reason, and you think a phony apology will make things right? You're—you're a *lunatic*, Frank Michaels, and so are these so-called men who ride with you." Levee swiped angrily at her traitorous tears. "Hiding behind your masks—why, you're nothing but cowards, that's what! Heartless thieves and—and cold-blooded killers. You'd *better* shoot me good and dead, right here where I stand, because, the very first chance I get, I *will* report you to the Texas Rangers!"

Her hysterical tirade silenced even the chorusing insects and the chirruping birds. Silenced the amused chortles of Frank and his cohorts, too. The men exchanged puzzled glances, and then the one called Tom said, "You want me to plug her, Frank, or d'you wanna do it?"

Frank rested one leather-gloved hand atop the other on his saddle horn, as if considering the idea. "I gave her my word, and I intend to keep it."

Tom snorted. "She'll probably die of thirst before she reaches the next town, anyway." Winking, he added, "If the coyotes don't get her first."

She'd been an unwilling eyewitness to what those mangy canines could do to a deer carcass, and in very little time, too. Levee pressed her fingertips into her eyes to block the grisly image, and, when she did, the picture of Liam's lifeless body took its place. A dozen thoughts flitted through her head. Could she have done something, medically, to save him? Why hadn't she seen the gunman take aim *before* he'd fired on Liam? If she had, what might she have done to prevent the shooting in the first place?

"Coyotes," she heard the rifleman say. "You're right, Tom. Not much chance she'll live long enough to tell anybody what happened here."

And then Mack's enraged voice broke through. "That was uncalled for," he grumbled. "The poor woman just lost her husband, for the luvva Pete."

As if she needed a reminder! *Please, Lord, please let this be a terrible nightmare. Let me wake up and realize that—*

A deafening explosion ended her prayer. She wasn't dreaming, as evidenced by the whiff of smoke spiraling from Frank's gun barrel—and the ghastly sound of Mack's body hitting the ground. "No-o-o," she wailed. "Not him, too! But—but you *promised*," Levee sputtered. "You promised not to—"

"I promised only not to kill *you*." Then, he coolly holstered his revolver and faced Tom. "Unharness the team. Now."

Frank and his men had ended four lives in little more than four minutes, and then, with four words, he'd dismissed the matter. The howling wind whirled around them, gathering the dust into tiny twisters that hopped across the prairie like jackrabbits. Levee buried her face in her hands, unwilling to let them witness one more moment of her misery. She had the rest of her life for that.

Life. She almost laughed at the notion. Sitting in the middle of the Texas prairie, waiting for only the good Lord knew what to kill her, wasn't her idea of *life*.

Suddenly, an idea dawned. Perhaps, if she got them good and angry, they'd shoot her, too.

Levee started hurling insults and slurs, shrieking like a fishwife and waving her arms. But she might as well have been a cactus or a tumbleweed for all the attention they paid her. Infuriated, she picked up rocks and sticks and hurled those, too, yet they continued to ignore her.

When the stagecoach team scattered in opposite directions, she bit back a sob. As they stuffed their saddlebags full of money, she admitted to herself that they really did intend to leave her out here in the middle of nowhere to wait for starvation and thirst—or hungry coyotes—to kill her. *Oh, Father, please let it be the coyotes*, she prayed. As painful as that would likely be, at least it would be quick. Until then, she'd have ample time to atone for her sin of selfishness.

"You're no better than the coyotes!" she called after them.

But her words disappeared into their cloud of dust and gleeful bellows. Hugging herself, Levee sunk to the dirt between the bodies of Liam and Mack and sat on her boot heels, rocking and groaning, groaning and rocking, as she waited for the tears to start.

But not a single teardrop fell—not for her husband or the baby they'd lost, not for the brave, young cowboy who'd died defending her, not even for herself, alone and afraid, somewhere in West Texas.

She didn't know how much time had passed when the sun began to sink behind the horizon, like a golden coin disappearing into a slot. A dark chill blanketed the plains, waking snaky shadows that slithered from bush to scrubby bush. Strange and forlorn moans spilled from Levee, ascended into the blackness, and blended with the cacophony of night birds and bugs and coyote howls.

By the time exhaustion rendered her silent, the moon was high in the sky, and Levee found herself cuddled up to Liam. And, though his lanky body offered no warmth or comfort, that's where she stayed, praying that before morning, the Almighty, in His loving mercy, would call her home, too.

CHAPTER TWO

December 1888 • Eagle Pass, Texas

Becky cupped a hand between her mouth and Samantha's ear. "See, I *told* you he's teacher's pet," she whispered.

Her seatmate rolled her eyes and sighed. "Shh, before your whispering gets us into trouble."

Levee tapped her pointer on the chalkboard. "Rebecca, Samantha, I'd hate to make you stay after school again."

"Sorry, Mrs. O'Reilly," the girls chorused.

Levee had done her best to look and sound stern, but her heart just wasn't in it. In the seven months she'd been in Eagle Pass, she'd developed a deep affection for every one of her sixteen students, from four-year-old Willie Neville to thirteen-year-old Tim Boone. "Now, let's pay attention to Billy's story, shall we?"

The boy picked up where he'd left off in his *Parker's First Reader*. "You have seen a picture of a cat and a house."

It was Samantha's turn. "Did you see a sound?"

"No," Tim, continued, "I can hear a sound, but I cannot see a sound."

As the children took turns reading the lesson, Levee's mind wandered. It was hard to believe that, just last April, she'd been in Boston, a happily married woman with a baby on the way. And here it was, just halfway through December, and she was a widow, forced to accept the only position available to make ends meet until she could afford the train fare back to Boston. If she hadn't spent most of her pay on supplies for the children, that's where she'd be right now.

You know better, Levee O'Reilly. Eagle Pass feels more like home to you than Boston ever did.

She perched on the corner of her desk as images of that terrible day on the prairie flickered at the corners of her memory. The stagecoach robbery, those awful men, the gruesome sight of her young husband lying so very still in the dust.... Levee clasped her hands and tried to shake the pictures from her mind with the knowledge that Frank Michaels was dead. Thank God for Kate Neville for firing the shot that killed him!

"Somethin' wrong, Mrs. O'Reilly?"

Levee felt her cheeks go hot. "Of course not, Tim. What makes you ask such a thing?"

"It's just, well, you looked powerful mad just now," the boy said, shuffling his well-worn boots along the floor beneath his desk. "I—uh, we're finished the page...."

So much for Reverend Peterson's assurances that you'd forgive that terrible man eventually. Forcing a smile, Levee glanced at the big, ornate clock in the back corner, which had been donated, along with a huge crate of books, by Matilda Montgomery. With only thirty minutes left in the school day, she saw no point in moving on to the next lesson. "You all did such a wonderful job. Just wonderful!"

Just as she opened her mouth to dismiss the class, Mack walked through the rear doors. "Howdy, young'uns," he said, hoisting a brown sack over his shoulder. "Look what your Uncle Mack has brought you!"

The girls giggled, and the boys shouted, and before Levee could say hello, Mack was surrounded by smiling children. He doled out rock candy, one chunk per palm. He looked so hale and hardy that it was hard to believe what sorry shape he'd been in when the two of them had arrived in Eagle Pass. If it hadn't been for his will to live, he would have died from Frank Michaels's well-placed bullet. The morning after the stagecoach robbery, his quiet whimpering had roused her, and she'd removed the bullet and patched him up using tools and tape she'd found in Liam's medical bag.

For two long days, they'd limped along the San Antonio Road, and with every painful step, Levee's hatred for Frank Michaels had mounted. Though it hadn't been his bullet that had killed her husband, it might as well have been. If not for Mack's strength and perseverance, Liam's body would have been food for the buzzards and coyotes. After helping her dig a grave using spokes from a broken wheel, Mack had fashioned a crude cross from the boards of the driver's seat of the stagecoach—hardly the grave or marker Liam deserved, but a long sight better than the alternative. How could any right-minded person—Christian or otherwise—think it possible for her ever to forgive the outlaw or his men?

Then, blessedly, a covered-in-dust stagecoach had appeared on the horizon. Levee had heard of mirages and thought that's exactly what it was. But the driver had stopped and said he was going as far as Eagle Pass, and, since his only passenger was a mangy mutt named Mischief, he'd delivered the trail-weary passengers to town, where they'd both been ever since.

"Penny for your thoughts."

Levee returned Mack's warm smile.

"I brought something for you, too," he said, holding up a thin, rectangular package. "Early Christmas present from me to you."

In the months since the robbery, she'd learned better than to argue with this bighearted, stubborn cowboy. "Just let me give them their homework assignment, and I'll be right with you."

Mack made himself comfortable in the seat closest to her desk as she instructed the children to practice their multiplication tables that evening. To the youngest two, who hadn't yet progressed that far in arithmetic, she said, "Recite your ABCs." Then, Levee hugged them all and stood on the schoolhouse porch, waving good-bye.

When she returned to the classroom, she saw that Mack had written "Levee O'Reilly is the prettiest gal in Eagle Pass" across the chalkboard. "Flattering as that might be," she teased, "you're not leaving here until you've washed that slate clean, Mack Burdette."

"All in good time. First," he said, holding out a package wrapped in brown paper, "you need to open your present."

She gawked at the small, flat rectangle. "But it's nearly two weeks until Christmas!"

Mack shrugged. "I'll probably be out at the farthest acres of the ranch by then, rounding up the strays."

Almost from the moment Dr. Lane had given him a clean bill of health, Mack had been a ranch hand for the Neville family at the Lazy N Ranch. He seemed born to the work, for in the time he'd been their employee, he had grown lean and tan, and his brown eyes glowed with power and pleasure. Though it made Levee feel conceited and vain to admit it, she knew that his happiness was in part because he'd taken a shine to her. His boyish grin, his impromptu visits, and his thoughtful little gifts for her and her students made it clear he hoped that she'd return his feelings someday.

But it had taken months to accept her fate as a widow. Had taken months more to decide that she never again would allow romantic notions to sway her from doing what was right. If she'd fought harder against moving to Mexico back in April, Liam would be alive today. And, since Mack had the same persuasive tendencies, she could not—*would* not—allow her fondness for him to grow into something more.

Gently, he wrapped his fingers around her wrist, pried her fist open, and laid the parcel on her palm.

"You really shouldn't have, Mack."

"Sure, I should've. Now, go on, open it."

She peeled back the brown paper and exposed a bar of chocolate.

"Imported," he explained, tapping its wrapper, "all the way from Switzerland."

Levee had seen the candies at J. W. Riddle grocery store and knew they cost far more than he could afford. "It's too much, Mack—really! You should take it back. I'm sure Mr. Riddle will give you a refund, or exchange it for something—"

He took the candy bar from her hand, opened it, and, grinning, bit off a corner. "Can't take it back now," he said around the mouthful, "so you might as well enjoy it."

He handed it back to her, and she took a bite, mostly to humor him. "I'll just save the rest. If I'm disciplined, it might just last until you're back from 'the farthest acres' so you can share it with me." Levee rewrapped the candy and tucked it into her canvas bag. "Thank you, Mack. But, really, you shouldn't have. You're too thoughtful and generous for your own good sometimes."

"No such thing as 'too generous' where you're concerned, Levee O'Reilly."

And he meant it. She could see proof of it all over his handsome, mustached face, could hear it in his voice. A blush crept into her cheeks, and, to hide it, Levee led the way to the door. "Will you be here for the children's Christmas pageant? I'm sure they'd love seeing their Uncle Mack in the audience."

A strange expression skittered across his face—a look of hope that told her nothing would please him more than to hear her say *she* would love seeing him in the audience. But it wouldn't be fair to mislead him. He deserved a woman who'd give him her all, not one who aimed to live out the rest of her days alone. "Wouldn't miss it," he said from the porch. "Not for all the world."

Just as she wondered what in the world to say to that, a rich, baritone voice called out, "Say, Burdette, you gonna stand there jabbering with the schoolmarm all the livelong day?"

Mack smiled and waved. "Hey, Dan. Finished at the granary, are you?"

"Yep."

How could she have been in town all this time without having seen the man before? Not at Sunday services or church socials, not in the shops in town or on the roads to and from Eagle Pass. As Mack threw his gear into the back of the wagon, Dan's gaze locked to hers.

If she'd ever seen bigger, bluer eyes, Levee didn't know when. Shining, golden curls peeked out from under his hat brim, and then he smiled, reminding her of how it feels to glimpse the sun after days of dreary rain. The warmth of it tingled from the roots of her hair to the soles of her stockings.